DISCARD

Praise for Robert Lane

and the

Jake Travis Novels

The Second Letter

Gold Medal winner of the Independent Book Publishers Association's 2015 Benjamin Franklin Awards, Best New Voice: Fiction.

"(Lane) has created a winning hero in Jake Travis, someone who is super-skilled, super-fit, glib, oddly bookish, funny as a stiletto..." *Florida Weekly*

"...A captivating book with lies and deceit as well as love and loss." *Readers' Favorite*

"Fans of Michael Connelly, Ace Atkins, and Dennis Lehane will likely find Lane's book satisfying on how it hits all the right notes of a truly suspenseful story." *SceneSarasota*

Cooler Than Blood

"Lane delivers a confident, engaging Florida tale with a cast of intriguing characters. A solid, entertaining mystery." *Kirkus Reviews*

"Gripping and highly enjoyable." *Foreword Clarion Reviews*

"Entertaining and enjoyable." *SceneSarasota*

The Cardinal's Sin

Finalist in the Eighteenth annual Foreword Reviews' INDIEFAB Book of the Year Awards.

"A cinematic tale...the prose is confident and clear, and the pacing smooth and compelling...readers will care about its characters. Another entertaining mystery from Lane—possibly his best yet." *Kirkus Reviews*

"It starts with a bang and never lets up...a sophisticated exploration of the relationship...in which the killing power of words vies with the powerful finality of the assassin's rifle. (An) exciting reading experience. Florida noir at its best." *Florida Weekly*

"This brilliantly calibrated thriller bests the leading sellers in its genre. Lane's writing is sharp, evocative, and engaging...a novel that not only entertains but enriches its readership." *Foreword Clarion Reviews,* Five Stars

"Engaging thriller...a compelling, quick-read novel." *Blueink Reviews*

The Gail Force

"The plot crackles with energy and suspense. The pace is breakneck... the writing is crisp. A consistently entertaining and self-assured crime thriller." *Kirkus Reviews*

"Charm and humor permeate the pages of this surprising thriller... there's little chance that anyone will turn the last page before developing a craving for the next installment." *Foreword Clarion Reviews,* Five Stars

THE GAIL FORCE

Also by Robert Lane

The Second Letter

Cooler Than Blood

The Cardinal's Sin

THE GAIL FORCE

ROBERT LANE

ISBN: 0692670440
ISBN: 13: 9780692670446
Library of Congress Control Number: 2016904964
Mason Alley Publishing, Saint Pete Beach, FL

This is a work of fiction. Names, characters, places, and incidents either are the product of the author's imagination or used fictitiously. Any resemblance to actual persons, living or dead, localities, businesses, organizations, and events is entirely coincidental.

Only for a little we live, and feel ourselves truly alive, with truth, and the Angel flaming sword comes to slash us out. Beauty and music there is.

Richard Llewellyn
How Green Was My Valley

ACKNOWLEDGMENTS

I find inspiration from, and wish to acknowledge, the places I travel to and write at. *The Gail Force* owes a nod to: the Alfond Inn, Winter Park, Florida; the Ritz Carlton, Key Biscayne, Florida; Casa Marina, Key West, Florida; Rosie's comfortable flat, Dublin, Ireland; and always, the Pink Palace, Saint Pete Beach, where, at this moment Jake Travis sits at the beachside bar, his cap low, his alcoholic encouragement in front of him, observing his stool mates as the low sun glitters silver the dark waters of the Gulf of Mexico.

THE GAIL FORCE

1

The Fat Man

Karl Anderson knew he'd made a mistake when he got a sex change and neglected to inform his wife.

"What the—"

"It's me, babe."

"What the—"

"Hey, you know we talked about it and—"

"Karl, you dumbass. What—"

"It's Colette."

"What?"

"Colette. You know, French. Thought we'd make a cute couple. Whatdaya think?"

"Oh, babe." Riley Anderson put down her grocery bag of fresh produce, fish wrapped in white paper—she suspected the paper was not as fresh as the fish it wrapped—and a loaf of French bread. She strode over to her husband and combed her hand through his hair, tenderly tucking a few renegade strands behind his left ear. "You're a blonde, babe. We talked about it? Remember? You'd look *so* much better as a brunette. Besides, a French blonde—they even make them?"

"Don't know why not."

"Name one."

"One what?"

1

"French blonde. Come on, Karl. They don't exist. It's like a happy Eskimo or—"

"Catherine Deneuve."

"Cather—OK, so you got one, but dead or alive, right? And look at your shoes. You got to start thinking differently."

"I'll be fine. Pretty sure she's still alive. Born in forty-three."

"You didn't, you know," Riley said with a coy smile, "touch the private equipment, right?"

They stood in a seaside bungalow, the late afternoon sun filtering through the slats of the venetian blinds, casting shadowed lines on the wall. A spiritual sea breeze swept through two sets of open patio doors, ushering in air that hung heavy with the gummy fragrance of saltwater. The front doors faced the Caribbean, and the side doors the courtyard and pool, one floor beneath them. "Some island south of Florida," the government man in the buttoned dark suit had retorted in response to Riley's earnest question as to where they were. That was three nights ago when they'd been dropped off at 2:00 a.m. in the middle of a weed-infested runway.

"No shit, Corky. Which one?" Riley had demanded.

"Brig-a-fuck-a-doon."

"Gotcha. Hey, thanks for the heads up. Now give me my phone."

"We've been over this. They can trace you. No phone."

"How long am I gonna be here?"

"Until you leave."

"Yeah? Well, let me tell you, if you come knockin' and I don't answer, it means I'm finally showing signs of intelligence. Got it, Corky?"

"Don't call me Corky."

"Corky, Corky—"

Karl had stepped in before Riley got wound up. He was always calming her emotions and outbursts, like throwing a blanket on a fire. He believed his wife's bravado stemmed from her diminutive stature, but he wasn't the type of man who gave thought to such trivial things. He simply loved her every way times ten.

"You know I didn't," Karl replied to his wife's question and gave her their last kiss. "It's just another precaution. We might even have fun with it." Their first kiss had been outside the prefabricated junior high classroom in Marion, Indiana, when they were fourteen years old. It'd been building for three days until finally, on the fourth day, Karl nearly knocked her head into the side of the building before attacking her lips with his own.

He folded her, all five feet and one inch, into his chest. She jerked back. "Boobs?"

"Little fakies. I'm thinking this might be a pristine opportunity for you to see if you swing both ways, you know, snuggle up to Daddy Big Tits, might find it rocks your boat. Make a real sorority girl out of you."

Riley smiled, glanced up at her husband, and said, "I don't think so, baby. You've been rocking my boat ever since the day you grabbed my shoulders, banged my head, stuck your lips on mine, and then dashed off like the Easter bunny being chased by a pack of starving coyotes."

While not poetic, and certainly not the finely crafted lyrical notes she would, if presented the opportunity, have chosen, nonetheless, it was a fine thing for Riley Anderson to say to her husband, as they were the last words he would hear her say. The last words she ever heard him say were coming around the corner like a downhill runaway truck.

3

Karl Anderson, who towered over his wife, gathered her back in his arms. He faced the open patio door. Riley, before looking up to his face, eyed the grocery bag on the kitchen counter. She wondered how she should prepare the fish but knew that Karl would likely step in and cook dinner. Maybe she'd slice up the French loaf, make garlic bread and croutons. Karl Anderson loved crispy croutons. Later, she would wonder if she *hadn't* glanced at the damn groceries if she would have seen the panic—the sadness—in her husband's eyes a split second sooner, and if that split second, of all the seconds the screwed-up world had ever known, would have made a difference in their lives.

When she did glance up, Karl Anderson was not looking at the object of his heart, but at the open patio door where a rotund, unwelcome guest stood blocking the salt air, the sun, the view, their future.

Karl, like a Polish weight lifter, jerked his wife over his head, took a giant leap toward the side patio that fronted the pool below, and heaved her over the patio rail and, with luck, into the pool's deep end.

"Run, baby, run," he screamed, praying that for once in her life, the little fireball would do the sensible thing and listen to him. That was assuming he didn't miss and Riley went *kerplat* on the concrete pool decking. Karl spun and dove for the shelter of a desk. Like a runner on third knowing he was cooked, he closed his eyes, thinking it would be less painful when the bullet found him.

It wasn't.

"Tsk, tsk, tsk," the Fat Man said on entering the villa. He glanced behind him. "Find her. Go." Two men were with him. The one who had shot Karl sprinted down the concrete stairs.

"*Mr.* Anderson." The Fat Man took several steps into the room. "Might I be mistaken or have you sprouted a pair of shapely—although the right one seems to be slightly off-kilter—breasts since our last meeting?"

"Eat me."

"Yes, yes, yes. If only you knew. Why not now, Johnnie, while he's still breathing?"

Johnnie Darling, who resembled the product of an incestuous relationship, slithered around his boss and snapped away with a Nikon D810.

"Fat little twerp," Karl Anderson blurted out. His left hand grasped his Tommy Bahama shirt that Riley had sprung on him yesterday as a present. He tried to stem the bleeding that was turning the gold silk shirt into a rust-colored premonition of death.

"Why the animosity?" The Fat Man tapped his cane on the floor. "Is that what the end brings you, tied up in a bow? It is different with all of us. You should understand. Our minds are so similar in some departments, but apparently—and this, most unfortunately does not bode well for you—sadly different in others. But what a marvelous picture you make, especially now that you've made yourself such a conflicted creation. You know how I feel about art. It stimulates our senses. That which we are rarely exposed to, that which we dream about and participate in only through the voyeurism of our dreams, stimulates us the most. So considerate of you and, I might add, so utterly unselfish, to be our *objet d'art.*"

"Go fuck yourself."

"Hmm…yes. Imagine the disastrous effect on the survival of the species if one could indeed finagle such an act."

Click. Click. Click.

The Fat Man prodded Karl Anderson's shirt with his cane. He nudged the blond wig off to the side, taking care to keep a piece of it on Karl's head.

Click. Click. Click.

"This is exquisite. Exquisite indeed. Death comes to what? A man? A woman? We don't know, Johnnie, what Mr. Anderson is trying to be. Perhaps one of your own. Death does not care, does it Mr. Anderson?"

Click. Click. Click.

The Fat Man stepped around Karl and toddled into the kitchen, his back to Karl. "I thought we were getting along splendidly. The beauty of numbers—their simplicity and brutal honesty. It's disappointing when those we trusted, our confidants, turn and drive a spike into our hearts. So sad. All of this, brought about by you."

Karl groaned.

The Fat Man picked up the bag of groceries. He positioned a chair before Karl, sat, and bent over, his face close to Karl's.

"Look at me," the Fat Man said.

Karl did not. Karl Anderson decided to go deep inside himself, to choose his place of death, to envision the dimpled face of his sweet Riley as the last thing he would see. *Did I throw her too far? I was afraid of coming up short. A short putt never goes in—oh God, please, I hope she hit the water.*

The Fat Man poked Karl's chin with his cane. "I said look at me."

Karl did not.

"Very well then." He leaned back and propped his cane against the side of the chair.

Click. Click. Click.

The Fat Man gave a dismissive gesture with his hand, his fingers trilling the air. "Be done, Johnnie, until the closing shot. Why, Mr. Anderson? Why couldn't you let me go? I told you that if you kept our secret, you would live. If not,

6

you would create this egregious situation. What part of that simple statement did you not comprehend?"

Karl curled into a fetal position and coughed up blood.

"Now you understand, don't you?" The Fat Man continued, undaunted by Karl's lack of conversational participation. "And your little Riley? My! What a throw that was. My guess is that she's bleeding out on the pink pool paver bricks. Pink. Pool. Paver. Bricks. What do you think, Karl? Or is it Pink. Paver. Pool. Bricks? Do you recall our number games? Of course you do. I got it right the first time, didn't I? Words with the fewest letters lead the way. We resort to the alphabet for a tiebreaker. 'Pink' before 'pool' as 'I' comes before 'O.' Remember? We constructed whole sentences in such a manner, although paragraphs were beyond the scope of even our advanced minds. I will miss your stimulating company. I digress—Riley.

"Perhaps that wasn't her fate; there's always the cabana, a somewhat softer ending. You know which one I'm talking about, don't you, Karl? Yes, that's right. The one where the lady in the black bathing suit was spreading oil on her breasts yesterday as if she were making love to them. Remember now? Judging by the trajectory, I think that is where your little trinket might have landed. Johnnie, would you be so kind as to glance out the door. Take a few shots of Mrs. Anderson. Show them to Mr. Anderson in your viewfinder."

Johnnie Darling went to the side patio door and peered down. He shook his raisin head at the Fat Man.

"Not there? Really—quite an amazing throw then. I'm sure Eddie will rope her in. Pity for her that she didn't hit the bricks. Didn't think of that, did you Karl? Really, have you nothing to add?"

Karl tightened his position, his arms and legs drawing into his center, as if in death, life compresses into you, growing small, dense, and close. Then, like a flickering flame reacting to a kindly puff, it was no more.

The Fat Man picked up the grocery bag. "I greatly admire your courage to control your last moments. Superb, actually. One never knows until the bitter end what kind of strength lies dormant in a man. With you, it is bottled animosity and structured silence. Think of the picture in his mind right now, Johnnie. The greatest art is that which we never see. Pity. Karl, are you tuned in?"

He reached into the bag and rummaged through the items. "I shall dine on your wife's shopping tonight. Let's see, Johnnie, French loaf, fresh produce, kiwi—excellent—such an integral component for a Caribbean salad." He unwrapped the fish. "Yellowtail snapper. Enough for two, which means just enough for me." He discarded the fish and stood, as if he'd instantly lost interest in it all. "I fear we've overstayed our visit, and we do want to be going before the police arrive; although I told them to give me an hour. One shot, Johnnie. With both instruments. Don't cheat and rely on the camera."

The Fat Man turned to leave.

"Shwell ill you."

He turned and was surprised to see Karl Anderson's eyes nailing his own. "Pardon me."

"Riley," Karl said with the greatest of effort, for he recognized his last breath. With that breath, he said, "She'll kill you."

"I think not. Johnnie."

Johnnie circled the corpse twice and settled on a position. He took his time with the Nikon. Johnnie Darling always took his time with the last shot.

Click.

2

Every thing's a game. Sometimes you win. Sometimes you lose.

I was twenty feet outside the wake of my boat, *Impulse*, getting ready to cut my Connelly slalom back across the double wake. I'd been clearing both wakes by launching off the first, and hugging my knees before letting the ski slap the water. I rocketed off the first wake and spotted another boat zeroing dead into my boat, *Impulse,* and Morgan, who was at the helm.

What the heck?

As Morgan swerved to avoid the other boat, the tip of my ski caught the water. My takeoff had been fine, the landing—not so much. My head and chest slammed into the water, and my legs flew up behind me, twisting my torso like a pretzel, which it was neither designed for nor accustomed to. I sprang free and somersaulted a couple of revolutions, although I wasn't keeping track. When I broke the surface in the bay, my house was less than a half mile off to my left. I glanced to the right where the Tierra Verde drawbridge should have been and—wouldn't you know it—there was my house again.

OK. Little dinged up. Got my bell rung. It happens.

Legs—check. Neck pain—the usual. No major problems. It was just my head, an overrated component of the

9

body, that was temporarily malfunctioning. I relaxed back in my vest, my face sticky with salt, and took in the blue Florida sky, allowing my mind time to surface at its own pace.

Morgan coaxed *Impulse* up along me. The kamikaze boat never blinked, and Lynyrd Skynyrd's "Tuesday's Gone" trailed in its wake, blaring out from a quad of rear speakers as the boat tore toward the open waters of the Gulf of Mexico.

"I needed to cut sharp," Morgan explained. "No choice. You wipe out? I didn't see."

"Might have flipped a few times."

"Shame I missed it."

"What's with Lynyrd?"

"Sunday boaters," he replied with a two-word summation that covered the lower end of the gene pool.

I glided the ski over to Morgan. He reached over and snatched it out of the water. I lowered the ladder and climbed over the transom and onto the deck. *Impulse* was a center-console Grady White, but Morgan and I installed a tow bar that spanned her twin engines with a ring in the middle.

"Idiot," I exclaimed as I reached into my pocket and pulled out my phone.

Morgan winced a smile. "You'll find out if the new water-proof case is what it's billed to be."

I shook my head in disgust. It had not been my intent to test the new case. I was rough on phones and merely wanted the toughest case. It flicked to life. After drying it, I placed it on the console in the shade.

I took a healthy swig from a bottle of water and yanked up my swim trunks as Morgan maneuvered *Impulse* back onto its lift. A double-barrel early season cold front had blasted through the previous week and tamed Boca Ciega Bay to the midseventies, but that didn't deter the full-bodied sun from biting my back like a razor blade. As Morgan raised the lift with the remote control, I held the pole on the aft port side of the lift to position and steady the boat.

A young woman approached us from the seawall. If she had been waiting for us on my lawn, I hadn't noticed. She strode with purpose down my dock, although I was certain I'd never seen her before.

"You Jake Travis?" she demanded as a way of greeting me when she was still ten feet out.

"You with the IRS?" I reciprocated her curt tone.

"What? No."

"DEA?"

"The wha—"

"March of Dimes?"

"We're not doing this. Listen to me. You have to find my husband before he kills more people."

"Your husband's a killer?"

"No. Before the Fat Man kills more people. I'm pretty sure he murdered my Karl, even though he changed his name to Colette, and we were going to make a run for it as a gay couple."

"Your husband had a sex change?"

"Not really. A fake, you know?"

"Fake?"

"Boobs, wig, shit like that. People do it all the time. Games and stuff. But that wasn't our angle. You need to stop him."

Impulse banged a few times onto the two-by-ten wood stringers and finally settled into her cradle as the lift continued its monotone climb. I leaned against the rear bait well and took another swallow of water. My head was still woozy, and with luck, when it cleared, the woman would have been a mirage.

The lady? Maybe a C-note in weight. A shapely red halter-top I failed to not stare at and shorts that covered a waist that never bothered to grow. She had a nasty bruise on her right shoulder; swirls of purple, red, and black, like a drunk tattoo. I could probably ball her up and toss her out of my life. Not a bad thought. She was interrupting our Sunday morning ski-and-drink time. I don't have many rituals in my life, but the ones I do have, I take seriously.

Morgan brought out a bottle of Taittinger from a cooler and gave me an inquisitive nod that I affirmed. He popped the cork—it resounded like a single stroke on a timpani drum—and poured two glasses. He resumed his finger on the remote, slowly raising me to Pixie's level. I offered my glass to her, wanting to be polite and at the same time wondering why.

"Are you listening?" she said as a reaction to my offer to share my bubbly with her.

I took a drink. I'd been looking forward to my Sunday morning champagne ski run since last Sunday. "I am listening," I confirmed to her, while contemplating how to politely inform her to march her bully attitude right back down the dock. "The Fat Man killed your husband, who was trying to become a woman. Correct?"

Pixie shook in her head in disbelief. "How can you stand there? He's a monster, a brutal killer. My husband is gone, and you're drinking champagne?"

"I offered."

Pixie hopped down into the boat—not an easy feat for most people. She was a nimble little number. She charged up to me, snatched my fine crystal flute, and tossed it into the bay.

"We were supposed to be in protective custody," she said while I pondered my glass drifting out of my life. "Someone told him—the Fat Man. He's connected beyond what we ever suspected. I'm pretty sure he killed Karl and know he's killed countless more. And you can bet your wet ass he's coming after me. Are you my guy? 'Cause if not, I'm not burning any more time here. Damnit, I'm talking to you."

I turned to her. "Have a seat, Pixie."

"It's Riley. Riley Anderson."

I extended my hand, and we shook. Her hand was a small quiet stone that got lost in mine. "Jake Travis. Have a seat, Riley Anderson."

She blew out her breath out and plopped down in the bow. I rummaged through the radio box and extracted a pair of sunglasses and a baseball cap. I poured more Taittinger into a plastic Krewe of Carrollton Mardi Gras cup and sat across from Riley. *Impulse* was safely above any potential wakes, and Morgan took the cushioned seat that backed to the console. I took a sip of Taittinger and said, "Take it back a step. Who told you about me?"

"An old man named Angelo."

Morgan and I exchanged a quick glance.

I sought to clarify. "Angelo who lives in Saint Kitts?"

"Yeah. He told me you ran on the cocky side, but to ignore your attitude. PI, right? Said you recovered stolen boats and do some shadowy government work, but he advised me to stay clear of that. Gave me your address."

Angelo is the ex-gardener of the Gulf Beaches Historical Museum. We'd met when I was investigating a lost letter from a deceased CIA agent, but that's another story. Angelo wanted to travel, and Morgan and I granted him his wish. We sent him to Saint Kitts about two years ago to do some fishing and cruising, and to help out at an Italian restaurant owned by a lady friend of Morgan.

Angelo was also the rightful owner of my cat, Hadley III. Some mumble jumble he fed me about the cat's lineage going back to Long Key for over a hundred years, and who was he to disturb that? While I knew that his temporary move was permanent, in my dreams he comes back for the pesky feline huntress. She is fond of lying low under the wild hibiscus bush in my backyard and, despite my two-hundred-pound advantage, springing at my ankles when I pass by. I've begrudgingly grown to admire her, maybe even like the huntress—but I don't know why.

"How did you meet Angelo?" Morgan wanted to know.

"We were to testify at a grand jury hearing in Miami in a week, and the government stashed us away in Saint Kitts. But Karl didn't trust the feds and was looking for a way off the island—you know, discreetly asking around, and he ran into an old man. Worked at an Italian restaurant. Said his name was Angelo.

"We got to talking, you know? We weren't supposed to do that, talk to strangers, but fu—jeez, you got to live, right? Karl said Angelo had a way about him. Sensed we were troubled. Karl confided in Angelo that we were on the lam. Government protection. We were being sequestered until we were called to testify against the Fat Man. But Karl didn't trust the feds. You can't hide from the Fat Man. He sees all, hears all. We told them that; those men in suits and dark glasses. We decided to make a run for it as a gay couple. Can I have a sip?"

"Not if you're going to pollute the bay."

She let out a harrumph, shook her head, and pouted her lower lip.

Morgan rose, fixed her a cup, and handed it to her. She drained it like water.

"Like I said, Karl didn't trust the feds. You can't hide from the Fat Man. He—"

"The Fat Man?" I cut her off.

"That's his nickname," she said with annoyance, like I was supposed to know. "Real name is Phillip Agatha. He's not gross or anything. It's like a combination of his weight and bank account. He's into blackmail art—that's what Karl called it. Who even comes up with that stuff? Splits his time between his boat, the *Gail Force,* and a condo in Miami. Karl and I did accounting work for one of his operations. Saw some stuff one should never see. We went to the FBI, and they whisked us to Saint Kitts to allegedly protect us until we can testify against him. But he found us. You got it now?"

"And you believe he killed your husband?" *Karl the cross-dresser,* I wanted to add but refrained.

She nodded. "I assume he's dead. I got away, but Karl said that if the Fat Man found us, he'd kill us both."

A pelican smacked the water off our starboard side. "How did you escape?" I asked.

She raked her fingers through her hair. Her forehead was pelted with sweat. "Karl tossed me over the balcony the afternoon the Fat Man found us. I ran to that restaurant, and Angelo took me by boat to Saint Martin, or whatever that island is that's split with the same name but spelled differently—I mean, way to confuse people, right? He bought me a ticket to Tampa. Gave me cash and your address." She paused and said, "That was a nasty spill you took out there. Why'd you flip?"

"Beats snapping in two." I wanted to know more about her husband's toss, but my patience was waning. Also, I was hungry. "What do you want from me, Mrs. Anderson?"

"Let's stick with Riley. Can you do that?"

"The question stands."

She started in but held back, as if a cosmic force were watching over her, controlling her emotions. She started to cry. Wonderful. I wanted to ski and drink, and instead I got a bawling, bruised broad and was down a flute. She brought her right hand up to her eyes and started to straighten up but relinquished her effort. She'd come far, and I was the end of the road.

She looked up at me with the prettiest obsidian eyes I'd ever seen, and I thought of her smooth and small hand. "Save me?" she pleaded. "I don't mean to be so damn melodramatic, but I know he's coming. They'll be no justice for those he's killed, and he'll kill more. I don't know where else, *who* else, to go to."

"You need to approach the police or the FBI," I instructed her. "How about the man who placed you in the protection program?"

"You mean like our handler, the guy who escorted us on the plane?"

"Sure. You got a way of contacting him?"

"You got a Ouija board?"

"Why?"

"Slumped dead against the garbage Dumpster. I passed him running from the pool. The only way the Fat Man knew we were in Saint Kitts was to have a plant—you know, like a mole, someone on the inside. I go to the police or the effing BI, and I'm dead. We went to them; Karl's dead, and I'm scrambling." She teared up again. Her breath escaped as she swiped her bangs away from her head. "Please." Her supplication was part speech and prayer. "Will you help me? I have no place to go. I—"

"Certainly." Morgan cut in before I was about to say— *we'll never know, will we?*

"I'm asking you." She nailed her puppy eyes to mine.

My stomach rumbled. Time to move on to the rest of the Sunday morning ritual. "I'll look into it."

"Promise me something?" Her eyes were bright and focused, and the tears were gone. *She been toying with me?*

"I don't know if—"

"When you find the Fat Man?"

"There's no guar—"

"Know how they put names on bombs?"

"I'm familiar with the attitude."

Riley Anderson stood up. "Put my name on the bullet," she said in a voice as clear as cold water. "The Fat Man. Let him know it was me—that Karl Anderson's girl got him."

3

Riley claimed she hadn't slept in two days and could no longer function without a few hours. She had only a small Pan Am duffel bag. It had belonged to Angelo and was his prized possession, gifted to him by a lady he worked for as a young man. I would make certain it was returned.

We went to the pink hotel a mile from my house. I gave the front desk clerk my member number, and told her to meet the needs of Mrs. Riley Anderson, although I registered her under a different name. I requested the clerk book her in room 406, if it was available. That room wasn't billed as gulf front, but only because the south pool lay between the room and the Gulf of Mexico. I informed Riley I'd swing by that night and take her out to dinner downtown with Kathleen and Morgan. Kathleen usually joined us for our Sunday morning ritual, but she had begged off to have brunch with her friend, Sophia, which led to our decision to dine out that evening. Riley promised the full story over dinner.

When I returned to my house, Morgan was on the screened porch, Jesse Winchester was playing on the 1962 Magnavox, and a fresh bottle of Taittinger was spewing vapors of fermented grapes into the air.

I stabbed a potato madly with a fork, and zapped it in the microwave. Afterward, I sliced it into quarter-inch strips and fried it in hissing olive oil, liberally coating the strips with salt and pepper. When the AMA comes out with a report in a few years and, reversing their decades-old position, states that salt is good for you, I plan to be way ahead in that game. I lightly floured a filet of gag grouper, seasoning it with pepper and fresh lemon. I pan-fried the fish, then mixed it in with soft scrambled eggs. A skillet of bacon, which had been spitting on another burner, completed the magnum opus. We took our positions.

We ate in silence, as silence to Morgan was not a void, but a presence, and one that often spoke the loudest. The lull between the sunrise fishing boats and daytime cruisers had quickly closed. Boats raced to the gulf, barely clearing the end of my dock, their wakes scarring the once calm water and crashing into the seawall like miniature rogue waves. Dolphins surfaced, and the osprey that crapped on my boat shrieked. A new album dropped on the turnstile, and Bryan Lee, a Sunday morning standard, filled the air.

I shoveled in a spoonful of egg and grouper and decided that the last thing in the world I wanted to do was get involved with Riley Anderson. But she'd hooked me with the bluster of her attitude and the vulnerability of her small, soft hand.

"Talk to Angelo?" I said after a swallow of eggs. Morgan had been on the phone while I slaved in the galley.

"I did. He confirmed what Riley said. He befriended them at the restaurant, and she chased him down the next night. Said she was hysterical and insisted her husband had been or would be killed—he wasn't sure of her exact words. He took her to Philipsburg to catch a flight."

His hair was tied back in a ponytail, and he had on a T-shirt with a pocket. I'd been a fan of T-shirts with pockets for years, and while not claiming to be a fashion trailblazer,

I'd convinced Morgan, who grew up on a sailboat, that they are one of life's basic necessities.

"New shirt?" I asked.

"Got it at the thrift shop." Morgan ran the local thrift shop that was open four days a week. I volunteered there myself—thought it might make me a better person.

"Do we believe her?"

"We do," he said confidently. "She tracked you down from a couple thousand miles away. She's scared, has no money, packs a wild tale, and professes to be in danger." Hadley III landed on his lap, took a sniff at the moon talisman around his neck, and settled her hindquarters down gingerly, as if she were mindfully considerate of his feelings.

"That reminds me," I said, although his comments had nothing to do with my wandering attention span. "Can you pick Riley up at the hotel and meet us at Mangroves? I'm supposed to be at Kathleen's at six, something about wanting me to look over a new class proposal."

"The digital revolution," Morgan reminded me, "and how it's accentuated the pace of change of the modern novel from 1998 to present."

"Come again?"

"That's her proposal."

"And you know this?"

"She told us both. Sitting here the other night."

"Interesting."

"Twice."

Hadley III leaped off his lap and sprinted toward a gecko. Morgan departed through the side door and circled around the bay side of my yard to his house next door. I placed a call to Natalie Binelli, an FBI agent whom I'd worked with in the past, and Brian Applegate, an information geek at

MacDill Air Force Base in Tampa, where SOCom is based. My partner, Garrett Demarcus, and I do work for our former army colonel and have used the base on numerous occasions. I left a pair of voice mails concerning Phillip Agatha and then found myself without physical motion, staring blankly over the water.

Riley Anderson, as Morgan noted, packed a wild tale. What the heck—I'd see where it went. After all, everything's a game. Sometimes you win. Sometimes you lose.

Sometimes you don't know what game you're playing.

4

I fed an orphaned meter on Beach Drive and took the lethargic private elevator as it grunted its way up to Kathleen's ninth-floor condo in downtown Saint Pete. The condo fronted Beach Drive and the expansive waters of Tampa Bay. On the way to her door, I stopped to return the book I'd borrowed from the common area she shared with the two other units on her floor. The area could be construed as either a living room with books or a library with couches: your pick. Each floor had a different theme, and we'd dubbed Kathleen's, which contained only war books, the Above Ground War Room. Until recently, the other two units had been empty, but Kathleen indicated she'd gained a pair of new neighbors within the past few weeks. I placed back the first edition of John Toland's *No Man's Land*. No titles caught my fancy. I had a better idea.

I rapped on Kathleen's door. She opened it.

"Forget your key?"

"Pardon the intrusion," I said with stiff formality, "but I've been struggling to choose between titles and wonder if you might step out here and lend a hand."

"Hmm, you would like me to go to the library with you."

Did she catch on fast or what? "I do. So many books, so little time. Do you recommend Chang's *The Rape of Nanking* or Gavin Daws's *Prisoners of the Japanese?*"

"That's a tough one, stranger. I suppose I could be of some assistance," she said, eyeing me warily, "but I don't know you, and I'm expecting a caller any moment."

She wore a summer dress with spaghetti straps. Her blonde hair, not yet collected, fanned out behind her. No shoes.

I took her hand in mine. "It won't take long."

"That's your line?"

"I'm proficient."

"*That's* your line? Tell you what, Proficient, let's have a drink in here. Both units are occupied and nine-B is the nicest—"

My mouth cut her off as I lifted her off her feet. I backed her into a wall of war books and battled the urge to gnaw her clothes off. She hiked her legs around my waist and leaned her head back, her right ear bent into John Colville's *The Fringes of Power*, which abutted *Last Letters from Stalingrad*. I yanked down her spaghetti straps, and her dress settled around her midsection like a patterned-cloth inner tube. We struggled to be quiet, but a couple of ancient tomes, as if vying for our attention, took a tumble.

My tongue found her breast and then traced up her neck until it touched her lips.

"Didn't you kill a man in this room once?" she said between breaths.

"In the elevator, actually. You're thinking of that now?"

"It's all around us, isn't it? The death, the brutality of the race, the—"

"They're just bo—"

"I don't like it." Her breathing was rushed and in crescendo. "Get rid of them. They're horror stories. Why are you slowing down? You said it would be fast. Come on, Proficient, come on, come—"

She was sucking my tongue when the door to our left opened.

"Mo pie," she said untangling our tongues, although I suspect she was going for "Oh my."

A thin woman—seventies maybe—fashionably dressed in jeans, a cream shirt, and layers of necklaces on her flat, suntanned chest, mildly observed us from the opened door of another unit. Kathleen's legs were still wrapped around me, my hands under her thighs, propping her up.

Kathleen swiveled her head to the side. "Mrs. Brandenburg. I'm so sorry. This is—"

"Sex in the library. Yes, dear. I can plainly see what it is." Mrs. Brandenburg commented. "Who is your friend?"

"Jake. Ah, Jake Travis. Jake, this is Mrs.—"

"Virginia Brandenburg. But please, just Ginny. Pleasure to make your acquaintance, Mr. Travis."

"It's Jake, Ginny," I said. "And the pleasure's all mine."

"Not if you're considerate."

"An excellent point, Ginny. I strive to—"

"Jake." Kathleen cut me off.

"Right. Well, I need to be going," I said and then turned my attention to Kathleen. "That'll be two hundred dollars, Dr. Rowe."

Kathleen puffed air in my face, and Ginny let out a giggle. If you didn't see her when she giggled, you would have pegged the sound as forty years younger. Do our laughs and giggles age? I decided they didn't, and it was good they stayed young. If you're lucky and figure this heartbreak carnival out before your number's called, humor should be the last thing you cough out on mother earth.

"I'll let you two rabbits go," Ginny offered, shattering my infatuation with her laugh. "I didn't really mean to interfere—nor, frankly, do I mind. I heard a ruckus, and I merely wanted to check it out. Very sexy legs—both of you. Kathleen?"

"Yes Mrs.—Ginny?"

"You know that dessert shop, a block down?"

"I do."

"That little machine that dispenses a ticket for the next in line?"

"Yes."

"Let's look into getting one for our private library."

Ginny Brandenburg gave me an ageless smile and gently closed her door. Kathleen's head collapsed on my chest.

"Proficient?" She spoke without looking up.

"Yes?"

She brought her eyes up to mine. "Where were we?"

Morgan and Riley took the corner and found us at our outside table at Mangroves. We made introductions. Riley was decked out in a resort-casual, sand-colored dress with a matching jacket. No way was it stuffed into Angelo's Pan Am bag.

"Nice outfit," I ventured.

"You like? Thank you *so* much. It was on sale, and I have nothing but rags in that travel bag. I know it's stupid, but I thought it would cheer me up. I've just been so depressed. I'll pay you back. It—"

"Nonsense." I scribbled a number on a napkin and handed it to her. "I have a membership there. It should be automatic, but make sure. Ten percent off anything. Food, cocktails, clothing, you name it. Be good to yourself." She cocked her head to the side, smiled, and stuck it in a brown purse.

"Thank you," she said. I couldn't imagine her internal battle—the world appearing so normal, yet twisted forever.

Applegate had gotten back to me. He had nothing on Agatha. Binelli had yet to return my call. I hadn't talked to her for over a year. What if she had no interest in continuing our tenuous relationship, whereby she used her resources at the FBI to unofficially aid me? If that were the case, I'd have to take whatever Riley dished out and try to sync it later with what I could unearth on my own. The colonel wouldn't help. He'd done me a mammoth personal favor once—when he arranged for Kathleen's new identity to hide her from her deceased husband's mob buddies—and he'd made it clear he was one and out. But that, too, is another story.

The waiter inquired if we'd like another bottle. His four pours had emptied the initial bottle. I nodded and told him to add a Jameson on the rocks. I treaded water while everyone got comfortable with one another, and then cut in. "Tell me about your bruises, from when Karl tossed you."

"Colorful, aren't they?" Riley stripped her jacket and pivoted her shoulder to display her discolored skin. "When the Fat Man found us, Karl and I were hugging and my back was to the door. Karl must have seen them come in. His eyes, they jus—I mean, next thing I knew, he had me over his head. He took a few steps, and I was airborne. Over the balcony and into the deep end of the pool. It was only one level below us, and I nicked the side going in. I tried to control where I went, like a flying squirrel—you know, what's-his-name. Rocky."

I arched my eyebrows. "Rocky was a cartoon character."

"Yeah? Well, let me tell you, I did my best Rocky."

"Karl say anything?"

"Yeah. He shouted, 'Run, baby, run.' Those were the last words my man said to me."

The waiter placed my Irish whiskey in front of me.

"Have a sip?" Riley said before my hand touched it. She was the type of person who liked to sample whatever someone else is drinking. Fine with me. Life's too short to just look at other people's drinks. I slid the tumbler over, and she took a double, wincing. "Run, baby, run." She glanced from Kathleen, to me, and back to Kathleen. "You never think about it, you know? What the last words you hear will be. And then you always have it because you're the one left behind." She gave a half shrug, just her right shoulder, the colors rising and falling. "That's what I got, and that's what I did." Her grieved eyes came back to me. "I ran to that restaurant where your friend Angelo works. Like I said, Karl befriended him earlier. He was the only person on the sandlot I knew. I ran into you and now—now, I don't know where to run."

I reached across the table and recovered my drink. The glass was already sweating with condensation—the water vapor in the air was cooling and turning into liquid. It imparted a cool dampness on my hand. Everything we touch, touches us. It struck me as a heavy thought I was destined to rendezvous with. I ditched it.

"You're not positive that your husband is dead, correct?" I wanted to clarify Riley's statements. "Is it possible they wanted him alive?"

"Believe me, I pray he's alive, but Karl knew too much. I told you on your boat; he told me the Fat Man would try to kill him. To kill us."

"About Santa. His name's Phillip Agatha, correct?"

"Right."

"How'd you meet?"

"OK, so Karl and I are—were—accountants. Benton Harbor corporate junkies, and that unfortunately came with Benton Harbor, Michigan, winters. Karl—shit, his mind was like a calculator on steroids—scored us, 'bout a year back, a job in Miami. Big art house, you know like Sotheby's, but private, and sweet fu—gosh, you just can't imagine the money. Listen, I'm sorry about my mouth; Karl keeps after me to clean it up."

"You were saying?"

"OK. So Karl just rocks with digits." Her cheeks ballooned as her breath puffed out. "They kept me on the legitimate stuff, but Karl? When they discovered his talent, he got promoted. They had him doing swaps, exchanges, buying art in one trust, gifting it to another—just about everything other than cash-and-carry. On Karl's side of the business there was rarely a name and address—never Mary Smith at 536 West Maple Street. It was always accounts that were shuttered immediately after the transaction. We rarely saw the art—painting, photograph, whatever—it was all a numbers puzzle. But Karl broke that. He was able to view what we were selling. Before that, each item was just a string of digits to us. Buyers, sellers, everything encrypted."

"Only Karl worked that side of the business?" I clarified.

"Right."

"When did you realize it was crooked?"

"Crooked? Is that what you think this is about?"

"Someone lifts a Raphael in Amsterdam, and it now hangs in a drug lord's cabana in Mexico."

Riley leaned in and propped her elbows on the table. Her black bangs formed a perfect ledge above her thin eyebrows. Her eyes drilled me. "Karl said we did that kind of stuff. I don't know any specific examples, but that wasn't the big bucks.

"Karl worked lone wolf one night and made a pattern out of one too many sets of numbers. He uncovered another business—blackmail. The blackmail pictures? They were the money machine."

"How did you, or he, know they were used for that purpose?"

"Geez, Louise, why else would a guy fork over five mil for a grainy picture of himself at half-mast with a woman in a bed behind him?"

I nodded in acceptance of her reasoning.

"My job," Riley continued, knowing her point had been made, "was balancing the books for the clean business lines. Karl discovered a man named Phillip Agatha ran the entire operation. Known as the Fat Man, but don't let him hear you call him that."

"Does the moniker fit?" Kathleen asked.

"Close enough." Riley's eyes darted to Kathleen and back to me. "He gets around, but with a cane. I met him a few times when he came in the studio. He wasn't in on hiring us, and he certainly had nothing to do with the daily grind of accounting."

"Ever meet him outside the studio?" I asked.

"That's when the problems started. We were at an employee party one night—the Ritz on Key Biscayne. We were on this big veranda of a restaurant that overlooks the lawn and ocean. The Fat Man—Agatha—rented it for the evening. Karl entered into a conversation with Agatha. They spewed numbers like tent-revival preachers quoting the gospel. They left me at the bar with a warm Chardonnay and Gino, the bartender, telling me he knew Bebe Rebozo back in the day. I'm like, who the hell's he, right? A clown? What kind of name is that? I mean, do you know?"

I gave a slight flip of my right hand to indicate it didn't matter. President Nixon and his entourage exited the arena long ago. She plowed ahead. "Karl told me later that night that Agatha had a brilliant mind, and coming from Karl, that puts him in a different sphere. Karl also said the more the Fat—Agatha—realized that Karl retained every number like it was branded into his brain, the more he seemed to reconsider Karl. As the night wore on, Agatha closed down, got more guarded. The next time Agatha dropped in, he avoided Karl. Karl became suspicious that if Agatha was worried about Karl's abilities with numbers, then those numbers must mean something. After that, it was game-on for Karl. A five-star Sudoku, baby."

I pulled out my cell phone. "Location and name of the art house in Miami?'

"The showroom's on the second floor of the Oceana hotel on Miami Beach. Name is Studio Four-Twenty. But words, not numbers. Big s, big f, big t."

"That's the name?"

Riley cocked her head. "Something to do to with—"

"The address?"

"No."

"Number of seconds in seven minutes."

"Yeah, that's what they said. How would you know?"

"Lucky guess. There was a book titled *The Seven Minutes*. Came out in sixty-nine. Explored the limits of pornography and free speech. The seven minutes refers to the time it takes for intercourse, and the book chronicles the thoughts in a woman's head during that time."

Riley reached over and took another drink of my whiskey as the waiter spread salads around the table. I pointed at my drink and gave him two fingers. He gave an understanding nod.

"Interesting." She reflected on my comment. "Something I should read?"

"Give it a go," I answered. "Critics panned it. Readers bought millions of copies."

"Whatever," she said, dismissing our mental diversion. "Four-Twenty was Agatha's baby. Had a goat for a logo. I mean, really? An art house with a goat for a logo? Karl discovered that Agatha owned the entire business. At first we thought he might have silent partners, but that wasn't the case. Hey, you with me?"

"Excuse me." I placed my phone away. I had texted Binelli requesting information she had on Studio Four-Twenty. I leveled my eyes on Riley. "So you cast your fortune with a bad lot. How did that lead to 'run, baby, run'?"

"Karl made a spreadsheet, you know, what numbers correlated to what photographs, and—listen, I don't really know you guys. We didn't ask for this, OK? Miami, right? Warm December mornings—I didn't even know there was such a thing. I mean the whole crazy thing sounded sexy, especially compared to tracking washer and dryer sales in Germany from a frozen office in Western Michigan. You know that's the western edge of the eastern time zone, right? In the winter, I'd be in my office for an hour and a half in the morning, and it would still be dark. They cranked up the heat to compensate, and I'm telling you, it was hot and dark, like the underside of a witch's tit in hell—oh, jeez." She punched the air with her right fist and shook her head. "I gotta clean it up. What I'm sayin' is—"

"Run, baby run." I tried to keep her focused.

"We understand, Riley," Kathleen said with empathy indigenous to her gender. "You didn't architect the story. You were deceived and purposely misled."

Riley, eager to have a caring ear, nodded at Kathleen. The waiter presented the new wine bottle and two tumblers of whiskey, each with a solitary round ice cube. Riley, without any acknowledgment to me for ordering her the drink, snatched hers off the table. She took a sip and squared her shoulders.

"We were in our condo in downtown Miami. It was night. Karl was on his computer, viewing pictures he'd decoded. I was standing over his shoulder, popping Sour Patch Kids, when this picture comes up. He pushed away from his desk, his face drained of color, and he said…he said, 'We got to go, baby. We got to get out of here.' I'll never forget that, you know? It wasn't like, 'Hey, look what I found,' or 'Let's think this through.' No, sirree. He knew right away that we needed out. My baby, I tell you, he was smart."

Our dinners arrived. Kathleen, who teases her food more than she consumes it, twiddled her fork and managed to spear a few bites. Morgan leaned back and took a sip of wine. He crossed his tan-slacked legs and cradled his long-stem glass. For a man who lived in T-shirts and shorts he always, per his deceased father's dictum, wore long pants while dining out. He'd ordered scallop appetizers for dinner. His diet, coupled with swinging around a sailboat like a monkey, explained his marathon physique.

My eight-ounce filet stood no chance with me. Riley had yet to acknowledge her lobster tail. Might cut that up and put it in scrambled eggs in the morning. Looking good for the world's second most important person.

"And did you?" Morgan inquired. "Leave that night?"

"Twenty minutes," Riley popped in. "That's what he gave us. He had us out of that condo and into a hotel—paid with cash—and in the local FBI office at nine the next morning. He said the FBI on account of all the international transactions we did.

"Karl told the FBI guy—guy's last name was Leonard, you know, a name that could either be first or last—what he'd seen, pictures of underage girls and the other photo, the one that made us run. Told him we had the bank accounts. Leonard said not to worry, said he'd take it from there."

I reached over and forked a chunk of Kathleen's snapper. Riley poked at her lobster tail, and then tore it apart like an osprey eating a pinfish. She bathed it in butter, and my mouth watered with regret over the scrambled eggs and lobster that wouldn't greet me in the morning.

I swallowed the fish. "What was the picture or pictures that Karl and you saw that caused him to flee? What you just referred to as 'the other photo'?"

She hesitated. "There was this one picture, but before we saw that he'd broken a series of numbers that unveiled five-, ten-, even several fifteen-million-dollar jobs."

"Do you have names?"

"Yeah, but Karl said that didn't mean anything. These weren't board-approved transactions, you know?"

"Leonard and the picture."

"I'm getting there," Riley insisted. "Karl asked if we were in danger, and Leonard said not to worry. We thought we overreacted. Karl felt bad about rushing me out the night before so we returned to our condo to get more clothes, maybe even stay. What did we know?"

She stuffed a chunk of lobster in her mouth and swiped a napkin across her mouth. She had thin lips, like Kathleen's. I was prepping to nudge her again about the picture that caused Karl Anderson to bolt, when she fired back up.

"We get back to our place; it was trashed—man-oh-man, it was pure luck we weren't there when someone came. We figured they knew we broke their code. But we'd taken our computers with us to the hotel. Not that it mattered; every number crunched by a machine is like a picture in Karl's head. Perfect recall. Karl figured Agatha knew that. 'You want your accountants to be bright,' Karl said, 'but not too bright, and I was too bright.'" She took the final bite from my breakfast and shoved her plate away. "Next morning, Karl's cell rang. It was an FBI agent, McKeen, or something like that. Two *e*'s. I know 'cause Karl asked. He said he was handed our case and had some questions. Told us he was swamped but to meet us for lunch at Hollandaise, downtown Miami."

"You, or Karl, think anything unusual about that?" I decided to let Riley travel at her own meandering speed.

She eyed me approvingly. "You would have liked my Karl. Yeah, he was suspicious, but the guy mentioned Leonard's name. Seemed legit—public place—right? We pull up, and Karl, he just says 'fuck,' you know, like that's the definitive word for the universe. Karl never cussed. Hell, I was salty enough for both of us, but I was, I am, trying to stop."

"He recognized someone?"

"No. Well, he did, and we didn't. We didn't know what this guy, McKeen, was supposed to look like in the first place. But the photo that made us run? The one you're bugging me about? Karl recognized one of the men he saw as the same guy on his computer screen. He was chatting with a slug-neck in a suit who had a holster, same as Leonard had, so we figured the slug-neck was McKeen."

I picked up my fresh whiskey on the rocks. "Sounds like the FBI was previously investigating Agatha, and you tripped across one of their agents. Maybe even jeopardized their operation."

"You think?"

"FBI scams are pretty elaborate," I explained after letting the whiskey dissolve down my throat. "Just because the man showed up in a photo doesn't implicate him. It's likely an intricate undercover assignment. They're on the verge of getting the evidence they need, and Karl stumbles along and blows it up. You need to approach the FBI again. I know an agent. I trust her, you—"

"We went back to the FBI office." She didn't even fake interest in my advice. "Karl wanted to talk to Leonard, the guy we saw before? He seemed real nice. But they told us he died. Hit-and-run the night before."

"I saw that," Morgan cut in. "Taken out by a swerving car as he left a barber shop."

"Could be coincidence," I suggested. "If they suspect that Leonard's death is in any manner related to his work, the FBI will go on the warpath. Until we know, we can conjecture all night."

"Conjecture?" She leaned in toward me. "Listen, dingleberry, when Karl asked for Special Agent McKeen, he was told that there was no McKeen in that, or any FBI office, in the state of Florida."

"The number McKeen called you from?"

"Karl was on that, too. Burner phone." She leaned back and took a drink from her glass, her face scrunching at the whiskey.

"Doesn't disprove the sting theory. Even makes sense." I stubbornly held my ground and returned to the event that launched Karl Anderson out of his chair. "The picture that Karl and you saw, the man he recognized at Hollandaise. Why is it so damaging?"

Riley folded her arms tight across her chest. "I just got a glimpse, OK? In the picture, this guy was standing next to a bed where a nude girl was lying. The girl, she...she was dead. Blood, just everywhere. There was a mirror on the wall, and you could make out the Fat Man and along with another man, whose face was hidden behind a camera. You know, one of those big ones. But the other guy—standing by the bed—his face was panic. He was the same man Karl recognized at Hollandaise, the slug-neck. The man who we assumed was an FBI agent."

She tossed back an ounce of whiskey and slapped her glass on the table. "Tell me now, Mr. Conjecture, how you like your FBI-stingy-thingy theory?"

5

I liked it just fine. Although, as names go, Mr. Proficient was more fun than Mr. Conjecture.

Undercover assignments oftentimes put agents in uncompromising and dangerous positions. It wouldn't be the first time, or the last, someone got stung in a sting, or got trapped in a situation from which they could not extricate themselves. Riley had revealed nothing to solidly dissuade me from my position that Karl and she had tripped over an FBI sting operation—possibly a busted one. But I wouldn't get anywhere by challenging her or trying to convince her that I, who had not witnessed any of this, knew more than she.

"Did you or Karl recognize anyone besides Agatha in the picture?" I pressed her.

"No. Karl said he'd bet his last chip they were blackmailing Panic Man with murder. Karl broke into the site again on Saint Kitts, but Agatha beat him to it. All the codes were changed."

"Would you recognize the man if I showed you a picture?"

"Recognize him? I'll need therapy to forget him. Besides, the point is, why murder? You'd think catching a guy with his pants down would be enough for blackmail, right? But Karl said Agatha was taking it one step further. Blackmailing someone with murder leaves no way out. The guy just can't just say, 'Oh, forget it. I was going to leave my wife anyway.' The ultimate blackmail, Karl called it. That picture—a man standing over a dead woman?—Karl traced it. It was a fifteen-million-dollar shot. Remember I told you he came across several fifteen-million-dollar jobs? He figured that was the going rate. You know, guy thinks he's getting laid and instead ends up with a murder rap unless he does what is required of him."

"And who wouldn't," I said, recognizing the perfect blackmail. "One will do whatever is required to avoid a life sentence."

A trolley car, with a half-dozen people on each side facing the middle and pumping their legs to propel the vehicle, passed us on Beach Drive. The interior of the trolley cart was a bar, and each human piston had a drink in front of them. There is much in this world that I do not understand.

"Did you tell anyone else that you were going to the FBI office?" Kathleen asked.

"Absolutely not."

"Denying the name," I reasoned, "would be standard procedure for an agent they had undercover, as would using a burner phone." I changed course before Riley had the chance to counterpunch. "How did you go from the FBI office to Saint Kitts?"

"OK, so we're back at the FBI office, right? This guy named Schum—one m—took us into his cubicle. Turns out they were preparing a case against Agatha. Don't give me any lip—that *does*n't explain Leonard's death and mystery-man McKeen, both of whom totally baffled the feds. Karl suddenly became the world's most important person."

I knew that was false. The world's most important person was to my left, dallying with her fork, although strangely, the pile of mashed potatoes the fish rested on had disappeared.

Riley let out her breath as if the evening had weakened her, and the finish line was finally within sight. "We never left their custody. They ushered us into a conference room. Summoned the team. I remember I liked that, safety in numbers, you know? Told us they were investigating Agatha and needed Karl to testify—some grand jury thing. Said we weren't in danger, but they wanted us out of the country. Karl accused them of having a leak. Asked them if the hit-and-run on an FBI agent was related to our case. Said he recognized one of the men at the restaurant as a client, or perhaps a victim, of Studio Four-Twenty."

"How'd they react to that?"

"Didn't give a shitbox about us, if you ask me, and you did. One of their own was down. Karl said we went from the pot into the fire, but we had no choice. They whizzed us off to Saint Kitts. Karl told me he didn't know if we were being hidden from Agatha or the FBI."

"Perhaps both," I said and decided not to claim a victory lap for previously insinuating that the FBI was already involved with Agatha. "If they were prepping a case against Agatha, it's likely they had someone on the inside, and Karl tripped a wire. The dead agents don't disprove the theory. They needed you out of the way. To protect you and their inside man."

"What happened next?" Kathleen asked before Riley had time to swoop on my statement.

"Karl told me to relax. Little hard to believe the whole FBI office was on the Fat Man's payroll, you know? They assigned Special Agent Lippman to accompany and protect us."

I said to Riley, "Is he that man you told me on the boat you found slumped against a garbage Dumpster?"

"You're dialed in now. Two dead G-men. Your they're-running-a-scam theory is taking on water. How do you—?"

"You just admitted they were preparing a case against him."

"By killing their own agents?"

I surrendered the point. It was likely a runaway sting, but there was nothing to gain by alienating her. I dropped it until I had the opportunity to talk with Binelli, assuming that call got returned. Either they were running an elaborate sting on Agatha—lining up an ironclad case to present to a grand jury—or they weren't. If they were, I was done. If not, then things got a little more interesting. I settled the chit and glanced at Kathleen. Our eyes met, and my world shrank. It's that simple. My eyes can chase skin all day, but my heart leaps only for her. My tail started wagging.

"How long you two been together?" Riley asked, catching our eye contact, or perhaps seeing my tail wag.

"Close to two years," Kathleen answered and gave me a matronly smile.

"That's nice. You look so relaxed together—ohhh—I bet you guys got it on be*fore* dinner, didn't you?"

I jumped in. "I don't—"

"*Totally* get it," Riley said, perking up, her knowing eyes flashing between Kathleen and me. "Karl and I used to do that all the time. Hitting the stars before dinner—that's what we called it—is *the* best way to enjoy a good meal. She leaned back in her chair and slapped her hand on the table. "Good for you guys. Super. I'm happy for you."

Kathleen squirmed in her seat, and I hid behind my whiskey glass. I had no idea that love in the library was public domain.

"Run, baby, run?" I prompted her in an attempt to wrap things up, while simultaneously taking the heat off myself. I wanted to ask her if she'd heard any gunshots as she fled but couldn't think of a delicate way to frame the question.

She hesitated and gazed at me from a different time zone. All evening, she'd been manufacturing happiness, as if she was trying to distance herself from her sad reality. The sadness, I knew, had become her new shadow.

"Karl," she said, "had on his new shirt I'd just bought him. I'd found it at...I had fresh fish that I...I—" She hung her head. "I'm sorry, I can't." Kathleen leaned over, touched Riley's shoulder, and shot me a disapproving look.

"Riley?" Morgan interjected. She raised her head, grateful that someone had summoned her. "What else can you tell us about the Fat Man, Phillip Agatha's, victims? The deceased girl; where did she come from?"

Morgan zoned in on the core issues faster than anybody I knew. The victim wasn't the blackmailed man who couldn't keep his hands off or his pants on, and who had likely, in the mindless pursuit of money, contacted Agatha to alleviate a business problem. The tragedy was the dead girl in the bed, and the one after that.

Riley, however, had no clue and had wrung herself dry. Studio Four-Twenty, she did add, maintained a respectable catalog of mainly South American artists. Above all, discretion and silence were expected from the employees. Anything less was met with a pink slip and a personal escort out the front door.

I told Riley I'd keep her informed, and we called it an evening. Morgan took Riley back to the beach on his Harley. Kathleen and I split a gelato from the dessert store next door. They did have one of those take-a-ticket machines. I asked the young brunette with the black apron around her waist how much they wanted for it. Kathleen punched me in my shoulder. Despite her PhD in English lit, she was fond of nonverbal means of communication.

As we entered her condo, she kicked off her heels and stripped the lightweight sweater she'd put on halfway through dinner. She let her hair down, and I wondered if she had a clue what that did to me. "What are you going to do for her?" she asked.

"Have a cigar on the patio."

"Way to face the music. You were a little insensitive back there."

"What part?"

"Whole part."

I replied by helping myself at the bar cart. A few minutes later, we sat in lounge chairs, facing the night, each with a two-ounce pour of twenty-year-old port. A yacht trolled south through the dark waters toward the mouth of Tampa Bay, a quarter moon holding water, tepidly lighting its path.

I took a drag of the cigar and offered it to her. She waved me off. "I think the secondary will suffice tonight." That surprised me. She was a sucker for a good cigar, and I was a sucker for watching her cheeks collapse inward when she took a drag. Dormant genes fired up at that sight. I imagined that stemmed from when our caveman forefathers gathered around the pit, passed the weed, and eyed the only woman who—

"What can you do for her?" Kathleen rephrased her earlier question, cutting off my intellectual quest to understand my highly disturbed, yet ultimately simplistic gender.

"Sniff around. See what Binelli at the FBI comes up with. If there's a leak in the agency, they've likely circled the wagons and choked off outside communication."

"The colonel?"

"Not in his area." Either the FBI was in control of Agatha or they weren't. If they were, they could take Riley Anderson off my payroll. Hopefully do a better job than they did last time.

Kathleen went to bed, but I stayed behind, high in the night sky. I finished both glasses of port before I got lost in the part of the clock that was suspended evenly between the falling and rising sun.

No man's land.

6

The sedan that shadowed my route rounded the corner in front of the Valencia. It kept a constant crawling speed up Beach Drive. If it were going to the hotel, it would have pulled in. Otherwise, that type of car had no business being downtown at 6:35 a.m.

I'd completed my morning run and was doubled over in Straub Park, staring at a woman's worn pink sandal with a black Nike swoosh. I wondered if she'd lost it while peddling on the beer wagon. Wine, whiskey, and tawny port sweated through my pores as if my body were emptying yesterday's poisons, knowing that in a few hours I'd reload and charge that hill once again.

I came out of my bends and starting limping down the sidewalk in my postrun gait. The sedan slowed beside me. The reflective, dark passenger window silently lowered, and a face appeared.

"Mr. Travis?"

"You got the wrong man."

"I don't think so."

"Perhaps you don't think."

"We'd like to talk to you."

"I'm all ears, Eliot."

"Get in the backseat," he commanded.

"Sweaty and all. Hate to stink up your ride more than it is."

"I'll spray it after you leave."

"With what? Perfume in your handbag?"

"Get in."

"Get lost."

The car stopped, and I faced my sparring partner. G-man to the bone: buzzed hair, plaid jacket, and a tie he got for Christmas fifteen years ago. "I don't know what they told you," I said, wondering why I let the guy goad me, "but if you expect 'get in' to pull my cord, your day's off to a disappointing start."

The back window lowered, and Natalie Binelli appeared. "If you didn't start with the premise that everyone was an enemy," she explained, "you'd have more friends. How's this: May we please have the pleasure of your company?"

If I didn't start with the premise that everyone I met was a potential enemy, I'd have been gone a long time ago. The army taught me to instinctively formulate a plan to kill people when entering an unknown situation. Try entering a Chipotle, and your mind, with no conscious prompts, takes out the room—barely hesitating for the junior-high kids in school uniforms—and maps your exit before the door shuts behind you. *And you want to integrate me back into your society?*

I capitulated and sauntered around to the other side. I got in and slammed the door.

"We got a few question for you," the tie in the front passenger seat announced while keeping his eyes straight ahead.

"Before you blow more air," I retorted, "here's a couple of guidelines. Buy a new tie every ten years, and I talk to Binelli only. You even acknowledge I'm here, and I'm gone."

"What do you think?" He nodded to the driver. "Class-A a-hole, just like the lady said."

Binelli's hand lightly squeezed my sweaty right thigh, and I instinctively glanced at her. It'd been, what, nearly two years? She wore jeans and a white blouse. A charcoal blazer covered most of the blouse, and her hair was a tad longer than I remembered. It fell just below the collar of the blazer, the tips caressing the cottony fabric. A fish-line necklace rested on her clavicle bone and disappeared deep into her blouse. Binelli was a theater major from Vassar who chucked the green room for the real show, but she still carried that persona; being the one on the stage everyone's eyes were glued to.

"Phillip Agatha," she stated.

"The Fat Man," I replied.

"What do you know?"

"Not much. You still packing two guns?"

Tie Man burped out a chuckle. Binelli let out her breath. Her layered, milk chocolate bangs rose and then settled in the exact same position, like opening and shutting venetian blinds.

"How'd you trip across the name?" she wanted to know.

Tie Man, still keeping his head straight, said, "Binelli, you're the candy that got him in the car. We do the questions."

"You didn't listen," I reprimanded him.

We hit a red light on Central. I gestured to the door and said to her, "On three. One, two." Binelli and I scampered out of our respective doors. She leaned over and stuck her head through the open passenger front window and said a few words I couldn't make out. The driver laughed, and the car resumed its mindless pace.

"What did you tell your friends?" I asked her.

"They're not my friends."

"I just contacted you yesterday. What did they do, pull you out of bed and shuttle you down here?"

"You could have been a tinge more considerate back there."

"They're not your friends. Besides, I don't ride those wheels."

"But I do." She planted her hands on her hips. "Where can we get a cup?"

"Walk with me."

We went to a corner grocery mart that did a brisk morning business. We corralled a table by the window, and the rising sun illuminated her chair. I went to the counter and purchased a bottle of water along with two coffees and a banana.

"Bagel," Binelli yelped from the table. "Everything. Toasted. Easy on the cheese. Not too easy. Double toast. But not burned."

I made one for each of us and returned to my chair in the shadows. It viewed the park across the street and the Saint Petersburg art museum a block south of us. It was a pleasant morning spot.

I took a bite of toasty-hot bagel and in midchew said, "Phillip Agatha."

She draped her tailored blazer over the back of her chair. Her gun rested in her holster above her left hip, the cinnamon leather strap cutting a swath of color over her white shirt. The top two buttons had the day off.

"He's above my pay grade," she said, crossing her legs. "The only reason they brought me in—and yeah, a two a.m. phone call, said a car would collect me in fifteen to take me to the airport—was because when I entered the name Phillip Agatha, from the text you sent, horns blared. Strobes flashed. They practically threw me into lockdown."

"What do you know?"

"We'll get there, Hopalong, but here comes my singular assignment for the day. Remember, shooting the messenger is a federal offense, not to mention extremely unfair."

"I'll save you the speech." I took a draw from the flimsy plastic bottle—they get any thinner, they won't be able to hold water. Ginny Brandenburg walked through the front door. She eyed me, cut a look at Binelli, rolled her eyes, and shook her head.

"You were collected," I said, focusing my attention on Binelli, "to put in a personal appearance in order to persuade me to drop my interest in Agatha. You told them I wouldn't listen. They told you to try. You will. You'll fail, although you won't tell them that. You'll end up actually helping me—aiding and abetting, they'll call it—but whether you admit that now, I don't know. You didn't mind the phone call because, frankly, it's a little boring at two in the morning, and you need the rush of the stage to feel alive. The curtain rises when you strap the gun on."

"Pompous ass."

"Did I miss anything?"

"Admitting your heart went pitty-patter when you saw me."

"What do you know about Agatha?" I asked for the second time.

"Why's he in your life?"

"You first, I can ride out of here without answering to superiors."

"No need to go to the mat with every comment, you know?" She took a sip of her coffee and held my eyes to make certain I'd received her message. "We've been doing an internal on Agatha—a lot of this I just got this morning. We had an agent, C. J. Leonard—Charlie Junior—in Miami, nicked into the deep sleep by a hit-and-run. Turns out he'd just taken a walk-in, man and wife, professing knowledge of Agatha's operation. Knowledge we'd been trying to gather for close to a year, and this guy, the husband, has it in his head. We're investigating Leonard's death. Maybe tied in, maybe not.

"Walk-in and wife double back the next day and claim that another agent, a McKeen, contacted them. No such man. Two e's, they insisted. Odd they knew the spelling for a man who doesn't exist. We questioned the guy on Agatha's business and verified that he was authentic. We whisk the couple off to Saint Kitts to keep them low until we sorted things out. We want them to testify at a grand jury that convenes in a couple of weeks. Our agent assigned to them ends up slumped against the Dumpster with a hole in his head. The man he was supposed to protect, the walk-in? Upstairs with the same wound. Ballistics says the same gun killed both, a Berretta 92. Sorry you asked?"

I finished off my bagel while it was still warm. I'd have to tell Riley there was a positive ID on her deceased husband. How much hope did she still harbor?

"So Agatha's a bad guy," I pointed out to her. "Go get him. That's in the job description, isn't it?"

She leaned across the table. "He's on our 'hands-off' list."

"I don't follow. Aren't you running a sting against him?"

"Not sure. Maybe—"

"It was a yes or no question."

"Then no," she admitted. "Apparently he's working with us, helping us net an even bigger fish, although murder's the shark of crime. He's been under suspicion for years, but no biggie there; international art galleries are under constant surveillance. I just know that somewhere, someone doesn't want anyone poking around."

"You got two dead agents."

"Like we don't know?"

"Here's what your agency doesn't know: whether to wear a suit or a gun. Consequently, you don't excel at either."

"I'd forgotten how sweet you are."

I left the table and returned with several napkins. I wiped my hands, which were wet from the condensation on the water bottle, and said, "The guy in the bureau, protecting him, running him, what does he say to that?"

"The women or men who operate those stings? They never step out of the shadow. Too much career risk if it lands in the shitter. From what I've been told, some faction of the bureau is insisting that Agatha can still lead us to bigger and better targets. Meanwhile, we don't have the means to make a credible case against him. We're not interested in prolonged and expensive court cases. We have a new mandate—unless the odds are heavily in our favor, we don't press charges. It's a budget decision. Life's a budget decision. So, to amend my statement, we're not sure whether he's hands-off, or we simply can't pin him at this time."

"No man's land," I uttered what was becoming a disturbing theme.

She nodded in acceptance. "That sums it up. How'd you happen to cross paths with Agatha?"

I leaned back and took a drink of coffee. Our eyes locked. "It's not in your best interest to know."

"I can take care of my—"

"You're my only contact in Hoover."

"I see." Her eyes glanced outside as she took another sip from her ribbed cardboard paper cup. A small smudge of red lipstick marked her entry point. "So, you know of Agatha from someone who came in contact with him."

I remained silent.

"OK." The right side of her lip curled up, like an internal challenge, not as an expression to others. "Let's retrace." She uncrossed her legs and leaned in. "Agatha's name floats up when a couple rings the doorbell of the Miami office. The agent they meet is the aforementioned victim of a hit-and-run. The couple, the Andersons, hit the bell a second time, and we put them in a quasi-witness-protection program—we need the Andersons to testify. The husband, Karl, with a K, holds a head full of data. We skirt them off to some island where even Magellan can't find them, and Karl with a K goes sunny-side up, along with the agent sent to babysit them. That tells me that the internal forces who are protecting Agatha have greater resources than the forces who were protecting the Andersons. The woman—wife— survived. She may or may not hold damaging information, and all of that would depend on what side you're on. Her name was Sissy, Casey—no, *Riley*."

She sat back in her chair. "How'd I do?"

"Pompous ass."

She came back in. She smelled good. It was the same perfume she had on the night we first crossed paths. Scent, unbounded from the dimensional world, is time travel.

She gazed at her cup, rotated it a few degrees, and then came back at me. "She found you. Didn't she? We sent them to Saint Kitts, and that's where you packed off that gardener, Angelo somebody, who worked with Escobar. You and your hippie neighbor spend time there. She, Riley, found you and told you a tale."

Ginny Brandenburg, on her way out the door, paused, and said with a double entendre smile, "Nice seeing you, Jake."

"Likewise, Ginny. Have an enjoyable day."

"You mean pleasurable."

"That, too."

"Friend of yours?" Binelli pried after Ginny was gone.

"Met her at a deli."

"Creepy. It's like she looked straight through you."

"I have that effect."

"Hmm...have you talked to her? Riley, not Miss Creeps."

"No."

She lowered her head like a disappointed teacher. "Still a liar, aren't you? Fine. My turn. You talked to Riley. Know where she is. But you won't tell me because you don't want to put me in danger. I can honestly say that I don't know."

I sat motionless, my hands tented in front of me.

"Give me a sign."

I pointed my finger like it was a gun, pushed my thumb down, and popped my lips.

"I need to tell the Boy Scouts in the front seat something. Any suggestions?"

I couldn't feign total ignorance; that would reek of covering up. Nor could I divulge that I had Riley Anderson stashed in the hotel. If the FBI was working both sides of Agatha, prepping charges against him while at the same time protecting him until those charges carried enough legal weight to convince a jury, Riley Anderson was prime material to toss under a bus.

"Tell them—" I started in, having no clue where I was going. We all do it. We engage our mouths before we engage our brains. Something's got to come out. It's oftentimes the raw truth. It's equally often pure garbage. "Tell them I'm coming after the Fat Man."

"This is serious," Binelli protested. "I just can't—"

I stood up. "What did you expect?"

"Sit down."

"Sorry if our first meeting misled you. The FBI doesn't know whether they stand for God and country or the devil and—"

"It's not that simple, and you—"

"I'm saddled and riding." I leaned over her. "They can sort out the moral questions and internal issues later. They lost control of the game. That brings other parties in."

She gave a slight shake of her head. Neither my words nor my posturing had fazed her.

"They can make your life difficult," she said quietly, as if she didn't want her voice to distract from her words. "You don't need them to be your friend, but you don't want them as adversaries. Why not help yourself? You don't prove anything by wearing red at a bullfight."

"My honesty with you does not necessitate that you share that attribute with them. Something will pop in that pretty head before you crawl in the backseat and they drive you around like a schoolgirl." I straightened out, giving her space back. "Tell them I heard a rumor, death in Saint Kitts, asked around, but not to worry, the real concern in my life is public-pension liabilities—be creative. Just help me get Agatha."

She stood. "Lord knows why I bother."

Why did she bother?

She took a step toward the door and dumped her plate with bagel crumbs into the trash can. I would have licked it first. She faced me. "I'll do what I can, but they got eyes on this one, and on me. Listen to me?"

"More than you know."

"Watch your hind side. Bodies are piling up, and our efforts are stymied from within. We got two dead agents, which means everyone's got their vigilante hat on. Don't underestimate G-men with six-shooters. They can give you religion real fast. Agatha has a magic field around him, which means no one trusts one another."

"I'll take your warning into consideration."

"No, you won't."

"What do you got?" I asked. "You didn't come here to log travel time with male chauvinist pigs."

She smiled and reached between her breasts. She pulled out a locket that hung on her long necklace, unfastened it, and handed a flash drive to me. "It's our basic material on Agatha. It saves you days of research, but more important, keeps you from blowing up my phone twenty-four-seven."

"Why?"

"Why what?"

"Helping me. Again. Going out on a limb."

"I'm bored."

"There's more."

"What are you now, a shrink?" She blurted it out defensively and then tossed out a dismissive, "I don't like bad guys."

She started for the door, a physical act intended to end the conversation. Binelli never did goodbyes, on the phone or in person. "What are you going to say," I said to her back, "so our stories mesh?"

She turned around to me. "They dragged me out of bed at two in the morning, stuck me in the middle seat of the plane and the backseat of the car. We checked your house and drove for three years before I remembered your penchant for early morning runs and that your lady was moving downtown. I was trying your cell for the umpteenth time when we spotted you. You run that fast every morning? By then the Scouts had clocked forty minutes of droning about everything from their golf game to passing gas during the Monday morning brief. Spitting out words like I wasn't even there." She nodded her head. "The pension line?"

"Yeah?"

"I'm going with that."

"Might be a long flight back to DC."

"I'll make them sweat."

"How so?"

"The old standard, sailor." She cocked out her hip. "I'll loosen another button."

7

"Have a good time." Kathleen sprang up on her tiptoes and gave me a peck. "Gallery-hopping in Miami."

I'd reviewed my plan with her, showered, and hustled home to grab my laptop before doubling back to the Tampa airport. Phillip Agatha wasn't likely to be hanging around his studio, and I'd even debated whether I wanted my face known. But if Studio Four-Twenty was the center of the maelstrom, I might as well jump in.

Traffic was kind to me, and the flight was delayed fifteen minutes. That granted me thirty minutes to kill before boarding. I got a table at a restaurant and ordered breakfast. I informed the waitress that her tip would be in direct proportion to the crispiness of the bacon and then inserted the flash drive.

Phillip Hartselle Agatha was raised on Bonaire, which along with Aruba and Curacao is part of the ABC Caribbean islands. His father was in hotel management and his mother part time in the same establishment. Agatha was the middle of three; he had an older sister and a much younger brother. Everyone else was anchored to the island, but Agatha tested off the planet in high school and snatched a full ride to Miami in Coral Gables. He majored in math but dropped out after two years, having already set up a profitable trading company in Hong Kong. Outside of sporadic visits, he never returned to Bonaire for an extended period of time. He spent most of his time either in his 4,139-square-foot condo twenty-eight floors into the Miami sky, or on his boat, the *Gail Force.* She was a 2006 164-foot luxury yacht from Proteksan-Turquoise shipyard. She'd been upgraded, at an estimated $2 million, when Agatha bought her three years ago. All funneled through Studio Four-Twenty.

Agatha's name was not connected to the studio until a Bermuda corporation that controlled the majority stake issued private stock two and a half years ago. A trust controlled by Phillip Agatha owned the entire float. By then, he was three tax identification numbers and two shell corporations removed. Also, my bacon was gone. I didn't remember eating the last piece. What's the point? I left a twenty on a ten-dollar breakfast.

Ninety minutes later I exited a cab, stuck my arms into my cream silk jacket and, after dodging pellet-size drops of rain, entered Oceana Hotel on A1A in Miami Beach. Riley had indicated that Studio Four-Twenty's showroom was on the second floor.

Oceana: an early 1940s project. Its current owners had done an admirable job of restoring to its opening day romantic luster. A restaurant was on the first floor, and the hotel's rooms started on the third floor. Behind the front desk was a wall of thick wood slots where messages and keys were placed. A cozy pub was off to the side and ran on the opposite wall behind the front counter.

Cozy pub: dark walls, a trayed ceiling, and a slick, shiny mahogany bar. It might hold thirty people, tops, but now served as sanctuary for two men. The wood backlit shelves of the bar framed amber bottles that stood like statuesque women, their dark mystery waiting to be unleashed in my body. I often find myself, immediately after exercising, looking forward to the Shangri-La part of the day, my mind skipping through the middling hours, hopping from one peak to another. I made a date with myself for that evening to do a little liver damage.

On the second floor, a glass door led into a pleasantly cool room with a gleaming parquet floor. A boy/man with dark skin and a tweed suit jacket sat erect behind a desk. His hair was the bastard child of a Beatle-bowl haircut and a marine: round and thick on top and a buzzed layer around his ears. The desk was an old door with a plate of glass on it supported by two wood horses. A phone and an open MacBook completed the ensemble. The phone was a black rotary, same time-period as the hotel.

"May I be of assistance?" he inquired as he twisted a ring on his right ring finger, my presence rudely interrupting his day. Nat King Cole crooned "Avalon" from ceiling speakers.

"I'm in town for the day, and a friend suggested I drop by. I have eclectic taste and thought your studio might be of some assistance to me."

"Honey, we're open by appointment only."

"Shame I didn't have the luxury of securing arrangements, but my lifestyle rarely permits such delicacies."

"Your friend's name?"

"Mr. Greenbacks."

"Naturally. And your name?"

"Travis. Jake Travis."

"My apologies, Mr. Travis, but we show *on*ly by appointment."

"Where's the Gail Force moored?"

"Beg your pardon?"

"Phillip's boat. Perhaps if you can't meet my most immediate needs, I can swing by, see if he can be of assistance.

Help him polish the rail." I tried to sound affable, but I could never hit that note.

His hands clutched into little miniature fists on each side of the laptop. He forced a tight smile, picked up the phone, dialed a single number, and said, "You listening?" He placed it back into its cradle and typed away on his computer.

"Does this mean we're done?" I asked.

He answered with a snotty smile.

I wandered over to a front window, taking in the Miami Beach scene. Miami's like a pot that every can of soup's been poured into. Sure, you might like bits and pieces, but the whole thing? Is it even digestible? For my money, I'd—

"I'll be taking care of you." A sultry voice lassoed my rambling mind.

I turned and faced a tall, slender bronze creature with waves of black, curly hair framing her high cheekbones, glossy forehead, and hammock lips. Her hair cascaded well below her shoulders. Sparkling brushstrokes of blue eye shadow covered her eyelids. She was in a black dress with a see-through mesh center. The see-through mesh didn't close up until south of her belly button, and down there she looked soft and vulnerable, like she was two different people. Her severe beauty was intimidating.

I moseyed over to her. She was taller the closer I got. Or I was shrinking. Some women do that to a man.

"Mr. Travis." She said it as a statement, not a question.

"Jake." I extended my hand.

She blew her breath out through pierced lips and then reached up her right hand and clawed it through my hair. She took her time, appraising me, considering my value. She took her fingers to the base of my skull, dug in, and nearly scratched me. I waited for a purr. Her hand then traced around to the front of my neck and she rested it just below my throat, her fingers hanging on my shirt above the top button. She gave me a little tug.

"That's how you shake hands?" I said, holding my ground.

"We all touch one another, it's just a question of how fast and how deep. Do you like my handshake?"

"Tough act for a politician to pull off all day."

No smile, and that disappointed me. Humor is the first thing I look for in a person. If it's not there, my interest dive-bombs. Garrett is the exception without explanation.

"Follow me." She turned and paraded through the door.

We entered a spacious bright room with a row of tall framed glass panes viewing A1A. One side wall held monochrome photographs. A girl with questioning eyes and small breasts. If she was sixteen, I was a hundred. Another shot was of two women touching each other while one of them glanced indifferently to her side, eyeing a large panting dog. It was typical artsy trash porn—not that I know anything about that. The opposite wall held oils that appeared to be serious art—not that I know anything about that.

My creature settled into a dark leather couch and crossed her enticing legs. I claimed the chair across from her. Nat was done with "Avalon" and a reggae throw down of "Crimson and Clover" filled the room. Tommy James and the Shondells catching a second wind in Miami. Maybe not such a bad town after all.

"I believe you were informed that we are closed," she stated.

"I need you to open up."

"I'm particular about that."

"As you should be. But if you want to do business—" I spread my hands.

"You don't have a referral number, do you?"

"Seven?"

"In fact," she said with an authoritative tilt of her head, "you know of no one who has visited our gallery or with whom we have conducted business. Is that correct, Mr. Travis?"

"Is Phil around? I'd like to have a few words with him."

"Mr. Agatha rarely stops by. Are you in town for the night? You could leave me your number."

I got up and took a seat next to her on the couch. I ran my hand through her hair, down her arm, and rested it on her exposed stomach. My fingers probed her skin through the mesh. I was practicing the golden rule: do unto others as they have just done unto you. I might be a tad cloudy on that.

She breathed in—low in the abdomen, like a singer—her stomach muscles rising and falling with the effort. She considered me with trusting eyes. I withdrew my hand.

"What's my prize if I have a number?" I said.

"Then you could enter our gallery."

"Aren't we in it now?"

"It's not a place."

"What might it be?"

"Close your eyes."

"If it's all the same to—"

She brought her left hand up and gently slid her fingers over my face, the tips of her fingers pressing the curvature of my eyeballs. She smelled heavy, like salt air with a dash of Marlberry flower. *Were Morgan and Kathleen going to have dinner together?* Kathleen had a late class at the college, and she usually dropped by afterward.

"What do you see?" she asked as her hand graced my cheek and then was gone.

"Amber waves of grain?"

"This—keep them closed—is our gallery. It is inside your head. Some artists create and sell their own passions. We understand the inherent disconnect of such a traditional and restrictive model. We urge our clients to imagine, to let free, their greatest fears, their lust, the dark secrets held in the inner chambers of their hearts that yearn for expression. Then we create the art. We put your feelings on canvas. What do you *feel*?"

"Jubilation as my enemies bleed out on the floor." I opened my eyes. "Can you arrange that? Place someone I need to control in a compromising position, a position that would entice that person to follow my every wish and command in fear that I would reveal a damaging photograph?"

She recoiled from me and abruptly stood. "Your number," she demanded. I gave it to her as she punched at her phone.

We eyed each other toe-to-toe. She'd need a gallon of paint thinner and extra-fine sandpaper to scrub the blue off her eyes. I'd apparently landed a right hook, so I followed up with a left. "Am I in the right place to have my needs met?"

She hesitated, as if she were in foreign territory. "If Mr. Agatha is interested, he'll give you a call."

"Business must be good."

She extended her arm toward the door.

"How about a name," I said. "Something to remember our time by."

"You may call me Christina."

I took a step toward her, our faces inches apart. "That's nice, honey. Now, tell me your real name." I wasn't sure why I said that, other than I was trying to throw her off her game.

She blinked. Twice. "Please leave now," she said in a pre-recorded voice, as if she was playing for the crowd. Or perhaps a security camera. I'd thought of dropping Anderson's name, but I could only play that card once, if at all. I'd stirred the nest. Time to see if any hornets came out.

"You don't have a special method of saying *au revoir* do you, similar to your greeting?"

"Sadly," she said flatly, "I just tell you to leave."

"Not even *auf wiedersehen?*"

"Not even *adios.*"

I bade my new playmate a good afternoon and took the stairs to the first floor. It was faster than the elevator, although I had no place in particular to be. Later that night at the bar, just as I reached for my second Jameson on the rocks, the first hornet out of the nest, a little Italian stinger, landed on my port side.

8

The stools on either side of me were empty, and then—poof—they weren't. A big fellow took my starboard side, the little Italian wasp, like I said, on my left.

I didn't pay much attention to the big guy; the brains are always in charge, and they are seldom housed in a prefab gym body. The smaller man, though, caught my attention. He had that aura that comes from knowing you need more than muscle when the action goes downtown. He wasn't much to look at. Without the threads, he'd pass for a drowned rat. But how many people, including yours truly, aren't a little freaked out by rats?

Little Italy snapped his hand up at the bartender, who quickly had a square lowball glass in front of him along with a basket of Cuban bread that I didn't recall seeing on the bar menu. Little Italy got served before the gorilla got his beer.

He took a bite of the bread and addressed the bartender. "Arnie, put a game on. They got one every night of the week now. Who wants this singing shit?"

On the high-def screen, a young woman was overproducing a song: her face anguished in emotion, dancers sweating behind her, flames shooting into the air, synchronized stage lights creating frenzied hype, and the people in the audience waving their arms over their heads as if they were celebrating a mass baptism on the banks of the River

Jordan. None of that masked her insufferable lack of tonality. The bartender switched channels and football players popped on the screen. Wherever the game was, it was cold and raining.

"What we got, Bowling Green?" My stool mate asked Arnie. "Who they playing?"

"FDU."

"Who?"

"Kent State. Four Dead U."

"*Gee*-zus, tough world. I ain't never heard that. What's the line?"

The bartender glanced under the counter. "Even."

"MAC teams—I burn them like Joan of Arc. What else we got?"

"That's it, Mr. Eddie. Later game starts in less than an hour."

"You make that up?"

"What?"

"Four dead."

"Don't believe so."

"Dunno how I missed that one. How's the pasta tonight?"

"Handmade today, sir."

"Cut me a center filet, you know, medium, little side dish of pasta. He knows how I like it."

The bartender tapped his computer. Eddie turned his head to me, his drooping eyelids masking indolent eyes. "You hungry?"

"Pardon?"

"Make it two, Arnie," he said keeping his eyes on me. "My friend here's gonna taste meat and noodles that'll make his dick shrink. You hungry, right? Sure you are, big guy like you."

Arnie folded black cloth napkins into a triangle and situated them in front of the three of us. The gorilla hadn't ordered anything, nor had Arnie seemed concerned with him.

"You from around here, Beach Boy?"

"No, I'm—"

"Youngstown, Ohio, myself. FMV—Fuckin Mahoning Valley. That's why I know the MAC like a hooker's back. Lot of guys, they get scorched betting what they don't know. Not me, Beachy, I stick to—what they call it? Circle of competence, right? There, but for the grace of God, go I, running around in my itty-bitty circle of competence."

I reached over his airspace and took a slice of Cuban bread. I dipped it in the tapenade next to the breadbasket and stuck a third of it into my mouth. Nice crust. A pinch of salt. With bread, it's always about the crust.

"You like my bread, huh? Arnie, our guest here needs manners and a basket for himself." He turned to me. "I can help you with one, pal, but not the other. You didn't tell me where you're from."

"You didn't shut up long enough for me to answer."

He sucked in his right cheek and nodded his head a few beats. "Ooooh...OK, OK. Speak with your balls. I like that. Why don't I sit here real polite and quiet-like while you chew my bread, and I can listen to you tell me where you're from? Think we can manage that?"

"West coast. Saint Pete Beach."

"Yeah, right, I know it. Saint Petersburg. Classic old joint. Like Youngstown, peaked, you know, on a relative basis, in the fifties, right? Marilyn and DiMaggio, you know they hung there, right? I never got that, you know? Naming some place in Florida after a Russian city. Gee-zus, I mean, what's that about?"

I shrugged. "According to legend, it was a coin toss between two of the founding men. The winner was born in Saint Petersburg, Russia."

He jerked his head away from me in a mock move. "Holy-schmoly, I can tell I'm gonna get smarter just sittin' by you. Yes, sir. Pick up IQ points just being downwind. Lucky day for me, ain't it?" He glanced up at the TV. "No way that's not pass interference. You see that? That DB had a handful of jersey." He came back to me. "Name's Eddie." He stuck out his hand.

"Jake." We shook, although I knew he was a man I did not want to touch.

"Ever play the game?"

"No."

"Too bad. Me neither, but I got an excuse. I can't hit one-fifty if I peed in my wet snowsuit. You look pretty healthy, livin' on a beach, like you're from one of those beach movies, you know like Frankie what's-his-fuck, and Annette... Annette...fuck-a-cello. Wonder what she's up to."

I ignored him.

"I said, I wonder what she's up to, that beach broad."

"Annette Funicello?"

He flipped his hands out.

"She's dead."

Eddie seemed genuinely surprised, even disappointed. "No. When that happen?"

"Few years back. She went the same day Margaret Thatcher did. Got buried in the news."

He leaned back and let out a series of chuckles. "What is this, trivia night? Who knows shit like that? You gotta love it, though, don't ya? Who'd ever think, really? The Iron Lady and the Beach Bunny checking out on the same day.

Bet the man manning the pearly gates got a kick out of that. Ja hear that, Henny?" He leaned across the bar and glanced at the thing on my starboard side.

"Ya, I got that."

"That's my buddy Hernandez, but who wants to call somebody a three-syllable word every time, you know? Too much work."

I glanced at Henny, but his head was down. His neck was a bloated piling. He had the personality, and the construction, of an Amazon box.

Our dinners came. Arnie gave Henny a burger—he must get the same thing every time. My filet was perfect, red in the middle but short of mushy pink. White circus tents of Parmesan cheese covered the side dish of pasta and marinara sauce. Eddie clammed up as his food demanded his total attention. He'd eventually get to the point of his visit, but his leisurely pace was of no concern. My only plan for the night was to hit my room early so I could do a pre-dawn run before heading off to the airport. Unless I got a call.

Eddie swiped his napkin across his mouth and pushed his plate forward. Arnie scooped it away, wiped down the counter, and deposited a new drink on a dry coaster.

"Let me ask you somethin', Jake." Eddie leaned back in his bar chair. "How long you in town for?"

"That's not what you want to know."

"No? Geez, you're a piece, you know that? Tell me what I want to know."

"Why I'm here in the first place."

"OK, so pretend I asked that."

"Heard this place has a good filet and noodle dish."

He rolled his tongue around in his cheek and checked out the game. Looking at the TV. Deciding what to say. "Do I know you?"

"No."

"Do you know me?"

"No."

"Here's the thing, Jake." He shifted his attention back to me. "You're a smart guy, got all the answers. Look at the stuff you laid down, Thatcher, a coin toss, a real know-it-all. Guy like you, why ask questions, right? But you did, Beach Boy, ask questions today. Right above me, am I correct? Course I am. Saint Pete, really, that's old Florida, some real retro stuff there, I understand that, you know? I love Youngstown, I mean I'd be a donkey's ass to live there instead of Miami, but I get it. So you and I, maybe we have some common ground. You follow me? 'Cause I'm working hard on your behalf here."

"Eddie?"

"Yeah, Jake?" He leaned in hard at me. Rubbing his hands together as if he couldn't contain his energy.

"Get to it."

"What were you doing in Four-Twenty today?"

"Shopping."

"For what?"

"Art."

"I don't think so."

"I don't care what you think."

"I introduced you to Henny, right?"

"Riveting character."

"You're a big guy, but he's bigger."

"Eddie?"

"Yeah, Jake?"

"If I was the type to admit fear, who do you think I'd fear: the sack of muscles behind me, or a guy that can't hit one fifty in a wet snowsuit?"

Eddie broke into a smile, leaned back, and slapped my back hard. "Gee-zus. I wish we knew each other in the day; you'd've loved my mother's spaghetti. Just enough sausage in the sauce to keep you wanting more." He quieted down and leaned back in. "I was right, you are one sorry, smart son-of-a-bitch. You've walked the road, I admire that, got dust on your feet, that's cool, but you didn't answer my fuckin' question, and my dinner's done. *Capisce?*"

I didn't want to hesitate, to show signs of indecision, so while part of my brain crunched replies and tabulated their consequences, planning a dozen moves ahead, I threw out, "I have a problem and was told Studio Four-Twenty could help resolve it."

"Yeah? Tell me about it."

"I told your girl upstairs. I need to own a man. Have him obey my every command. Are you my answer or not?"

"Beachy," he said, spreading his hand, "we're purveyors of fine art."

"I don't think so," I volleyed his earlier reply back at him.

Arnie dropped by. "Another, Mr. Eddie?"

"Not tonight, Captain." He glanced up at the screen and held his gaze there. "You know Jimmy T's president of Youngstown State now. Bet he spends half his time with *x*'s and *o*'s. Frickin' gold pants, you believe that? Up in Tallahassee they got rape charges and hit-and-runs coming out the greasy wazoo and everybody loves 'em.'" His eyes turned to me. "We treat everybody the same. I need a referral. You didn't approach by regular channels. That doesn't mean we can't do business, but it means you and I are at a dead end here tonight. You understand?"

His dinner jacket was a striped cut of cloth, which despite the challenge of his coat-hanger frame, draped perfectly over his shoulders and neck. There was no bunching of cloth usually associated with off-the-rack coats on narrow shoulders. He had on a pair of blond leather tassel loafers. No socks. For a drowned rat, he had nice threads.

"I need to check with my source," I said.

"Your source?" His interest genuinely piqued.

I finished off my whiskey. "I represent a third party. I'm here strictly as a middleman. You're wary of us, we are equally wary of you." An alcohol-emboldened plan was formulating as I talked. "Before I divulge more information to you, is Studio Four-Twenty the answer to my problem?"

"And your problem is what, again?"

"We need a certain individual to be more cooperative in a business deal. A photograph, a work of art that will convince him to see things our way."

"Haven't a clue what you talking about, my friend. You approach us through the channel markers, and maybe I do. Understand? You get outside my channel, you got a problem. The man I work for likes things neat and proper, and I live by a code: never turn on the man who pays the tab."

I handed him my business card. "I'll be back in touch within the week."

He nodded his head without glancing at my card. "You do that, Jake. You get back in touch. Go through our site and then call upstairs, tell 'em you want to talk to Eddie from Youngstown State, got that? But I got to tell you, you know, be honest with you since we spent this quality time together.

If you don't check out, I don't wanna ever see you in Miami again."

"It's a big town."

"Just sayin'."

He stood. I remained seated. I had nowhere to go. "And if it does work out," I said, striving to end the evening on a positive note.

Henny, whose contribution to the dinner repartee had been "Ya, I got that," rose out of his seat. He was a tad bigger than I'd envisioned and had dwarf ears. "If it does," Eddie said, "it shows how we get along despite our differences, 'cause I weren't too happy when you reached over me, helping yourself to my bread. That told me you truly don't give a shit. I know that attitude. That's what I learned in Youngstown before I left all that frickin' rain. Hey, you remember Maurice Clarett?"

"Can't say I do."

"Youngstown boy. When the Buckeyes beat Miami—you know, championship game? Miami intercepts this pass—could turn the game, right? Maurice? He tackles the DB that has the ball and wrestles it right out of his arm. Just beats the guy up for it, right there on the field. 'Canes, they never knew what hit them. Twenty-two guys on the field and one of them from Youngstown." He shook his head. "They never had a chance. Anyways—where was I goin' with that? Oh, yeah. What I was sayin' is that I brought that attitude to Miami with me, and guess what?"

He waited so I went in. "What?"

"It was already here." He coughed out a laugh. "That's how they built this sweat-hole. No one gives a flying crap. Tore the heart right out of what used to be Florida and made a new one of concrete and glass. Gotta love it. But it's my

home now, and you're in my circle now of competence—
remember that."

"You're from Youngstown, but missed Four Dead U."

He slowly bobbled his head. "Yeah, yeah, I did. You
know, I'm gonna give you that one. But listen up, Beach
Boy; there'll be something you miss someday, too, my friend.
And you'll be lucky if it's that harmless."

He waved his hand at Arnie as he strolled out the door.
"Later, Captain. Tell cook it was wonderful."

9

Miami's not bad—while everyone sleeps.

It was dark the next morning when I went for a run. The beach was no good as it was high tide and the sand soft and lumpy—an ideal situation in which to twist an ankle. I switched to the boardwalk, but the wood treadmill left me boxed in. I settled on the middle of the A1A. I found my stride as Miami and the sun still snoozed. A woman in a silver thong glided past me on rollerblades, wires flying out of her ears.

After four miles, I cooled down in the park across from Oceana. My breathing resumed its normal rhythm, and I took a seat on a bench in the shade. A pamphlet stapled to a pole advertised a navy Blue Angel air show. About two weeks out. I didn't know people still went to that stuff.

I'd stayed at the bar last night and mapped out my next few moves. Beyond that, the possibilities exploded exponentially, and I had no clue what the board might look like. But that didn't stop me from planning and believing I could steer those events once they came into focus.

I'd deliberated sharing my plan with Binelli last night, but I wanted to sleep on it, and more important, run on it. No idea if my plan would fly, or if it did, if I could pull it off. But it was the best bad plan I could come up with, and it had grown on me, step by step, down A1A.

At 7:30 a.m., I dialed Binelli.

It went to voice mail. I disconnected and hit her button again. I repeated the process six times. She finally caved in.

"You better be bleeding on a street," she said in lieu of hello. "I was in a meeting, and yes, they are important."

"I want to go in as a plant for the FBI."

"Whatdaya mean?"

"Agatha. Studio Four-Twenty. I've already made contact and planted the seed. I just need you to legitimize it."

"How bad's your wound?"

"I got their attention last evening. Said I represented a third party who was looking to blackmail someone—not those words—and heard they were my ticket. They insisted I needed to approach by regular channels."

"And what is it you want me to do?"

"Set me up," I explained. "Whatever you think will work. Maybe I work for the military industry. Peace is offending my bottom line, or perhaps there's an imminent shift away from the door handles I manufacture for fighter jets. You figure that end out. I'm someone who needs a congressman in my pocket, maybe Ways and Means, maybe not, but somebody who requires a compromising picture that will help me maintain my bottom line. You catch Agatha in the act, shut him down, we all go home."

"Weed legal in Florida?"

"It's a good plan, and you know it. One your outfit might already be running, but it's busted and needs fresh legs."

"We can't—"

"You can." I stood and started pacing as a homeless person wearing enough clothes to survive a Minneapolis winter shuffled past me.

"You're not a—"

"That's not the issue." I turned onto a side street past a drugstore that had a liquor department twice the size of the pharmacy. Make that three times.

"Who to trust," she threw over the airwaves.

"Who to trust," I repeated. "At best you're a divided house. You run this past the wrong person, or it leaks out, and Agatha, assuming he has inside friends, knows I'm coming. You need to approach someone who is beyond question and limit my proposal to as few people as possible."

"Why are you doing this?"

"I'm bored." I pitched back the same answer she'd given to my question—why she was helping me—that I'd asked her over coffee and bagels.

Not skipping a beat, she echoed my reply, "There's more."

"Because your outfit is too cross-eyed to do it the right way itself." As my words spilled out, I knew I would revisit my decision. I had no natural interest in shoring up government slack.

I explained how I saw the game unfolding. She warmed up to my plan and said she had one particular person to pitch it to. We disconnected. I called her back and gave her a description of Eddie and Henny. Told her to see if she could identify either one.

At the hotel, I grabbed a newspaper and enjoyed a fresh farm breakfast on a fine Florida morning. On the way to the airport, I checked my phone over and over—like TJ and the Shondells—but nothing from Binelli.

"What are we eating?" I asked Morgan that evening as he came through the screened porch door lugging a small Styrofoam Buccaneers cooler with a busted handle. Kathleen sat next to me, her head buried in her work.

"Trout. Ninety minutes out of the water. Exact same three-day period the last four years." Morgan kept a chart of every edible fish he caught, meticulously plotting the time, weather, and tide at the time of the catch.

"What can I do?" Kathleen asked without looking up from her stack of papers.

"Nothing," Morgan and I chirped at the same time. Her offer to help with dinner was nothing more than common courtesy that she had no desire, or ability, to fulfill. Kathleen in a kitchen was a sailor in a rodeo.

Sunset was at 5:58 p.m. Night encroached from the east, chasing the day into the western edge of the sky. My hut faces southeast, and in the late fall evenings, the sky, like a play without a curtain call, darkens quickly. The red-flashing channel marker came on, Hadley III yowled and pounced on Kathleen's lap, Morgan fired up the Weber, and I knew the FBI would be thrilled with my plan. If a sucker is born every minute, I've put in my time. For a smart guy, I make my share.

After dinner, I lit an Ashton and passed it to Kathleen. She inhaled the entire west coast of Florida and slowly exhaled through pursed lips. A waft of smoke stalled in the cooling night air.

"I always regret it in the morning," she mused.

"What's that?"

"The cigar—the rancid taste in my mouth when I wake. Why is the splendor of the night the spoil of the morning?"

"I'll pass on that."

"A wise man, indeed." She smiled and handed me back the cigar. "Give it to me again," she said, her head back in the cushion.

"I'm proposing to go undercover, with the FBI's blessing, in order to secure a deal with Agatha."

"Why?"

"Shut him down. Save future victims. Avenge the death of Karl Anderson."

"OK. If it doesn't work?"

"FBI's problem."

"No, I mean—and you know I mean—what danger to you if it doesn't pan out."

"Not much," I softened the truth. Maybe even infringed on lying. She knew that. I suspected she also knew that I knew that. After that, I got plumb tired of thinking.

"You're—let's call it 'fabricating'—this time," she said.

"It is a kinder word."

"These people killed Riley's husband and two FBI agents, right?"

I propped my feet up on the glass table next to my Tinker Bell alarm clock and tapped ashes into the Copacabana ashtray. I often set Tinker Bell to five o'clock to keep myself from indulging before then. I lie to her, as well, but she's an alarm clock.

"I'll look both ways before I cross the street."

"It's not funny." She shot me a glance. Her hair was down, and the flame from the candle she'd lit danced shadows on her face. She wore a scoop-neck loose T-shirt and jeans. And socks. The summer humidity was long gone, and she didn't tolerate chilled feet. One of those socks, the right one, gently rubbed against my outstretched left leg, in a slow, constant beat.

"Hear me?" she said.

I met her challenging gaze. "I'll be approaching them as a client, not an adversary."

A sailboat searching for wind came in from the gulf and eased past the end of the dock. The only sound it emitted was a patient rendition of Gabriel Faure's "Pavane." The music faded, leaving a gap someone needed to fill.

Morgan said, "Is Riley safe?"

"Can't imagine how they would trace her here," I said, struggling to keep the haunting notes from infecting my head. "We need to get her in front of photos of senators, congressmen, lobbyists—the whole bag of chips. See if she recognizes anyone in the photos."

"I got that," he volunteered as he stood. "I'll start gathering pictures tonight, take her for a sail tomorrow. Be good for her to be out on the open water."

I needed to describe Eddie and Henny the Amazon box to her to see if she recognized them. Also needed to tell her that the FBI identified Karl's body. That wasn't an item to outsource.

Morgan bade us goodnight and slid out the side door. It latched quietly behind him as he crossed the lawn to his house. The bay was still but I knew its tranquility was deceptive, a ruse. It's a twenty-four-hour struggle to eat or be eaten. If you're born into it, you don't have a choice. Maybe we are no different, but our high intelligence versus other species deceives us, convincing us that we have more control over our actions than we'd like to admit.

Kathleen went to the bedroom while I cleaned up. I need to be greeted by a spotless house every morning. Realizing there is part of your life you can't control is no excuse for not taking responsibilities over the parts you can control. In the bedroom, I opened the window and cracked the venetian blinds.

Kathleen's voice turned me. "Not too much."

"Window or blind?"

"Window."

I shut it some more, although likely not as much as she would have preferred. The moon broke free of a cloud, and the room brightened.

She climbed on top of me, her hair falling down on either side. The light on her face was doubled filtered through the blinds and her hair. It rendered a golden glow to our face-to-face world. I pulled her nightshirt over her head and dropped it on the floor.

"You have a choice," she said.

"I know."

"You barely know her."

"I know."

"You *don't* know her."

"I know."

"Yet you're getting ready to go back in."

"I know."

She brushed her hair off my face. Hadley III jumped on the bed, and I kicked her off with my foot.

"Tell me you'll be careful."

"I'll—"

"No." She placed a finger over my lips. "Tell me you'll remember us."

I kissed her and rolled us over, and at the point of no return, when I didn't think conversation was even possible, she broke away and in a raspy, husky voice, said, "Say it Jake. Say it."

"Remember. Us."

Afterward, we lay awake in the cool night air. I pulled the sheet over us so she wouldn't get cold and question me on how much I had actually closed the window.

"I like her," she started in as if we were in the middle of a conversation.

"Riley?"

"Mm-hm. I think she had a good thing with her husband, like us, I mean. It helps, you know, liking her, trying to see a little justice in her world."

Kathleen was not an "I mean," or "you know," type of woman. She was struggling with our reoccurring theme: my inability to handle the banality of life and the risk I assume so that I may feel that I have truly lived. The central themes of our lives are fountains raining down on us, soaking everyone we care about. A pitiable predicament.

Sixty minutes before sunrise, as I was lacing up my running shoes, my phone signaled an incoming text. I changed clothes, packed, and left Kathleen a note.

An hour later I viewed with dismay the marathon-long line at the Starbucks in Tampa's bustling red terminal. A pleasant-looking brunette in a turquoise business suit was three spots away from payday. I gave her a twenty, my best smile, and my order. I told her to keep the change.

"Where you headed?" she asked me when she handed me my coffee and my change that she insisted on not keeping.

"DC. You?"

"Frisco."

"You'll look great with flowers in your hair."

"Thank you," she said through a cute schoolgirl smile.

"Have a great life."

"You, too."

10

I was thirty minutes early for the meeting. Binelli's pre-sunrise text, which included my flight information, instructed me to meet her and an "associate" at "12:30/ Tony's/N/upstairs." Tony's was an Italian restaurant in a converted 1800s house on N Street in Washington, DC.

The hostess led me up the rickety narrow steps, where I found the spot I suspected Binelli had in mind. It was a solitary table tucked into the front corner by a window that overlooked the upstairs balcony. The window was open as it was an unseasonably mild late fall day. A breeze, like a blow dryer on low, funneled through the window.

I stepped out onto the slanted balcony. It was barely wide enough to hold circular two tops where people could gather around and place drinks. Had a young lady in a Southern belle dress once graced the wide-plank flooring, listening to the clopping of horseshoes on the brick street below? Perhaps she waved at a young man and hoped he waved back, or at least be more assertive and confident than he had been at the last social event. What themes rained down in their lives?

Why did Kathleen even attempt to talk to me after sex? *She knows better.*

Back inside, I adjusted the table and opted to wait at the downstairs bar. I told the hostess—a sturdy woman who commanded her post like a battalion leader—to hold the upstairs table and took a high-back stool. I ordered a Bloody Mary from the bartender, a man in black pants, a starched cuff-linked shirt, and a bow tie. It was a nice bar, and he made it even more so. Dressing up never takes a place down.

Binelli and associate were ten minutes late, which is less than an ideal way to commence a meeting with me. I survived by convincing myself that I wasn't waiting—I was drinking at a bar.

I stood as they approached. She was wrapped in a bleached-maple dress that wasn't quite the bomb for a night on the town but was a stitch too tight for a day in the office. The gentle slope of her neck melted into her shoulders.

Her companion was ageless—between fifty and seventy—old for one and young for the other. His hawkish nose accentuated his deep-set eyes. His shirt cuffs protruded a perfect inch past his jacket. A pair of navy cuff links anchored each sleeve. He was a corporate, in this case, government, clone that kept the wheels both turning and clogged. You might accuse me of being harsh and quick to judge people; you might be right.

Binelli made introductions. Cuff Links was Edward Kent Franklin, an assistant director of the FBI. Probably a third or fourth tacked to the end of his name, as well. I wouldn't be surprised if he were a direct descendent from a minuteman who held his ground on the North Bridge.

"Please," he implored me, "just Kent." I led Binelli and Just Kent back up the rickety steps. I claimed the seat against the wall that faced out over the restaurant. It had plenty of legroom; that's why I'd jiggled the table on my first trip up.

We suffered through obligatory small talk, and then Kent kicked the ball. "Your scheme intrigues us," he said. He fastidiously unfolded the linen napkin, placed it on his lap, and slowly, as if there were a penalty if he concluded his task too hastily, positioned the utensils that had been wrapped within the napkin.

"I bet." I crossed my legs. "I'll also wager that you're willing to send me in with your full blessing." I'd forgotten to text Kathleen and make sure she'd seen my note. Out of sight, out of mind. Travel does that to me. Is that why I like to travel?

"That's a different key than you were singing yesterday morning," Binelli pointed out. "What happened?"

"You tell me."

Her eyes, under finely stenciled eyebrows, never dropped from mine as she replied, "You don't have to do this. We can have lunch and go our separate ways. Bothers us not one bit."

"We can protect you," Franklin threw out the worn phrase in an attempt to appease me. His gaze was both attentive and opaque.

"Did he just say that?" I kept my eyes on Binelli.

"Just you and I. Your call."

"Show me the blueprint."

"Kent?" She glanced at Franklin. They were relaxed sitting next to each other, but I couldn't place the relationship. Not sexual. Someone she could trust. A mentor, perhaps, or a father figure. Franklin scooted his chair closer to the table and then brushed his hand down the front of his suit. The waitress dropped by, and we placed our orders. She asked if I wanted another Bloody Mary. I said yes, but not to bring it.

"We've wanted to nail Phillip Agatha for years," Franklin started in as if he were addressing a board meeting. "We believe he conducts blackmail for hire. He's managed to thwart us, but we have a high degree of confidence that he has blackmailed numerous government officials, as well as those who come in contact with primary decision-makers, both here and abroad. Furthermore, we believe that the death of two of our agents—Ms. Binelli has notified me that you are familiar with some of this material—were at the hands of Agatha. He may even have someone in the agency. If that's the case, it's an ill-conceived operation that has spun out of control, and it's unlikely anyone will step forth. We tend to bury our mistakes, and we don't take kindly to those bearing shovels. We tolerate this unspoken arrangement as one never knows when one might be in need of such consideration."

I shifted my eyes to Binelli. "You implied to me you weren't running a scam on Agatha."

Franklin jumped in and defended her. "Agent Binelli has just recently been brought up to speed. She was not entirely inaccurate. We're not positive someone is protecting Agatha. Therefore, if we send a plant in, we need to be quiet. Invisible. An outsider is ideal as he is less likely to draw attention. The time has come. The man has appeared." He nodded at me and smiled wryly.

If Edward Kent Franklin referred to two dead agents as "this material," I knew that, if he learned of my death in the morning, he'd forget my name by lunch. The man didn't give an elephant's ass about me.

Franklin placed both his elbows on the arms of the chair. "Are you familiar with Zebra Electronics?"

"Are you familiar with an elephant's ass?"

"Pardon me?" His eyebrows furrowed.

"Tell me about Zebra Electronics."

He hesitated and then said, "Plano, Texas, firm that does missile guidance work for the navy. The contract expires the end of this year. The navy is taking its business in another direction."

"You a navy man?" I jutted my chin at his links.

"Oh, those? No. I've got so many different pairs. West Point. Class of seventy-nine."

"How much of the contract is Zebra losing?"

"Whole deal."

"The navy contract is meaningful business for Zebra?"

"Correct. The navy, and certain work Zebra does for the bureau—which is why we are privy to this classified information—accounts for nearly seventy percent of their revenue. The founder, Daniel Vigh, planned to go public a few years back, but the market of oh-eight torpedoed those plans. He couldn't file this past year because the Street knows this contract was coming up. With the cancellation notice, four weeks away from going public, his dream is sunk."

"Is he aware of this?"

A siren wailed down N Street. Franklin waited until it passed.

"No." He shook his head. "Nor are you to initiate contact with him. Standard procedure. These operations function best on a need to know.

"You'll be going in as an intermediary working on Vigh's behalf. Agatha runs a background on Zebra Electronics and verifies what I've just told you. You need blackmail on a specific individual who will convince the government to keep the current contract with Zebra. Best of all, we have the urgency of time on our side. The high-probability operations are the ones blessed with speed. Time exponentially increases the probability of a snafu."

Our lunches came, and I took a bite of my salmon and spaghetti. It wasn't on the menu, but salmon was, as was spaghetti and meatballs. A languid breeze wove in the window, and I wished Binelli would change perfumes. My gaze wandered from her bare shoulders to her eyes. They were waiting for me. She flashed them back to her plate.

I stuck a fork of braided spaghetti in my mouth, took a few chews, thought of Kathleen's spaghetti straps, sex in the library, and said, "What if Agatha checks with Vigh, even contacts him directly?"

"He has no reason to," Franklin replied. "Even if he did, what would Vigh say if Agatha did send someone to see him? He, Vigh, would deny it. No way would he implicate himself to a man he doesn't know, and who is accusing him of trying to blackmail a government official. Agatha knows that. That's why he places strict adherence on prospective clients approaching him through the proper channels. He has no means of authenticating such a person."

"About those channels. I was directed to approach Studio Four-Twenty in such an official manner."

"A series of numbers and a password."

"How do you know this?"

Franklin pampered his lips with his napkin and leaned back. "We had a gentleman who made contact with Agatha, but chickened out. Didn't have the guts to go through with it. He'd already deposited his down payment, a hundred-k, and came singing to us wanting to exchange information for fifty thousand dollars. We told him we had a better idea: he'd give us the information, and we wouldn't press charges of attempted and premeditated blackmail."

"He couldn't implicate himself," I pointed out.

Franklin spread his hands. "So we misled him on his rights. That's what attorneys are for, and he, somewhat ill-considered, approached us solo."

"Yet here I sit."

"I think your case is a little—"

"He gave you the numbers?" I had no interest in his assurance.

"He did. Two sets. Good for another thirty days, we hope."

"Who's the mark?"

"Man called Devon Peterson."

"Government?"

"K Street," he clarified. "Peterson is a close friend of Charles Walderhaden. Walderhaden's a weed-toking Monkey Business Democrat from Colorado. He sits on a subcommittee that makes recommendations to the Way and Means. They stamp whatever comes out of that committee—they'd approve funding for a V-six on a baby stroller. Peterson and Walderhaden go way back, played football together at Michigan. Attended the other's kids' weddings. Tennis partners."

"And if Peterson," I continued the thread, "is caught in an embarrassing pose and is informed that extending the Zebra Electronics contract will make his problem vanish, you're betting he'll go to Walderhaden to bail him out."

"Most assuredly. Put pressure on a guy *under* the guy you need to get to. Walderhaden has nothing to risk. Furthermore, he'll desire to stay clean; he won't require further detail. The Zebra contract isn't that big, half a bil. That's not even gutter gum in this town. But if you own your own shop, half a billion a year on a five-year contract with a twenty percent margin is—"

"Half a billion to David Vigh." I calculated, placing my nearly clean plate on the table next to me. I don't recommend salmon and spaghetti after a Bloody Mary.

"Something like that. Even more if he can go public. Odds are that the conversation between the former Wolverines won't hit the five-minute mark. Peterson will say he's got a personal problem and extending Zebra's contract will allow the sun back in his life. Walderhaden won't want to know the details. Ignorance is more than bliss—it's money, power, and, most important, the avoidance of jail. They'll ask about each other's wives and then grouse about their draw in the doubles match at the indoor tennis facility where they play every Saturday morning this time of the year."

"What's Agatha going to do to Devon Peterson?" I directed my question to Binelli to see if she had the stomach for this tasteless business.

She swiped away her bangs as if she been caught off-guard. "Nothing that Peterson hasn't already done to himself. He can't go two weeks without summoning a woman to a hotel room. His marriage is rocky, and his mother-in-law just passed, leaving over six million to her only child. Peterson, for the first time in his life, has sail-away money. He's been telling his partners that he's out in a year or two. A couple of pictures, and his wife, who has threatened before, dials her attorney."

"Walderhaden and Peterson play tennis on Saturday mornings?"

"Yes," she answered tentatively, not knowing where I was going with my question.

"Around ten?"

"Ten thirty," Franklin cut in.

Binelli narrowed her eyebrows. "What's this—?"

I kept my eyes on Binelli. "I bet you know what he does Tuesday afternoon in August."

Binelli rolled her tongue in her mouth poking out her right cheek. Kathleen favored her left with the same move. Franklin stepped in for her. "We keep tabs on certain individuals whose wanton lifestyle may endanger—"

"Save it," I said. "They don't call it the Hoover building for nothing."

Binelli suffocated a snort, but Franklin was humorless. Like Christina. *Wonder what she's doing now?*

"Do I suggest Peterson as the mark to Agatha?" I directed my question to Franklin.

"Absolutely. You get in, drop the name, and you're done. We take it from there."

I glanced at Binelli, and this time her eyes didn't divert from mine. "I bet I made you a hero; someone like me willing to risk the gallows."

"I wasn't the one who called you six times."

I shifted my gaze to Edward Kent Franklin. The knot of his tie was a rock under his chin. I didn't even know the man, and I was already bone-tired of him. He seemed like a straight-up guy, but I often find such lusterless people to be boring and wearisome. I got to the page we all knew was waiting for us. What I realized *after* I volunteered to Binelli. Why I knew her superiors wouldn't hesitate to grant her the green light.

"Problem is," I said, "Agatha, as you've insinuated, is likely the target of a busted sting. That's how he found the Andersons. He learned of their visit to your Miami branch, and less than twenty-four hours later, the agent they met was dead. You jet them to Saint Kitts, and Agatha's waiting, tapping his toes. Another agent down. Whoever is running him has grossly underestimated Agatha's capacity for violence and consequently can never let it be known that he, or she—the agent—was running Agatha. Someone in your cubicle has family blood on their hands. At this point, your agent would be wise to shut his operation down to preserve his career. Maybe he/she already has. But you're not sure.

Maybe there is no internal operation against Agatha. Perhaps he's simply paying someone in your house for information.

"You know all this," I continued with my soliloquy. "You run the data. You crunch the numbers of who, so disturbingly soon, could have known when the Andersons first dropped into the Miami office. You crossed those people with those who had knowledge of the Saint Kitts vacation. Put your best team on it. Stanford grads ran programs. Hierarchy held a dozen meetings in two days—arranged clandestine rendezvous meetings in parking garages. Nothing. Whoever was running Agatha, or is the recipient of his money, has buried his identity in a nuclear bunker." I leaned in toward Franklin. "The bureau can't afford to send another man into that bunker. It's a suicide run."

Edward Kent Franklin gave a slight tilt, an acknowledgment, of his head. "Your deductive reasoning is quite impressive, Mr. Travis. I'll be succinct. We would rather lose you than a third man. That is why we are so excited, and supportive, of *your* suggestion."

11

Remember us.

That nearly did it. My left leg gave an involuntary twitch, as if my instincts were registering a vote. Instead I went with, "Tell me what you're going to do to mitigate my risk." It didn't sound like me. The answer would be hollow, so why ask?

"No one not at this table knows this meeting is taking place, except for those whom you have told." Franklin responded with a double negative. He was fond of them, telling me earlier than Binelli was "not entirely inaccurate."

He continued, "If you agree, and as agent Binelli indicated, the decision rests solely on your shoulders, I will handpick those who will share in this knowledge. Two, three others, tops. You will be granted tremendous anonymity.

"The downside, I'm sure you see, is that you will have very little—I'll be honest here—virtually no support once you're in the field. Agent Binelli will be your only point of contact. She will contact me, and only in person."

I detested the implications of the phrase, "I'll be honest here." I controlled myself and asked, "You have a dossier for me?"

"I do." He reached toward the floor and brought up a tired brass-buckled leather doughboy. He flipped the buckles, extracted a manila folder, closed the case, and placed it back on the floor. He ironed his tie with his left hand, as if the act had unruffled him. He slid the folder across the table to me.

"You will, of course, be using your real name. No need to do otherwise even if you hadn't barged in on them. I understand at times you are...in the employment of your former SOCom commander."

He waited, but I had no comment.

"Of course. You can see why we are particularly impressed with your generous offer and attributes—my crass remark concerning your expendability, which you took quiet gallantly—notwithstanding. Agatha won't find anything on you. I looked into you. You are, Mr. Travis, as I am sure you are aware and have indeed cultivated, a ghost of a man. Our ghost. That will prickle the hairs on his neck but also provide him some comfort if you play your cards properly. I don't think you need instructions from me on that point. Are we agreed?"

"Is there anything else you need to tell me?"

"I believe that covers it."

"A moment alone with Special Agent Binelli, if you'd be so kind."

He hesitated. Edward Kent Franklin was not accustomed to being dismissed from a meeting. "Certainly." He stood, and I did likewise. Franklin didn't carry an extra pound on his angular frame. His groomed hair was combed back, and tufts of gray highlighted his ears. He'd likely spoken to his barber more last week than I did mine last year. He reached into his inside coat pocket and handed me a card. I gave it a cursory glance. His title was longer than his name. He had a long name.

"Mine's a little simpler," I said as I gave him my card. It contained my name and cell.

"It's not the title," he assured me. "It's the man. And I'm confident we got the right one. Pleasure, Mr. Travis." He stuck his hand out, and we shook. I invaded his space, still clasping his hand. I spoke privately to the man.

"If the opportunity ever arises during our time together?"

"Yes."

"Do not double-cross me."

"You have nothing to worry about."

The breeziness of his stock reply indicated that I'd not properly conveyed my message. I fortified my comment. "Allow me to rephrase myself. Fuck me on this, and I will rip out your fingernails."

That earned a blink. His jaw tightened, but Franklin wasn't a virgin. "I am entirely capable of interpreting your words the first time around. I am confident of your success. We will be in your debt." He glanced at Binelli. "I'll have the car fetched."

I stepped back, and he negotiated the stairs behind me.

"How'd you fetch him?" I asked Binelli as I reclaimed my seat.

"Stop it. He hired me. Was one of the few on the inside track years ago to become director, but withdrew his name. He likes the job and hates the politics, and the higher you go, it's all political."

"Who else will know?"

"Not sure. Likely one or two of his own men. It's a tight group. You don't have anything to worry about."

"Tell me you didn't—"

"Withdrawn." She smiled and leaned in, bringing those damn shoulders across the table. "Read it," she nodded her head toward the manila folder just enough for her bangs to swing out and back again. "If you don't like it, burn it and let me know."

"What questions am I not asking?"

"Read the dossier. Give me a call. Or not."

"Does your buddy know about Garrett?" I asked her. Binelli had met Garrett only briefly when she was working undercover on a case he and I were assigned to—the aforementioned lost letter of a deceased CIA agent.

"Not that I know—"

"Don't tell him."

"Why? Garrett might—"

I reached over the table and cupped the back of her neck with my hand, the thin chain of a necklace gently biting my hand. I brought her face in toward mine, and her eyes flinched. "You either have my back or you don't. I trust you, no one else. Do you understand that?"

"I—"

"Do *not* tell him."

She hesitated. I liked that. She wasn't making an emotional decision that she'd easily back out of. I let her go and settled back into my chair. It didn't escape me that I'd been staring at her for an hour and had composed a reason to touch her.

"I got it," she said. Her voice was subdued, yet with conviction. Less guarded. Forget it. It was three words.

I explained I had some time before I headed to the airport and planned to stay at the restaurant awhile longer and read the file. I stood as she maneuvered around the table to leave. She headed toward the stairs.

"Seven," I said.

She spun her head over her left shoulder. "Pardon?"

"I called you seven times."

She held my eyes for a few seconds, and then like a fog, evanesced down the steps.

I stepped onto the narrow balcony and observed as Franklin held the door of the fetched car for her. She climbed into the backseat. I took my phone out and snapped a picture of him. He cruised around to the other side and let himself in. The car leaped off the curb. Back into the rat race. What's the point? You might win the race, but you're still a rat. I went back inside, sat, and positioned the manila folder in front of me.

I couldn't summon the energy to open it. After a while, I, too, went down the steep and narrow steps and wondered how Binelli made it look so effortless.

The change of venue at the airport, along with a frosty mug of beer, energized me, and I buried my head into the dossier.

A hundred thousand dollars, seed money, had been deposited into a bank account. Kent must carry some weight to get that cleared so fast. There was enough background on Zebra Electronics to fill a 10-k. All from a source that may have reason, and motivation, to filter what I know. Garbage in, garbage out.

I called Mary Evelyn, Garrett's secretary. She had thirty years in at a law firm that kept offices on three continents. Her network of associates and information-gathering capacity made Google look like Atari during its Pong heyday.

"Mr. Travis," she answered in a tone somewhere between a tease and authority.

"Please, just Jake."

Mary Evelyn and I had an ongoing battle in which I tried, always unsuccessfully, to get her to address me by my first name. The only times she crossed the line had been when I was emotionally vulnerable. It pains me to acknowledge such a state.

"Mr. Travis." She managed to enunciate my last name as if it had three syllables. "Some of us are obligated to remind the world that decorum is alive and well."

"After all we've been through, you rest on decorum?"

"A better world would evolve if all parties rested on decorum."

"I'll donate to that cause. Any other fund-raisers in mind?"

"Joan of Arc is having its forty-eighth annual festival this weekend. Weather is just beautiful for this time of the year. Two months from now, and Erie will be ice. Why don't you drop by, Mr. Travis, I'll be collecting tokens, as I always do, at the fresh doughnut stand. Only the alcohol booth provides more funding for pre- and postschool care."

"Many who likely have parents with substance abuse issues," I said.

"It is a circular world."

She certainly had a different take on the Maid of Orleans than did Eddie. *MAC teams—I burn them like Joan of Arc.* Mary Evelyn was east-side-Cleveland-Ohio-never-married-Irish-Catholic. She knew everything about Garrett and me. That had been his call. I thought he was nuts. He wasn't. I met her once— asked her if she had conflicts between her beliefs and what we did. She informed me certainly not, and that I didn't understand religion. I told her to tell me something I didn't know.

"Call me Jake, and I'll work the tent with you."

"Wear an apron?"

"Hand out balloons to children."

"Hmm...a strong move, a tempting treat. But I'd hate to inconvenience you, not to mention putting such a terrible fright into the children. What can I do for you, Mr. Travis?"

I asked her to gather information on Zebra Electronics, Daniel Vigh, and Edward Kent Franklin, the third.

I was about to say goodbye, but instead said, "One more name."

"Certainly."

"Natalie Binelli."

"Spell it."

I did.

There's an Italian phrase I've never forgotten: *Fidarsi è bene, non fidarsi è meglio.*

"To trust is good, not to trust is better."

12

I get high twice a day.

In the pre-dawn hours, I push myself to the edge, my heart racing to 175 beats a minute, electrified endorphins charging my brain, my pores oozing with salt and sweating away yesterday's illusions. In the evening, the alcohol puts it all back in, and my insides boil it down to where I rule my world, and my dreams and aspirations are a touch away, just one more step, one more sip.

Flush and reload. Flush and reload.

It was the next morning, and I stood naked under my outdoor shower as the cool water displaced heat and salt from my body. I'd run barefoot to the beach and continued my pace into hip-deep water, where, like an amphibious vehicle, I'd converted my body to a swimming machine. A half mile later, I emerged and continued my run, the saltwater creating a crusted surface on my skin that sweat cracked and eroded. I returned home, and feeling at the top of my game, launched a kayak and stroked out to Shell Key and back. It was a harebrained decision. The trip out required minimal effort as the tide was with me. Returning was a Sisyphean experience. I was exhausted, famished, and stupid. Two out of the three could be easily resolved.

I took a gulp of my second bottled cold beer, closed my eyes, and raised my face up to let the water drown my head.

Mary Evelyn had sent me an encrypted message at 2:37 a.m. I planned to take it to Sea Breeze to read while I emptied their industrial refrigerators. Despite it being my idea, I was fifty-fifty on the whole undercover gig. Going into a divided house, where no one trusted anyone else, and neither side gave two shakes about me, was a borderline suicide mission. What was I thinking? Sometimes it took more guts to say no than yes, and this might well be one of those times.

"Jesus Jenny. What do we got here?" Riley Anderson stood by the open white gate that led to the front yard. Her hand rested on her hip, and her right elbow pointed out.

"Where'd you come from?" I quipped.

"Don't you own a bathing suit?" She made no effort to move, or alter her stare.

"Don't you knock?"

"I rang your doorbell, and there was no answer. I know you like your porch, so I thought I'd walk around. Jiminy Christmas, don't just stand there. Put that towel around your waist. Make yourself decent."

I grabbed the towel draped over the top of the wood-slat fence that separates Morgan's and my houses. I wrapped it tightly across my midsection and tucked it in. "Anything else I can do for you?"

"I'm depressed. Take me to breakfast?"

"How'd you get here?"

"I biked," she announced triumphantly, as if she were eager to leave her depression behind. I imagined she tried on every coping mechanism in the catalog. "They rent them. It's a swell way to get around the island. I took off yesterday and was gone most of the afternoon. Did you know there's this place where they serve—jumpin' beans, listen to me—you live here, you know."

"'Jumpin' beans'?" I said, wishing I'd dried my hair before circumferencing my waist with the towel. "'Jesus Jenny'?"

"Karl says I cuss too much. I'm working on it."

She had on a wide-brim hat and a beach cover-up that gathered at her waist. A rope served as a drawstring. I needed to inform her that the FBI confirmed Karl's death, although she still referred to him in the present tense. She assumed as much, but I suspected she still held a remnant of hope.

"Give me a minute," I told her. "I'll grab my bike. We'll pedal to breakfast."

Although Sea Breeze was less than two miles from my house, when we strolled in, I felt as if I hadn't eaten in days. I know the feeling.

"Booth?" Riley said.

"Counter."

I asked a slumped unshaven man to scoot down one. He did, but his dog didn't. "Thunder don't mind," Unshaven said, as if reading my mind. "She sleeps through 'bout everything." I positioned my four-legged stool over the mutt whose only reaction was a bored blink. Riley and I faced the pine-panel walls of the restaurant that had been serving breakfast for nine decades and, thank goodness, had resisted the urge to ever alter the décor. Peggy halted her swirling motion in front of me and spattered, "Who's your new playmate?" Her eyes hammered Riley.

"Friend of Kathleen's and mine." I didn't need her lip about not being faithful. I needed food. Fast.

"What would you like, honey?"

Riley gave her order. "Usual, Jake?" Peggy shifted her judging eye to me.

"Bring two."

"Two what."

"The usual times two."

"Don't think you're gettin' no ten percent off."

A few minutes later, four eggs, six strips of crispy bacon, four slices of dry toast, and a potato field from Idaho blotted out my counter space. And bless Peggy, a small red bowl—the one with a chip on the rim—of sautéed onions that found an instant new residence over the eggs and potatoes. A spoonful of pepper followed. One of the egg yolks broke, and a creeping puddle encroached the potatoes, like an invading sea of yellow molasses. I reached for my fork, and Riley said, "What are you doing about getting the Fat Man? You weren't even home yesterday."

I started shoving eggs into my mouth, wiping my chin with a napkin to mop up the drippy yoke.

"You don't care, do you?"

For Pete's sake. I glanced at her. Her black-olive eyes were waiting for me. "Give me just a sec," I begged. "Can you do that?"

"You're the promised land?" She blew her bangs with her breath. "Eat away."

Three eggs later, my survival assured, I said, "Did you sail with Morgan yesterday? View some head shots?"

She nodded. "I'll puke—sorry—if I see another picture. Afterward, he took me to Fort DeSoto. He dropped anchor, and we took his tender to shore and got ice cream. Then he sailed us offshore, I could barely make out the land, but he seemed pretty confident. Said he was raised on a sailboat. How does that work?"

"How does what work?"

"Being raised on a sailboat."

"How does it work anywhere?"

"I mean, no sports."

"He swims with the dolphins."

"Friends."

"There's a whole community of sailing families. They're out there now; you don't meet them doing the eight-to-five tracking appliance sales in Germany."

"Geez, some of us got to make living, you know. He ever go to school?"

"No. And I know of few who are greater read or possess a keener mind. Before he was permitted to leave the boat, he was required to read a hundred books selected by his father."

She spread her hands in mock surrender. "Fine."

I took advantage of sixty seconds of silence to scoop up potatoes drenched in egg yolk. She clocked another silent sixty, and I finished up, although I failed at being a clean-plater; too many spuds. She suddenly emitted a muf-fled sob and brought her napkin up to her nose, her cheeks trailing tears.

"Riley?" I hesitated and then put my arm around her. It's not a smooth move for me, and I feel like a broken toy when I do it.

"I'm OK." She blew her breath out, and her chest col-lapsed. "It's just…it's just that he's gone, and I am here, and the gulf was *so* beautiful, and it's so unfair—unfair that's he's gone and unfair that I can never enjoy any of it again."

Her tears, under her superficial layer of joy, didn't sur-prise me. "Look at me," I said.

She swiped her eyes with the back of her left hand and did as commanded.

"What would Karl want you to do?"

"Oh please…that old chestnut? I know—you're sup-posed to go on in the manner your loved one would want you to do. Some fart-knocker shrink, who never even had a pet hamster die, came up with that sorry-ass, jerked-off, piece-of-shit line."

"Hey, jiminy Christmas."

"What?"

"Look at me," I repeated.

"No."

"Jenny Jesus."

"Leave me alone. It's not funny."

"Fart-knocker."

She relented, her cheeks flushed, her eyes wide, as if to say, "You want me, here I am."

"Screw the shrink," I advised, "but know it's true. Don't tell me you didn't imagine Karl on the boat yesterday. When you got ice cream, you saw his favorite flavor under the glass in the gift shop of Fort DeSoto, and he was there. He's rolling his eyes right now at your last outburst. We both know that when you tried on that cover-up—don't even think of paying me back—that you appraised yourself in front of the mirror in the hotel and asked his opinion; he told you he likes it."

"I bought it at the thrift store."

"I'm saying—"

"I know what you're saying." She reached out and touched me, physically and verbally conveying her point. "But I can't. Don't you see? Don't you understand?"

"Tell me."

"Not when he's out there. Not when the Fat Man sails the same water, views the same sunset. I can't go on with Karl next to me while that man still lives." She wiped her eye and turned away. "He might as well have killed us both. God forgive me, but I want him dead. Oh, I know that's not right, but it's right for me. It's the only way it will be right for me."

The woman next to me and I unabashedly shared a dominant gene in the inner chambers of our hearts: revenge.

"I was laying some groundwork yesterday," I said. "I'm not going to find Agatha around here. I'll be in and out for a while."

She remained subdued. Nothing like her cocky zinger on my boat: *Put my name on the bullet. The Fat Man. Let 'im know it was me.* I didn't know how the hours were treating her, but my guess was they were lengthening every day, ticking by slower and slower. What if someone took me out? Would Kathleen get stuck, unable to move forward? I had Garrett; he would step from the shadows and right her world, let me rest in peace. Shoot first. Ask questions later.

Riley said, "He didn't do that."

"Who do what?"

"Karl. He doesn't roll his eyes."

"Didn't or doesn't?"

She granted me an acknowledging smile. "You're sweet. You have your moments, despite yourself. I hope and pray he's still alive. Sometimes that hope is the only thing that rouses me out of bed in the morning, yet I know that if I get the official word that he's gone, my heart will die twice."

She paused as if she expected me to say something and then continued. "You're working on it, right?" Her eyes lit up in anticipation, and she shifted toward me on her stool. "Finding the Fat Man?"

"I'm fully engaged in your case, Mrs. Anderson."

She placed her hand on my arm. "Thank you. Thank you so, so much."

Guess I'd made up my mind. Truth is, I didn't have the guts to say no.

Nor did I have the guts to tell her that Karl's death had been confirmed. Not that I thought it would be easier to tell her later, I just couldn't do it that morning—sever that gossamer thread of hope and kill her heart for the second time.

I slid off the side of the stool, mindful not to awaken Thunder.

13

That evening I figured out what I like about cats.

"Why are you going to Miami via Dallas?" Kathleen asked as we sat in the screened porch.

The sunset charter sailboat *Magic* keeled over at the end of my dock. A woman's playful laugh carried over the water. "If Agatha has someone watching me at the airport, I want to be seen coming in from Texas. I already spilled to Eddie where I lived, but a physical trail back to Zebra wouldn't hurt."

"That's extreme caution—think it's necessary?" Her hair was tight in the back, but was slightly off-kilter and resting on her left shoulder. No earrings. No discernable makeup. She wore shorts and an oversize gray pullover sweatshirt that came out of my corner of the closet.

"Doesn't hurt," Morgan took the question while stroking Hadley III's back. She was purring loud enough to power the ceiling fan. "On more than one occasion, we'd be entering a harbor when the wind would kick in from nowhere. My father would pilot the boat in like he always did. His expression never changed. He tells me to approach every port the same. 'Caution and force,' he says. 'Always go in with caution and force.'"

Morgan's switch to the present tense was not unusual when discussing his deceased father. Would Riley keep refer-

107

ring to Karl in similar fashion once I gave her the news? Thoreau was afraid to discover, on dying, that he'd never lived. I'd begun to believe that for the living, the dead never die.

"There you have it." I directed my comment to Kathleen. In her mind, words from Morgan originated on Mount Sinai.

"You'll receive a warmer welcome than last time?" She said it in a tone that indicated the answer she was searching for.

"No doubt," I quickly answered to alleviate her worries. "I entered two ten-digit numbers into their website. At two tomorrow, I have an appointment. The correct pass-word, and I'm in."

"And that is?"

"'Eddie from Youngstown State.' That either unlocks the door or gets me run out of Miami."

"Know when you'll be back?"

"Day or two."

"Afraid of no?"

"No. And no."

A center console with a dog sticking its nose into the wind ripped past us, coming in from the gulf. I wouldn't be surprised if half the fishing trips I witness from my perch have a dog aboard.

My mind got sucked into the vortex of the material I'd compiled from Binelli's and Mary Evelyn's reports. Franklin—this tidbit was courtesy of Mary Evelyn—did have III after his name. He was a lifer G-man, as was his father before him. He'd been bumped around between Los Angeles, Dallas, and Chicago before doing the last thirty in DC. Her report contained the street address of every house he'd lived in. He was divorced, although a gag order prohibited his wife from discussing the particulars. He was, due to outside business interests, independently wealthy. Whether, as Binelli indicated, he shied away from advancement due to political indigestion, or he was never invited to sit at that table, could not be ascertained.

Eddie from Youngstown was Edward L. DiCampano. Not much more on the man from MAC country. Never married. Did time as a youth and showed up at Agatha's side around three years ago. They were an unlikely pair: an oversized IQ and a street-smart Italian. Mary Evelyn reported that his name came up as a partial owner of several parking garages in the Mahoning Valley.

Henny the Amazon box: Nothing.

"—I said I'm pregnant." Kathleen jarred me out of my thoughts.

"Excuse me?"

"Twins. Or maybe sextuplets. I forget what the doctor said."

"We could use the help at harvesting."

"Where are you?"

"I was going over the cast."

"Fine, I'll tag along—nothing else to do," she said with enough bite that I got the message. "Who's up?"

"The lead. Phillip Agatha."

"The Fat Man."

"The same. He started Studio Four-Twenty five years ago. Before that, little was known of him. Highly intelligent and on the FBI's ten most watched list for white-collar domestic issues. Recent events strongly suggest he is one step ahead of the bureau."

"More like two miles," she observed. "Anyone else?"

"Johnnie, with an 'ie,' Darling—a new name. Official title is artistic director, Studio Four-Twenty. There's a single picture of him exiting Oceana. He looks like a wet joint."

"That's pleasant," Kathleen commented. "Your FBI buddy, Binelli, give you this information?"

"She and Mary Evelyn, although, surprisingly, it was Mary Evelyn who dug up Darling. The feds don't know about him."

"I'd like to meet Mary Evelyn one day. Anyone else on the playbill?"

"No," I lied. In this case a good attorney would vindicate me.

Mary Evelyn had also sent a few pages on Natalie Binelli. It had included a picture of her in the role of Fantine at Vassar. It was an artsy theater photo seething with shades of twilight gray and muted sexuality. Binelli spent two years tramping around off-Broadway and then chucked it all for a life fighting crime. She was thirty-one years old and had seven years with the bureau. It came at the end of the report: Binelli's parents were innocent victims of a turf war in New York City between warring drug lords. They were in the Big Apple to see their youngest daughter in her first, albeit small, Broadway role. Binelli's ticket onto the stage turned out to be her parent's ticket off the stage.

Three months later, Binelli took her last bow.

When she picked me up in downtown Saint Pete after my run and we shared coffee and bagels—she'd thrown her crumbs away, a criminal act I never would have committed—I had asked her why she risked herself, her career, for me. "I'm bored," she'd replied. I didn't buy it, even questioned myself earlier in the conversation why she was bothering to help me. She'd hesitated, added that she wanted to get the bad guys, and then ended the conversation by walking away. Was she contemplating telling me more?

Why didn't I share that with Kathleen? Out of respect for Binelli's past?

Would Riley, even if I were successful, gain closure, or like Binelli, would a violent, random event redirect her life's passions? Binelli never hinted at the trauma behind her decision to forego the theater in favor of packing a Glock; although it likely played a major part in her willingness to support me—and the rogue justice she felt I represented. Garrett had suffered a similar tragedy when his long-time girlfriend was shot in the head while riding in the backseat of her friend's car on the interstate; the Cleveland police said the stray bullet was fired from outside a bar four blocks away. We were deployed at the time. There was never an arrest, and subsequently Garrett never rested. The event created a "before and after" Garrett. Was there a "before" Binelli that I would never know? Garrett had zero tolerance for the mere smell of criminality and would—

"It will be interesting," Kathleen disrupted my thoughts.

"What's that?"

"Meeting these people. Seeing what they're like in the flesh versus your image of them."

"I suppose."

"I suppose?" She gazed at me, stood, and said to Morgan, "Morgan, next time you fix conch chowder and fresh bread for dinner, do us both a favor? Invite some engaging company—you know, conversationalists." She leaned over and kissed him on the top of his head. "Thanks for dinner." His hand floated up as he kept his face toward the bay, and she gave it a squeeze. She went in the house and Morgan called it a night a few minutes later.

That left the cat and me.

Hadley III pounced on top of the Weber and gave a condescending stare over her domain: dolphins blowing in the dark; birds squawking over territorial rights; the occasional night traveler, some in boats of silence, others in boats of music. The channel marker pulsating its nightly warning. It was a domain she understood so little about. Nonetheless, she showed no fear, only curiosity enforced by presumed superiority.

That is what I like about cats.

14

The Fat Man

"Johnnie, be so kind, will you?"

Johnnie Darling shambled over to the condo's sunken living room bar. He measured two shots of whiskey into a solid glass tumbler. He smashed two fresh cherries and added them to the tumbler, along with a single translucent cube of ice. He stirred his creation with a swizzle stick and added a third cherry, its stem still attached. He took a cloth and wiped down the side of the tumbler and, with the cloth still wrapped around it, presented it to Phillip Agatha. Agatha took the tumbler, and Darling kept the cloth.

"Thank you, Darling." Agatha turned away, faced the darkening Miami skyline and Atlantic Ocean, and then added, "Go on, Eddie. What else did he say?"

Eddie replied, "Said that Saint Petersburg, Florida, was named in a coin toss."

Agatha let out a bastard sound between a hiccup and a laugh, his stomach involuntarily flexing up and down with the effort. "And so it was." He adjusted his feet so he faced Eddie. "So it was. But you are not in my employ to catalogue meaningless trivia. Tell me things about him that you are good at, that special talent that makes you so valuable to me."

Eddie put down the racing forum for Gulfstream Park and took a sip of his drink. "I watched the tape—when he first came in? He toyed around with Christina. Not a man at all unsure of himself."

"She notified you?"

"Yes, sir. She got a bad vibe from him. Called me soon as he left."

"Any particular words or phrases that struck you, or our lovely Christina, as odd?"

"I'll recite it to you." Eddie placed his drink on a coaster. He leafed through a stack of papers that were spread out on the glass table that was supported by a marble mermaid. Eddie had been with Agatha the day he bought it at Saint Armands Circle. He never knew anyone to spend $17,000 on a coffee table. It was six months before Eddie put a drink on it, coaster or not.

"Here it is. He says this to Christina…no wait, this is before he sees her. He says this to Charles, that's who I got on the front desk."

"Go ahead."

"'Where is the Gail Force moored?'"

"And Charles?"

"Oh no, sir. He didn't say a thing. He's a good man."

"He said *something*, didn't he Eddie?"

"Yes, sir." Eddie glanced down at his paper. "He said, 'Beg your pardon?' That's what he said. 'Beg your pardon?'"

"Continue."

"And then Beach Boy—Travis—said, 'Phillip's boat. Perhaps if you can't meet my most immediate needs, I can swing by, see if he can be of assistance.' After that Charles dialed Christina. His, Charles's, last words were, 'You listening?'"

Agatha took a drink and let some of the mashed cherry work its way around his mouth before he swallowed it. "The Gail Force."

"Yes, sir."

Agatha again turned to view the outside world. Lights flicked on in the neighboring towers as if someone were lighting giant vertical birthday cakes, a candle at a time. He did not notice that as much as he contemplated the black water of the Atlantic and, above it, the cold and endless space. Phillip Agatha knew the sun was nothing more than a lit match in a walk-in freezer.

"It's not a secret boat, is it?" he said with his back toward Eddie.

"No, sir. It's just that most people who approach us don't know nothing of her."

Agatha seemed to consider that. "Don't know nothing?"

"Yes, sir."

Agatha pivoted around to Eddie. "You mean they are ignorant of her existence."

"Yes, sir."

"And your enigma man led with that card. Doesn't tell us anything, though, does it? Perhaps he's fond of boats; perhaps his referral source desires to remain anonymous. There are countless possibilities, all meaningless unless he presents himself to our world. And when is that? At two tomorrow?"

"Yes, sir. He entered the twin ten-digit codes, followed by his last name."

"But your suspicion lingers, does it not? I keep you wrapped up in my life for your sixth sense. It does you no good, weakens your attractiveness to me, if you piddle around being anything other than what you are. Out with it."

Eddie shifted his weight. "Most guys, when they approach us? They're…maybe not scared, but cautious. They should be. If not, they're too dumb for us to do business with. Most guys we do business with…they're more like me, sir, than you. But Travis? Gee-zu—pardon me, sir. Who the heck knows, or cares, that Annette Fun-a-cello and Margaret Thatcher died on the same day." Eddie said Funicello's name deliberately, as if he were in a school play and had rehearsed it for days.

"He told you that?"

"Yes, sir."

"Not common knowledge, but hardly disrupting. Continue."

"So the guy's smart, see what I mean?"

"No crime in that."

"No, sir. But there is a crime, in my old neighborhood, in this: I've got a basket of bread, off to my left, right? Travis is on my other side. He reaches across, like no cares in the world, and helps himself. I know that type of guy. You pay me for my instincts? This guy don't care. He's smart, and he don't care. That's not our usual customer. In fact, Mr. Agatha, I'm not sure what he is if he ain't danger."

"I see. But you don't think he carries a badge?"

"No—that's the problem. He's worse. He carries himself like he's above someone who carries a badge. A real badge man? Those guys would have made me squirm. Those guys hate people like me and look down on my kind. If he was law, he would have stuck his righteousness in my face. This guy was cool. No qualms about being squeezed between Henny and me. Oh, I almost forgot. Henny? I point out to Travis that's he's with me, just in case he didn't catch on—"

"You've just told me how smart he is."

"That's correct. And this was after the Annette-Thatcher comment. I was trying to rattle him, 'cause my antennae was up."

"Proceed."

Eddie spread his hands, palms out. "He couldn't care less about Henny. Basically told me *I* was of interest to him. Some stuff about if he were to be scared, he would fear me more than Henny."

Agatha let out a series of rippling chuckles. "No wonder you're suspicious. He's like you, Eddie. He has good instincts. Knows how to rattle people. Perhaps your self-recognition is the core of your nervousness. What did you tell him?"

"Told him next time he called to say he wanted to talk to Eddie from Youngstown State. But that just means he doesn't have a legitimate referral, just the codes."

"Or that he likes you, or a dozen other conclusions that cannot be made with certainty at this point. He had the numbers. Did you run a background on him?"

"Yes."

"Nothing there, correct?"

"Correct."

"We will proceed with the meeting."

"Yes, sir. Bring him to your office, a little after two?"

"No," Agatha drew his words out, "I don't think so." He resumed his pace. "This man intrigues me. You say he's smart but has no fear, an incongruity that arouses your senses. Every man has a monster under his bed. Your fear, Eddie, is of violence, a common and elementary definition of the word. But fear is far more pervasive and deeper than bodily harm. *Real* fear creates our character. It molds us and forces our actions. You said he mentioned the Gail Force?"

"Yes, sir."

"Bring him aboard. Tomorrow at eight we shall throw a party, and your new friend will be in attendance. Round up Miami's finest. Be imaginative. Do I need to tell you anything more?"

"No, sir. Our usual inaugural treatment for Mr. Travis on the Gail Force?"

"Most assuredly. Christina?"

"Waiting outside."

Agatha fluttered his fingers. "Have a pleasant evening, Eddie. You may tell her she can come in now. Johnnie? Another, please."

15

The black SUV dropped me in front of Oceana. I had reservations there for two nights and had not booked a return flight to Tampa. I didn't know whether I needed three hours, or a week. They had assured me that they were not full, and if I wished to extend my stay, it wouldn't be an issue.

At two o'clock, I presented myself to my friend with the Beatle-bowl-marine haircut.

"I'm back."

"Hmmm...as the world turns. We've been expecting you, Mr. Travis. Your password?"

"Eddie from Youngstown State. Or maybe it's George from the jungle; I get the two confused."

"Yes. I see how you could be challenged by such things." He reached into a drawer and handed me an envelope. "It's George *of* the jungle. Open it, please."

It was an invitation to attend a party on the *Gail Force*. Tonight. Eight o'clock. Formal attire required. It contained a bar code.

"This is my meeting?"

"I was instructed to present the invitation to you."

"Can I meet with Mr. Agatha earlier? My business is urgent. Besides, I left my tux in the cab."

He smiled at me as if I deserved pity I didn't understand. He reached again into the drawer and presented me a business card.

"You did no such thing, sweetie. See Marlo, two blocks north. That's a left when you go out the front door. If you hit Bennie's Bar, you've gone too far. He can take care of you within the hour. Tell him Mr. Agatha sent you. I suggest you go straight forth. The afternoon is already late."

I glanced at the card. Marlo. No last name. Just an address.

"Will there be anything else?" he asked. Like he had a dozen things to do.

"Bennie's a nice place if I want a sandwich?"

"Totally. Best Cuban on the block."

"See you tonight?"

"In my dreams." He blinked.

Marlo was on his knees pinning a man's trousers. The man jabbered away into his cell phone, a diatribe of Spanish syllables flying out of his mouth like snow in a blizzard.

I took a seat and picked up a men's magazine that professed to know a woman's eleven hot spots. I put it down. I picked it up. I peeked at the hot-spot article. Really. I had no idea. Plus, they missed two that I know of.

"May I help you?" Marlo said as the Spanish tsunami blew out the front door. Marlo ate pasta and bread every night for dinner. His measuring tape was draped around his neck and the first few buttons of his shirt were undone revealing a chest of curly hair. He had natural dark skin tone that, at that very moment, Anglo-Saxon girls just a few blocks from me were trying to replicate by offering their unprotected bodies to the fireball in the sky.

"Mr. Agatha sent me. Apparently I'm not up to his standards."

"No, you are not."

I expected a smile and was a tad disappointed when one never materialized.

"Please." He signaled to the box that fronted three mirrors. "The occasion?"

"Formal. Tonight on his yacht."

"Black. Yes?"

"Do I have a choice?"

"White is accepted," he admitted while taking a tape around my chest. "But it is no good. You will go in black. And shave. A man should not degrade his clothing." He did my inseam, arms, and asked my shoe size. An Asian man brought out a shoebox. I took a seat on a cloth bench and tried them on.

"You need sock?" the assistant asked.

"I do."

"I have sock for you."

"Five o'clock." Marlo cut in. He turned to his assistant. "Don't forget to get all the pins out."

"How much?" I asked, reaching for my wallet.

He was considering a sizing chart and didn't bother to look up. "It is taken care of."

"I insist."

"You have no choice." He glanced up at me. "Five o'clock. Don't be late. It's poker night."

"Mr. Marlo," the assistant cut in, "never misses poker."

"Don't forget the pins," Marlo reprimanded him.

His assistant gave me a playful smile. "I always forget pins."

Outside, the Miami heat melted me like I was a stick of butter on Alligator Alley. I took a left, ducked into Ben-

nie's Bar, had the best Cuban on the block, and was bliss-
fully ignorant that Marlo's assistant would so greatly alter
the course of events. Twice.

16

The *Gail Force* was docked directly across from downtown Miami off the MacArthur Causeway on Miami Beach. She rested at the end of the pier, just inside a break wall. I could envision bringing her in, but it had to be double black diamonds heading out. At the marina's black wrought-iron gate, I presented my invitation from the backseat of my limo. The gates swung open like flower petals in a slow-motion film.

The yacht was preened in blue. Her deck lights were blue, as were her underwater lights that ran the circumference of the yacht. All the cabin lights were on. Florida Power and Light was making a few bucks off her. She also looked like a shopping mall on Black Friday; she was jammed and hopping. A live band was set up on her aft deck.

A pair of offensive linemen in tuxedos parked themselves on the pier at the base of the gangplank. I presented my invitation again, but this time it was scanned; Agatha knew I'd arrived. The couple behind me received the same treatment.

I headed straight to the bar in the aft deck and ordered a Jameson. The bartender plopped a cherry in it. All the drinks received a complimentary cherry. The band, dressed in formal black, broke into a sinuous rendition of the Doors, "Riders on the Storm." The deck lights dimmed, as if someone had sprayed a mist of aphrodisiac into the already sultry Florida evening.

A lady with a pair of breasts leading the way—they reminded me of the dog pointing its nose over the bow of the fishing boat—approached with hors d'oeuvres. A black bow tie choked her neck, and then nothing until her black dress took over. Top to bottom, the dress likely measured no more than two and a half feet.

"Filet?" she asked as she presented a silver tray to me. She was missing a fake cyan-colored fingernail.

I helped myself to several cubes of red beef. "Hang around a sec, will you?" I said as I discarded toothpicks on her tray.

"There's a buffet table inside, would you like me to lead you to it?"

I popped another cube in my mouth. "I'll manage."

I wanted to get the schematics of the boat before I met Agatha. I hiked her 164-foot length around the deck and then entered the main aft stateroom where the buffet was spread out. Sliding glass doors led to a smaller inside stateroom. The sliders were wood and contained stained glass. No way was she launched with those. Agatha had detailed her to his liking, and there were enough wood built-ins that an Amish community must have taken up residence for six months.

I chatted to a few girls, defended my bachelorhood against both sexes, and was about to take the circular back stairs up to the next level when from behind me came, "Mr. Travis."

I turned. "Christina."

She, too, was festooned in blue, with layers of thin blue necklaces that seemed to generate their own light. Her deep-blue dress scraped the floor, and a slit on the right side appeared to go to her hip. She wore blue bracelets, and her hair was black with streaks of blue. She was a walking billboard for the primary color that stood for loyalty, peace, and trust. But it was also Picasso's color of depression and sadness, used during a specific period of his life. The Blue Period.

"Have you taken a tour?" she inquired.

"I was about to investigate the upper level. Care to join me?"

"You've seen the lower level?"

"I have not."

"I suggest we start there. It would be a pity, your first time aboard, not to experience Mr. Agatha's masterpiece."

"Will you be my tour guide?"

"Try to endure," she answered tonelessly.

She strode off, a model on a runway, not the least bit inhibited by her high heels. There are two types of women in the world: those who can truck along, their enthusiasm for each step undiminished by the spike in their heel, and those whose each successful step is treated as an answer to a silent prayer. Kathleen was of the latter, Christina the former.

"The Gail Force, Mr. Travis," Christina turned up the volume over her shoulder, "is a piece of art." I pulled up beside her. "The yacht," she lowered her tone, "is incomparable in design. Mr. Agatha spent over two million dollars on the woodwork and furniture. That does not include the art you will see on the walls." She stopped and adjusted my bow tie. "You would have looked impressive in white."

"Marlo didn't think so."

"He's so old-school, but Mr. Agatha likes him."

"He also told me to shave."

"Respect the clothing?"

"Close enough."

I ran my hand over a polished varnished exterior door. "Didn't the yacht originally have reflective glass doors?"

"Mr. Agatha replaced all the reflective glass doors."

"Why is that?"

"That's a question for him. Shall we?"

She sashayed down the steps, and I followed, maneuvering around two women who needed to get a room.

The lower level didn't suffer from lack of activity, although one of the doors had a "Shhh…we're sleeping" sign hung on the hand-carved door handle. I studied one of the knobs as we passed it. It was a whittled palm frond.

"Washington Palm," I observed.

"Excuse me?"

"Each doorknob is a carved Washington Palm frond."

"Mr. Agatha changes them every six months."

"Why is that?"

"Mr. Agatha appreciates the beauty of ordinary objects."

"The previous door handles?"

"A feather."

"What's next?"

She turned to me. "I don't know. It's part of the fun of working with a great man."

"What makes him a great man, beyond rotating door handles, which in the annals of history would hardly seem a challenging exercise, or a worthy endeavor, for a prodigious mind?"

"You've not met him. You may wish to refrain from sarcastic questions that on later reflection will cause you to feel foolish for voicing. This way, please." She extended her arm into a kitchen roughly the size of my house. It was crammed with help staff. "Mr. Agatha was fastidious in planning the kitchen."

"Hence his nickname?"

She turned sharply on me, her hair chasing her face in an attempt to keep up with her. "I suggest you keep that to yourself."

"How many work in the kitchen on a regular basis?"

She hesitated as if she'd been expecting me to react to her advice and was slightly thrown off when I didn't. "Two. They are full-time."

"But he doesn't live aboard."

"The market in Miami is very competitive. Whether he needs them or not, they are on a yearly salary and work only for him. That is the only way to maintain good help."

"Is that what you are?"

"Pardon?"

"Good help?"

"I'm your tour director. Notice the two ovens." She motioned off to our left where twin stainless steel behemoths stood. She stopped in front of a wood door. "And of course, the wine cellar." She reached to the top of the doorframe and collected a key. She unlocked the door and dropped the key in her purse. "The door is from a farmhouse in Italy. Mr. Agatha keeps his extensive collection in his condo."

I followed her into a small climate-controlled room. It was a tight fit.

"Do you know your wine, Mr. Travis?" She freed a bottle from a leather strap that kept it snugged in its place and presented it to me.

"There's red," I answered thoughtfully, "white, and—tell me, do they make a blue, like you?"

"What do you think of this?" She ignored my juvenile posturing and stuck the bottle out, forcing me to take it from her. It was a 1999 Mouton Rothschild.

"Red French," I said. "Stick a candle in it and watch the wax drip down its side."

"That's Chianti, Mr. Travis." She tilted the bottle. "This is what's being served at the top deck. You can buy a Lamborghini with the wine that Mr. Agatha will share with us tonight."

"What does that mean?" I asked her.

"What does what mean?"

"Him serving a Lamborghini to people—many I doubt he even knows?"

"His intensity on the pleasures of life is unmatched."

"And this?" I brushed past her and selected a bottle that was held tight by a wooden rail. It was a 1973 Chateau Montelena Chardonnay. It took first place in the 1976 Judgment of Paris. The tasting, arranged by a wine merchant, forever changed the perception of American wine. Its value? I couldn't imagine. A 1973 Stag's Leap, the overall red winner, rested next to it.

"I don't know about that one. Perhaps, when you meet Mr. Agatha, you can ask him yourself."

"When will I be meeting Mr. Agatha?"

"When he wants to meet you."

"When might that be?"

"Do you find our time uninteresting?" She took a step toward me.

"Not in the least bit. Where else can you view priceless red and white wines, finely crafted door handles, and a stunning woman in blue?"

She nodded slightly, as if to acknowledge my compliment, and followed it with a smile. "Follow me."

We exited the wine room, and I said, "The key."

"Excuse me?"

"To lock the door."

That sparked an embarrassed grin and a split second of self-consciousness, like when you open your mailbox as the neighbor's walking the dog, and it's empty. Something about her wasn't right—wasn't her. She fumbled in her dainty purse, pulled out the key, and hastily locked the door. She returned the key to the top of the frame.

We picked our way back through the kitchen and up the circular staircase to the main deck, where the band in black was doing a Latin beat. The dance floor was a tribal frenzy. I followed her up to the next level, where a studious-looking man stood guard outside a door. As Christina approached, he opened the door without comment. We entered the third-level stateroom. The live band died with the latching of the door.

"Beachy."

"Eddie." I pulled up to him and shook hands like old chums as I succumbed to the charm and taste of a man whom I'd yet to meet. "I haven't run across my host yet."

"You see the end of that game?"

"Game?"

"Bowling Green. You see it?"

"I did. Enjoyed another drink after you and Henny left. Where is your outspoken friend?"

"Let me get you a fresh one." He reached out and took my glass.

We strolled over to a bar, where he raised his left index finger for the bartender. Odd. He was right-handed. There were fourteen people in the room, most of them sitting around a table that I assumed served as a second dining area.

Eddie handed me my drink, said, "Salute," and we clanked glasses. Mine didn't have a cherry in it. They must be running low, although Agatha didn't strike me as a man to tolerate the slightest imperfection.

"Tour the pilothouse?" Eddie suggested.

"I'd love to."

He led the way to the front of the room, through a door and up a half flight of steps that were more function than design. I glanced over my shoulder to see if Christina was joining us. She was gone. I nearly lost my footing at the top.

"How many in her crew?" I asked as we entered the pilot-house. The forward wall was solid electronics fronting two separate captain chairs. The room was dark, except for under-counter lights and the glow from outside. A desk sat in the far corner. It was an odd thing to see in a pilothouse.

"Seven including the domestic. That's not including Mr. Agatha's entourage."

"All full-time?"

"Yes."

"That's got to be a hefty operating budget."

"Everything has its price."

Eddie wasn't his usual wiseass self; he must bottle up when his boss was around. I moved over to the helm to get a better view of the electronics. I steadied myself on the port side captain's chair as if the boat had encountered a swell. *But we were tight against a break wall, so tight I'd marveled at how the captain could dock the boat.* It would be nice to talk to the captain—milk him for a little information.

"To our business together." Eddie was behind me. We clanked again, and both took another sip.

"I'll tell you, Beachy, when we first met? I thought I might see you again, you know? You being the type of guy who don't usually show up unless you got a purpose in which you aren't easily dissuaded from. You listening?"

"I am." I was a little light-headed, like when you get up too fast.

"So when you came through with the code, I wasn't surprised. Tell me, who you working for?"

"What?" I stumbled toward a chair.

"Tell me who you work for. Who you really work for."

No cherry. Signaled the bartender with his left hand.

"I was told to see Mr. Agwatha." My tongue was thick and heavy. The glass fell from my hand. *He's trying to get it out of me, who I really am. Can't be trusted to talk. Got to shut up.*

"Who told you about us, Beachy?" His breath was on me, his gnarled hands grabbing my shoulders. I took a swing at him, but my arm was sluggish, like I was swinging under water. He slapped it away. "Why do you really want to see Mr. Agatha? Look at me." He stuck his hand under my chin. "That's better. I didn't believe a word you said when we first met, so you tell me here and now who you are, and I'll have Christina take you home. You like that? Look at me. I said, you like that? Maybe she can show you one of the rooms below; just tell me who you work for. Come on now, Beachy, stay with me. She's all woman, woman like you've never had. Who are you?" He slapped me across the face. "Look at me, you fuck."

I didn't trust myself to talk, nor could I guarantee my silence. I started singing. "God bleth Amereeecaaa."

He slapped me again.

"Wand of the fweee."

Fweee? What is this? The Elmer Fudd hour? Where's Rocky and Bullwinkle? Who said Rocky? Who said that?

He raised his hand. I stumbled away from him and toward the door. I was singing, but I didn't know why. The room spun, and the door vanished. Just as I started to go down, Henny—*where'd he come from?*—caught me in his arms, and I folded into him like he was a giant box. My world went dark, and for some delirious reason, my last thought was Amazon, and life seemed so disappointing if that's what it all came down to.

17

My right eye sprung open to a blond wood ceiling with a strong grain pattern. *The inside of my coffin?* No. Sunlight streamed through the slats of wood shades. A few seconds later, my left eye followed suit, although it took a conscious and prolonged effort to pop it open. I was lost, like when you wake up from an afternoon nap and momentarily have no idea where you are or what day it is.

This was an extended-play version of that sensation. I lay in bed, staring at the ceiling. It was pretty wood—if I spent the rest of my life staring at it, it would be a peaceful existence. My mind started flipping through the names of people in the twenty-seven club—those who died at that age. It seemed vitally important to me, although I couldn't imagine why.

Let's see where it leads. Beats staring at a wood ceiling the rest of your life.

Jimi Hendrix. Janis. Kurt. Rupert Brooke. *He laid down some heavy lines, and those punk-rockers don't even know his name.* Winehouse. Morrison.

The Doors.

Took their name from William Blake: "If the doors of perception were cleansed everything would appear to man as it is, infinite." *Naw, that's a dead end—not bad, though, pulling that out of sleepy town. Gee-zus, am I good or what? Who says that—gee-zus? Is it that little twerp in a wet snowsuit? No, no, no. I don't think so. Change course.*

Door handles?

Why does that feel like progress?

A cherry-less drink. An Amazon box.

A hum of engines.

The Gail Force.

I sat up in bed as it came into focus. I was naked except for my underwear. I took a deep breath and then another. I was in a small stateroom. I stood and opened the blinds. There was nothing outside my porthole except endless water that fused on the horizon with the blue sky, as if they were a singular item with a creased fold. A small nightstand next to my bed held a steaming coffeepot, orange juice sludged with pulp, and a croissant.

Did I tell Eddie about myself? I didn't think so.

I showered, going between hot and cold water, and ending it as cold as it came. After shaving, I smeared lotion on my face, but it had a sweet odor, so I washed it off. My tux was neatly hung in the closet, and next to it were two pairs of long pants and two shirts. The pair of beige linen pants fit perfectly, as did a maroon short-sleeved silk shirt. I ate the warm croissant and poured a cup of coffee. A pair of new pliable leather loafers were also the correct size. I told my feet not to get too used to them. I unplugged my phone from a charger—someone was surprisingly considerate. It was 9:50 a.m., the following day. Hopefully my limo driver had thrown it in and headed home.

I latched the door behind me and traipsed around until I ended up on the aft deck of the main level. The sliding doors were open, and a tropical breeze ribboned through the space. Agatha was perched at the teak dining table. He stood.

"Mr. Travis, I'm so delighted to see you. Phillip Agatha."

Agatha lumbered a few steps toward me. He used a thin cane more for style than for purpose, as it was no match for his body. We shook hands. His pudgy fingers were warm, and his face had baby-smooth skin. His eyes danced as if the moment was magic. His thin dark hair was slicked back, not a single strand free. His rotundness, distributed evenly over his frame, was masked by his youth.

"I apologize for sleeping in." I freed his hand. "It appears your liquor cabinet was compromised."

"Please have a seat." He sat back down, and I took a chair to his left. He picked up a damp cloth and wiped his right hand. "I'm in an unusual business, Mr. Travis, and thus have unusual customs. I assure you, you were not treated differently than anyone else. I see you found your clothes this morning."

"I did."

"Excellent. If you care to look in the top dresser drawer you will also find swimwear and folded shirts. No shorts, though. Outside of swimming, I don't tolerate men in shorts. I do hope you don't mind. Also, when we dine, do keep in mind that I admire promptitude."

Agatha's voice carried the timbre of a grown-up choirboy who had maintained his youthful innocence and purity. It floated with the confidence of a sorcerer, as if he knew where the conversation was headed, each word a precursor to events that he could clearly see.

"Those are the house rules?" I challenged him. "Long pants and be on time?"

"A man would do well to live by those."

"And if I do mind?"

"I beg your pardon?" He took a sip from his coffee.

"Being restricted to long pants?"

"Then I'm afraid you would suffer from unusually warm legs for the duration of our trip," he noted wryly.

"Not the most difficult of conditions for a man to endure."

"I should think not."

"About our trip," I said as my eyes scanned the horizon. "Where are you abducting me to?"

He chuckled pleasantly. "Dear Mr. Travis, you carry a delusional sense of self-importance. Do not flatter yourself; this is hardly for you. I'm going to Freeport to view a piece of art. We'd thought you'd like to tag along. Your presence ensures that we are granted an unencumbered opportunity to adequately enjoy each other's company. We'll be back in Miami by nightfall. Are you hungry?"

"I could eat this yacht."

Another chuckle. "Yes, well, see, we've found common ground already." He flipped his left hand up, his stubby fingers paddling the air. A uniformed steward, who'd been standing like a metal coffeepot, spoke into a handheld device as he dashed away.

Christina joined us from the aft deck. She wore a bikini top and a swath of flowered orange cloth around her waist that ended just beyond her knees. A single gold necklace strand rested on her chest, where beads of perspiration glistened like liquid diamonds.

Agatha appraised her. "Did you give Mr. Travis the tour last night, dear?"

"Yes, Phillip. I even showed him the wine room." She sat on the chair across from me, erect with her hands on her lap, her attention on her master. "His interest resided with that."

"Deplorable abuse of opportunity. What did he think of our modest collection?"

"He professed knowledge of red and white, and wondered if there were any blues."

Agatha swiveled his head toward me. "Mr. Travis, I—"

"Jake."

"Excuse me?" he said with an edge. Phillip Agatha did not appreciate being interrupted. That was good to know.

"Call me Jake. If I hear 'mister' prefacing my last name one more time, I'm swimming to shore."

"We're still forty miles out...Jake."

"Tide's in my camp."

"As is your glib attitude. Eddie was right, you've got that spark. Jake it is, and Phillip to you." Agatha leaned back in his chair. "The wine room, Jake, did you like it? Wine is the ultimate art. It is the rarest form of human artistic expression; it is fluid—that alone places it on an unoccupied field—it naturally appreciates over time, and best of all, we destroy it when we consume it. Imagine Michelangelo creating a fresco knowing that to properly enjoy it, it would need to be eaten."

"Will Eddie be joining us for breakfast?"

"No, just us. And Christina, of course. You're a man who appreciates dictating the subject, as am I. Do you like Christina?"

I glanced at Christina, and her eyes met mine. She showed no hint of self-awareness or discomfort, but it had to be there. At least in the world that I knew, but I was beginning to think the *Gail Force* sailed a different sea.

"I do." I returned my gaze to Agatha. "She's a beautiful woman."

"Wine and women. The greatest forms of art that man will ever know. Why would a man accompanied by Christina pass an empty bedroom? Certainly she lubricates your senses and weakens your moral certitudes."

Our breakfasts arrived. Christina received a bowl of fruit and yogurt. Agatha and I received plates with soft-boiled eggs, hot salmon, thick slices of fried potatoes, buttered toasted Italian bread, and grilled asparagus on top of a whipped squash.

The server hovered over me. "What type of juice would you like?"

"Grapefruit would be fine."

He proceeded to a cart where he sliced two grapefruit, squeezed them in a hand juicer, poured the contents into a glass, and handed it to me.

After a few bites of salmon, I said, "Are you accustomed to people answering your blunt personal questions?" The salmon was cooked medium with a tinge of teriyaki. The grapefruit was chilled.

He gazed at me through narrowed eyes, as if by squinting, he would gain a larger measure of me. "Have I offended you?"

"Perhaps you offended Christina."

"Why don't you ask her? Christina and I are quite comfortable, *Mr.* Travis. It is you who is being ornery."

I ignored his salutation. "Perhaps I woke up not only on the wrong side of the bed this morning but in the wrong bed. I don't appreciate being drugged and kidnapped nor see the purpose of such an inconsiderate act."

"Come now. Such a beautiful—"

"A federal offense." I purposely cut him off.

He squirmed in his seat and then spread his hand over the table. "It's a precaution we take with all potential clients. A party is no venue for business. I loathe repeating myself, but as I stated earlier, this grants each of us the other's unswerving attention. I'm doing my best to get us off to an auspicious start, despite your enfeebling remarks. Would you like to return to shore? I can arrange for a helicopter to gather you in the Bahamas."

"What I'd like is more juice, please." I glanced over at the server. He sprang to action on the beverage cart, and I returned my attention to Agatha. "Mr. Agatha," I stated.

"Phillip." He gestured with his left hand. He gave me an approving smile, although it was a smile of someone who had forgotten, or perhaps never knew, what a smile was. Rather, he mimicked the facial expression, as if he were trying to copy what he'd seen others do, but in itself was foreign and beyond him.

"I'm not familiar with your method of business, but if you think I should be anything other than alarmed and disturbed by your opening gambit, then perhaps—despite my employer's keen desire to engage in your services—we should part ways, and I can seek other means to achieve my objective."

It was a gutsy move. I certainly didn't want him to toss me overboard, nor did I want him to think that I was eager to conduct business with him at any cost.

Agatha leaned back. I was considering how to salvage my mission if he went against me, when he acceded, "Yes. Well, I suppose if someone slipped something in my drink I, too, might be a bit miffed, although I trust I would never be impertinent to my host. I hope your accommodations, coupled with exquisite hospitality wrapped in congeniality, will more than compensate for, as you said, my opening gambit. You play chess?"

"I know a king from a queen."

"I'm sure you do. And you know a great deal about wine, don't you, Jake?"

I spread my hands. His question didn't warrant a reply.

"You selected and held the 1973 Montelena. You know its significance."

I shot a look at Christina, but her eyes were on her yogurt. Did she inform him or was there a camera in the wine cellar? Or both?

"An erudite knowledge, I assure you."

That seemed to pique his interest. "The Paris Tasting of Seventy-Five," he said. "Am I correct?"

"If you say so."

"It pains you, does it not? To agree with something that is so blatantly wrong."

"I am your guest, and one who apparently needs to work on his impertinence."

"And a polite one at that, despite your tempestuous protesting. Your deportment shifts from aggression to courtly manners with speed and delicacy. I commend that. Go ahead, correct me. We both know my blunder was by design."

"The Judgment of Paris. Seventy-six. Do I get a treat?"

"Erudite knowledge, indeed. As if the first word in some manner deprecates the second." He took a final bite and signaled the waiter, who swooped his plate off the table, removed the placemat, and poured coffee into his cup. "Christina, if you don't mind."

Christina stood and, without granting me a glance, headed toward the lounge chairs on the extreme aft deck.

Agatha rose. "Let's also make ourselves more comfortable."

He picked up his cane. A carved animal's head served as its cap. A sheep, a dog, a goat? I couldn't discern it. We relocated with our coffees to where overstuffed couches and chairs were strategically placed around tables in an area that had no walls. A tongue-in-groove wood ceiling with a pair of rotating fans shielded us from the sun. Agatha settled in a couch that relinquished its form in recognition of his weight. I took a wide chair, overlooking Christina. The churning wakes trolled behind us, each side a foaming replica of the other.

He opened a wood humidor. "I suggest these." He reached in and handed me a Davidoff. "They are excellent for the morning. Extremely mild, with an aged Dominican leaf and a Yankee wrapper, they blend exceptionally well with the coffee bean."

I torched it, took a drag, crossed my legs, and considered the merits of enjoying the cruise and tossing overboard the whole undercover shtick.

"Eddie doesn't like you." Agatha said and then blew smoke into the air, where the breeze whisked it away like a lost child.

"He'll get over it. He's peeved because I reached across him and helped myself to his dinner bread."

He chuckled. "Quite perceptive. Yet I would be more comfortable doing business with you if you secured his stamp of approval."

"I'd be more comfortable if I could trust what drinks you give me."

"A stalemate, then."

"I don't think so."

"No?"

"Eddie's not the decision-maker."

"What is it you want from me, Jake?"

I took a leisurely drag and exhaled in a similar tempo. Music came on, like we were at a resort where it would come on at the same time every day. "Splendor in the Grass." A Pink Martini number that I always admired.

I gave him the quick and dirty on Zebra Electronics. Told him I flew in from Dallas. I slipped in that I lived in Saint Pete but traveled extensively. As I'd previously told Eddie where I lived, I wanted to quell that incongruity in case it troubled him. I explained that my employer had identified a target that would make our problems disappear, and we saw no harm in the effort. He inquired how I came across his name. I replied my source didn't want to be associated with any names, and that Agatha came highly recommended as a man who would get things done, however they needed to be handled. It was the right answer. He listened patiently; that was hard for him.

When Agatha's coffee was done, the waiter brought him a tumbler, wrapped in a napkin. No cherry. Perhaps they were reserved for the afternoon hours. Agatha had an oral fixation. In the short time I'd known him, the purpose of his right hand had been to constantly present offerings to his lips. His senses were continuously imbibing food, smoke, and liquids.

Agatha took the glass, and the waiter kept the napkin. He took a sip and said, "Are you with a law enforcement agency?"

"No."

"Do you report to or work for a law enforcement agency?"

"No."

"And if you did, what would your answers have been?"

"No and no." I'd given Kathleen the same line. Was she really upset with me last night? That line to Morgan about dull company?

"Precisely. You see my dilemma?"

I snuffed out my cigar in a bamboo ashtray shaped like the open palm of a monkey's hand. It would look nice on my dusty glass table in the screened porch next to the Copacabana tray.

"Not really." I uncrossed my legs. "You face this predicament with nearly every transaction into which you enter."

"I do. But Eddie—how shall I put it—we have little in common. Yet he is an invaluable resource to me. How do you explain that?"

"I don't have to. He works for you, not me."

He took another sip and placed his drink on a coaster on a wood table off to his side. His naked right hand rested on the couch, his fingers drumming.

"You know about cats?" he said.

"I have one."

"Certainly you jest."

"I would never joke about a cat."

He paused then broke into a riotous laugh, as if he'd just heard the best of the Marx Brothers for the first time. "You?" He managed to exclaim between guffaws. "I cannot see that at all. You did not acquire the hunter through any desire of your own, am I correct?"

"A friend asked to me look after her." *The same friend who sent Riley Anderson to me so that I could put a bullet in you with her name on it.*

"A friend indeed." He let out a soprano giggle that was incongruous with his body mass. "Eddie is my cat. He possesses a sense that is foreign to me, or at the very least, I am deficient in. I embrace all people, love all people, and wish harm to no one. Eddie is crass. A ruffian. His language is deplorable, and his table manners need constant tending, but no mistake, he is my radar."

"Perhaps I could buy him a drink. Like the one he gave me."

He straightened up. "Let's not tote old baggage all day, shall we?"

I leaned forward. "Am I on the right boat or not? Time is of essence to my employer."

He paused, as if to voice his distaste at my urgency. "I'm never in a rush, nor is there ever a deal I cannot live without. I am intrigued by your predicament and yes, you are on the right vessel. Shall we review the terms? There's no need to waste our time if our association is ultimately doomed by the vagaries of details. Ten million US dollars upon completion, wired to an institution of our choice. A million up front that is nonrefundable in the event that we are unable or unwilling to fulfill your requirements. I trust this is not an issue?"

My hundred grand wasn't going to cut it. I'd worry about that later. "My million dollars. You could take it and walk."

"I could. If you're worried about such an item," he pointed out sharply, "than we have no business doing business."

"If my employer didn't worry about such items, he'd never have made his first million."

"Your logic is specious. We are not discussing either's first million. Will it be an issue?"

"I can sell it. What's our next step?"

"We drop anchor in Freeport in about an hour." He stood. "I'll be ashore for two hours or so. You're free to disembark, of course, but my business is private and you will be on your own. We leave with or without you, so if you do take off afoot, be it not far."

I rose, and he plodded past me and into the main stateroom. He hadn't answered my last question, at least not in the context we both knew I had phrased it in. Like a wizard,

Phillip Agatha commanded and controlled every aspect of his world. I shifted my gaze aft and caught Christina's oiled bronze body frozen in the sun.

It'd be nice to have a lunch mate in Freeport.

18

Christina twirled her hair while studying the menu. I ordered a beer, fries, and a grouper sandwich. She twirled some more, and I told the waiter to make it two. "No," she glanced up and handed him the menu. "Substitute a rum-runner, on the rocks, not frozen, for my beer. Salad for fries. No dressing. And bottled water."

We sat on a plank-floor porch outside a Caribbean yellow-walled restaurant. The windows behind us were open, and on closer scrutiny, I noticed there was no glass, just shutters that were latched on the outside on rusted hinges that had likely never been touched. When you're in a part of the world that doesn't need doors and windows, you're in a good part of the world. The *Gail Force* rode anchor in the harbor, and we'd taken a tender to shore. Christina had informed me that, as a reminder, she would receive a text fifteen minutes prior to the tender returning to the yacht.

I wanted to learn as much about Agatha as I could but assumed after our conversation at breakfast that every word would be relayed back to Agatha.

"What's her name?" she asked. Her seat viewed the marketplace and harbor while I faced into the restaurant, patrons brushing behind me. A lousy seat, but I'm not comfortable at a table with a woman unless the woman has the better view. My good seat at Tony's, in which my back was to the wall, and Binelli stared into that wall, was an exception. I didn't know who she was bringing and therefore wanted to view the upstairs and the steps.

"Whose name?" I said to her question.

"Your girlfriend."

"What makes you think that—?"

"Please." She angled her head and smiled. It was a nice smile, a girl-next-door smile, but it didn't go with the rest of her. It was like something from her past that she'd forgotten how to do, or snuck out when her guard was down. "I'm not unattractive," she added.

I leaned in, elbows on the table, and placed my chin on my overlapping hands. "Frankly, my dear, I find you repulsive."

She hesitated and then mimicked my position, our faces a foot apart. I tucked a rebellious strand of hair behind her ear and wondered why I did that.

"But not repugnant?" she said.

"Revulsive."

"But not repellant?"

She was good. I was running out of Rs. "You'd do well at Scrabble."

"I spent hours doing so with my mom," she said proudly. "Spill it. Who is she?"

"A certain lady."

"Lemme guess, more than six months. But less than two years."

"Does your cynical observation stem from experience?"

"Hmm...let's say two parts observation and one part experience. Redolent."

"I'm more interested in the minor than the majority. Revolting."

"Redolent's better, and you know it," she said defensively.
"Not in points."

"It's not fair. Obscure words should be given more credit."

"Redolent? I hear it a dozen times a day. Besides, you
should be penalized for words that sound like plaque-infested
varmints."

Her lips curved into a relaxed smile. In some manner,
we'd moved a step closer to each other, or at the least, elimi-
nated a layer that was separating us. The drinks arrived, forcing us to split away from our midtable powwow. Her hurricane glass was capped with an umbrella a golfer in Saint
Andrews would die for. I drained a third of my bottle on my
first pass.

"And you?" I said.

She took a sip by bending over and positioning her mouth
on the straw. "My experience is that the *really* good men are
as common as four-leaf clovers."

"One could say the same about women."

"I wouldn't know. I need a man to open the door for me, to
look at me as if he owns me, although he knows he doesn't, to
be the world to him, although I have my own world. To catch
my eye from across a crowded room and to search no more."

"That's on your resume, under 'goals'?"

"Your certain lady?"

"Yes?"

"Ever ask her how she feels when you open the door for
her and she strides through, while you stand at attention?"

"I have not."

"Do so. And no, it's not on my resume."

"What is? Moving up in the Agatha Corporation?"

"It's a good gig—no, it's a fabulous gig. I get an Amex
card for my wardrobe, attend all types of functions that

require me to look pretty, and get paid more than I should. Exorbitantly more."

"And in return?"

"I am loyal to Mr. Agatha."

"I need to engage him for business. Will you put in a good word for me?"

"Such as?"

Our lunches came, and I ordered another beer.

"He, or at least Eddie, doesn't trust me," I explained. "I'm under pressure from my employer to consummate a deal. I need to impress on Mr. Agatha that it's a simple business deal, and I'll be on my way."

"Suggestion?"

"I'm open."

"Dummy down, and don't walk so attractively...confident."

I responded by taking a swig from my bottle. She continued, "Mr. Agatha is always looking for someone to have mental duels with. Your knowledge of wine? That just excites him. May even cause him to lengthen your negotiations just to keep you around, like a cat swatting a mouse. And your attitude? 'Call me Jake, or I swim?' Most people who approach us bring a dose of uncertainty. What do you really want?"

"I'm here to strike a deal for my employer."

"Really, you can—"

"Eat your fish."

"—trust me."

"I do trust you. I trust you to tell him you were a good little girl, poked me for information, and that I desire to transact my business and move on."

She shuffled in her seat as if she were about to say something, but instead she forked a sliced cucumber—with far more gusto than the cucumber warranted—and stuck it in her mouth. She used utensils to eat the fish off the bun but didn't finish her fruit and politely asked for a container to go. We had about twenty minutes to kill and, per Christina's suggestion, we drifted over to the bazaar that occupied the street behind the restaurant. A cruise boat was in the harbor, and the marketplace was bustling with excited tourists eager to experience pictures they'd seen in brochures or on bright computer screens. Everyone always heads south, trying to stay a step ahead of their problems, chasing their golden future, only to discover their problems are tethered to the sun and are the last item to spill out of the suitcase.

The local venders at the bazaar, most of them black women, vied for attention by chattering nonstop as American dollars flirted around their booths. Christina paused at a table that displayed necklaces, bracelets, hairpieces, and disparate knickknacks.

Two women, likely off the cruise boat, were in front of us, and one of them had two items in her hand. The proprietor wanted fifteen dollars for the two, insisting that normal price was ten each.

The lady holding the merchandise adjusted the strap on her Burberry crossbody bag. She was adamant that ten dollars for both was as high as she could go. The vendor was a large woman with a purple-flowered peasant dress that a stiff breeze would shred. She insisted on fifteen. Burberry stuck with ten and started to back away.

"OK. Ten dollars for you. Such a pretty woman."

Burberry shot a sly smile at her companion, whose ring finger had a walnut-size diamond on it, and spun around to the table. She handed the lady a twenty and stood with her hand out. The vendor gave her two dungy fives and said, "Would you like a bag?"

"Please."

"What do you think?" Christina said, demanding my attention. Her left hand held a copper necklace against her chest where earlier that day, beads of sweat had taunted my eyes. Her right hand held matching earrings and a bracelet.

"Looks good on you," the vendor said, although the question was directed at me. "You are a nice couple, very beautiful. Such a woman, you need to take care of her."

"They look very nice," I said to Christina.

"But do you like them on me?" Her voice carried a tone that was both genuine and indecisive. Neither the question nor the tone fit the festooned-in-blue female warrior who had dug her fingernails into the back of my neck when we'd first met.

"Need to take care of your woman." The vendor jumped in. "Treat her well."

I glanced at the necklace and then into Christina's searching eyes. "I do. I like them on you." She reached for her purse. "Allow me." I withdrew my wallet. "This way I can feel as if I'm obligating you to put in a good word to Mr. Agatha for me."

"Is it always about business?" She sounded disheartened and dropped her face.

I palmed the vendor a bill from my closed hand and said, "Your work is beautiful. It would sell for much more in other places." I reached out with my other hand and clasped it around her hand that held my bill.

"Thank you, mon." She reached into her tattered purse, but I quickly steered Christina away. She hollered after me, but her voice was soon lost to the buzz of the marketplace. About a third of the way back to the marina where our tender was docked, Christina exclaimed, "My fruit. I left it at the necklace stand. I'm sorry. I'm always forgetting things."

"I'll walk back—"

"Nonsense. Better me be late than you—trust me. Get us settled. Have a drink waiting for me, will you?"

We took off in opposite directions.

Spero, the bartender on the *Gail Force*, informed me he was blind in his left eye from birth and preferred to have people approach him from the right. I informed him my left ear was on permanent strike courtesy of an explosion during a tour in sand-land. We exchanged sympathetic nods, and I started to explain what Christina ordered in Freeport. He cut me off, insisting he knew exactly what the lady liked. He made a tall drink in a short time.

An evening blow kicked in. I retrieved my jacket from my room and draped it over the back of my chair. When Christina boarded, I presented her with her custom rumrunner, and we settled into lounge chairs in the stern. Streaks of light, like angel children playing with flashlights, lasered out from behind massive thunderheads that hung like underbellies of floating continents in the sky. She folded her arms across her. I stood, peeled my jacket off the back of my chair, told her to lean forward, and wrapped it around her. We kept Spero employed and chattered with an ease you're lucky to find with another person.

That spell cracked when Eddie planted himself in front of us, scratched his scarred chin, and said, "We'll be in contact."

I peered up at him. "Will I being seeing Mr. Agatha this evening?"

"You know that's not what I said, Beachy. Mr. Agatha's occupied. He wants me to tell you that he enjoyed your chat this morning."

"You understand that there's an element of urgency in my request."

"You understand the meaning of 'we'll be in contact'?"

I wanted to throw out a barb about him slipping me a bad drink—that won't do—I wanted to pick him up and toss him overboard. Instead I asked, "When? I need to know in the event I'm required to make alternative arrangements."

"You'll have to make that call on your own. Christina will see you off the boat."

He sauntered away as if he hadn't a care in the world, or there was nothing in the world he cared about. They sound so similar. They are so different.

As we entered the Government Cut channel, Christina and I stood and went to the rail. I drained my whiskey and said in a mock chivalrous tone, "Our time together draws nigh."

"Will you survive?" she said, going along, but then she turned serious. "Don't be despondent. He's unpredictable. If he had dinner with you tonight, I'd have been shocked." She took a step into me. My jacket hung on her. Her eyes were glassy from the booze—her hair heavy on the shoulders of my jacket. She looked like she'd stepped out of a 1940s film. I would have followed her back into it.

"That was sweet, what you did back there," she said.

"Back where?"

"The bazaar. I went back to get my fruit container. The lady in the purple dress? That was thoughtful of you, especially after how rude those two women were. She told me what a good man I have, to never let him go. What a happy life we have in front of us."

"A real fortune-teller."

She came in another step. Our bodies were inches apart. We were like two repelling magnets, feeling each other's force and knowing that at any moment we might violently collide. Six hours of boozing were now in firm control of our senses. Our intellect tucked in tight for the night.

"You gave her a fifty," she said, her voice roped with alcohol, "and hustled me out of there. You didn't want me to know. She was relieved to see me—wanted to make sure you didn't give it to her by accident."

"An honest lady," I said.

"I told her you knew what you were doing—that you always seem to know what you're doing."

"They're poor people. I don't like it—Americans, the richest species on the planet—practicing their negotiating and bickering skills with people who were born poor, live poor, die poor. It doesn't sit well with me."

A half step and she was on me, her mouth pressed against mine. I took her probing tongue but then let her go before her kiss, like a good whiskey, spread deep throughout my body.

"Take me with you," she breathed into me, her body pressing hard into my chest, her breasts like cushions between our two rib cages.

"I don't know—"

"They're bad, evil people. I need to get away. I don't know why you're here, but you're not one of them. I know the kind he does business with. It's not you."

"I don't—"

"You've got to help me," she rambled on. "I'm afraid for my life. You have no idea." Her eyes frantically searched my face, but they lacked conviction, as if she were unsure of herself, of her role.

"Listen, lady." I shoved her away. "I had a good time with you today. If you think palming a fifty makes me a saint, dream away. I'm here to do this deal. If you tell me these are nasty people, then I'm on the right boat."

I walked away from her, although every instinct I had told me I should have picked her up and hauled her off the boat. Later, when I went down the gangplank, she handed me my tux in a garment bag. Our eyes never met.

My limo had left. I summoned Uber, and a kid in a Nissan picked me up. The road was undergoing construction, and as we juddered along, he chatted nonstop about European soccer until I slammed the door on him at Oceana, disgusted with it all, but nothing in particular.

19

"You need what?" Binelli spit out over the phone.

"A million for the down payment." I juggled my phone while trying to peel a banana. "That's assuming I get a callback. You were in theater, sometimes that phone doesn't ring. Can you front that type of money?"

It was two days later, and I was back home. I'd sprinted five miles on the beach and rinsed off under the shower on the boardwalk at the hotel just as the day was trading places with the night. I changed clothes in the hotel's locker room, fixed a cup of Columbian dark, and ate a banana. I pocketed another one that looked like a giraffe's speckled neck and went out to the second-floor balcony overlooking the resort's two pools and the Gulf of Mexico. The resort's blue umbrellas were raised, the matching cushions laid out on the lounge chairs. A yoga class was stretching on the beach, and two men were setting up the beach cabanas on freshly raked sand. The smell and chatter of breakfast floated up from a restaurant to my right. The bar directly below me still had its steel curtains down, but a deliveryman was carting booze through the side. A girl on a paddleboard had the flat gulf to herself. I took a seat on the concrete bench.

"I dunno," Binelli responded to my question for more money. "You negotiate?"

"I'm a man in a hurry. I have no negotiating position. He knows that."

"I dunno."

"You're repeating yourself."

"I. Do. Not. Know. You like that better?"

I managed to get in a bite of the giraffe banana. "If I get the call, he may want the funds wired before we meet again, *if* we meet again. Tell Franklin to pony up the dough. What's the plan if it all plays out?"

"We'll give Peterson a heads-up that someone's coming after him. We want to corral the perps who blackmail him and work up toward Agatha. You'll testify as to your arrangement with him."

"Starts with my million." I took a final bit of the banana and tossed it at the seashell garbage can.

"I heard you. I'll—"

"If you can't, call me. Today. I'm not staying on the ship if it's taking on water."

She hung up on me.

I knew even if Binelli struck out, I'd reconnoiter with the *Gail Force*. See what I could find, settle the score with Eddie; maybe even whisk Christina out of there. She was a different woman when she stepped out of Agatha's shadow and didn't have her sex on. Still, she was a hot body with a cold mind, and I trusted her like a neighbor's pet snake.

I got up, picked my banana peel off the gray concrete floor, and dropped it in the garbage can. I can never make that shot.

At the house, I hauled out all the notes I'd collected on Agatha's operation and personnel. Morgan popped in and wanted to know if I needed anything from the hardware. I told him to check the list on the fridge. He said he'd already grabbed it. He also volunteered that Riley was striking out in identifying who she and Karl saw in Hollandaise—who had also been the same man on Karl's computer screen. He snatched the truck keys and took off.

The names rolled over my mind. Agatha, Eddie, Franklin, and the dead G-men; Lippman and Leonard. Did they know something? I switched gears: Daniel Vigh, Devon Peterson, Charles Walderhaden. What if it all traced back to Zebra Electronics? Follow the money. I couldn't see that. Kathleen called.

"Early lunch?" she said.

"Certainly."

"Mangroves in thirty?"

"Meet first in the library?"

"Don't think so."

"Let's give Ginny Brandenburg a lunch special. I read about these eleven spots that a woman—woman, you still there?"

She wasn't. Like Binelli, she'd hung up on me.

I went for my truck key. Right. Morgan was at the hardware. I entered the code to his garage and mounted his Harley. Thirteen minutes later—the hog hums at 110 on the 375 exit ramp—I tripped the kickstand in front of Mangroves. Ten minutes after that, the most important person in the world sat down across from me, and I said, "You look better than Christina," and she said, "Tell me about her," and I did.

I left the kiss out. It was a one-way job. Mostly.

"What will you do if they don't call?" Kathleen asked after the waiter cleared the table and I'd brought her up to speed.

"They will."

"So sure."

"Ten million dollars. His yacht eats that in a month. Besides, I gave them no reason not to call."

"You said Eddie didn't like you." Her white long-sleeve shirt was partially rolled up as the sun had finally answered the opening bell. She had on jeans and no jewelry. Her hair was down and she exuded that laid-back album-cover hippie style. I always dug that style; I'd pass up a limo of Victoria's Secret girls for a maiden in the grass.

I took a sip of iced tea, and an ice cube slipped into my mouth. "He gets paid not to like people."

"I see. You going to make me ask it twice?"

"If the phone doesn't ring," I said and cracked the ice, "I'll meander down to Miami, stir things up a bit. At the very least, I'll get an audience with Eddie."

"You don't meander."

"I can learn."

"Don't do that by yourself."

"Learn?"

"Miami, silly."

"I'll bring my friend."

"What does he say to all of this?"

"I haven't told him yet."

"You just said—"

"I'll call him today."

"Morgan?"

"Might enlist him as well. Keep an eye on Riley?"

She gave me sloppy salute.

"I told Morgan to place pictures of the Washington zoo in front of her, see if anyone strikes a bell. If he hasn't the time—"

"I'm on it, Rodger-Dodger," she said. "I'll go to the hotel, rent a cabana, treat Riley and me to lunch—dinner later on—sip eighteen-dollar rum drinks, buy the bar a round or two, flip through the pictures with her, and do a little shopping in the lower level." She tented her hands in front of her and rested her chin on her knuckles. "After all, you get ten percent off." She batted her eyes. That was a new move for her. Kathleen brings a little mystery every time.

"Sure you don't want to go the library with me?" I, on the other hand, hold little mystery.

"You never put me up in a hotel carte blanche."

"To do what?"

"Just pointing that out. I'm proud of you—giving her support. You're being generous."

"Rhymes with dumb."

"Not even close."

"Some language, somewhere."

"If that's the way you want to see it."

I settled the check, and we rose. I gathered her in my arms. The greeting pecks we exchanged when she arrived didn't cut it. I wrapped her tight and kissed her. It was a penetrating kiss usually associated with the deeper end of the day, a few drinks down the road. But I didn't need alcoholic props or a digital—or analog—clock, to arouse my passion and make my heart go thumpity-thump-thump.

We pulled apart, and I said, "A new goal: we need to get arrested for doing it in a public place." I traced my finger over the corner of her mouth where the thin edge of her lips gave way to her soft cheek. Where age was just starting to show. No magazine in the world knows of that spot. Or ever will.

"Remember, we did it behind the beach museum," she reminded me.

"And in the gulf."

"The library."

"Where next?"

"It's a marvelous world."

"It is a marvelous world."

"Let's stay in tonight," she suggested. "You cook."

"You can't."

"I know."

"You know something else, don't you?"

"I do, but I never tire of it."

"I am spec*tac*ularly in love with you."

"No, you've got it worse than that," Kathleen informed me.

"Worse?"

"You're a *sucke*r for me. Do something?"

"Yeah?"

"Let 'em know we were here today." She said it in a husky voice that knocked my knees out.

Behind us a car honked, and there seemed to be other distractions as well, but then everything faded except the pounding of her heart on my chest. Seven billion of them in the world, and if you're lucky, real lucky, you get just one of them close to you, so close that you feel it more than yours and feel it even more when it's not there and that's what keeps it close to you.

I never cooked for her that night and wondered, like a parallel universe, what we missed. How things would have played out if he hadn't called. We can play that game every day, but sometime it carries greater weight. Greater consequences.

Eddie rang and said a room was waiting for me at Oceana. On the way to the airport I called Kathleen, but it went to voice mail. It seemed an empty conclusion to what had been a promising day. I told Morgan to saddle up and that Kathleen would take over the Riley project.

I hit Garrett's number.

20

The Fat Man

Phillip Agatha took a drink and, before his glass found the table, raised his other hand and made a chaser out of inhaling his cigar. "You've made it quite clear," he said, "you are wary of the man. I, on the other hand, see no reason why I should avoid a simple and highly profitable business deal because of swagger."

Eddie stood at the side of the teak dining table, his hands folded in front of him. Christina approached the table from the opposite side and stopped. Eddie said, "Unless you really need the—"

"My business, in that sense, is no business of yours." Agatha held his cigar over the bamboo monkey-hand ashtray and gave it a courteous tap. "You called him?"

"Yes, sir."

"He'll be there?"

"Yes, sir."

"Excellent. Christina, have a seat," Agatha said benevolently. "You are stunning in white. I'd like to see that more often. You are a dark-haired angel atop a Christmas tree."

"There are dark-haired angels?" Christina questioned him.

"There are now, my dear."

She settled into a chair off to Agatha's right, facing Eddie, and crossed her slender legs. She sat straight, for her mother had told her that a woman's spine should never touch the back of a chair.

"Anything else, Mr. Agatha?" Eddie asked.

"Listen to what Christina has to say." Agatha shifted his gaze to her. "How did it go, my princess? Did you, as I instructed, try to pry open our new clam?"

"I did."

"And?"

"I pleaded with him to take me with him."

"Was he tempted?"

"He is a dispassionate man. I kissed him and told him that I was afraid for my life, that, as you suggested, I was surrounded by evil people."

"You said that?"

"What?"

"Evil?"

"Yes. I thought you—"

"No, no, my dear." He rolled out a chuckle and stole a glance at Eddie. "It's fine. Did he show any compassion, anything in his eyes?"

"He didn't take my kiss. He said that if the people on the boat are nasty, then he was on the right boat. He insisted he was here only to do a deal."

"And did you believe him?"

"I did."

Agatha took a sip from his drink. "Tell me about the lunch you shared with him the other day."

Christina shifted her body ever so slightly in her chair. "Mostly small talk. You know, the tourists, the cruise ships that unload every day. I did challenge him once on what his real purpose was, but he kept to his line. Said he wanted to strike a deal."

"Did he call anyone or talk to anyone out of your earshot?"

"Not that I know of."

Agatha pivoted his lollipop head toward Eddie, as if it rested on finely engineered German ball bearings. "Tell me what you're thinking."

Eddie rubbed his chin.

"I am more inclined to engage him now. He's certainly focused on his task, and Christina's talk of evil didn't bait him into enlisting her to cooperate with him, in the event his intentions are other than what he says. But his—what do you call it?—sense of propriety bothers me."

"Your caution is appreciated and duly noted. As for the man's propriety, I find it not the least bit alarming," Agatha said. "I shudder to think that I've relegated my life to conducting business with society's lowest common denominator, those who lack propriety." He dismissed him with his right hand. "Thank you."

Eddie pivoted and marched off, a soldier relieved of his post. Agatha pulled himself up in his chair and, in a somewhat difficult maneuver, crossed his legs. He took another sip from his glass tumbler and said to Christina, "You didn't return to the boat with him. Why was that?"

"I'd forgotten something at the bazaar. I had fruit for lunch and couldn't finish it. They put it in a container for me, and I'd left the container on a stand in the market. Forgetful me."

"He didn't go back with you?"

"I told him to go on ahead and have a drink waiting for me."

"Very good. Just curious. I hope you don't mind my meddling. The bazaar, did you purchase anything?"

Christina smiled and traced her hand over her necklace. "The earrings as well." She dipped her head and swept her hair over her shoulder, exposing the elegant nape of her neck and a round earring.

Agatha motioned her closer, and she leaned over. He fondled the earring, but never touched her skin. "Such simple craftsmanship. Crude, yet as original as an El Greco. Did he buy them for you?"

"He insisted." She returned her head to an upright position, although her hair still cascaded, like a still waterfall, down her right side. "Twenty dollars, but he got them for fifteen."

"Bickering with the poor. Perhaps I should not have dismissed Eddie. He is so stubbornly convinced that our Mr. Travis is cast from a different lot. It would be good for him to hear that Travis is more colloquial that he thinks. Was it there? Your container of fruit?"

"It was."

"Anything else you wish to add?"

"No."

"When he returns, you'll be his host. I don't need to remind you, but the devil is in the details. Anything unusual, come straight to me."

"Of course."

"Now, my dear," he added, signaling the waiter, "I believe there is a chaise lounge yearning for your body."

Christina parted with a weak smile. She reclaimed her favorite lounge chair and picked up her book. She turned to the dog-eared page and started reading. She closed the book and dropped it on her lap. She stared across the transom and into the marina.

"Would you like some shade?" Spero asked. "It's much too bright to be reading in the direct sun."

"Please."

Spero raised the umbrella, but Christina did not raise her book.

21

"You Travis?"

"You Nicky?"

"One and only. This babe what you're looking for?"

"Everyman's dream, Nicky."

It was a few hours before check-in time at the Oceana, and I stood on the aft deck of a boat in a Key Biscayne marina. If the *Gail Force* pulled up anchor with me aboard, we wanted a chase boat. I'd called ahead to secure the vessel, but the boat's owner, Captain Nicky, wasn't there when we arrived. Morgan and I had taken the opportunity to check out *Fishy Lady* on our own. She was a thirty-three-foot cuddy cabin with a yellow finish that mirrored her surroundings. She sported classic lines, an eleven-foot beam, Garmin's latest catalog on her dash, and a trio of Yamaha 300s on her transom. A man can marry a boat like that.

Nicky had a two-day beard, sun-wrinkled skin, shorts held together by the pockets, and a sleeveless Dolphin's sweatshirt that was a veteran of numerous oil changes. His face was round, like that of a stick-figure.

Nicky jumped aboard his girl, and we pumped hands like lost friends. "She'll do just fine," I told him. "How often you wax her to keep her like this?"

"Hard, twice a year on the vernal and autumnal equinoxes, and twice each time."

Morgan swung around from the bow and introduced himself. Nicky unlocked the interior; it would sleep two, but Garrett, at six three, would need to curl up. Nicky reviewed the electronics with us. I informed him that it would be Morgan, and not me, operating the boat. He shifted his attention to Morgan and asked him how experienced he was on the water. Morgan explained he had a captain's license and had never spent more than three contiguous weeks on land since before he was eighteen. Morgan became Nicky's idol, and he peppered Morgan with endless questions while I completed the paper work.

"She didn't come from the factory with the three hundreds, did she?" I asked as I handed Nicky his clipboard with the paper work attached.

"Two-fifties. I traded them in. The extra one-fifty lets her skim the waves. I've never had no one complain of too little power. Lot of these guys who chase the game fish pay for speed. I figure I'm making my money back." He turned to Morgan. "Where you headed to?"

"Knock around the Bahamas for a few days."

"But no return date?"

"That's why," I interjected, "you can keep my card open, per diem."

"I got it booked next week. Starting Tuesday."

"We'll dock her before then."

"I gotta ask, you know?" Nicky scratched his stubble. "You fellas seem straight up, but this here's a fishing and cruising boat, know what I mean? Nothing funny, no drugs, we cool on that?"

"Perfectly," I said. "We're meeting some friends. Little tough to have a tight schedule when the intent of each day is lobster, beer, and stoking coals on the beach."

"Would you like a call," Morgan placated him, "after the first day or so, to give you an idea? I wouldn't want my boat out with no return date."

Nicky nodded at Morgan. "I'd appreciate that."

We parted ways, and Morgan and I headed off to rendezvous with Garrett at the marina's restaurant. It was a fish house and bar that hung out over the water supported by crusty pilings. Garrett strode in wearing stonewashed black jeans and a black short-sleeve T-shirt that blended into his skin. He dropped his duffel on the floor. I brought him up to date.

"You got the bag?" He directed his question to Morgan. He was referring to Morgan's red spinnaker bag that carried an assortment of passports, currencies, firearms, and communication equipment, among other items.

"Locked up on the boat."

Our lunches arrived. Yellowtail snapper sandwiches all around. Water for Garrett, iced tea for Morgan, iced tea and a beer for me. Don't tell Tinker Bell.

Garrett, after a swallow, said, "You got Riley looking at mug shots, see if she recognizes anyone?"

"We do." Morgan took the question. "I assembled close to seven hundred pictures of senators, congressmen, aides, and lobbyists. Kathleen is going to finish taking her through them."

"The leak?" Garrett turned to me, catching me in mid-pull from the longneck.

I placed the bottle on the table. "Franklin thinks someone in the bureau was, or is, running an operation against Agatha. When it resulted in two dead men, whoever that person is likely shut it down—covered his trail so he couldn't be traced."

"You buy that?"

"That, or Agatha's simply paying someone to feed him information and turn a head."

Garrett was silent, obligating me to press my case.

"The agency is capable of spawning operations so heavily cloaked they get lost within themselves. It's possible, if someone instructed Franklin to back off and Franklin balked, he'd be told that inquisitive minds are not conducive to employment security."

"You trust him?" Garrett came back with a variation of "you buy that?"

"No reason not to. Binelli vouches for him. I'd vote in his favor."

He considered that and said, "What's victory for us?"

"Agatha is brought up on murder charges for the death of Karl Anderson, or at least as an accessory to his death. His blackmail shop is padlocked."

"You won't be making any new fans with your heroic efforts," Garrett pointed out, in the event I'd suddenly gone brain-dead. "You find a bad G-man, and they'll suffocate this operation. They'll have you sign a gag order to never discuss it."

I'd been fondling my beer and withdrew my hand. "Franklin's ex-wife signed a gag order. A nonsense item, but I'm curious. I can't go to Binelli with it, she's too close. Mary Evelyn can look, but usually those are sealed documents."

"You just said you trusted the guy."

"Standard paranoia. We—"

"I might be able to help you there," Morgan interrupted me, an act he rarely commits. We both stared at him. His ponytail was tied together with a string that his father had used on his hammock when he served on a destroyer in the Vietnam War. His sandals looked as if one of the twelve disciples had padded around in them, and his faded pink T-shirt was likely a castaway from the thrift shop. He appeared an unlikely candidate to gain access to sealed divorce documents in Washington, DC.

"How?" I challenged him.

"My sister's last cruise," he took out his phone and started texting. "Said it was three couples, divorce lawyers, and wives, or husbands, either Baltimore or DC. High-end firm. Second year they came during the same week. I'll see if she can ask around."

Morgan's sister ran the family's charter sailboat cruise business, mainly around the British Virgin Islands. Morgan had been involved in it for years before he decided to see what all the hoopla was about living on land.

"They'd respond, no offense, to the captain of the boat they sailed the BVI with?"

"You can't imagine. When I was in the business, those corporate couples? That week was the week of the year for them. We'd see the same faces the next year, and you better remember them because they certainly remembered you." He punched his phone. "Just a thought."

"A good one." Garrett backed him up and then turned to me. "What's the blueprint if the Force takes off?"

"I'm open—got anything?"

"B, B and G."

Bold, brief, and gone. It was from the army. In whatever we do, be bold, brief, and gone. Never tiptoe through the shallow waters of indecision. We'd rather fail with confidence than succeed with timidity. We formulated a plan and contingency plans, but like nonbelievers in a church, we didn't take them seriously.

A champagne bottle in a slim, ornate silver floor cooler waited for me in my room at Oceana. A cheese and fruit tray, covered with a clear wrap, was on the table next to it. An embossed card from Agatha said he was looking forward to continuing our discussion on wine. I was in, but as far as I knew, I was still nine hundred thousand short of having a chair at the table. I called Binelli.

"You got my money?" The corked popped off the champagne bottle.

"Was that a gun?" Binelli exclaimed.

"Champagne cork."

"It's the middle of the afternoon."

"Depends what time zone you're in."

"We're in the sa—"

"I've been summoned. You got my money?" Misty white vapors swirled out of the decapitated bottle.

"Same account, but you're cleared to a million."

"You guys trust someone like me with that type of dough? I don't know whether that's good or bad."

"Validate us. What's on your agenda?"

"Sip champagne." I took a bite of sharp cheddar. It was good. None of that low-fat stuff. "And nibble on cheese until my phone rings." There was a knock on my door. "Or there's a knock on my door. Hugs and kisses to Franklin." I hung up on Binelli, giving her a taste of her own medicine.

I sprang to open the door. Christina appeared like a hologram, wearing jeans and a cream, moderately transparent, sweater. The sweater threatened to slide off her right shoulder, and a thin black bra strap highlighted her bare skin. The makeup was at a minimum, which maximized her attractiveness. She flashed a nervous smile a split second too late, as if she wasn't quite prepared for the door to open. Similar to when she'd forgotten to place the key back above the wine cellar door on the *Gail Force*, she seemed more normal when she was nervous. I didn't know what that meant.

"Nice necklace," I said. It was the one I'd bought her in Freeport.

"Thank you and thank you."

"Champagne?" I stepped back and extended my arm. She brushed past me, bringing a faint smell of honeysuckle into the room.

I filled two glasses and handed her one. We clinked our glasses, and I said, "To our business deal."

"You'll need to take that up with Mr. Agatha," she reminded me.

"Tonight?"

"We'd like you to present yourself at the Gail Force tomorrow morning at ten."

"We sailing or using it just for our meeting?"

"Are you asking questions all afternoon?"

"What other activities do you have in mind?"

"Take me gallery-hopping. I have the day off, and Mr. Agatha likes me to view the other studios on a regular basis."

"A shame to leave the bubbly behind."

She smiled, went over to the minibar, opened a cupboard, and grabbed two paper coffee cups. I did a generous pour into both and said, "Is this why my meeting's not until tomorrow? Gives you further opportunity to know the client, loosen him up, see what falls out?" I handed a cup to her. "How many times have you been in this room? Enough to know where the cups are? The sun's angle in the early morning? I bet you know what time housekeeping knocks on the door."

It came out harsher than I intended. The heck I care anyway?

My thoughtless comments earned me a wintry smile and a clenched, "Do you think you could be nice for a few hours?"

"Let's find out."

She spun and flounced out the door. I wrapped some cheese cubes in the cellophane and stuck it in my pocket. On the way down, we stood in opposite corners of the elevator, like two wary animals. I opened the front door for her, and we got sucked into the hot and claustrophobic sidewalk traffic of Miami Beach.

22

The chili dogs did the trick, although in the end, I hated them as much as I had liked them.

It took a seventy-minute hour for the champagne to kick in and initiate a thaw. By then, I'd realized traipsing around in a funk and not trusting—who was she, my guide, an accomplice, Agatha's snitch?—was no way to idle away an afternoon.

We ducked in and out of a half-dozen galleries. Several of them, notably the ones that refilled my cup, were half-decent. She was guarded at first, and we kept the conversation on safe ground, meaning neither of us learned a thing that would advance our respective causes.

After the walking and the boozing, and viewing enough $10,000 numbered aluminum beach and sea-villa prints to fill a gymnasium, I suggested we give our overloaded senses a reprieve and grab some grub.

We window-shopped several restaurants, their *maître d's* posted at sidewalk menu stands, hocking us to come in. I wasn't in the mood to go from overpriced art to overpriced fish and wine. On a side street, a block away from the action, were outdoor tables that sprouted Smirnoff umbrellas. I took Christina's elbow in my hand and guided her around the corner. I pulled a chair out for her facing back toward the action we had just escaped and took the chair across from her. I dragged an empty chair to my right and propped my feet on it. If I entered an art museum in the next two decades, it would be too soon.

"Tell me about yourself," I said, having exhausted every other avenue of conversation with her.

"Mr. Agatha—"

"No. No. No. Your story does not begin with Mr. Agatha."

A waiter dropped off two menus. Christina gave hers a few studious minutes and then frowned as she placed it back on the table. "You ever have a chili dog?" I said.

"A what?"

"A hot dog with chili on it."

"*No*. Why would anyone do such a thing?"

"Once upon a time someone couldn't decide between the two, and the world's been a better place ever since. Three chili dogs," I instructed the waiter when he paused at our table. "French fries, ketchup, malt vinegar, beer, and a Chardonnay."

He left, and Christina asked, "How do you know I'll like it?"

"Only the Chardonnay's for you. Where were we? You were telling me about your childhood."

She smiled. "I was doing no such thing."

"Pretend you were."

"You don't give a damn."

Ouch. That landed pretty hard. Guess she wasn't over my ungentlemanly remarks in the hotel room.

"What am I supposed to think?" I said defensively. "You play the part. You—"

"I don't care what you think. You can keep your thoughts to yourself. Why are you so kind to a poor merchant you don't know in the Bahamas and so crass to me?"

I put my feet on the pavement, leaned across the table, and held her eyes with mine. "Try this on, girl: I understand the relationship, the brief encounter, with the lady in Freeport. I don't understand your role, other than to keep tabs on me."

"That *is* my role. What do you expect? We don't know you, and we have to be careful, selective. That doesn't mean I don't have feelings."

"I'm sor—"

"I have *ne*ver heard housekeeping knock—"

"I didn't—"

"I'm gone long before then."

I didn't know what to say, so I clammed up. The chili dogs came, and she picked up her utensils. I recalled her dissecting her fish sandwich in Freeport.

"That won't do," I said as I reached across the table. I placed my hand on hers and lowered it to the table. "Like this." I picked up a chili dog and took a quarter of it in one bite. I swiped a napkin across my mouth.

She took a deep breath, like she was prepping to dive into a cold pool, and gingerly fingered her chili dog cradled in paper. She lifted it to her mouth, closed her eyes, and took a bite.

She chewed patiently and was about to say something when she went back in for seconds. I doused half the fries with malt vinegar and squirted an anthill of ketchup on the edge of the platter.

"You're right," she said, uncharacteristically talking while eating.

"How's that?"

"The world." She smiled as she dotted her mouth with her napkin. "It *is* a better place."

After several sacred minutes of consuming chili dogs, during which a heavenly choir broke into the "Battle Hymn of the Republic," I said, "Your childhood."

"Really?"

"Really."

She took a sip of wine and placed the glass back on the table, her eyes following the glass as if to make certain it was firmly in place. She glanced up at me. "The lady at the bazaar? That's my mother, but we're from Aruba. My mom sets up shop every day in Oranjestad, by the water where the cruise ships come in. Aruba, Freeport, Saint Somewhere, it doesn't matter—they're all the same. Every day she takes half of what she's gotten that day and deposits it in the Aruba Bank.

"I'd help her out. I have two younger sisters; my father sailed off one day, and we never saw him again. I never knew him. My mother used to be a schoolteacher, but my father, before he stowed a ride, beat her too much, even when she was pregnant with me. It was nip and tuck for her giving birth to me. She missed too many days after that, and the school let her go. She has no money; the half she keeps back is barely enough. She's sacrificing her todays for her daughters' tomorrows. Have you had enough?"

"No." I thought of asking her what her sisters' names were but decided that could wait.

"Sure you have. You're too polite to bow out."

"I don't recall anyone accusing me of being too polite. I'm sorry about your mother. How did you get from there to here?"

She considered the question, as if she were contemplating different paths to embark on. "There's a book, Pride and Prejudice." She held my eyes with an intensity that I'd not witnessed in her. I involuntarily straightened up in my seat.

"Jane Austen's romantic novel of manners," I observed.

"How—why do you know that?"

"'A young man of large fortune.'" I flipped up my right hand. "Go on."

"My…never mind."

"Tell me." I sounded like a schoolboy on a first date. I started to reach over the table to her but stopped. I placed my hands on either side of my plate. "It's not hard."

She looked as if she wanted to believe in me but couldn't, and I wondered what that said about me. She stole a glance at her wineglass, as if the object would offer confirmation or in some manner strengthen her resolve.

"My mother loved that book. Said she read it long before I was born." She raised her face, her eyes latching on to mine. "When I was a little girl, she read me her worn copy, told me that's where she got my…she'd read to me in bed, the windows open to the wind rushing in and my mind rushing out. Out to the sea and visions of a land with grand estates and noble and kind men women swooned over. Men who treated women with such courteous respect and proper deference. A fantasy world to me. I don't need natural laws to bend." Her eyes wandered. "My fantasy was, perhaps even still is, so much simpler.

"Phillip came by one day." She dabbed a french fry in vinegar and stuck it in her mouth. "Two years ago last May. A Disney ship was at port. That's really good. Do people really eat fries with vinegar?"

"They do."

"Not bad. I missed that. I missed a lot. What did you call it? A novel of manners?"

"It's a genre. The book rests heavily on the customs and behaviors that were prevalent in a certain class of people. The characters struggle internally between what they feel and what society expects of them."

"Like today?"

"Like today. The Disney ship?"

"Right." She hesitated, her eyes going past me. "I'll have to tell my mother that—a novel of manners. I think that will endear it to her even more." She folded her hands on her lap. "OK, so a Disney ship was in port. Those are the money days, when a boat comes in. I was helping my mother, and Phillip dropped by. He was kind, such a gentleman, polite, well spoken." She smiled as the thought hit her. "A man of manners. He was from Bonaire, just next to us. A neighbor, you know? He took me to lunch—told me he ran an art studio in Miami and that he was looking for an assistant. He pointed at the Gail Force and said, 'She's mine. Be my assistant. Come sail with me.' Something about experiencing beauty and music. I didn't take him seriously, but when I told my mother, she glanced at the yacht and said, 'Go. Now. This instant.' She practically threw me off the island. I went home and packed. I send money back every month." She gave a dismissive shrug of her right shoulder. "Are we going to split that last one? I mean, if you want, you can have it."

I cut the last dog in half. I picked up half and held it up to her mouth. She took a bite, our eyes never losing contact. She giggled as a chunk of it failed to meet its fate. She wiped her lips with her napkin, and I decided to attack an incongruity that had been brewing within me.

"The first day I saw you?"

"Yes?" It came out muffled. Her sweater had given up the good fight and had slipped off her right shoulder, leaving only the strap of her bra to interrupt her unblemished skin.

"Your unusual method of shaking hands."

She rolled her eyes and swallowed before continuing. "Ohmygod. That's Phillip. He urges us all—those of us who work at Studio Four-Twenty and meet potential clients—to be creative. To touch people. It sets us off from the other galleries, although I'm sure you've noticed everyone has their bag of tricks. Did you pick up in that one gallery? I forget— oh, what was the name?—Vincent's. Remember? The man with pork-chop sideburns who offered us the use of their back room? The talk is it's a bedroom with video equipment. Then afterward, to commemorate your afternoon delight, they hope you pick up a five-thousand-dollar artifact on the way out the door."

"I don't recall Pork Chops. Did they give us refills there?"

"I don't think so."

"Those places didn't hold my interest."

"I did observe a direct correlation between your appreciation of art and the level of champagne in your cup."

"Do you like what you do?" I steered the conversation back to her. She took a sip from her long-stemmed wineglass.

"I do. And do you?"

"Pardon?"

"Like what you do?"

"It's interesting." I measured my words. "The business I'm hoping to conclude with Mr. Agatha, is, or may be construed by others, to be somewhat distasteful. You realize what he does, what I require of him?"

"That's your business. My mother wears the same clothes she wore the day she saw me off on the Force. Everything that woman does is for her children. At the pace I'm saving money, both my sisters will be able to attend school in the States. In less than two years, I'll be free and can do what I want. That's my business."

She didn't address my question, but I let it go. Instead I said, "Your parting comment to me on the boat—your theatrical, 'Take me with you. They're bad, evil people.'"

I'd dismissed her comments as an act, likely called for by Agatha to see if I would seize Christina's comments as a means to recruit her, thus exposing myself as someone other than who I claimed to be. Still, I wanted to hear it from her. Her words had jolted me that night, and I'd nearly succumbed to an alcoholic urge to sweep her away.

She crinkled her nose. "Phillip, again. Sorry. I'm not sure why. Something about seeing if you were sincere in your desire to conduct business with us. Apparently you're sincere, and I should avoid the performing arts and stick with my passion—the visual arts."

"You're a painter?" I asked. She'd started calling Agatha by his first name. I interpreted that as a thaw in our relationship, but she was still Agatha's employee.

She fingered her hair and cocked her head to one side. The earring that I bought her in Freeport swung out and, like an obedient pendulum, circled back. "I'd like to go to art school. I've been accepted at Savannah College of Art and Design, but as I said, I need to put it off for a year or two, depending what I can work out with Phillip, to save more money. My sisters are counting on me."

"Saving money for your family justifies being supportive of Mr. Agatha's business taste?"

She retreated into her chair. "Who are *you* to question *me*? I'm not the one paying ridiculous sums of money to put someone in a squeeze, and for the record, that is all he does—squeeze someone, usually a man who has been unfaithful. I told you about my father? Breaks my heart if someone gets caught and actually has to atone for their transgressions on this side of heaven."

"You're aware, then, that he blackmails people?"

"That's why you're here, right? You want someone caught in bed with someone else so you get your way in some business deal. Yes, I know. Phillip told me. And no, I'm never the bait. He would never ask me to do that."

"I never in—"

"You wondered."

"Does he do more?"

"What do you mean?"

"Does he stop at artistic blackmail pictures, or is there more?"

"I haven't a clue what you're referring to."

"I think you do."

She shook her head, her eyes challenging mine. "You're big on that, aren't you? Like when you asked my name, that first day, and then didn't believe me when I told you. Why ask the questions if you have all the answers?"

"And you're guilt-free? You just asked me, when you were talking about yourself, if I had enough, and when I hadn't, you overruled my answer."

She gave me a disapproving smile, as if we both needed to do better, and said, "Why the added interest in Phillip?"

"If things go according to plan, I'll be wiring him a substantial amount of money. I'd be an idiot not to be curious." I didn't want to come across as too interested in Agatha's extracurricular activities, nor did I think she was aware that his business model extended beyond traditional blackmail.

We chatted some more, and she waved off my suggestion for dessert. I impressed on her that it was a century-old tradition to follow chili dogs with cheesecake. She accused me of making that up. I countered that the century started today. We split a slice of cheesecake that was not made on the premises, although that didn't deter us from sparring over the last bite.

Afterward, we hiked it off, sidestepping the swelling foot traffic that heated up when the sun went down. She inquired about my childhood, and I insisted the only thing I recalled were little green men kicking me out of the capsule—wishing me the best of luck while laughing riotously. She said that explained a lot but was undeterred. I resisted. I had a few items in that suitcase that I'd never unpacked—never even told Kathleen, although I knew the longer I went before telling her, the harder it would be. Only Garrett knew.

We soon found ourselves in front of Oceana. A two-man combo, tucked behind the hostess stand, played Latin music. The porch was crammed with diners. A security guard stood on the sidewalk, arms folded, keeping a dull eye on anyone who dallied too long.

"See you at ten." I said. "On the boat."

"It's loud out here."

I opened the door for her and followed her inside. The dining room to our left was subdued. The bar where I'd met Eddie and Henny was bursting, but at a miniscule volume compared to the front porch and sidewalk. A few paces in, she pivoted and faced me.

"He's never used me," she stated.

"So you said."

"I can't think of a kinder man. He's never asked me to do anything against my will. He's the epitome of manners. He knows my dreams. He supports me far more than is required. I told you, I plan to put my sisters through college, help out my mother."

"That's great. I—"

She melted into me like a warm blanket on a hot day, her breasts flat against my chest. She draped her arms around me and planted a kiss that tasted like chili dog and malt vinegar. There's something about a dirty kiss, one that's not washed in toothpaste and fresh lipstick, but carries the remnants of the day, the grain of the alcohol, the insides of a body. A dirty kiss is a damn good kiss.

She quickly, professionally, stepped back.

"What was that for?" I asked. My chest felt hollow and lonely, my breathing heavy.

"So you know me," she explained. "Know how I taste and remember that sensation when I ask you a favor. I don't know you, but I side with Eddie. If it were me, I'd pass. But Phillip? He rises to the challenge."

"You're wrong about me, but I don't get what you're asking."

"Don't hurt me. Don't hurt him. I'm too close to walking away."

"I—"

"Promise me. Let me have my plan. I need it for my family. I'm all they have. Don't take it from me. Leave him alone."

Maybe it was the string of loose hair that hung over her right eye. Maybe it was the moderately transparent mesh sweatshirt and that thin bra strap that had been driving me fucking crazy all day, or maybe it was my desire to make her happy. Certainly the liquor had a hand in it. There's always booze.

Whatever the reasoning, I responded, "I promise," knowing that I was lying.

She dropped her arms and turned. She took a step, and I said, "Hey."

She spun back around.

What now?

185

I was stuck between "hey" and wanting to take her upstairs and into my bed, where the narrative would end. In the morning, when housekeeping knocked, it would take four or five raps before our eyes opened. But she would be gone by then, right? I didn't think so. I didn't think so at all. A traitorous feeling swept over me. The only question was, would it be transitory or permanent?

You never know when your path takes you deep into no man's land.

Remember us.

"See you at ten," I said, repeating myself. The words were much heavier the second time around.

I expected a quick smile, but instead she looked right through me, like there wasn't enough of me there to hold her interest, and vanished through the door. It was the first door all day she passed through that I hadn't opened for her.

At a corner stool in the bar, I ordered a Jameson, and told Arnie to deliver a fresh one every fifteen minutes. Maybe the whiskey would wash away her kiss. It was different than the one we shared on the *Gail Force*. It wasn't just because her breath was stained with the day, her tongue embedded with cheesecake. It was *her*. The one on the *Gail Force* was mechanical, flesh upon flesh with no meaning. Not this last one. Screw it. I was done. Keep her at a distance. Get the job done. Haul ass out of Dodge. Still, I wish I hadn't lied and thrown out that shit promise that I'd leave Agatha alone. It was one I had no intention of honoring. My actions would drive a stake into the heart of her dreams.

Damn chili dogs.

23

He whistled.

I turned. His ragged clothes were draped over him like royal garments. His beard masked his face, although his deep-set eyes sparkled. Behind him, the first hint of dawn brightened the eastern horizon, chasing away the dark like a silent army.

The homeless man was still swathed in layers of threadbare coats. It was the next morning, and I'd just completed my run. The man, as he trundled toward me, swayed his head side to side, as if he were pondering the onerous plight of humanity. What was it like to at one time have been so cold that you fear it, even in the heat, for the remainder of your life? Why did I care so much for the woman in the bazaar, but observed my homeless acquaintance as a middling statistic? I don't understand empathy—where it comes from, where it goes, why it inexplicably surfaces.

"The Blue Angels are coming," he announced when he finally took notice of my presence, although I was not sure his comment was directed at me or voiced as a general decree.

"What?"

"They fly high, and they roar, and they're gone."

"Cover your ears."

"No need to kill them," he urged. "They challenge the flaming sun and die on its sword. The beauty and the music, all gone."

Idiot. He'd likely gotten spooked in the past by the navy's Blue Angels air show and realized they were returning in a couple of weeks. Nut-head needed more than coats and empathy.

"You can't hide," he called after me as I headed across the street, his voice ascending like the sun. "The Blue Angels are coming."

I had the fresh farm breakfast I'd enjoyed on my previous visit. It's reassuring having a routine on only the second trip to a new place. It's an instant way to ingratiate oneself. Over coffee, I checked e-mails on my phone, switched to news, and my browser came up with the first page of *Pride and Prejudice.* I didn't remember doing that. I must have sailed pretty far down the lonely river last night.

I called Kathleen to see if Riley had any hits viewing mug shots. She assured me that if she had, I'd be the first to know. She asked if I was behaving, and I assured her that if I wasn't, she'd be the last to know. She countered, "Hence the question," which led to me confessing that I passed out late yesterday and woke up in a harem of naked twins. She opined that part of my brain had never left the Neanderthal period. I congratulated her on finally being keyed into roughly half of the world's population.

I didn't tell her about the kiss. (That's two now.) I was pretending I didn't enjoy it. You're allowed to do that—look it up—when your brain is stuck in the Neanderthal period.

Garrett called, and we reviewed our nonplan, contingency plans, and save-our-rear-end plan.

At 9:45 a.m., I gathered my over-the-shoulder leather bag. It contained my laptop and a couple of burner phones.

Nothing I couldn't explain or that would incriminate me if Agatha decided to search me. I headed out to the *Gail Force.*

"You do know," I said when I confronted Henny at the top of the gangplank, "if they're ever short an anchor, they can tie a chain around you."

His mouth twitched. "Spin around."

He frisked me and searched my bag. He asked why I brought my laptop. I replied I was addicted to online shoe shopping and asked him what size he wore. He snapped it shut and handed it back to me.

"Follow me."

He stopped a dozen feet short of the dining table, as if he were not permitted to enter the inner sanctum. Phillip Agatha, reposing at home base, guffawed into a phone that was suffocating in his thick hand.

Music came on. "Splendor in the Grass." Ten o'clock sharp. Agatha started every day, at least on the *Gail Force,* with the same song.

I took a swivel seat viewing the aft deck. All the seats reclined and swiveled. The good chairs were not limited to the polar ends of the table. Agatha concluded his call and granted me his attention. "Forgive my rudeness. Have you had breakfast?"

"I have."

"So early?"

"I like worms."

"Ah, yes, But the early worm gets eaten. No one ever tells that side of the tale." He flipped his hand, animating the same statue who had waited on us before.

"You inaugurate every day with the same song," I said as a fact, rather than as a question.

189

"Observant of you. 'Splendor' has been a staple for a while. What would your choice be?"

"Send in the Clowns?"

He barked out a laugh. "We could have quite some fun with that, couldn't we? I won't challenge your hypothesis. I'll be changing it shortly, although Sondheim's morose piece is not up for consideration. You see, I like shaping my world to the extent I can. Why not know that at precisely ten o'clock, I will be reclining in this comfortable chair, enjoying the morning and assuaging my senses with an arrangement of musical notes that I have chosen, firmly in control of my destination."

"Your destination?"

"The greatest destination carries no map, for it is not a place, but rather it is the ability to apportion one's time as one pleases."

"I had a pleasant day with Christina yesterday, as I'm sure she informed you."

"You do like jostling the topic, don't you? Your free time with Christina is your business." He paused to take a sip of coffee. "I assure you that her time is her own as well."

"We conducted an academic comparison of your commercial competition. Do you do enough retail business to warrant such concern?"

"Most definitely," he said with conviction. "Studio Four-Twenty does remarkably well on its own."

"Not this well." I spread my hands.

"No. This requires more creative and interesting arrangements."

"Did she bring anything to your attention that your competitors are engaging in?"

"I have not spoken to her, although I doubt you believe me."

I wanted to give him the opportunity to slip and reveal more about Christina's role, but Agatha was not a man to make unforced errors. A Caribbean-skinned steward who I'd not seen before approached me. He proffered a bottle of champagne. "May I, sir?"

"You may."

Agatha said, "Eddie is still worried about you."

"That scalawag still not in my camp?"

His eyes narrowed. "Scalawag?"

"I believe it was you who referred to him as a ruffian."

"So I did. Excellent." A smile spread over his face. "I do enjoy your company. No fear. Eddie, as you pointed out, works for me and not vice versa. It would be asinine of me not to consider his opinions and equally deplorable, and ultimately costly, to follow his every whim."

"Does this mean we have a deal?"

"We looked into Zebra Electronics. Your nonpublic knowledge of them losing the navy contract adds credibility to your case and its urgent resolution."

"How did you acquire this 'nonpublic' information?"

"We have our means. In our business, it is extremely important to cultivate channels of information."

"Can you help us?" It was a good line, direct and to the point.

"We are still conducting—"

"Can you help us?" I repeated, having fallen in love with it.

Agatha adjusted his weight. "You are the icon of impatience."

"I have a task with a deadline."

"Indeed. You gave us a target, yes? A Mr. Peterson."

"Devon Peterson."

"How did you come upon that name?"

I spread my hands just as a flute of pink bubbles was placed in front of me. I was getting my month's quota of champagne in two days. "Mr. Vigh," I started in, "also cultivates necessary channels of communication. It is paramount for him to know not only who has his hand on the government spigot, but also how to influence those people without endangering their careers. He is accomplished in the art of ebbing and flowing in others' circles, his presence undetected, in order to secure his objective.

"He knew the contract was subject to renewal the day it was signed. Like any successful businessman, he desired, and worked intelligently, to mitigate that risk. The shifting monetary winds of Washington require him to plan accordingly as one never knows when the government teat will be removed."

That was a sermon for me, and I rewarded myself by bringing the flute to my lips. I needed to buy more. The bottle that Morgan, Riley, and I shared was my last.

"And you concluded," Agatha surmised, "that Mr. Peterson is a likely candidate to secure your objective?"

"We did."

"We usually need to take it on ourselves to secure, in the case of Mr. Peterson, such a perfect mark," Agatha observed.

"Are you offering to reduce your fee?"

He laughed, his chin rippling in joy. "Hardly, although I would think less of you had you not inquired."

"The people you use, are they local?"

"You mean am I sending Christina?"

"I meant no such thing."

"Of course not. You like her, don't you?"

"Why do you care?"

"She means much to me. She has goals that I am helping her achieve. I would not—"

"Then I suggest you keep her out of harm's way."

Agatha's eyes narrowed, and he collected himself by taking another drink of his coffee. "Do you have any other advice for me, Mr. Travis?"

"Not at this time. The personnel you employ?"

"Not your concern. They are discreet beyond measurement. Your job is to wire the money at the inception and again upon completion. You understand that by 'completion,' I do not mean Zebra Electronics getting their stocking stuffed. I mean pictures that we will provide to you. We have no control over the course of events after that. Are we in agreement?"

"We are."

I still didn't know whether we were concluding our business today or pulling up anchor with me aboard. If we weren't cruising, Garrett and Morgan didn't need Nicky's boat. The precaution, however, was necessary. We couldn't afford to wait until the *Gail Force* eased out of the harbor and then start scrambling for a chase boat.

"And your Mr. Vigh, is he content with that arrangement?" He brought a clipped cigar to his lips, and the waiter whizzed to his side and torched it. "In fair disclosure, we will place Devon Peterson in a situation that will cost him dearly if he does not extricate himself from it. He will, as you noted, have an easy way out. You will be out ten million dollars, and our job will be finished. But…" He paused and inhaled, tilting his head back as if in some manner his posture contributed to the enjoyment of the cigar. "We are irrational creatures, no? There is no guarantee that your Mr. Peterson will follow protocol and engage in rational thoughts and actions that, while they seem clear to such splendid minds as our own, for some unfathomable reason, he may avoid."

"And my employer is out ten million dollars."

He tapped his cigar on the monkey ashtray. "You disappoint me."

I corrected myself. "If Peterson does not act in his best interest, I am out of time. The contract expires, and Mr. Vigh loses potentially half a billion dollars of profit over the next five years."

"You understand I will never contact Mr. Vigh. If he is tempted, impress on him to reciprocate similar disinterest in me. Are we clear on that point?"

"Crystal."

"Very well. What is your contingency plan? In the event that Mr. Peterson does not react in the method that you seek?"

"I was hoping you could help me there." I said picking up the trail of the conversation. "I need to meet my objective. You get paid," I raised my hand upward in a subtle motion, "for blackmailing Peterson with artistic poses. I get paid for results."

"What if he's thinking of leaving his wife," Agatha challenged me, "and despite her inheritance, this is all meaningless to him? What if his career and paper money have lost their place in his heart, his midlife compass unexpectedly calibrating a different true north?"

Agatha's knowledge of Peterson's situation was impressive; he'd certainly done his homework.

"The thought has occurred to us." I said as I leaned in toward him, confident that we were getting to the crux of the matter. Too bad I wasn't wearing a wire. Why hadn't Franklin suggested that? Perhaps he foresaw the rubdown I received upon stepping onto the boat. "What other means do we have to facilitate our deal?"

"We could arrange for criminal charges," Agatha explained. "For example, an arrest that could carry jail time. The shadow of the gallows tends to focus the mind."

"What type of jail time?"

"Life, if he's lucky."

"If he's lucky."

"That is correct."

"Additional cost?"

"You realize," he said, "the charges against him that I'm alluding to?"

"Only one charge carries such a draconian sentence."

"Only one charge, then, guarantees our results. Or, to be precise, allows us to discharge our responsibility with the full knowledge that we have done everything within our scope to achieve our objective. That we have, indeed, played our best card."

"That is all one can ask."

"That is all one can do."

That was the hammer hitting the nail. Agatha took a draw from his cigar and followed it with a sip of coffee. He gave a slight push of his plate, and the waiter cleared the area in front of him, wiping the surface with subdued flare.

"Tell me, Mr. Travis. Is Mr. Vigh intimate with your aggressive side? That is to say, if we reach an agreement, is he on board?"

"He is intimate with my reputation. He doesn't wish to know the methods of my trade. He worships ignorance. Pays for results."

He nodded. I'd given him the answer he wanted.

Agatha continued, "I take it you and he have a slightly different agreement than I have laid out for you. That is, you get paid a nominal amount, but nothing compared to what you receive *if* he gets the contract renewed."

"I have a job to do. Are you my man?"

"I am not a violent man, Mr. Travis."

"But you employ such men and realize that violence is a historically progressive force."

"A *holy* historically progressive force. If one is to quote Trotsky, one should not omit the key word. Do you know when he said that?"

"I do not, but I'd guess it was prior to Franck Johnson taking a pick axe to his head in a Mexico City suburb in 1940." *Why do I play up to this guy?*

"A fine answer. A tip of the iceberg, I'm sure, of what you can discuss on the matter. The Bolshevik Revolution was indeed a pivotal point in the history. Nineteen-sixteen. That is when Trotsky recorded his observation. Do you know why I remember that?"

"How would I know why you remember anything?"

"My apologies," he said with a slight dip of his head. "My question was erroneously posed. Do you know the importance of nineteen-sixteen?"

"The Easter Rising?" I threw out an event my great-grandfather participated in.

"No. I'm thinking of greater scope."

"I acquiesce."

"Please don't, for I detest dispirited conversation. Nineteen-sixteen, Jake. That was the first year the GDP of the United States surpassed that of Great Britain. The torch was passed from the old to the new. Simultaneously, the bear in the east was rising. But the new world, fired by unfettered capitalism, was about to roar even louder and, nearly a century later, stand idly by as the bear crumbled under its own voluminous corruption. But the bear had a task to perform and did it frighteningly well. It bestowed an incredible gift upon the world. Do you know what that was?"

I remained silent. The question seemed more of a conversational pause than a legitimate supplication.

"Do you, Jake, know Stalin's greatest gift to the world?"

"Stalin's greatest gift?" I said, realizing I was off the mark on my assessment of the earnestness of his question. "That's a black trifecta of words. I'll go with door number two; sacrificing forty million of his own people so that Western civilization would not succumb to the tyranny of the Third Reich."

Agatha leaned back. "Precisely, my man." The topic energized him, and he quickly leaned back in. "The Great Architect presented Stalin to the world so that he could maul Hitler. You see the grand synchronicity, don't you? The macabre justice? So few do. It took one ugly creature to destroy another so that the world's advanced democracies could survive. Do you know what that means?"

His questions were prompts for his own train of consciousness. I remained silent, having no intentions of encouraging him and wondering when the conversation would get back on track.

"There is no meaning," he reasoned, answering his own question. "Nothing is written. I have my own philosophy—spin, you might say, to those encompassing three words; do not impose anything on the canvas, and you will see how blank it truly is. You will learn to appreciate its blankness. Do you agree?"

"I wouldn't disagree."

"You prefer the simple declarative and are reluctant to engage in lengthy verbal exchange."

"And you prefer concluding your statements with a question."

"Hardly a grievous fault for either of us. Nonetheless, I shall adapt your clipped style, after all, words tend to dilute themselves. We both know there are no laws. A gift of forty million Russians. Do you know any by name?"

"Pardon?"

"The forty million. Name one."

"I cannot."

"Have you ever shed a tear for them?"

"I have not."

"Nor does it matter," Agatha said as if he'd scored a debate point. "They are collectively a fly upon a wall. Their names and the lives they represented are no more than a puff of air in a hurricane. Do you see my point?"

Agatha was eager to find someone to validate his thinking. But I'd reached the end of my patience with his masturbating intellect and prattling summation of humanity. I repeated, "Are you my man?"

He hesitated, either caught off guard by the abrupt change in direction, or unwilling to leave his pontifications on history.

"I am." He reclined back in his chair.

"Additional cost," I asked for the second time.

He placed his hands on the table, each one void of an object that would provide him with pleasure, and said, "Have you've been to Russia?"

Here we go again. "I have."

"I would like to go there sometime to view their great works of art. Additional cost? This is a delicate task that needs to be performed properly the first time. The inclusive price is fifteen million."

It was the same price Riley mentioned for the job that Karl had tripped over and eventually led to the Andersons' fleeing and Karl's death. Riley had mentioned three such transactions. How many more had she not found?

"I could get a street job for a fraction of that," I said.

"And you are free to do so, although you would never pick a surgeon with that reasoning. We do not compete on price, but on thoroughness. You need never worry about the deed coming back to you."

"You are confident this can be accomplished in time?"

"Most assuredly."

"When?"

Phillip Agatha picked up his cigar, took a long pull on it, and blew out smoke. His eyes never left mine. His round head never moved.

"Christina is waiting for you inside. You will wire a million within the hour."

"That type of money deserves some acknowledgment of my question."

"Soon. I'm quite certain you understand, given the nature of our work, we never divulge precise times. And my question, Jake, that you ignored, equally deserves acknowledgment. The nameless forty million Russians? The puff of air? Do you see my point?"

"I do not know a single name," I admitted, "Yet that does not render them any more meaningless than a meal I ate three years ago but no longer recall. Try living without eating." I threw his style of questioning back at him. "Do you recall every meal you've ever eaten?"

He gave me a disgruntled look and then flicked his left hand, but the waiter didn't move. Henny, who I erroneously thought never approached the altar, maneuvered behind me. In a startlingly quick and smooth move, he slipped my leather bag off the back of my chair and gave it an Olympian heave overboard. I held myself just in time from reacting, allowing him to complete his assignment. It was not unexpected. He turned to me, crossed his arms in front of his body, and sneered. "No new shoes for you."

"My phone, my computer," I started to protest, wishing I was a better actor than I was. "I need it to complete the wire."

Agatha stood. "We both know that's not true. Terribly sorry about that *ruffian* display. But it's a scurrilous affair we have embarked upon. And Eddie? He doesn't trust you and, frankly, he had an excellent point. If you are to be trusted, then sacrificing your leather bag and using our equipment to facilitate your communications—that is, by the way, a procedure we insist on—is an insignificant price to pay for the rewards you will reap. I'm quite certain you not only understand our position of caution, but taking a moment to be in our shoes—online shopping, really—you realize you'd do the same thing. We pull up anchor in fifteen minutes. We'll tend to further business later on."

He waddled inside without waiting for a reply. My bag sank slowly, as if it couldn't decide whether it was a birthday balloon or a rock. How did he know of my earlier comment to Henny? Was Henny wired? No time for that. I had greater issues.

If I read Agatha correctly, I'd just agreed, and would be guilty of, accessory to murder. Somewhere, some young unfortunate girl's number would come up, and I'm the one that put that play in motion. Eddie's prophetic parting comment to me the first night we'd met rang in my head. It was after I called him out for bragging about his circle of competence, although he didn't know, despite being from the area, that FDU was Kent State University.

There'll be something you miss someday, too, my friend. You'll be lucky if it's that harmless.

24

The *Gail Force* broke clear of the channel and into the open waters of the Atlantic Ocean. *Fishy Lady* followed us, although she was soon lost in the armada of pleasure craft.

I had wired the money earlier using a computer that Eddie provided as he hunched over my shoulder. It was my belief that for an extra five million, Agatha's plan was to arrange for a dead woman in Peterson's bed, much like the picture that Karl Anderson had stumbled across. Agatha would then explain to Devon Peterson that having his college chum Walderhaden extend the Zebra Electronics contract would commute his pending life sentence. Agatha was correct in his assessment that one never knows how another will react in a particular predicament. However, offering Peterson a method to avoid spending the remainder of his life in prison provided the highest probability that Peterson's decision would be conducive to our goals, no matter how uncalibrated his compass might be.

Agatha had been mum on his timeframe. Binelli needed to be notified of the actions I'd initiated, and the FBI needed to be ready for Agatha's strike. But I was temporarily without means of communication.

We motored into Nassau and dropped anchor just as the night was clipping the heels of the day. Christina and I avoided the hectic market of Nassau and headed toward a second-floor restaurant above a closed real estate office. I'd been there twice before with Morgan. We entered by means of rusted steel steps that ran up the side of the building. The steps had a jagged, pronged surface, normally used for better traction in snow and ice. It was an odd thing to see in this part of the world. There was a small landing at the top, and when I opened the door for her, her body backed into mine before she stepped inside the room.

I was in beige linen pants and a short-sleeve brown silk shirt. A steward had informed me that my clothes were mine to keep. I'd asked him if I could keep the yacht as well. At least I was getting a new wardrobe out of the gig. Christina wore ridiculously tight jeans with a wide silver buckle and a white long-sleeve shirt with seams of fluffed cotton. The baby cauliflower humps of cotton ran the length of her front buttons, bunched up around a high collar, and decorated the end of the sleeves. We steered clear of dissension, which included any discussion concerning Agatha, Studio Four-Twenty, or herself. We politely picked over our fish dinners, the meal sadly empty of the curiosity and giddiness when we had consumed the chili dogs.

I didn't dare tell her of Agatha's intent, although if it came down to the final seconds, I could always supplicate my case to her. My goal was to testify against Agatha on suspected murder charges. Based on what Riley Anderson saw and my conversation with him, I could make a strong case in front of a grand jury. Whether it was sufficient would be decided by the pleas of dueling attorneys and the judgment of a jury. If they voted in our favor, Agatha would be brought to trial. Riley would, despite her desire to kill the man, have closure and vindication for what the Fat Man did to her life.

The central question still remained. Who was Agatha's inside man? Unless I unlocked that door, I feared that I'd entered a dark labyrinth, where objects, once set in motion, remained in motion. With a nod to Newton's first law of physics, Jake's first law of life is this: a body in motion produces unintended consequences.

Morgan and Garrett entered the restaurant fifteen minutes after us. They made a beeline to the bar, never glancing in my direction.

Christina's eyes wandered over to Garrett. With his height and alopecia areata—outside of thin eyebrows, no hair graced his skin—Garrett was a chiseled and polished dark figure who could pass as a storefront mannequin. She diverted her attention back to me before her casual glance became a stare. I was waiting for her, and her eyes fell from mine, knowing she'd been caught. I remained silent, as I didn't wish to draw further attention to them.

When Garrett went to the men's room, I excused myself.

The two stall doors were still swinging when I entered. I assumed he had kicked them to ensure that we were alone. "They tossed my bag overboard," I offered as a greeting.

He grunted. "The same little job that slipped you a drink?"

"His big brother. Fifteen million for a hit. A dead body on a bed with a picture of Devon Peterson standing next to it. Agatha's suggestion. Claims that is the surest method to encourage Peterson to act in the manner we desire. Riley came across several fifteen-million-dollar transactions."

"When?"

"When what? She came across the pictures, or when Agatha—"

"Our deal."

"Don't know."

"Find out."

"Won't tell."

Garrett took a moment and then said, "What if he's fast? Next forty-eight? Does Franklin have that type of speed? Plus—"

"We have to assume he's that fast."

"—there's an innocent woman to be considered. We can't let her die."

I went to the washbasin and splashed water on my face. I snatched a rough paper towel from a beaten-up metal dispenser and dried off. I wondered if his last statement was fueled by his personal tragedy of when his girlfriend died.

"I'll press Agatha," I said. "But if I were he, I wouldn't give a specific date. Contact Binelli. Tell her twenty-four a day on Peterson. They could entrap him anytime, and she needs to have people on him to prevent the murder and to capture Agatha's men."

He handed me an extra burner phone on my way out the door.

Christina had a fresh drink in front of her. We continued to dance around each other with inconsequential conversation until I ventured in. "How fast does Phillip work?"

"I wouldn't know," she said curtly.

"Is my business, and our association, over in a day or a week?"

"I said I wouldn't know."

"Can you find out?"

"No. I don't want to be involved."

"But here you sit."

"I *told* you. I'm—"

"There are other ways, you know."

She twirled her hair. "Other ways for what?"

"To make money. To help out your mother and sisters."

She flipped a strand of hair out of her hand and gazed at me as if she were considering her options. She settled for, "We need to be going."

Her sharp declaration was disappointing. She was loyal to Agatha. I relinquished my effort to turn her—for the time being.

"Where?"

"Downstairs," she instructed me. "He has plans for you this evening."

"You won't be joining us?"

"I wasn't invited."

"Why is that?"

"It's not for me to ask. Perhaps, afterward, you can tell me."

"Then you can report back to Agatha."

It came out a little nastier than I intended, but being rude to a tightly jeaned woman is a highly effective, albeit, shameful trick to maintaining a monogamous relationship. Her lips parted as if she were about to speak. But instead, she marched out the door leaving me feeling cheap—the cost for being highly effective.

25

"**M**r. Travis, slide in, will you?" Phillip Agatha beckoned from inside the car after Henny opened the door of a limo.

I crawled into the back. I'd never seen the driver, but Eddie sat in the passenger front seat. Johnnie Darling, whom I recognized from a picture, sat across from me. Eddie was not a big man, but Darling was even smaller. The man I'd described to Kathleen as a wet roach had a sallow face and disappeared into the leather seat like a fold of a blanket. Henny clambered in behind me and took the seat by the door. The car, like a boat, registered his weight.

"Your pleasure?" Agatha said, nodding toward the bar.

"Whiskey."

"Your girl is Jameson, I believe."

"The entire species enchants me." Through the rear window, I saw Christina walking away from the limo.

He chuckled as he used metal tongs to pluck two cubes from a small stainless steel cooler. He dropped them into a tumbler he held with a napkin and then added a pour of whiskey—a word believed to be derived from "water of life." He stirred it with a swizzle stick, used a fork to add a lone cherry, and handed it to me. He discarded the napkin.

"Where are we off to?" I said, tipping my tumbler to him in appreciation.

"Dancing."

"Shouldn't there be womenfolk along?"

"I don't believe that will be an issue. Our venue is already well stocked with that other species you so admire."

Ten minutes later, the limo pulled up at the rear of a single-story cinder-block building. There was an unmarked metal door a Tomahawk missile couldn't blow through. A security guard opened it as the entourage approached: Agatha, Eddie, Henny, Johnnie, and myself. Inside, Agatha worked his way to a spacious booth while Eddie and Henny took a side table. Johnnie disappeared.

A band, two guitar players and a bass, occupied one corner. The music was low, which made conversation easy. Cigar smog clouded the dark air. Alluringly clad women danced with one another on a slightly elevated stage, wove among the crowd, and nestled on men's laps, whispering into their ears. One leggy woman wore jeans and nothing else. The clientele had big rings and bigger stomachs. Nice shirts. Expensive shoes. Some wore gold necklaces. Men who wear gold necklaces do not come across their money by honest means.

"This entertains you?" I said to Agatha as a redhead with a seahorse tattoo on her right front shoulder presented him a drink, wrapped in a napkin. She wore a loose halter top that stopped between her breasts and waist. I scanned the room and doubted Garrett and Morgan would enter. They wouldn't want their faces known to Agatha. Garrett and I knew the advantage of operating as a team while the opposition had no clue there was another member. It's like playing chess and having an extra queen that your opponent is not aware of. It is an incalculable advantage.

"It is all entertainment," Agatha addressed my question. "We are, however, here for business. We need to procure a new employee. Are you offended?"

"Deeply."

"What do you think of red, our waitress?"

"She has a seahorse on her body."

"Beyond that?"

"I got stuck there."

"Does she interest you?"

I wasn't sure where he was going with the question. "I find her fascinating."

"Play along, will you? And there—" He nodded out toward the room. "The blond-haired girl, what about her?"

"Mesmerizing"

"You're not cooperating."

"I don't know the game."

"Why the palpable display of indifference? We're merely doing a little male bonding to celebrate the day." He raised his glass, "I'll get the festivities going." He took a sip and then craned his neck like a turtle as his eyes scanned the room. "I select that thoroughbred—see—over there."

My eyes followed his hand. A tall, athletic black woman stood behind a man, rubbing his upper arms. Her hair spilled over the man's head and onto his face; her breasts rested on his shoulders.

"If I could dance," Agatha mused, "I would ask her. But you do not want to see me dance." His eyes momentarily left me and then returned. "For you, I should think...oh, come now, indulge me. Put your penny-ante feelings aside and point at a young lady that suits your taste."

I searched the room and took in nine girls. I took the one in the middle—the five spot. She was a small-boned brunette whose last two meals kept her from being officially malnutri-oned. She wore a lace bra and baggy pants.

"You like her?" Agatha pressed me.

"Mom would approve."

"Point at her?"

"Excuse me?"

"Give her a sign. These girls dance for money. You'll be putting food on her table. Look at her. She could use a little pudding."

I obediently brought my hand up and pointed a finger in her direction.

Click.

Johnnie Darling and his camera skimmed into view and vanished just as suddenly.

"There, that wasn't so hard, was it? Agatha said. "Stellar choice—not only attractive, she's delicious; a *profiterole* you can taste from here." He waved his hand and the redhead was again at his side. "Theresa, the little cream puff, over there."

Theresa's gazed out into the room. "That's Lucille, Mr. Agatha."

"If you would." He nodded toward me. "Our prudish friend here needs to stretch his legs." He slipped her a bill. "It's good to see you again."

Theresa strolled over to the young woman and whispered in her ear. Lucille glanced at me, beamed a fresh smile, and finished serving drinks. She came over and without preamble, snuggled in next to me, her right arm caressing my neck, her fingers smoothing the hair around my right ear.

"You like to dance?"

"Terribly sorry, but I'm missing my legs."

"No," she said, running her free hand up my thigh. "Plenty of leg there. Yes, sir, plenty of leg."

"Actually, I was in Verdun—"

"Good grief, man." Agatha vehemently cut me off. "Verdun, really. Get 1916 off your mind. Dance with the child. Celebrate life. Embrace trickle-down economics."

I didn't know what his game was but surrendered my resistance. I slid out of the booth, took her hand, and led Lucille to the dance floor where other couples were melting to the tune of the classical guitars. She threw her arms around my neck and pressed her body into mine. She ran her hands down my arms, found my hands, and tucked them in under the band of her terry cloth pants.

Click. Click. Click.

Johnnie Darling stalked us with a wide-lens camera in front of his face. I instinctively lowered my face.

Click. Click. Click.

Not wishing to be a prude—*when did I become considerate?*—I gave Lucille a few minutes and then excused myself. She followed me. Halfway to the booth, I handed her a fifty, told her it was the time of my life, but that it was over between us. She started to protest. "Vamoose," I said as I gave her a spank. She turned and refocused her attention on the table she'd been working when Theresa the Seahorse requisitioned her.

Our table looked like midnight on a cruise ship. Lobster tails, fried chicken, waffles, scallops, and pink chateaubriand were laid out in a seashell platter. Agatha, with a napkin sprouting out of his neck, was deep into his pleasures when I rejoined him.

"Quite a spread," I commented.

"Yes," Agatha said proudly. "I am not one to limit myself to hospital food, figuratively or literally.

I took a seat. "Why did Johnnie take my picture?" I knew I'd blundered before I'd finished my question. Agatha didn't skip a beat.

"How do you know Johnnie's name?" he replied coolly.

"Christina."

"She introduced him to you?"

"No. She mentioned his name when I asked who would be joining us tonight. It's the only name she mentioned that I didn't recognize; therefore, I assumed that man is Johnnie. Am I mistaken?"

My mind raced ahead. I needed to have Christina vouch for me. I'd have to get to her before Agatha did as I would need to explain to her how I knew Johnnie's name. I'd tell her that my contact who put me in touch with Agatha mentioned a man who took pictures and went by the name of Johnnie Darling. That would work. I should have gone with that just now instead of Christina. Too late. It was a stupid mistake. Two stupid mistakes.

Agatha considered my response while he finished his chew. "No," he said evenly. "You are not mistaken. Johnnie Darling is my artistic director."

"But his name is not on Studio Four-Twenty brochures or website."

"*Internal* artistic director."

I nodded as if it meant something and rephrased my question. "Why did your internal artistic director take my picture?"

Agatha adjusted his weight and said, "I'm not sure. Perhaps Eddie can enlighten you. Johnnie's always snapping away." While at times verbose and enchanted with the sound of his own voice, Agatha was impeccable with his words. *Perhaps Eddie can enlighten you.*

I grabbed a lobster tail, picked up a knife, and carved out a chunk of crustacean meat. I dipped it in butter, but instead of enjoying the taste, I felt a sense of unease manifest within me. Agatha's earlier comment concerning a new employee came back to me. I was losing control of the game.

"You mentioned," I said, dabbing my mouth with a warm, damp cloth napkin, "that you are here to procure a new employee. For what purpose?" It wasn't my smoothest delivery, but it would suffice.

Agatha put down his fork and dragged his napkin off his neck. He straightened his collar, although it was perfectly fine. I'd never noticed him touch an article of his clothing.

"Do you know how I came to name her, the Gail Force?"

I spread my hands. "This answers my question?"

"You actually have two questions in the queue, Mr. Travis. Why did Johnnie take your picture—I suggested that Eddie could assist you with that—and for what purpose do I seek a new employee. You're being unusually inquisitive this evening. But, unless you've made other arrangements, and that would sorely disappoint me, we are here until the boat leaves."

I leaned back and crossed my legs. "How did you come to name your magnificent ship?"

He positioned his hands in front of him like the paws of a great sphinx. He was as motionless as I'd ever seen him. "When I was very young, nine specifically—ages are such crude markers of one's maturity and intellect—nonetheless, I was nine, I came across a goat. You are aware I grew up on Bonaire?"

"I was so informed." I'd settled on the evasive answer as I'd already stumbled in revealing Darling's name. I feared he'd question the source of my affirmative reply, but he rolled on, his eyes on a distant shore.

"Finding a goat was no big thing. Chickens, goats, dogs, they roamed freely. We thought nothing of it. It is the same today. But one day, my older sister and I came upon a goat that was being eaten by wild dogs. Not a pack of dogs that would be dangerous to us, but domestic hungry dogs following genetic code."

"It was injured?"

"It?"

"The goat."

"It was a 'she,' and she was bleeding quite profusely."

"The dogs were attracted to the blood."

"That is correct. My sister tried to beat them off, but it was not to be. There were three or four of them. Considering my mind for numbers, I cannot recall exactly how many dogs there were, nor was the number of dogs the focus of my sister's and my attention. The goat was bleeding because she was in the process of giving birth. As the dogs were eating her alive, killing her, her body was quivering, trying to push out her calf.

"We finally succeeded in beating away the dogs with sticks, but it was too late for the goat. She bled out. She lay there, dead. And then," he leaned in, pushing away the seashell platter of food and clearing the table in front of him, "the most remarkable thing occurred. Her body, there on the dirt ground, surrounded by her own insides, convulsed. The carcass spasmed and the calf came out, not entirely, you understand, but enough that my sister and I started to tug on its legs and were able to complete the messy task."

He leaned back. "A most incredible thing, no? The muscles had just enough blood in them to shudder life from death."

"A good tale," I agreed, not having a clue what the bloody goat had to do with the christening of his yacht.

"My sister and I took the baby goat—the kid—home and raised it. We bottle-fed it, bathed it, let it sleep in our room. We brushed it daily and took it for walks. We named her— for it was also a she—Gail, after the wind, although we kept the feminine spelling. My sister was taking sailing classes as the time, and she liked the flag that signaled a gale wind. Do you know it?"

"Double red."

"Yes. A single flag is for smaller craft and a double red is for gale winds. Recall, we were born and raised on an island, therefore, there was absolutely no excuse *not* to be accomplished in the art of harnessing the breath of Aeolus. Therefore, while it was to be avoided—one would be feeble-minded to intentionally set course into gale winds—we were instructed, nonetheless, not to fear the double red banners.

"Her instructor in sailing class had her take a boat out, in what only can be construed as highly tempestuous seas, in order to acquire a taste so that in the event she got caught in a gale force, it would not be all together unfamiliar. She did exceptionally well."

"And you?"

"Pardon?"

"Did you sail the tempestuous seas?"

He seemed to reflect on my question. "I, and at a young age, I remind you, not that I boast, believed it dangerous to go into such seas, to believe one could control a vessel in a gale force, for it is the gale force that controls you. Nor was it easy for me to maneuver in a sailboat, although that served as a rudimentary reason, an excuse of convenience. I did not go out. I was content to exercise my intelligence rather than my body. What do you think?"

"About what?"

"Our discussion," he admonished me in an impatient tone, as if I weren't keeping up in class. He reached to the table and took a leisurely sip from his glass and delicately placed it back. "That sooner or later, a life worth living will be caught up in a gale force, and prepare as you might, you are bound to relinquish control. Why purposely go there? The gale force is waiting for us all on its own terms. Do you grant homage to the dictum that that which does not kill us makes us stronger?"

"Nietzsche was an optimist," I pointed out. "Blindly following his observation would leave most of us vegetables in a hospital ward."

He chuckled in agreement. "Nothing poetic about that, though, is there?" He eyed me as if measuring me for the first time. "I was, as I said, nine. I believe I truly loved that goat. At least I had a feeling for her that has yet to be replicated. But such are the feelings of a child."

"You named your yacht after her."

He let his breath out and his body shriveled in like a bloated raft that had sprung a leak. "My mother—and I in no manner hold her accountable—said the goat had to go. Gail, you see, grew, and goats, well…" He rolled his head to the side and smiled drolly. "They are not exactly house creatures, even on an island. My sister and I took Gail to a man who raised goats. Oh, but you must understand, it was an event for us. We bathed her and brushed her for the final time. I packed her toy. It was a stuffed sock that I had colored a face on. We made great ceremony out of her leaving the house. 'You're a big goat now, time to be on your own, we'll come visit you.'" He waved of his hand. "Things you do as a child before the world demands that you hide your emotions and bury your trampled heart.

"We arrived at the man's small farm, a windswept acre of worthless dirt." He punctuated the last part of his statement with unbecoming bitterness. "He instructed us to put her in a fenced area with other goats. 'We'll see what happens,' the man said. 'We'll see what happens.' He knew. I, of course, had no idea. No idea at all. It was, looking back, my last moment as a child."

He perked up, and straightened his posture, as if the adagio part of the movement had passed. "We opened the gate, and Gail trotted in. She froze, as if she didn't know what to do. There was a male goat on the far side. He saw the new goat, lowered his horns, and as my sister and I watched, he charged our little goat. He gored her while my sister screamed. Gail bled out. Just like her mother did. I wanted to scream, but I could not. Does that strike you as odd, that I could not scream?"

"I'm not—"

"Nor could I cry. Then or now. All I do is rationalize. For as I passed from a child to a man, I thought, such is the life of a goat. Such is all life. There is beauty and music, and then it is gone."

I wasn't sure what to do with his story and was about to toss out an obligatory remark when he jumped tracks. "Do you like snow?" Agatha said.

"And you accuse me of jostling the subject?"

"If your challenged attention span will bear me out, you'll see that I've done no such thing. I've not seen snow—have no desire to be imprisoned by winter. They say each snowflake is unique, different from all others, although our minds know the improbability of such sweeping declarations. I've often thought that our lives must be like snowflakes, different and unique."

"But those flakes," I countered, remembering his treatise on the forty million and picking up the sniff of his trail, "end up in a cold pile, ultimately indistinguishable from one another."

"Yes!" He became as animated as I'd ever seen him and the table shifted as he leaned in. "Precisely. You see it too, don't you? The snow? Stalin's masses? My pet goat? It does not matter. Only when floating down does our uniqueness shine, and then we are piles of snow. Gail was born to a dead mother and gored to death six months into her life. A tragic tale, would you agree?"

"If you say so." I searched the room for Johnnie to see if he was taking more pictures, but I couldn't locate him.

"But do you agree? Everyone who hears it offers their condolences to me, my sister, and even to Gail. Do you not feel the same way?"

"My condolences."

He touched his right ear lobe with his hand. It was another new move for him. He leaned back and studied me. "You are a conflicted man, Mr. Travis. Your intellect crusts your heart, giving you a false streak of emotional impoverishment, as if you wish to exude insentience. But it is the stoic man who hides a torrent of emotions."

"We're discussing a goat," I reminded him.

"Yes. And my tale?"

"You were a child. It was a goat."

"You see nothing else?"

"You're wrestling a story for a phantom meaning."

"My dear man, I could not have stated it simpler."

He torched a cigar and offered me one with a gesture of his hand. I declined. Theresa the Seahorse dropped by and cleared the table. Agatha kept his gaze on me. "I have a proposition for you." He shifted forward and lowered his triple chin as if challenging me. "I'll pose a riddle. There'll be a meaningful reward if you provide the correct answer and reasoning."

"And if I'm wrong?"

"No penalty. Oh, for the sport of it, let's say you need to tango with Lucille again."

"If I'm right?"

"If you're right, I'll knock a million dollars off our agreement. I would be gravely disappointed if you passed that along to your employer, therefore, it is a million dollars for you."

"I'm certainly not doubting your honesty, but for a million dollars, if I were you, I'd change the answer."

He eyes struck me as if my response had mortally wounded him. "You besmirch me, accusing me of being a common cad. I assure you, Mr. Travis, I am a man of my word. Shall we?"

"Double it."

"I'm sorry?"

"Two million if I'm right. I pay you a million if I'm wrong."

"Why?"

"If you're good on your word, then I'm betting on myself. I like that chance."

"Delightful. My first impression of you was of someone who might be all hat and no cattle. Clearly, that is not the case. So be it. One for me should I judge you wrong and two for you if I judge you right. Shall we?"

"Fire away."

"Did the goat have a happy life?" Agatha asked.

"That's the riddle? A fifty-fifty shot at two million dollars?"

"Your reasoning, I remind you, as well as your answer, must be correct."

"And you know the answer because you've spoken with the goat, Gail, from beyond?"

"Your answer?"

I gunned down my whiskey and decided not to overthink it. Agatha viewed history as a blur; people held no more value than trodden leaves on a forest floor.

"On the surface," I started in, "it is a tragic tale. The dogs eating her mother during birth, the goat's quick demise when being corralled with other goats. But I'll cast a yes. Your goat, Gail, had a wonderful life. She did not know her mother was killed before she was born. She was a goat. You and your sister were her mothers. While alive, her needs were met, she never wanted for food, shelter, or attention. She did not consciously think of life or death. She was not aware of the great divide. When death came, she did not know it was early, nor did she know its face as it charged her from across the yard. Her beginning and end have no relevance to her life. The short happy life of Gail the goat. The only relevant word is happy."

Agatha settled back, his face clouded with solemnity. "Bravo, my man. Bravo." He drew the vowels out, like a singer taking a diction class. He resumed his pace. "The 'Gail Force,' Jake, is being truly alive. The sheer joy of wild and uncontrolled winds. Our death, or the death of others, is not of consequence to the life we lead. Forty million Russians, a fly, and a goat; they are the same. There is only the moment, and we must seize it with everything we have, for we are doomed by the unsustainable nature of our pursuits."

What hogwash shit, I thought but kept my lips zipped.

"Congratulations." He dipped his glass to me. "You just clipped a two-million-dollar coupon. I've made the wager with others, but this is the first time I've had to pay. It is a pleasure to do so."

"The reflective doors that originally came with your yacht?" I said, my temperature rising.

"I beg your pardon?"

"The outdoor wood doors on your yacht."

"What about them?"

"The nine-year old boy who witnessed this and couldn't cry? He became inured to the world and created his own stage that allows him to repeatedly avenge the death of his pet without repercussions of guilt, or visions of a disapproving Being. A capitalistic, narcissistic jihadist. That's why you had the reflective doors removed from your yacht—you don't want to see yourself."

Agatha's jaw clenched, and his gaze narrowed. I'd hit home, and at that moment I understood the man: life to Phillip Agatha was tawdry and empty, a mistake of a beginning, a random interlude, and a meaningless conclusion.

"Why must you," he pleaded, "after such an impressive reply, sully our evening with *that?*—as if *you* are qualified to pickpocket my mind. I do not assign death a specific feeling, nor, do I exclude it from life. I'll do our relationship a favor and strike your cold-blooded and churlish comment from my memory. It is true; I replaced the doors, but hardly for the reasons you flatter yourself with. I simply do not like the minatory sun glaring on them. Enough. It is a tale of a goat. No? Nothing more."

Agatha, in a huff, promptly announced that we were departing. Before we left, Henny approached Lucille. He said something to her, and she grinned and nodded. He palmed her some bills. She glanced at me and smiled. I knew then what the purpose of our visit had been. The answer to my twin questions to Agatha: why Johnnie had taken my picture and why Agatha needed a new employee.

26

I'm not fond of waking up on boats; there's no place to dispel my energy.

I did a few laps around the deck, poured a cup of coffee that had not been brewed when I first passed it, and took a chair. The sky brightened as the steam rose from my cup as if they were related events.

I hadn't seen Christina after we left the nightclub and needed to explain to her that my source had mentioned Johnnie Darling's name and that, furthermore, I'd erroneously informed Agatha that she had mentioned the name to me.

She found me on the aft deck, where I was reading Halberstam's posthumously published *The Coldest Winter.* I'd spotted it on an end table in the main stateroom, as if it had been placed there by an interior decorator. Christina took a lounge chair next to me and declared. "You were rude last night." Her hair was tied back, and a gold sweatshirt, one size too large, billowed in the wind.

"I'm rude a lot." Then, realizing I wasn't helping matters and needed her help, added, "My comment was harsher than I intended. We have a delicate relationship."

"Is that what we have?" Her eyes searched mine. "A relationship?"

"I need to conduct—"

"I lied for you."

"Pardon me?"

"I confirmed to Phillip that I told you about Johnnie Darling."

I nodded slowly as her words, and her decision to cover for me, sank in on their own pace. Agatha had not wasted any time in verifying my story. Christina was flirting with being a double agent.

"I was mistaken," I confessed. "My source who led me to Agatha had mentioned Johnnie and gave me a physical description. I erroneously mentioned that you provided the name."

"I lied for you."

"No need to. Like I said—"

"I lied *for* you, and now you're lying *to* me."

I put my book down and faced her. Our knees slightly touched. It didn't feel awkward. That's not saying what it did feel like.

"What did you say?"

She brushed her hair off her face, the breeze quickly mocking her effort. "Phillip asked me if I gave you Johnnie's name. I told him that you asked who would be joining us on the boat. I said that Johnnie might, and you cut in that he was a name you didn't recognize. I told him he was the artistic director. I kept it short."

"He asked you directly if you gave me Johnnie's name, not what names you gave me?"

"Yes. 'Did you give Mr. Travis Johnnie's name?' is what he said."

I was surprised that he gave Christina a leading question versus asking her what names she gave me. Agatha *was* capable of unforced errors. I'd also told Agatha that Christina dropped Johnnie's name when I inquired who would be joining us after dinner last night, not who would be joining us on the boat. I doubted he missed that. If he brought it up, I'd chalk it up to a fuzzy memory.

"Did he believe you?"

She didn't answer but shook her head. "How did you know Johnnie's name?"

"My source, who led me to Agatha, gave me a rundown on his personnel."

"Don't do that again."

"I won't."

"I mean, draw me into—"

"I know what you mean."

She stood. "Eddie's waiting for you in the stateroom." She started moving away.

I felt I owed her an apology for mentioning her name. "Hey," I said.

She turned. "You said that once, and there's nothing behind it." She walked away. I picked up my book and pretended to read. But the cold months in Korea held little interest for me.

A few minutes later, Eddie called out from behind me. "Beachy. You got wax in your ears?" He came around and took a seat next to me. "Christina told you to double-time it to the stateroom. You wanna do business or not?"

"You found me."

"Still ticked about that drink, aren't you?"

I put the book down and sat up in the lounge. I scooted it back as I adjusted my weight. No need for our knees to touch. He held a manila folder in his hand.

I spoke into his blank eyes. "When can I tell Mr. Vigh that our job is complete?"

"When we tell you."

"He'll want to—"

"You understand what I said?"

"You understand I'm the client in this relationship?"

He gave a slow nod and sucked in his cheeks so they made sinkholes on both sides of his face. He held that for a moment and then said, "I got something I need to share with you." He reached into his folder and extracted several eight by ten photographs. I knew what they were before I saw them. I knew when Henny approached Lucille before we left the nightclub. I hoped I was wrong. I'd done that before—hoped that I was wrong about something I knew to be true. So far it's never worked. That's never daunted my efforts, or my enthusiasm, to keep deceiving myself.

He slid over a round teak table and laid a picture on it. It was of Lucille and me dancing, my fingers disappearing into the lower part of her bare back.

"What do you think of that, Beachy?"

"Johnnie needs some tips on using the f-stop on a thirty-five millimeter."

He laid out another; me handing her a bill, although it would be difficult to prove the denomination, not that it mattered. The third and final was of me, taken from behind. I was pointing my finger in the direction of Lucille. She was clearly in focus in the background. Johnnie slammed that one.

"What do you think we use these for?" he asked.

"Show and tell?"

"You know, don't you? Sure you do. Bright guy like you? Saint Pete named from a coin toss?" He shook his head. "Gee-zus, I'm gonna remember that. Sure makes me a better man." He pointed at the pictures. "These, you see, are our insurance pictures. You follow me, don't ja?"

"Little minds rarely go anywhere."

He smiled, like he was just getting warmed up for his favorite part. "Beachy, Beachy, Beachy. It's not where I'm goin', it's where you already are. My job is to explain your predicament. Your situation. I'll make it clear, so even a bright guy like you can understand. You see Lucille, here?"

He held up the picture of me dancing with Lucille. My chest tightened with pain. I fought the urge to dig my fingers into his spiny windpipe.

"I said—"

I cut him off. "Come out with it."

He shook his head. "Man, I hope to never see you again after today. When we're done, we are done." Eddie laid it out exactly as I feared. "Lucille's our new employee. She's thrilled, I can tell you that. Gets to go to Washington D and C. High-class call girl; more money than she ever dreamed about. Right now? Her friends back on the island will be planning a big farewell party.

"Unfortunately, her professional career will be cut short when she's strangled to death. You know, her first customer, a Mr. Devon Peterson, he don't know it, but he's gonna get a little too physical with her. Unfortunate, really. Girl like that has a lot of potential.

"You see, don't you? You ever—I mean a week from now or twenty years from now, it don't matter—decide to grow a conscience, or get ready to meet your Creator and start thinking you got some suitcases that won't fit through them pearly gates—you know, them gates that your buddies Thatcher and Fun-a-cello squeezed through on the same day?" He nodded at the picture. "You remember we got those. You come after us, and we say—what do you think we say? We say, this guy knew. Look, he picked out the girl. Points right at her. Rubs his big paws all over her scrawny baby ass. Hands her money.

He was in on day one, knew he fingered her to die. You follow me?"

"A little blackmail on me to ensure that I don't cave in."

"Yeah. Your f-stops working pretty good."

"I could tell the truth."

"You could." He nodded again at the pictures. "But we'd pay someone to testify that you told our Lucille here, and she told her girlfriends that night, that you had a job for her up in DC. You see now, don't you?"

"You treat all your business associates like this?"

"No, but you ain't the first, so don't get your feathers all ruffled. We do it when we need extra precaution. You earned that on account I don't like you."

"Eddie from Youngstown?" He nodded. I tempered my aggression. "It's been a pleasure doing business with you."

"That's what you say, tell me what you think." He stood, and I did likewise.

With great effort, I repeated, "It's been a pleasure doing business with you."

"You disappoint me, Beachy. First day we met, reaching over and taking my bread? I know it's inside you."

"That day?"

"Uh-uh."

"I smelled you before you even sat down."

He sucked his cheeks between his teeth again. "That's more like it. You better not be out to screw Mr. Agatha."

"You have nothing to fear." I slapped my hand hard on his shoulder. It knocked him back half a step. "I'm a business-man, and despite your and my proclivity for distrust, I have the utmost faith that our arrangement will be mutually beneficial."

He considered that and said, "I'll give you a call when we need the funds wired." He reached into his pocket, pulled out a cell phone, and handed it to me. "We'll text you a picture, our proof of completing our end of the bargain. You're a smart guy, but listen to me; destroy the phone the second you get the text. You'll wire half the money by nine tomorrow morning, and the remainder when you get the text. I understand that Mr. Agatha cut you a deal, knocked two mil off the top. You owe seven mil now and seven when you get the text. That's fifteen counting the one mil down. *Capisce?* Give us your account number, and we'll wire two back out to you. That way your employer will never know. You know it don't make me too happy, rebating seven figures to you."

"That's the best part of the deal."

"If it was up to me, I wouldn't give you the steam off my piss."

"Charming. You trust me to wire the additional seven?"

"Me? I don't trust you worth shit. Thought I just told you that."

"Anyone not pay?"

"Why? You thinking?"

"Just asking."

"Since you did," he invaded my space, not in the least bit put off by his lack of height and hundred-pound disadvantage. "We had this one guy. Said he was in a squeeze, would need a few more weeks to secure his funding."

"Did he?"

He spit out a cackle. "We never found out, Beachy. Never found out. Turns out the guy couldn't swim. Who knew, right? Not even a dog paddle, but holy shitsky, you should have seen the little fucker try." He shook his head. "Gave it everything he had. Mr. Agatha, he likes that story. Says it saved us a lot of hassle, you know? I tell our clients, when some smartass like you broaches the question of not paying the second installment—hey, you like that—'broach'? I'm startin' to sound like you and that 'proclivity' shit. Gee-zus H, I'm lost again—oh yeah, we had one guy, after we tell him, he insisted on paying us all up front. I'm glad you asked, you know why?" He waited a beat. "I said you know why?"

I remained silent.

"I'm hopin' you don't pay. It be my pleasure to bring a little Mahoning Valley justice to your doorstep."

"I'm afraid you're destined to be chronically disappointed in me. I'll pay—on time—and then be out of your life."

As I spoke I was looking forward to paying Eddie a visit after we shut it down. Might even get an Advent calendar to mark the days. A revenge calendar. Do they make them like that?

"Seven million. Nine o'clock," he said and trudged away. He picked up the pace the farther he got.

"When?" I said after him. He turned and spread his hands. "When do I tell Mr. Vigh that his problem is taken care of?"

"When you get the text."

He took off, but this time his step gained a light, insouciant swing. I'd asked Agatha the same question. It was a question I wasn't going to get answered. It was likely a moot point—my job might be finished. I doubted the feds would cough up seven meganotes unless they had a reasonable chance of recovering the money.

After we docked, I summoned a ride, fed my driver false directions to make sure we weren't being followed, and eventually told him to head to the marina where *Fishy Lady* was docked. Despite the meandering drive, my thoughts were clear, focused, and straight. I'd fingered an innocent girl to die.

Another snowflake for the pile.

27

"**I** need seven million," I told Binelli on the phone.

"When did you start doing stand-up?"

I was camped out at the bar in the marina's fish house while I cuddled a diluted Bloody Mary. No sight of *Fishy Lady*. I'd given Binelli a description of Lucille and instructed her not to let Peterson out of her sight. I was worried Agatha would act before I wired the first installment. I doubted he was concerned about my credit score. He would strike at the earliest opportune moment, speed and surprise combining to offer the least amount of risk and the greatest chance of success.

I reiterated to her that I needed the funds wired by nine.

"I'll pass it up," she said. "If it gets knocked back down, we'll have to go with what you have, but it'll be your word against his. We'd be lucky to find a prosecuting attorney who doesn't barf her lunch laughing at us."

"Who all knows?"

"I don't follow."

"About me. Who has Franklin told?"

"No one that—"

"Put some vodka in that, will you?" I said to the bartender as he passed me. I shoved my drink to him and he registered his distaste for the world by grabbing my glass and not looking at me.

"You're kidding, right?" Binelli said. "It's not even lunch time."

"You wish you were me, don't you?"

"Don't flatter—never mind. No one knows. Until our conversation today, there was no need for others to know. There is now. I'll try to get a tail on Peterson this morning. We won't need to say why, so it's possible that even then, no one will know. But when we barge in on Peterson with his pants down, word will leak."

"Don't try."

"What?"

"Don't *try* to get a tail on him. Get a tail—"

"Lemme handle it."

"Natalie?"

I don't think I'd ever called by her first name. Why do we have some relationships where we rarely invoke the other person's name? And when we do, does it unleash squelched feelings? Who keeps track of that crap besides me?

She said, "You know my name."

"I do. Do I need to tell you the only thing that matters to me?"

"Stop Lucille from getting murdered."

She knew I'd put a young girl, whom I didn't know and wished no harm, in grave danger. And I groused over a weak Bloody Mary.

"You got it." I affirmed her statement.

"Never play cards," she added.

"Say it."

"You always lead with your heart."

She hung up. The bartender dropped my drink in front of me. I started to reach for it. I stopped.

What's the plan, Stan? Sit here and hope it all turns out right?
Bitch about a weak drink? Let the gale force blow you around?

A few minutes later, Garrett and Morgan burst through
the side door. I gave them the lay of the land—told them I
had girl issues, that I'd set things in motion, and that Lucille
had a date with the Grim Reaper.

"You're responsible," Morgan stated in a rare accusatory tone.

Garrett piled on. "Time to get your ass out of the backseat and grab the wheel."

What a pair of chums. I told them what we were going
to do.

We split at the airport. Morgan headed back to Tampa to
expand the number of photos that Riley was viewing in an
effort to identify whom she and Karl saw in Hollandaise and
on Karl's computer. Our ongoing failure on that front in no
manner absolved us from pressing on.

Garrett and I boarded a 737 to Washington. From my
aisle seat toward the front of the plane, a hundred torsos
passed me on their way to the rear of the plane. One was a
woman's thin waist with a thick belt. The western-leather
strap had holes with tarnished brass grommets. Her white
shirt was tucked into black jeans. I nearly glanced up to see
her face, but caught myself. What if she, too, would die by
my mere acknowledgment of her?

I leaned my head back to relax, but it did no good. Normally, calmness possesses me as a jet thrusts down the runway. Instead, I'd become a fevered brakeman on a southbound
train, a chain around my neck, my fist tight on the lever, in
an effort to stop a death that I, and I alone, was responsible
for setting into motion.

28

The Fat Man

"Tell me, again my dear, pre*cise*ly what he said."

They sat around the teak dining table on the aft deck. Christina gazed down at her cottage cheese with fruit and then quickly back up at Agatha as if she was aware that the lack of eye contact implied guilt.

"It was exactly how I already told you, Mr. Agatha. He inquired as to who was going to be on the boat."

"There is no need for that tone or stiff formality. I'm just tying up loose ends. I apologize, my dear, for questioning you again. And your reply?"

"Something about the usual crowd and that Johnnie might be joining us. He said he didn't know that name and—"

"Yes, yes. We've been over that part. Did Johnnie's name surface again in your conversation with Mr. Travis?"

"No. I think maybe he asked me, over dinner that night, when I told him that you had plans for him? He asked who else would be joining us and I said Johnnie, as well as Henny and Eddie."

"You gave Johnnie's name to him at the restaurant, before we went to the club?"

"I think so."

Agatha hesitated. "So you mentioned Johnnie's name twice to him. You didn't indicate that during our initial conversation."

"Yes. I suppose I did. It's not like I kept track, or anything. Did I do anything wrong?"

"Of course not, dear. I was merely curious, nothing else." Agatha flipped up his right hand. "Thank you for your time."

Christina gave a parting glance at her plate and stood.

"Take it with you, dear."

"That's all right. I'm not really hungry."

After she left, Eddie came out of the stateroom and stood off to Agatha's side.

"You heard?" Agatha prodded him.

"She gave a different story than this morning."

"Yes, but one that is entirely believable."

"She changed her story. He got to her and told her what he told you and now she's covering for him."

"Your cynical and doubting roots run as deep as anyone I've known."

"That's why I'm here, sir. If I may?"

"Please."

"Beachy—Travis wouldn't ask twice. I don't mean to be the slightest bit disrespective, sir, but you're enchanted with this guy. I think it's clouding your judgment."

"Irrespective, Eddie. I do like him. But that does not necessarily predicate a lack of sound judgment on my part nor, may I add, does his mentioning Johnnie's name indicate a Pandora's box. He could easily have gotten the name from his original source, whom we do not know. Due to the unfortunate delicacy of our job, we insist, as you know, that our clients never reveal themselves to one another, and I've thought it an unavoidable Achilles heel of our business model."

Eddie remained silent. Agatha added, "Talking myself into it, is that what you're insinuating by your silence?"

"No, sir. But, I think we should call Mr. Philby. Let him know we might have a plant. At least give him Travis's name. Tell him to be on the lookout. I know he's ticked over his two guys that we wasted, but emphasize to him that we was protecting him. Acting in his best interest. See if he knows—"

"Yes, yes. I don't need to be lectured on how to handle him."

"We got nothing to lose, that's all I'm saying."

"Very well."

Eddie started to turn but stopped. "And Christina?"

"What about her?"

"I don't trust her," Eddie declared.

"She's fine. She would never engage in any activity that would undermine us. I'll grant you the battle, not the war."

29

Natalie Binelli was slouched against a wall next to an ad for the Washington zoo when Garrett and I cleared the secured gate area at the airport. She was oblivious to the ferocious lion hovering over her right shoulder.

"How'd you—?" I stopped as I realized who I was talking to.

She raised her eyebrows. "Kent would like a meeting." She straightened up. "Got a minute?"

"He here?"

"Dispatched me to fetch you. He's meeting us at a pub, fifteen minutes out."

"When you did the search, did you—"

"Relax. I only did it on you. I didn't know Garrett was with you, and I don't sing." She cut Garrett a look. "You still single?"

"You still pack two guns?"

"I do."

"I am."

It was time for someone to step up, tell the two birds it was OK to smile at each other and that they shared a grievous past. Neither of them knew of the tragedy in the other's life. Not that that would guarantee love's flush, but there's magic in the stars that is a step ahead of us as we follow in the dense. Realizing this, and being the great matchmaker I am, I turned to Garrett and said, "You got the rental."

He sprinted off, and I followed Binelli, getting a whiff of her perfume.

"Why are you here?" she said.

"Make sure we're on the same page."

"That's the line I gave Franklin." She shot me a disbelieving glance. "Thought you would have called first."

"Who doesn't like a surprise?"

"I'm not fond of them. If I ask you the same question again?"

"Same answer."

She grunted and picked up her pace.

Edward Kent Franklin sat in a stitched deep-burgundy booth with a mirrored wall behind him. Two thick cloth chairs rested on the opposite side. A single lamp, no more than four inches in diameter, dropped from the ceiling and softly illuminated the table. He pulled himself to his full height as I approached, and we did the good-to-see-you-fake-smile-we-both-know-we-don't-have-jack-shit-in-common handshake.

A cold front had shaved twenty-five degrees from my last visit, and I wore jeans and a camel blazer. The restaurant was stuffy, and I placed the jacket over the back of my chair. A porcelain-faced waiter with a dour disposition inquired what he could "do for you." Franklin indicated we weren't eating and ordered coffee. I ordered an iced tea for myself and a double Bloody Mary for Binelli. She overruled me and quickly changed it to coffee. I said to Franklin, "Why was I fetched?"

"You have a large appetite."

"Seven million."

"That's heavy beef."

"It's a hammer in the desert fiasco—"

"That's a different department."

"Can you do it?"

"It'll take time."

"Agatha wants it by nine tomorrow morning," I told him. "You in or out?"

Binelli squeezed my left thigh.

Franklin's chest expanded and slowly relaxed. He took a sip of his coffee and said, "Tell me everything."

I did. Sort of. I left Christina out of it, but gave him the rundown on Agatha, Eddie, and Henny.

"When is this supposed to happen?" he inquired.

"I don't know."

"This girl, Lucille?"

"What about her?"

"You think they selected her like a sacrificial lamb?" He fidgeted in his seat.

The knot of his tie was flawlessly smooth and rested just under his chin. He had on the same navy cuff links he'd worn to our previous meeting. His hair was bolted into place. He was not a man to fidget. Maybe all the years behind the desk made him immune to the crimes he was paid to prevent. Maybe he had hemorrhoids.

"We're discussing a person," I reminded him, "not an animal. You need men on Peterson. Now. Eddie's suspicious of me. I'm sure he's shared his concern with Agatha. Agatha will act quickly; in the event I'm a plant, he won't give me time to set up a defense."

"First, they—"

"There is no first. If I'm Agatha, my men are waiting. When the money hits, they move."

"They have to scout Peterson," he reasoned. "They'll want to know his habits, his routine. They need to get with your girl and drop her in some madam's rotation. That all takes time."

I turned to Binelli. "You want to tell him how the wheels on the bus go round and round?"

"I don't know—"

"Tell him."

She cast me a thanks-for-putting-me-on-the-spot look and focused her attention on Franklin. "It's likely that Agatha has done all that," she explained in a placating tone, "or at the very least, is conducting those exercises as we speak. He would have done it before he took the job to ascertain how difficult it would be and to measure his risk. When the money hits the account, he makes a phone call. Maybe even before."

Franklin spread his hands. "Perhaps I've been off the street too long. I'll defer to both of you, as I'm clearly out-numbered."

"The money?" I prodded him.

He hesitated and then said, "We'll wire it by four today."

"Peterson?"

"You want someone on Peterson before—"

"Immediately."

"I'll see to it."

My breath eased out. I hadn't been aware that I was tense. "What do you require of me?" I directed my question to Franklin, but my eyes wandered to the mirror behind him. Binelli was there, studying me in the mirror. Our eyes met. I expected her to drop her gaze, as she did at Tony's, but she held fast. Do I let her know that I discovered why she joined the bureau? How would I explain my background check on her?

Franklin was rambling away in his response to my question. "…furthermore, we'd like to have you make a statement today to Special Agent Binelli. It will be instrumental in preparing our case for the grand jury. With what you've told me, and when we catch Agatha's men, Eddie, Henny…" *I could tell her that it was standard operating procedure; she's a tough nut, heard that line a few times.* "…and their photographer, Johnnie, Phillip Agatha is finished. Stand down. You've done us a great service. Agent C. J. Leonard? We now believe his murder was orchestrated by Phillip Agatha. Same with Lippman."

Something Franklin had just said struck me as odd, but the thought vanished like a shooting star. Should I mention Christina, in the event they raided the house and took all the girls? No. I'll get her out early. *That's it. Haul her out of there.*

"Are you following me?" Franklin asked with a measure of impatience.

"The leak within?" I responded trying to mask my mental drift.

He paused, as if my question was not in line with the discussion. "We may never know," he said. "And as before, no one not at this table knows of this meeting. I see no need for concern."

"What if Agatha tells his informant about this operation?" I asked.

"Why would he do that? Even if he did, it doesn't lead back to you. Outside of us, we, as in the bureau, don't even know you're working for us. Your anonymity is a blessing. Now, if you'll excuse me, I have another meeting to attend." He slid off his booth.

We stood and shook hands.

Franklin said, "We owe you."

I countered, "Remember what I said about your finger-nails."

He nodded and marched out the door, his arms in front of him, likely working his coat buttons. It wasn't that cold, but Franklin was a man who relished the days he could wear a dress coat, the long tail flowing behind him, a testament to his status. Such men rush summer, yet secretly urge its demise. I took the booth where Franklin had sat so that I was across from Binelli. It was still warm. I slid over a spot.

Binelli said, "What's with the fingernails?"

"We've been texting pedicurist names."

"You mean manicurist."

"Right."

Before Binelli could seek clarification, Dour dropped by and delivered a monotone, "Anything else I can do for you?"

"Bring me a cheeseburger, fries, salad, and a beer. You?" I glanced at Binelli.

"I can't. I need...sure, make it two, but skip the beer."

"A Chardonnay for the lady," I said.

"No. I'm fine."

"Do it or die," I commanded the waiter. I intended to make my voice light and breezy, but it didn't work. He let out a nervous garble and scooted away.

"What the heck," Binelli said. "Might as well see how you live. Every time I talk to you, you're boozing."

"Really? I think it's every time I talk to you, I need a drink."

"Ha-ha."

A middle-aged couple claimed a booth on the far wall. The second the waiter delivered their menus, they both buried their heads, either desperately hungry, or desperately bored. Two-thirds through my cheeseburger, Binelli said,

"We'll need you to make a statement. We'll take a back door into Hoover. You'll need to call Garrett; tell him it might be a couple of hours."

"About that." I finished my bite and chased it with a beer. "A couple—no make that three things. First, a cheese-burger and beer make any day a better day. Second, we both know you didn't believe my reason I gave you as to why I came here." I took a drink of iced tea and rolled a cube of ice with my tongue. "And third, that part about me making a statement? Hate to put you in a bind, Vassar." I cracked the ice. "But that ship's not going to sail."

Her face froze, and then she shook her head. "I knew you were lying. Do *not* do this to me."

"Here's what's going to happen."

I gave her the plan.

She fired a fusillade of words one should never hear in public. The desperate couple switched tables.

I told her to relax. Find an inner beach.

She told me that I was placing her whole career in jeop-ardy, and referred to me as a "shit bird."

I shot back that she was the one that accused me of lead-ing with hearts.

She said that was only because I didn't have a brain.

Dour sauntered over again. Halfway through his encore performance of, "Anything else I—" Binelli, without alter-ing her attention on me, blistered him. "Beat it, fugger-nut,"

I reminded her that the FBI had a leak; to do anything *other* than what I proposed was suicidal.

She repeated choice words from her previous salvo and added a few I hadn't heard in a while. Said she'd think about it and got up to leave. I told her I was being considerate; I didn't need to tell her any of this. She announced she was done with me. I confessed I liked her perfume.

She instructed me to "Eat crap," and stormed out of the restaurant.

I didn't follow her command, but I did pick over her fries. Fries are always better off someone else's plate.

30

Garrett and I were camped three houses down from Devon Peterson's Arlington colonial home. We were stuffed in a rental car that, although was billed as full-size, reinforced my deeply embedded commitment to own mammoth, environmentally endangering, petro-burning wheels.

I'd explained to Binelli—this is what set off the fireworks—that we were taking it off script. No way were we abdicating our responsibilities for a young girl's life. It was the only way to ensure that we (sounds much better than "I") weren't guilty of sending a young girl to her death and to simultaneously capture Agatha's men. I'd just finished giving the play-by-play to Garrett.

"How'd she handle it?" he asked, keeping his eyes on the house. A yellow leaf fluttered down, swaying back and forth like a swing on a short chain, until it came to rest nestled on the wiper blade. I fired up the engine so the heater kicked in. A squirrel, with a nut in its mouth larger than its head, hopped over the pavement in front of us. It froze, as if it had momentarily forgotten its place in the world.

"Bit of a fit," I said. "Told her I'd give a statement when it was over."

"She still on our side?"

"She stalked out on me after telling me to eat—here he comes."

I gunned the car, braked for the squirrel, who got the message, then swung into Peterson's driveway. His garage door was rising as he continued driving into the garage. I stopped a few feet short of his rear bumper. Garrett and I sprang out of the car as Peterson exited his vehicle.

"Devon Peterson?" I said.

He turned around, a glossy new briefcase in his hand. An eggnog-colored muffler hung around his neck and draped evenly on both sides against his black topcoat.

"Yes?"

"We'd like a moment of your time."

"And you are who?"

"My name is Jake Travis. This is my associate, Garrett Demarcus. We're here on our own accord to prevent you from being blackmailed within the next week." We'd thought about not revealing our identities, but the basis of our plan was raw honesty. Top to bottom.

"I don't know what you're talking about."

"Some resourceful people want your roommate, Walderhaden, to pass some funding their way. They plan on blackmailing you to get to him."

"Who are you? I'll call the police."

I took a step toward him. He stole a glance at Garrett and then back at me.

"We were retained to arrange a sting. We've had a change of heart and now desire to prevent that from happening. We don't care about you, we're only here because we decided that it's in our best interest if we control the play. We need you on our side to help prevent a murder."

His eyes narrowed with the first hint of fear. "The hell you talking about?"

"They plan on killing the next girl you're unfaithful with. She'll bleed out on the bed. There'll be pictures of you standing next to her. If your heart survives that traumatic moment, you'll be instructed to ask Walderhaden, your Saturday morning tennis partner, for funding for a defense contractor. Refuse, you'll spend the rest of your life in jail. That's why they're playing the murder card. Outside of suicide, it leaves you with no way out. Do you understand what I said, Mr. Peterson? I cannot make it any simpler."

"How…how do you know this?"

"I selected the girl you're going to presumably kill," I admitted.

"I don't believe you."

"I'm going to wire seven million dollars to set this in motion, and not a Yankee dime of it gives a damn what you believe."

Devon Peterson dropped his shiny briefcase.

I didn't have a clue what a Yankee dime was.

31

Peterson insisted on continuing the conversation in a public place and driving his own car. We followed him to a Starbucks with grid windows viewing a deserted patio where abandoned tables gathered leaves around their legs. Like the restaurant, it too was stuffy. As if at the first hint of fall's demise and winter's impending arrival, everyone ramped up their heaters. We gave Peterson the synopsis.

"You never answered my question," he argued. Peterson's clipped speech matched his grooming. Did DC make men like him, or did men like him make DC? He'd gotten a coffee at the counter and kept glancing at it. "Who are you?" he said. "You with the FBI?"

"We are not," Garrett answered. "And you're done asking who we are." Peterson eyed Garrett, nodded weakly, and said, "Fine. But back it up, Hardy Boys. Why should I believe a word of what you say?"

"Your mother-in-law died," I said placing my elbows on the table and clasping my hands in front of me. "She left your wife six million. You've told your firm that you're within a year of slamming the door. You're unfaithful at every opportunity you get, and if your wife finds out—she already knows, so what we mean is, if she tosses you out—you lose half your money, get slapped with alimony payments, and never touch a penny of the six million."

"Whoopee-dick," he rallied to his defense. "So you know me. What? You think there are secrets in this town? You didn't answer my question, numbnuts, so I'll rephrase it for you. Why should I trust you?"

"Listen." I leaned back and decided to take a different tack. "You're doing a good job here. If it were me, I'd be sweating a sauna, hearing what we just laid down. You have a choice to make. Either we're blowing smoke about this whole thing, the seven mil, the girl bleeding out on the bed, you smiling for the hidden camera, or we're not. Consider the consequences if what we say is true. What do you have to lose if you trust us?"

"You're missing the salient point," Peterson ricocheted back. He had disturbingly flawless teeth. "I can thank you for your advice, keep my zipper zipped, and eff off to all your threats. And you."

"Devon, Devon, Devon." I drummed my fingers on the tabletop. "Did you not hear what I just said? Your buddy is Walderhaden. Your wife, as we speak, is one foot out the door. You are the perfect mark. You've got a bull's-eye on your back. You think they need your consent to do this? Maybe have you audition for the part?" I shifted forward and lowered my voice. "You're an idiot. They'll slip something in your drink. Flash you pictures the next morning over your bowl of Lucky Charms. They'll smile. You'll vomit. You'll suddenly understand how people wake up minus a kidney, and the last thing they remember is a girl at the bar who they couldn't believe was that into them. But you? Your kidneys will be fine, it's your freedom that will be missing. A murder rap throws a wrench in retirement plans. You'll learn too late in life that a stiff dick is your worst enemy. Got it now? 'Cause we don't have all day, and you're starting to bore me."

Peterson's lip quivered. I felt bad for the guy, and then I felt like crap. I'd voluntarily gotten involved in a vile piece of business. A college-age couple took the two-top next to us and opened textbooks.

"What do I do?" His eyes pleaded with me. He had cast his vote.

I gave him the plan, as the couple marveled that *Othello*, *Lear*, and *Macbeth* all came out within two years of one another. Their table represented the human race better than ours.

"How do I know you'll be there, that you'll show up?" Peterson pressed.

"Blind faith," I replied.

"That's my point. Give me something that shows your motivation, proves your change of heart. I don't buy that you got involved and then didn't have the stomach for it. Nothing personal," his eyes darted from Garrett to me, "but you two don't strike me as candy stripers. You knew what was in store for you."

"The girl they plan to kill?"

"What about her?"

I remained silent.

"I see." He nodded methodically, as if each nod brought him a little closer to the truth. Cracked the door just a bit more. "You told me you fingered her, right?"

"That's correct."

"That wasn't in the job description, was it?"

Again, silence was my best voice, as my position was too painful to concede.

He gave a slight smile and followed it with a snort. "A conscience. It does tend to muck things up, doesn't it? You're here to make sure her blood's not on your hands. You don't give a fiddler's fart about me."

"Thought he made that clear," Garrett cut in.

"You dialed in now?" I kept my eyes on him.

He hesitated, as if he were still processing the new information. "What does she look like?"

I described Lucille and gave him our plan.

"You see her," I lectured him, "and at that moment you will trust me with your life and know that every word is true. I don't know when, but I'd guess within the next few days. Call me. Do *not* go down that path by yourself. We good?" I handed him a burner phone and my card.

He took the phone. "Do I have a choice?"

"You tell me."

"My wife. I don't—"

"Nothing from us."

He held my eyes as if to seal my last statement. He stood, the burner phone in his hand. "I can call you anytime, right?"

"Day or night."

"And you're watching over me?"

"We are." His insertion of "over" into his statement, versus the omission of the word, told me he'd capitulated. "Watching over me" and "watching me" are two different statements.

He shook his head and gazed at the floor. He held that pose for a moment as if he'd never considered a floor before. His coffee cup was loose in his hand, and I thought he might drop it. He brought his eyes up to mine, turned, and headed toward the door. At the door, he hesitated and then pivoted. "Don't let me down."

I gave a nod, and he was gone.

"Think he goes to the police or the bureau?" Garrett said.

"It's a risk, but he's got nothing but a tale told by an idiot."

There was no need to share with Garrett the rest of Shakespeare's statement on human existence. Garrett's literary taste ran strictly to hard news. But the final line of Macbeth's soliloquy upon hearing of his wife's death rang in my head, as if condemning my plan—condemning me, for after all, I'd just referred to myself as an idiot: *Full of sound and fury, signifying nothing.*

"You need to contact Binelli," Garrett insisted. "This could go down tonight, and she hasn't confirmed a makeup artist. No artist, no deal. I'm getting some air." He bolted for the door, and I punched Binelli's number.

She picked up after the first ring. "What?"

"Can you come out and play?"

"I don't have a choice, and you know it, you shit bird."

"What *is* a shit bird?"

"You."

"Did you tell Franklin what I asked you to tell him?"

"I told him that I'd be surprised if you didn't shadow Peterson; that was your nature."

"And?"

"He was paranoid you'd interfere with the endgame; Peterson meeting with Walderhaden. Franklin's adamant that it's crucial they go through with their meeting."

"The tail?"

"Plans to have a crew tailing him ASAFP."

"When? An hour? Later today?"

"I don't know."

"What good does it—?"

"I. Do. Not. Know."

"Makeup artist?"

"I placed that call," she told me. "He's on standby. What do I say to Kent after it's done? He's bubbling with questions. He'll know I abetted you, like you said I would."

"Tell him—"

"Skip it. Why do I care? You used me."

I didn't contend her point but said, "Tell him the truth. My obstinacy changed the game. You had no choice if you want Agatha. I'm prepared to save Lucille and go home. You'll be a hero for cooperating with me."

"Shit bird."

Devon Peterson called at 8:34 p.m.

"She's here." His voice was breathless. An image of his perfect teeth flashed in my mind. "At least this chick looks like your description. Said her name is Sandee. But it's her. Told her I was beat. Did a four-mile run. Said my legs are tired, like you told me to. She gave me the same line. You know, saying I had plenty of leg. I had a drink with her and excused myself."

"Where are you?"

"Patriots, where I usually go."

"Afterward?"

"Same hotel, Park Suites, like we discussed."

"We'll be there. Call me if it doesn't happen."

"You'll be there, right?" His voice trembled, looking for confirmation.

"We'll be there," I repeated with an effort to sound confident and calm, neither of which I was. We disconnected.

"Time to hustle," I told Garrett.

"Let the sound and fury begin," he said.

I glanced at him, expecting a smile, but his blank face signified nothing. I'd known him since I was twelve, and what I knew was this: I still didn't know the man.

32

"There's three of them," Garrett said from the passenger seat. A tablet cast a soft glow over his face. The top of his head rubbed against the roof of the car.

"Three what?"

"Park Suites."

"You joking?"

"I don't joke."

"Incredible. Closest one to the Patriot Pub?"

"Park Suite West. Two blocks. Others are miles away. Take a right at the next light—you just blew through it. Make that two more."

"Can I turn on the next—?"

"One way, wrong way. Right in two lights."

I punched out my breath as I sped through a yellow/red light, wondering what other simple items we'd overlooked—and if DC had red-light cameras. Peterson told us he always used room 328. He often stayed in the city during the week instead of driving to his house—drinking and dining were major components of his job—and his firm kept the room. We'd been lucky that he pulled into his driveway.

It wasn't surprising that Agatha moved so quickly. It confirmed my hypothesis that he mapped out the operation soon after I met him, if for nothing else, to gauge how dif-

255

ficult it might be. Once he committed, he'd act immediately, for time alters the accuracy of any operation.

We pulled into the valet parking, and I hesitated. I didn't want to wait on a valet to retrieve my car when it was time to leave but saw no other option. "Take good care of her," I said to the less-than-enthusiastic young man as I handed him the key to the rental. "She's my dream machine."

Garrett stayed back as I approached the front counter. I inquired if Devon Peterson had checked in, telling the efficient-looking uniformed young woman that I was supposed to meet him in the bar for a nightcap.

"I always liked that phrase." She studied her screen.

"Excuse me?"

"Nightcap." She gave me an exploratory smile that's illegal in seventeen states. I couldn't decide whether she was another man's daughter or a predatory cat. "It sounds so old-fashioned."

"Devon's that type of guy."

"I suppose."

"You know him?"

"He's a frequent guest, but I haven't seen him this evening."

"Perhaps he'll be arriving shortly. He uses his firm's suite, three twenty-eight, I believe."

"He won't be staying there tonight," she said with confidence.

"Oh?"

"That's what I was checking. Another gentleman from his firm checked in earlier to their suite."

Swell. Peterson had yet to arrive, and we were already on the contingency plan.

I caught myself leaning in on the counter and backed off. "I'm sure Devon's planning on spending the night. He doesn't like tooling around after his nightcaps. Where will you put him?"

"No" she demurred. "He's seldom fond of tooling around after his nightcaps. I don't know. You'll have to check with him. We're not full, though. That won't be an issue."

I thanked her, turned away from her, and took a seat on a circular couch that stiffened its resolve when I sat on it. It was off to the side and out of the main traffic flow, although I still had a clear shot of the revolving front door. Several couples gathered as if waiting for another party. To my left, a solo woman sat studying her computer screen at a long high-top table with a power strip running down the middle. I doubted Agatha would send Eddie and company; he likely would outsource such work. If so, however, I had a bevy of cards up my sleeve. In aggregate, they didn't add up to much more than a pair of twos. Garrett took a seat in the chair across from me, a newspaper in front of his face. A plump lady approached, eyeing my couch. A couple of coughs and a quick nose wipe on my sleeve sent her in search of more sterile pastures.

"Three twenty-eight's taken," I said to Garrett without looking at him. "No sight of him—take that back. Coming through the door."

Garrett stood, lost the paper, and went to his position by the bank of elevators. Peterson's eyes surveyed the room, found me, and just as quickly glanced away. Lucille was at his side, her arm around him. Not quite the material you'd envision taking into Park Suite West, but not the material you say no to after a drink or two. I buried my head in a magazine so she wouldn't see me. They went to the front counter, and Peterson turned his head over his shoulder as if searching the room. My old-fashioned girl must have told him someone had just been at the desk inquiring about him, maybe even pointed me out to him. Peterson was good. Calm. So far, he was doing exactly what I'd instructed him to do during our meeting at Starbucks.

Peterson and Lucille headed toward the bank of elevators. Garrett and Peterson exchanged words. The door opened. Peterson extended his arm. She didn't know to go in first. The woman who'd been studying her laptop screen bolted in to join them. Part of Agatha's team? Likely a lead person dispatched to follow Peterson to see what room he entered. How would Agatha's men plan to enter the room? If it were I, I'd stick on a serving jacket and knock on the door while holding a bottle of champagne.

I kept my eyes on the front door. Two men entered and headed straight to the bar. A man pulling a carry-on suitcase with a busted wheel was next. He tramped through the lobby, his suitcase clacking on the marble floor with every rotation, like waypoints marking his progress through the foyer. He was far from home, had likely battled the corporate/government world since 6:00 a.m., and had surrendered his cause. Not every day gets a checkered flag.

Here's what I didn't see: G-men coming in to protect Peterson. Just as I feared, Franklin hadn't moved fast enough.

Two suits came through the revolving door, their eyes professionally scanning the room. One held a rectangular box, the type that a champagne bottle comes in. The other held flowers. They didn't look like the type of men to deliver flowers and bubbly. They headed straight to the elevator.

I called Garrett and hit the stairs.

33

It was pretty dull after that, except Peterson peed in the bed, but you can't really blame the guy.

And Lucille screamed like a deranged banshee when they painted her dead, but you can't really blame the girl.

And Binelli proved she was more mature than me, but that's such a low bar, you can't really give her credit.

We never intended to let Agatha's men in the room. Then what? Barge in with pistols popping? It would have been nice to catch them in the act, but the consequences of misjudging the line that separates the intent of murder from the act of murder are harrowing.

I rounded the corner. Garrett had his arms straight out, gun level at the chest of Flower Man. I shouldered my gun and frisked them. The champagne box contained a gun, plastic gloves, and a thin, metal cord that could nicely slice a neck. The flowers were real, as was the camera and gun that Flower Man packed in his coat.

"I'm trying to deliver some posies here," Flower Man said when I pocketed his piece.

"And if they don't like them?" I confiscated his camera. We needed it. "You fire off a few rounds and tell them to appreciate nature?"

"Tough neighborhood, you know?" He eyed me with alarming confidence. "You guys are a perfect example of what

I mean. We go to deliver champagne and flowers and what do we get? The Oreo boys draw their piece on us. You got nothing. You know you got nothing. But me? I got something. I got a license, so how about you handing it back."

"No champagne in that box," I reminded him. "You might want to file a complaint with the liquor store."

"Frankie-T, you know there was no juice in that box?"

His partner eyed me. "Really? Chintzy little chink. Know something? The immigrants of the old days? They built this country. This new batch? They learn too fast, just wanna rip everyone off."

Someone rapped on the door. "Travis, that you?" Peterson called from the other side.

I told him we were secure and to open the door.

We followed our prisoners into the suite. Garrett kept his gun on them, but they posed no threat. The downside to our let's-not-take-any-chances-and-get-someone-killed plan was they had committed no crime. They knew this. Furthermore, they showed no signs of unraveling.

"Stinks in here," Flower Man said. He glanced at sheets that were yellowed, and then at Peterson. Devon Peterson stood by the bathroom door in tighty-whities. Lucille was in the bed with a sheet wrapped around her. She eyed me with recognition but remained frozen in confusion. "Jesus, man," Flower Man complained, "you know they got a toilet for that, right?"

"Can I go now?" Peterson asked me.

"Looks like you already did," Flower Man retorted, and he and Frankie-T shared a barroom chuckle.

"Not yet," I said, biting my cheek. "We've got a little work to do." I turned to Flower Man and Frankie-T. "You know the drill, face on the floor, hands behind your back."

"How 'bout this," Flower Man banged back. "I go home to my wife—"

Garrett took two steps and was in front of him.

"—and kids."

Garrett flashed a knife at his throat.

"Hey, hey, hey, take it easy there, midnight. I don't—"

Garrett nicked him in the neck.

Flower Man's hand shot up to his neck to apply pressure. "What'ja do that for?"

Garrett said, "Carpet."

The men eyed each other and then went face down on the green carpet. *When did green come back in style? Why?*

"Get the show going," Garrett instructed me as he stepped back. Like it was my problem.

I called Binelli. Painted the scene. She was miffed that no G-men were protecting Peterson, but we decided to sort that out later. It was actually easier without another set of alpha males in the room. Within twenty minutes, though, she arrived along with the two charmers who taxied her around downtown Saint Petersburg. There was also a third man who I presumed was the makeup artist. He tugged a hefty briefcase and avoided eye contact.

"Stinks in here," said the FBI agent who had sat in the front passenger seat. His comment was directed at me.

"You ever shower after that run?"

"That's the same tie, isn't it?" I lashed back at him.

"We got this now. You and Butch can skedaddle."

I didn't move. Decided to stay calm; count to ten and let him diffuse on his own. *One, two—*

"Hear me? Time for you to hit the door."

Three, four, five—

"We're the law, dickwad. You're amateur hour. Pack up and—"

Binelli cut in. "Give it up, Sanveski. Franklin says he can stay."

Six, seven—

"You need beauty queen to fend for you?" He dared me.

Eightnineten. "You mean this little lady you whip your dragon over every time you—"

"Stop it, you *flip*pin' idiots," Binelli commanded and knifed me a fiery look. I was disappointed that I'd let him get under my skin. I should be better than that. I plan to be someday—does that count?

I went over to Lucille to get away from it. I'd had a conversation with her while waiting for the rear guard to arrive. "Remember what I told you?" She nodded. "You'll be fine, but you won't be going home until it's all settled." We couldn't have Lucille hightailing it back to her friends and telling them grandiose tales about her trip to the States.

Sanveski confiscated their wallets. I was surprised they carried them. Binelli ran backgrounds on Flower Man and Frankie-T. Their arrogance morphed into silence when she read their records. Lucille's eyes darted frantically around the room, searching for anything of solace. Binelli instructed her to get back into the bed. The top sheet was pulled over the stained bottom sheet. The makeup artist approached her. Although I had told her this was coming, as he started his craft on her neck, she broke down, her body convulsing with sobs.

Then she did the banshee thing. Flopped around like a catfish on land. I physically restrained her while Sanveski idly smacked his gum.

Binelli intervened, murmuring soothing and indistinguishable words to her. Whatever she said took hold. The makeup artist performed his art, and we had a dead girl. Lucille had a gruesome wire cut across her neck and lay on bloodstained sheets. Rallying to the role, she rolled her open eyes back, as Binelli snapped away with the confiscated camera. A real Hallmark moment.

It wasn't without points of contention. I insisted that the shot look *precisely* how Agatha would expect it to appear. Angle. Lighting. Number of pictures. Otherwise, Agatha would smell a rat. Not only did we need Flower Man's cooperation for that, but we also needed him to send the picture, sans any code that indicated a problem, to Agatha via the regular channels.

I foresaw their cooperation as being problematic, and they did not disappoint me.

"What's in it for us?" Flower Man had demanded.

Sanveski finally got off the bench and said he'd put in a good word for the two of them—get a prosecuting attorney to lighten their sentence. They thought it over and claimed they were innocent. Sanveski explained how it wouldn't look that way when he reported they both assaulted him. He dutifully explained the charges for assaulting a federal agent. Brought up lost privileges under Homeland Security. Emptied the bag on them. They considered, thanked him for the lecture, but said they would like to talk to their attorney. They also inquired if we knew of any good coffee shops that were open late. These boys had been to the dance before.

Garrett had been leaning against a dresser. He uncrossed his arms and picked up Flower Man's wallet that Sanveski had left on top of the dresser. He stepped into the man's face and held the wallet in front of his nose.

Garrett eyed him from inches away. "You brought it on a job?"

After his girlfriend died he had zero tolerance for evil—even went looking for it.

"Why not? Delivering flowers, right?"

"You won't make that mistake again," he said in a matter-of-fact tone. Garrett flipped through the wallet, dropped it lazily on the man's feet. "Married? Kids? Mother still living?"

Flower Man blinked. Clenched his jaw.

"When I visit them, any message you'd like me to convey?"

"You don't have the balls."

"Is that your message?" Garrett said with a lace of diabolical sympathy that sent a shiver up my spine. "Because that's what they'll hear."

Flower Man sucked his cheeks in and nodded a few times as if he were digesting the man in front of him. Seeing for the first time someone in the room who spoke his language. Lucille whimpered, like an animal sensing danger.

"You're not law here," he calmly reasoned to Garrett.

Garrett kept his eye on him. "Let's see if that's an issue."

Sanveski smacked his gum.

One.

Solitary.

Pop.

I didn't like Sanveski's smart mouth, but he knew when not to use it, or in this case, how to use it.

"Bubble gum," Flower Man kept his gaze on Garrett. "What kind of deal we talking about?"

Sanveski threw out some vague promises, and they'd cooperated after that, instructing us on what shots to take and how to send the pictures.

Binelli explained, in addressing a question I had, that a bogus accident report would be generated that should keep them under the radar for a week, or enough time to bring in Agatha. I argued for them to be able to exercise supervised communication with Agatha, but I lost. Franklin had dictated the orders, and the two were to have no communication, beyond forwarding the photos. The theory being that the FBI would move quickly and wrap things up in a matter of days, before the absence of communication from his team aroused Agatha's suspicions. Binelli stated that Franklin—who was blazing hot over my ad hoc actions—was planning to meet with Peterson to ensure Peterson went through with his meeting with Walderhaden. Peterson needed to sell his case and support the illusion. Franklin didn't want to leave any room for doubt in the minds of the grand jury. I contended it wasn't necessary but saw no harm and gave in. Things had gone remarkably well. It felt odd, unsettling. As we departed the hotel, I whistled "Dixie."

I stopped. It was a jaunty, silly, and upbeat song that in no manner conveyed the future horrors of the Confederacy.

34

The Fat Man

"**S**plendor in the Grass" filled the air on cue as Phillip Agatha perused the *New York Times* that Eddie had collected for him. He neatly folded the paper and placed it on the teak dining table of the *Gail Force*. He maneuvered it slightly so that the fold was running at an exact parallel line to the edge of the table.

"The pictures," Agatha said.

Eddie handed a folder to Agatha who placed it on his left. He took a sip of coffee. The casual observer would not notice that the coffee cup sported an extra-large handle to accommodate his fingers.

"Anything unusual?" Agatha asked without opening the folder.

"No, sir." Eddie stood with his hands folded in front of him.

"Normal channels?"

"Yes, sir."

"You completed the payment to the team?"

"Yes, sir."

"If I wanted obedience and manners, I'd get a poodle. Out with it."

"There's a particular shot of the room. A wide angle."

"The point?"

"Johnnie told me this operative, he never do—did that before."

"And we should be concerned?"

"I'm just saying, this is his third job for us, and in the past, Johnnie said he never sent a wide angle shot like that."

"Johnnie has already informed me. Yet, he does not share your concern."

"I wish we could have sent Johnnie."

"I can't spare him for every job. He had his own exigent matters to attend to. Tell me, Eddie, would you change course because of that single photo."

"No. But I would because of this: I can't contact my team."

"Must I prod you for every word?"

"I called 'em. Sent encrypted e-mail. Nothing. I picked up some news item about an accident last—early this morning, a few blocks from where this went down, some pad called Park Studio. I believe it was their car. Report says two men in satisfactory condition. But I searched the hospitals, can't find anything."

"You've been up early."

"You see my point? What if they was—were set up? They been tucked away, and we can't talk to them."

"What if they were in an accident?"

"What if they *wasn't?*"

Agatha paused as if he were reconsidering his priorities. "You have not forwarded the pictures to Travis, is that correct?"

"Not until you tell me to."

"Very good. You showed him the pictures of him and Lucille?"

"Yes, sir."

"Invite Mr. Travis back on board. If there is any foul played involved, I trust you believe it stems from him. Tell him we'll deliver the final product in person and inform him that he can wire the money at that time. Place the picture of the eternally resting Lucille next to the pictures you took of them together."

"He knows we have them—those pictures. I don't think that will rattle him."

"Rattle him? Perhaps not. But if he is being the least bit disingenuous in his relationship with us, it will cause him to reevaluate what is truly important to him."

"We need more."

"Pardon me?" Agatha settled his coffee cup squarely on a coaster. He adjusted the round coaster so that it was approximately an inch from each side of the table. Not satisfied, he gave it a final nudge.

"Beachy—Travis, he just waved off the photos I showed him, the ones of him and that dish. All due respect, sir, I don't think placing those photos next to each other will mean anything to him. Did you talk to him? Mr. Philby?"

Agatha reached for an unlit cigar. He brought the clipped cigar to his lips and the waiter was at his side, torching it. He inhaled deeply and then spewed a cloud of smoke. "Nice to see you're holding me to my responsibilities. Yes, I spoke with him. He assured me he never heard of your nemesis, Mr. Jake Travis. I do believe your imagination has gotten the better part of you."

"What if he's running him?"

"Travis?"

"Yes, sir."

Agatha chuckled. "I amend my statement. Your de*li*rious imagination. Yes, what if, indeed? But rational minds must carry the day. There is no reason to believe that to be the case. He is quite upset—'ticked,' I believe you said. Killing his man in Miami was one thing. Double-dipping in Saint Kitts was entirely unfortunate."

"It was the only—"

"Do not interrupt me—you are not to blame. We did what we had to do. He could have fudged the first, but twin coffins have put him in the most delicate of situations."

Eddie crossed his arms in front of himself. "He can't touch us. His association with us guarantees that we own him for life."

Agatha balanced his cigar in the monkey ashtray. "Let's backpedal," he said evenly. "That is an interesting hypothesis you just raised. What if, indeed, he is running Travis? While we control Mr. Philby, he also possesses us, even more so if your theory that he is conducting his own operations bears any weight." He tapped the cigar needlessly on the edge of the monkey's palm. "Fascinating possibility, really. Using us without our knowledge for a greater purpose than what we pay him. Delectable. It is growing on me. What new meanings do past events carry if that were to be the case? Tell me, Eddie, where you're from, that part of—" Agatha swirled his hand in the air.

"Ohio."

"Yes, in the part of Ohio that is you, how long could such a relationship endure? A relationship where each party held a gun on the other party, unsure of each other's knowledge and intention?"

"Sometimes quite long."

"And then?"

"It would end," Eddie admitted, "as all things do."

"How?"

"Violent and fast."

"And the winner?"

"The first one to see it coming."

"Have a seat. Allow me to tell you what I foresee."

Eddie DiCampano took a seat at the table with Phillip Agatha.

35

"You need to get one of those outdoor heaters that restaurants have," Kathleen complained as she rubbed her arms.

"Just another thing to break," I replied and took a forkful of fish.

Kathleen, Morgan, Riley, and I sat around my outdoor table finishing dinner. I'd asked Riley earlier, before Kathleen arrived, to walk out to the end of the dock with me. She balked. Asked me why. I told her I had official news for her. She planted her feet. Said she wasn't going to walk that dock. She cried. I held her. She said are they sure? I said yes. She cried some more, or maybe it was one long cry; I don't know much about that.

"How long have you known?" she said, struggling unsuccessfully to stem her tears.

"Few days." *Would she be upset that I didn't tell her immediately?*

"Thank you."

"Thank you?"

She had sniffled and given me a weak shrug. "Those days."

When Kathleen finally arrived, she noticed Riley's running eyes and blemished face. She cornered me, and I confessed that I'd confirmed Karl's death. She scolded me for not waiting until she was there to break the news to Riley.

She placed her arm around Riley, and they both cried. They had walked to the end of the dock where they remained until Morgan gathered them.

The temperature fell with the sun. It was seventy, but it felt like sixty.

"I'm buying you one for Christmas," Kathleen insisted.

I shoved my plate away. "A wine of the day membership?"

"No, boofus. An outdoor heater."

"Too big. No place to store it. It'll break, and I'd rarely use it."

"It's not for you."

"You mean you're buying yourself one and shipping it to me."

"That's what I said."

"Does that mean we've said 'I do' to each other?"

She smiled. "No. It means I'm cold."

I got up, went to my bedroom, and returned with a heavy sweater. "Arms up," I said from behind her. She leaned forward and raised her arms. I dropped the sweater over her arms and tucked it down her back.

"I don't get it," Riley said to me as I reclaimed my seat. Her composure had returned, although dinner had been a subdued affair. While I'd prepared dinner, Kathleen and Morgan helped her decide how to inform family members. Kathleen also made plans to pick her up at the hotel in the morning and spend the day together. "You're just waiting for Agatha to call?"

"That's the arrangement," I said. "He texts me a picture of dead Lucille, and I wire the remaining funds." I leaned in and held her eyes. "Don't be surprised if that doesn't occur and some other instructions are communicated."

"Like what?"

"Don't know."

"Then what? After the money thing?"

"I, and you, will testify before the grand jury. We should have enough to bring him to trial. At that point, we're done until the trial."

She shook her head and took a sip of Irish coffee from my Goofy/Mickey/Donald cup. The three of them were silhouettes marching single file in front of an American flag, with Donald bringing up the rear. She had selected the cup herself, and I thought it immature of me to tell her it was my cup and that no one ever touched it except me. She was coming to terms with her dead husband, and I was worried about Donald Duck.

"You make it sound so simple," she said, holding the heavy cup with only two fingers. "I think you underestimate him. You ever find who he has on the inside?"

"No. You want to take another shot at the photographs Morgan and Kathleen showed you?"

She rolled her eyes. "I'll go *wonk*ers if see another picture. I must have flipped through a bazillion."

"We're up to nearly eight hundred," Morgan backed her up. "That's about every senator, representative, and staff photo we could come up with. We discard the women and focus on the men." I recalled that earlier Morgan had indicated he was close to seven hundred pictures. He was expanding his search.

"Nothing?" I directed my question to Riley.

"Zilcho," she said. "Oh, I mean some looked a teeny-weeny bit familiar, but only due to the sheer numbers. I didn't see anyone I could pin as the man in Hollandaise and on Karl's computer. He's got to be in with Agatha, don't you think?"

"I do."

I still harbored a theory that the man she and Karl recognized was an undercover agent. I'd tried to convince her of that when we had dinner at Mangroves and hadn't made any progress. I wasn't going to rehash it with her. If she ever did finger the man, my first stop would be with Binelli to see if that person was on the payroll. I'd bet heavy dough that was the case. I poured myself a refill of red wine and felt strangely indifferent to it all. I said, "Keep looking." It was a wasted comment, intended to fill my empty thoughts.

I'd been out of sorts all day. Despite the improv with Lucille and Devon Peterson, things were going swimmingly well. Yet the whole affair felt like a single note that had gone slightly flat while the original tone remained, creating a disharmonious and dissonant timbre. Maybe I was being irrational; what's wrong with a plan that goes the distance every once in a while? I'd even taken a late afternoon stroll on the beach, hoping for an epiphany. The tide was out, and the receding water had left shallow pools and narrow streams that cut miniature canyons into the sand. Dolphins were jumping in the shallow water, and that rarely happens. I took a few snaps with my phone, a sure sign of the doldrums, although I got lucky once and caught Flipper clean out of the water. I'd told Morgan about it—my picture of a dolphin jumping in shallow water—and he'd said he'd witnessed it himself on only a few occasions.

Riley splintered my thoughts. "How long do I need to stay in the hotel? It's great and all, but I need to see some family."

"For your protection, likely a couple more days," I told her, "depending on when and what we hear from Agatha."

"Will I be safe from him even if a grand jury indicts him?"

"As safe as you'll ever be." It sounded weak, and I scrambled to add some substance to it. "He'll know that the feds are watching him, and that more than one person is testifying against him. His lawyers will instruct him to batten down the hatches."

After dinner, we relocated to the screened porch. Kathleen lit a solitary candle and Hadley III slithered through the cat door that Morgan had recently cut into the aluminum bottom of the screened door. A mortally wounded gecko was in her mouth, and she treated it with great concern, as if she wished it no further harm. She placed it under Morgan's chair and then hesitantly lowered her hindquarters, as if she hadn't a clue what to do next.

The burner phone that Eddie gave me signaled an incoming text. I had an audience, so I read it out loud. "Beachy. Jobs done. Mr. Agatha enjoys your company and would like to personally present the finished product to you. Tomorrow. Four o'clock. The Gail Force."

"No picture?" Morgan said.

"That's it."

Kathleen's eyes were on mine as she asked the simple question we all use when we cast a wide net of concern. "Is everything OK?"

"I'm sure Agatha just wants to gloat," I replied as my thoughts forged ahead.

Another trip to Agatha would require additional planning on our part. Garrett had opted for a night run in lieu of dinner, and I was eager for him to return. He often exercised more than once a day or at odd times; I'd known him to do five miles at midnight. He believed it foolish to condition your body to expect peak performance within a tight window every day. I thought it was foolish to exercise during cocktail hour. Plus—and you can also check this out—one of the lost tablets explicitly forbids exercising past 5:00 p.m.

He finally came around the corner, after rinsing off under the outdoor shower. We crafted our next move. Morgan called Nicky, who informed him that, fortunately for us, his party—the one he was concerned we have his boat back for—had cancelled, and *Fishy Lady* was available. Morgan secured morning tickets while I convinced Kathleen that it wasn't too cold to sit at the end of the dock. She begrudgingly agreed, although as we strolled down the dock hand in hand, it was like tugging a reluctant pet.

"It *is* cold out here. Gusty." She grumbled as we sat next to each other on the bench, her arms wrapped in front of her, tightening the sweatshirt. She had a point—the end of the dock always caught the razor's edge of the wind. "Get up," I ordered her as I stood.

I took her hand, gave her a heave, and led her a few feet out from the bench. I positioned us on the dock; my back against the bench with Kathleen nestled between my spread legs. She leaned into my chest. I wrapped my arms around her and brought her deeper into me. Her hair frolicked in the wind like wisps of electricity, tingling my face.

"This," she said as she tilted her head back onto my right shoulder, "is nice. We haven't done this before, have we?" The moon's light reflected off the scrubbed surface of the water and created a sea of silver flashes. Beyond the red channel marker, and across the bay, the drawbridge was rising.

"Don't think so."

"I'd remember."

"I'd forget."

"No, you wouldn't," she countered.

"I know."

"Why do you think he wants to see you?"

"Entertainment. Who knows?"

"Will she be there?"

"Who?" I was upset with myself for playing games with her.

"You know."

"I suppose. She's constantly by his side."

"You like her, don't you?"

I moved my head back and tried to look her in the face, but she kept her head buried.

"Don't," she said. "This is easier not looking at you."

"Where's this coming from? I told you everything about her."

"I know you did. That's how I know you like her. You confessed like a guilty schoolboy."

"There was nothing to confess. Listen—"

"Jake?" She jerked her head away and looked at me. She positioned herself Indian-style and faced me, the wind blowing her hair toward *Impulse* as if it were reaching out to touch the boat. "Always tell me, OK?"

"You know I—"

"Even the little things."

"Relax. I don't worry about you and that toad-faced biology professor who shows up at all your class readings."

Her hand shot to her mouth. "Oh, my gosh, who told you? Sophia?"

"Funny. I'll break his glasses."

She dropped her hand. "I'm not you."

"What does that mean?"

"You don't have to worry about me."

"Then why the double standard for—"

She silenced me by touching her fingers to my lips. I took her head in my hands and brought her face close to mine. "There's never anyone else," I said. "I'm not interested in eking out crumbs of emotion and slivers of commitment."

And then Kathleen threw this down: "I wonder if it's sustainable, if disenchantment is inevitable."

Swear to almighty, when things are humming along in your life, a woman will throw up speed bumps. *Disenchantment?* I didn't see it. At best, life's a hundred-yard dash. Who even uses that word?

An intelligent reply didn't surface, so I went with, "You stupid, crazy girl. Shall we apportion our lust for the sake of sustainability?"

She shook her head with a salacious smile. "We shall not."

She settled back down facing the water. She lifted her hand and pointed out toward the horizon that the tarp didn't block. She did a twirling motion with her finger.

"Dialing God?" I asked.

"I've rearranged the stars and carved our initials in the sky. If you ever feel yourself drifting, look up."

"At the stars?"

"Maybe they're angels—what do we really know?"

"For starters, stars are exploding balls of hydrogen and helium that—"

"No, they're not. Besides, what can a poet do with hydrogen and helium? You think those gases can stir the soul and fire the heart?"

I didn't have an answer, but I knew what her salacious smile stirred. I rolled over on top of my mystery girl and was deciding whether to initiate the dock—it *was* chilly and other people were present—when the decision was made for us.

"Ahem."

Riley Anderson towered over us for such a diminutive girl. Just as she had crashed my outdoor shower, the woman displayed conspicuous timing.

"Morgan said you saw dolphins jump today." She shrugged as if to indicate her untimely interlude was Morgan's fault.

"I did." I sat up. Kathleen did likewise and, in a wasted effort, brushed her hair off her face.

"He said you got lucky on one, got it completely out of the water."

"I did."

"I asked if I could see it. He handed me your phone." She pulled it out of her sweatshirt pocket like she was extracting a hidden gem. "So he gave it to me. I hope you don't mind." She hit the screen a few times and showed it to me. "You took this today, right?" It was a picture of a dolphin.

"I did."

"I scrolled through your pictures. Pretty hard not to, know what I mean?" She crinkled her face.

"I do." That's a first cousin of "I did," so my streak was still alive.

"I came across this." She shoved my phone in front of my eyes. It was the picture of Kent Edward Franklin III walking around the car outside of Tony's on N. I'd taken it, on a whim, from the upstairs balcony as he and Binelli were leaving.

"What are you telling me, Riley?"

"It's him."

36

"Him?"

"The man I saw at Hollandaise," Riley gushed out impatiently. "The same man Karl recognized as being in a picture with Agatha, you know, with a dead girl on a bed. Who is he? Why's he on your phone?"

"A high-ranking agent in the FBI. Listen to me." I stood, leaving behind what might have been. I'd been doing that a lot lately with Kathleen. "I told you at Mangroves that the FBI was likely running an operation against Agatha. This confirms—"

"Why would he be at the crime scene, you know, the picture on the computer?"

"I don't know. I'll find out."

"You know him?" She sounded hurt, like I'd been playing her, holding back.

"Met him only briefly," I lied. "Took the picture on a whim. I have a contact in the bureau, and she introduced us. I'll get in touch and see how he's involved."

While I'd been talking to her, my mind had raced ahead, trying to keep up with the game. Franklin had kept me in the dark. I didn't dare tell Riley that. Not yet. It was coming into focus; he was the man running the operations against Agatha and was responsible for two dead agents. He needed a home run to salvage his reputation. I was his slow pitch down the middle. I could only assume that he'd chosen not to tell me, as I didn't qualify under "need to know." Furthermore, had I known, I might have passed on the assignment.

Did Binelli know? I doubted it. He fogged both of us.

We marched down the dock and ran into Morgan at the seawall coming out to see us.

"My sister's cruise mates finally got back to her." He directed his words to me.

"Who are you talking about?" I said.

"The divorce—"

"Right. The gag order. This must be Franklin's night."

"Why's that?"

"Nothing. What do you got?"

"The divorce attorney said Franklin used to be married to the bottle and struck his ex a few times. He's a teetotaler now. But during the divorce he didn't want to take any chances that she'd bring it up. He wanted it buried along with some miscellaneous business deals."

"They told your sister that?"

"Exchanged it for the third week of March. Prime sailing time."

"Tell her I owe her."

Nothing Morgan had said gave me any concern. It was easy to understand why Franklin didn't want his duel with alcohol known. Nor were outside business interests a concern. It would be shocking if a man in his position and steerage had not tumbled across business opportunities in his lifetime. Mary Evelyn's report had previously indicated that Franklin was wealthy beyond his pay stub.

An osprey, caught in the moonlight, cleared the top of the palm trees. A fish in its talons waved its tail like a busted rudder of a bomber on a night raid. The fish had no knowledge of its predicament. "Do me a favor?" I said to Morgan, deciding that knowledge was an underrated power. "Go back in. See if you can find what those business relations are. Names, partnerships, LLCs—anything you got, we'll take."

"I'll try. But she suspects they only gave her quasi-public information, and that well's running dry. It's likely the issues with his ex and the bottle made the rumor mill long ago. I'll call her in the morning."

I gave a disapproving shake of my head.

"Right."

He left a voice mail and then ran Riley back to the hotel. On her way out the door, she hummed an up-tempo rendition of "The Boxer." Garrett went to Morgan's, which is where he stays when he visits. He insists on giving Kathleen and me our privacy and keeps clothing and gear at Morgan's, including his kite-surfing equipment. "Call her," he instructed me on his way out the door, "make sure she's straight with us." Kathleen, still in my sweatshirt, decided to return downtown; something about work she had to finish. She took off after telling me not to be a stranger. I wondered what she meant by that. That would have to wait for another day. That's a specialty of mine—saving the big issues for another day.

I was alone and wandered out to the seawall, a solitary figure in the ghostly moonlight. The tide was out and the air thick with the lusty smell of saltwater. The channel marker's reflection cast a flashing red straight line on the water. It followed me as I paced the seawall, as if its beating message was for me, and me only. I punched Binelli's number. I spilled what Riley said before Binelli got a word in, telling her that Riley identified Franklin as the man at Hollandaise and in the picture on Karl's computer.

"I know," she finally managed to squeeze in.

"Come again?"

"He told me—"

"When do I become privy to this information?" I started pacing as the palms rustled in the breeze.

"Easy, OK? He just told me this evening."

"What exactly did he say?"

"He's running Agatha. I was getting ready to call you. He—"

"Little turd ball lied to both of us." I'd needed to maintain calmness and a sense of control with Riley. Not so with Binelli, and my insides churned with disgust that the man had used me.

"Give me a minute?"

"I'm off your payroll, doll. You can talk all day."

"You think I'm happy about—?"

"You used me."

"I did—"

"You're Franklin's vixen." I regretted it the moment it came out, but it was too late, like trying to stuff the toothpaste back in the tube. It just doesn't work.

"Piss off."

I blew out my breath. "Tell me." I picked up a palm frond and tossed it into the bay.

The air was quiet. A dolphin blew. Then another. I sensed the cruciality of the next few seconds in our relationship and was relieved when she came back in. "Do not interrupt me. He's been trying to get Agatha for years. Franklin even showed up at one of the crime scenes when he was undercover. But it was after the fact. He never had enough to get it past a grand jury. The whole thing went back-burner. When you appeared, he fired it up again."

"Riley thinks there was a dead girl in the bed. Why not finger Agatha for murder at that point? Wrap it up?"

"A body was there when Franklin arrived and gone by the time agents came. No body, no murder."

"Hollandaise—the restaurant in Miami where the Andersons where instructed to go?"

"They would have been fine if they kept that meeting. Franklin said McKeen was an alias for an agent he thought about sending in. Then you—"

"Why not tell us?" I demanded.

"Need-to-know basis."

"Anything in the world that doesn't cover?"

"Not in my universe. Think of it. Franklin doesn't know you, and he wants to protect my career. He told you, and me, what we needed to know. That's how these guys operate."

"Why the urge to confess tonight?"

"He said it would come out at the grand jury hearing, so you and I might as well find out now. He assumes you'll get a picture, and your job is wrapped up. And don't give me any of that pissy-ant stuff that I withheld anything from you. You have no right talking to me like that."

"I didn't get a picture." Something large stirred the waters.

"What?"

"No picture. Instead, I got an invite to appear on the Gail Force at four tomorrow. Presumably to see the picture."

"So you get the proof tomorrow. It doesn't alter the outcome. Listen, I had no idea."

"Forget it," I said. "I'm bad—we're good. Do we trust Franklin?"

"He was under no obligation to tell me this. He could have waited until you were ready to confront the grand jury. He told us as soon as it was practical to do so."

"Isn't he a little high up to go undercover?" I inquired, although I was already tiring of my questions.

"Franklin started as a field agent—it's in his blood. He used his divorce as a ruse that he needed money. He arranged for a chance meeting. You know the guy he told you about who snitched on Agatha? Guy who provided us the code? He put Franklin and Agatha together without Agatha knowing he was being run. Franklin gets a monthly stipend to keep the feds uninterested in Studio Four-Twenty. In return, we've been trying to collect enough evidence to put Agatha, and his clientele, away for a long time. A sweet little thing when you view it from above; Agatha is paying Franklin so that Franklin can eventually shut Agatha down. The money goes into the widow fund."

"Two dead agents," I reminded her to temper her admiration. "He's creating the widows he's raising money for."

"Yeah, well, we're not the first to get swept into that circle. I'm better off not knowing, and he…he's been instrumental in my career. He knows there's certain knowledge that will only be detrimental to me. He's got to be on the hot seat for it. I don't *want* to know."

Franklin had likely overplayed his hand and provided Agatha with too much information. He had no way of knowing Agatha would take such draconian action.

"I'll need to complete the final wire," I said, returning to Binelli and business.

"The money's good—Franklin's confident he can recover it all. I'll text you the instructions."

"Franklin still got the reins, or is someone else driving the Conestoga?"

"Franklin's trying to hold on to his job. You got it now? He needs to wrap this up, not lose any more men, get the money back, and have a rock-solid case to present to the grand jury."

We disconnected. During the conversation, I realized the fleeting thought I couldn't hold during my second meeting with Binelli and Franklin. I'd gotten distracted, my eyes meeting Binelli's in the mirror, neither of us backing down. I had told Franklin about my meeting with Agatha, about Eddie and Henny. But I'd left Christina out. There was someone else I left out. Not by design, but by simple omission.

Franklin: *With what you've told me, and when we catch Agatha's men, Eddie, Henny, and their photographer, Johnnie, Phillip Agatha is finished.*

I had never mentioned Johnnie's name. Positive of that. Furthermore, the feds didn't know about Darling; Mary Evelyn had unearthed his name. Franklin had made the same mistake I'd made while talking with Agatha. That slip-up alone should have led me to see the connection, and I wondered, again, what I was missing now.

37

Morgan, Garrett, and I headed to the marina where Nicky was waiting for us on *Fishy Lady*. He forewent the documents, and we settled on a handshake. We had no way of knowing if the *Gail Force* was going to pull anchor or not. If so, Garrett and Morgan would again shadow me. If not, they'd never untie the boat, although we would compensate Nicky for the time.

Binelli had texted me during the night to confirm that Peterson had delivered. He met with Walderhaden, and as Franklin had prophesied, Charles Walderhaden had no interest in the details. Zebra Electronics would keep the contract. I'd reevaluated my earlier doubts and was glad Franklin had insisted that Peterson follow through with Walderhaden. If Agatha harbored any doubts regarding my authenticity and decided to investigate, at least the deal I brokered was legitimate. Daniel Vigh had become a wealthy nonparticipating beneficiary—another unintended consequence. My desire to help Riley Anderson was rippling into a tangled affair.

Henny frisked me at the base of the gangplank. I told him I found the cutest pair of sneakers for him. He didn't even validate my comment with a grunt. He led me to the aft deck where Agatha conducted his business. He wasn't there, nor did I see Christina. I collapsed onto a lounge chair in the shade, leaned my head back, and closed my eyes.

I'd spent most of the night auditioning wild scenarios in my head of what I was missing. Nothing earned a call-back. Toward morning a mad theory, born from boredom, a penchant for creativity, and a desire to vindicate a sleepless night, metastasized in my sleep-deprived mind. My theory had no beginning, but the ending was a classic; a boat-load of money docked in someone's account. Daniel Vigh. *What if that wasn't an unintended consequence?* I tried to work backward from there, but nothing broke free from the cobwebbed thoughts.

"Mr. Travis," Phillip Agatha beckoned from behind me. A spasm tingled my skin as a light sleep vacated my body like an intruder who had been caught. "I didn't mean to wake you."

Agatha sat on his throne, cocktail in hand. I joined him at the table.

"Mission accomplished?" I said.

"Up late last night?" He sallied back at me.

"I find your boat unusually relaxing."

"Delightful. I can think of no greater compliment."

"I never received a picture."

"I assure you, the mission—as you say—was a success. Eddie will provide you shortly with solid proof. You will then wire the remaining funds, and I shall honor my word and rebate you two million. Would you care to unwind? We're taking an overnight journey to the Keys. There's a gallery in Key West that is importing some items for me, a unique new talent in Colombia. I would find your company most welcome and stimulating."

"Do I have a choice, or is Eddie fixing me a drink as we talk?"

"That again? Certainly such a minor vicissitude won't derail our relationship. The choice is entirely yours."

"I'd be honored."

Another twenty-four hours on the *Gail Force* would be advantageous. It would provide me the opportunity to gather more information about Agatha's operation that could prove useful when testifying before a grand jury. It would also allow me a final shot to convince Christina that her future was elsewhere. I had a home-run plan for her, her sisters, and her mother that might entice her to leave. If she stayed, I feared the legal system would derail her dreams for years. That was putting an optimistic bent on her future.

"Christina will be accompanying us. You do so enjoy her company."

Did the man read minds? "You mistakenly believe I have more than a casual business interest in Christina."

"Do I? Recall our conversation when I told you about my pet goat? The gale force tests us in many ways, Jake. The rushing wind of emotion, in the presence of another person, makes it difficult to hold onto those whom we leave on far-away shores."

"I'll make a note of it."

"Your insouciance does not fool me."

"Baffles me."

"Perhaps, you, too, avoid the reflective glass. There will be a few other guests—art patrons and dedicated buyers—joining us. Dinner will be at eight." He checked his watch. "We depart in twenty-two minutes. You will have your usual room."

"Do all your fifteen-million-dollar clients get a bon voyage cruise?"

"You are thirteen, remember?" He stood up. "Eddie will be formalizing the conclusion of our business. I look forward to spending the evening hours in your company."

He took a few steps and twisted back to me. "It's formal. You'll find your closet sufficiently stocked to meet your needs. White, I believe, although that wasn't my call. Do let the staff know if there is anything you require."

He walked away, waving his cane like a drunken conductor's baton. I started to help myself to a drink when Spero appeared and insisted on performing the task himself. Despite our bonding over the infirmaries of our respective left sides, my eyes never left his hands. I took a seat in a shaded cushy aft chair as the yacht's diesels emitted a throaty rumbling from beneath me.

One drink later, Eddie plopped down across from me and tossed a red folder onto a table between our chairs. He placed a shoulder bag on the deck next to him.

"Open it," he commanded.

"You're not carving the roast beef at dinner tonight, are you?"

"Open it."

It contained eight-by-tens of Lucille in the bedroom. There were also pictures of Lucille and me the night I'd selected her—in case I'd forgotten or misconstrued that salient point.

"For my photo album?" I asked as I winced and quickly turned away from the pictures. I didn't want Eddie to think I wasn't shocked by the brutal act.

"You killed her."

"You treat all your clients in this manner?"

"That ain't your concern. This is: wire the money." He extracted a laptop from his bag and placed it on the table, facing me.

I hoped Binelli came through for me. I punched in the numbers and turned the laptop back around so that it faced Eddie.

"Your turn, MAC Man."

"You wire us the money?"

"I did."

"What you do, remember all those routing numbers and stuff?"

"God does not distribute his gifts evenly," I told him. "You owe me two million."

"Not so fast. Your money lands. Then we wire."

I reached into his bag. He started to protest but caught himself. I rummaged around, found a pen, and scribbled some figures on a piece of paper.

"Here." I shoved it at him.

He took it and shook his head in appreciation. "Hey, you wanna keep these?" He picked up one of the pictures of Lucille wrapped in bloody sheets and held it up.

I walked away before I lost control.

In the pilothouse, I yakked with the captain until nearly seven. If he was concerned that anyone was following him, or even aware, he didn't let on. He was a man of the water and a welcome reprieve from the rest of the boat.

Dinner at eight meant cocktails at seven. I wasn't sure what the pairings were, but a couple of the women appeared to be top-shelf trophy wives or hired companions. The men were older and bored with the sound of anyone's voice except their own. A guitar player, perched on a stool, strummed away, his shaved head down, swinging slightly side to side with the beat of his own instrument. Next to him, a square-shouldered man with a Texas field of greased hair had Christina backed up against the rail.

"Excuse me," I squeezed between her and Vitalis. She was in a strapless white dress that had a slit on her right side that stopped halfway past her knee. The top of the dress gathered under her breasts and was sequined with small, jagged colored stones. A bracelet on her right wrist bore the same stones. "Sorry for the interruption." I touched her elbow. "We need to talk. I'm—"

"You're interrupting," Vitalis protested.

"I apologized, Slick." I shifted my attention to Christina. "I'm not comfortable with an abortion. Let's search for a common ground."

Vitalis cut judgmental eyes at Christina and grunted. "You two apparently have some discussing to do." He stomped off to the bar.

"There's no need for that," Christina chided me, although her face battled a smile. "I'm entirely capable of handling myself. It's my job to be polite and entertain the guests."

"He's a dull and stupid man."

"You don't know that."

"I'm a guest."

"Tell me, for I forget, where we are in our relationship. Oh, that's right, I'm a snitch for Phillip."

"You do kiss the man's robe."

"I do no such thing."

"Just an observation."

Her eyes narrowed. "Is this why you were rude to our guest? To come over here and be rude to me?"

"No, I came over here because there's no one else on the boat I'd rather talk to than you."

"Then say something nice."

"I respect your opinion. If you want the abortion, I'll support you."

She swatted me on my arm, and her smile broke free. "Thanks to your comment, everyone's going to talk about us.

Don't look, but he's already spreading the virus. The woman he's with is trying not to stare. Besides, it's not funny. Phillip's not paying me to be the butt of innuendo."

"Who are our houseguests?"

"Potential buyers. Phillip wines and dines them on the way there and back. Most have previously expressed interest in purchasing multiple pieces." She snatched a wisp of hair prancing in front of her eyes and then let it go. "You came up in a conversation I overheard he had with Eddie."

"Tell me about it."

"Buy me a drink."

"They're free."

"Pretend they're not, will you?"

Although I assumed her last comment was meant to be light banter, that was not how it sounded.

We meandered—recall, Kathleen didn't think I could do that—over to the bar where Spero presented Christina with her signature drink. I placed my tumbler on the bar, and he poured a Jameson on a single rock into a new glass. "Special Reserve," he said. "I ordered it for you."

"Sláinte," I said and raised my glass. It was awkward knowing the man would soon be searching for a new job. Employment aboard the *Gail Force* would be a difficult gig to replicate.

I was about to probe Christina for what she overheard, when a waiter maneuvered through the crowd, ringing a bell. Like actors in a play, we all straggled around the table, peeking at embossed name cards that were folded on charger plates. The plates bore double red flags inside a wide blue brim.

It was boy, girl, boy, girl. Christina was to my right. On my left was a woman with butch blond hair, rouged lips, and a diamond shaft around her neck. She introduced herself as "Brooklyn." As the waiter leaned over and removed her plate, Brooklyn inquired if I'd brought any weed on board.

"Afraid not."

"Do you think we can score some in Key West?" She sounded like a kid on Christmas Eve.

"Score?"

"I've never been there. Perhaps you can help me."

Agatha rescued me as he ceremoniously rose and presented an opening toast. During dinner, Brooklyn and I chatted with our neighbors across the table, a pleasant couple from Lantana, just south of Palm Beach. He had just unloaded his nursing homes and purchased a new house from a couple whose children were moving them into a nursing home. He rambled about nursing homes all night. Christina worked the group to her right. We exchanged niceties during dinner but said little else. Our legs touched a few times. I wanted to know what she overheard between Agatha and Eddie, but didn't dare question her during dinner. I kept my face plastered with pleasantness, never cussed, learned a lot about nursing homes, and was duly impressed with my conversational agility. Still, the nattering was drudgery. Being physically constrained by a seat made it strategically difficult to withdraw from the droning conversations. At best, I would have lasted a day in Victorian England. Agatha concluded dinner by proclaiming we were free to "mingle…get to know those whom we are blessed to share the sacred passage with, and fill our lungs until they burst with the sensuous tropic air."

"Take a walk with me?" I half-asked and half-instructed Christina when we stood.

"You heard my orders." She smoothed her dress. "It's mingle time."

"Mingle with me. I have an offer to make you."

"Let me guess. I tell you first what I overheard Phillip and Eddie talking about, and then you make your so-called offer."

"Were you always this cynical?"

"You're rubbing off on me."

I didn't know whether that was in reference to our junior-high leg contact during dinner or not. We finessed away from the crowd, although the chords from a guitar followed us.

"Your guess is wrong," I told her when we stopped. Her back was against the gunwale of the yacht. "My offer comes first. I want you off this boat."

"I can't—"

"Listen to me." I stepped into her. "You need to leave. I can find you another job. Money's not an issue."

"Why?"

"Because this is a foul business. I'm fine with the job that Agatha did for me. But these things have a way of ending abruptly. You could be out of work very quickly."

"No, I mean, why do you care about me?"

"Do I need a reason?"

Good God, Jake. Can you possibly say anything with less heart?

She spun around and faced the dark waters, her arms crossed tight in front of her.

I wanted to say something, but my mind was racked with too much self-doubt to formulate a coherent thought. I took a step so that I was beside her, both of us facing the empty sea.

"He said you were too calm," Christina said, staring out over the water.

"Who?"

"Eddie. That's what you want, right?" She spun her head to me. "Me to tell you what I overheard?" The breeze, added by the *Gail Force* doing eighteen knots into a steady southwest winds, strung her hair out wildly behind her, like it was trying to pull her away from me. "They didn't know I was listening. I was coming into the stateroom and stopped just outside. Eddie said you barely flinched when he showed you the picture. Said you were too calm. What picture did he show you?"

"I can't say."

Her eyes narrowed. "Why don't you trust—?"

"Because you need to trust me." I was so deep into the forest of lies I had no clue where I was.

Keep it simple.

She needed to be off the boat. When the ship went down, she would be drilled endlessly about her knowledge of Agatha's affairs. I wasn't sure what she knew, but at the very least it would be the end of her gravy train, not to mention legal expenses and possible jail time. An overzealous district attorney might even go after her for accessory to murder. My conundrum was that I couldn't tell her about Agatha's extracurricular activities without imparting information that might come back and be used against her should she decide to stay. Furthermore, like that neighbor's pet snake, I didn't entirely trust her. I'd come too far to blow the mission during landing. The less she knew, the better off she was. The better off I was. Keep things on a need to know. The Franklin manifesto.

But a darker fear lingered in the peripheral of my imagination.

Agatha was a highly functioning, yet deeply disturbed man—an iniquitous combination. A real whack-job. If she learned he employed murder to meet his objectives, he might make a picture out of her. He had to keep knowledge of the inner sanctum of his operation within a tight circle. Christina was a bright woman, but my bet was that Agatha had worked hard to deceive her and not allow her entry into that circle.

I plowed ahead. "When we get back to Miami, let's—"

"Eddie said you were too calm with death."

"What?" I stalled, knowing where she was headed.

"He told Phillip that you were 'too calm with death'—those were his words—and 'that wasn't right.' What did he mean by that? Too calm with death?"

"I don't know—"

"Who died?"

"I don't—"

"Stop lying!" She shoved me away with her hand.

"Come away with me." It came out before I had a chance to consider the implications of the words.

She froze for a second and then demanded, "Why do you say things like that?"

"I care for you. We—"

"Stop it! Do you hear me? Do you hear you? *Care* for me? You have another."

"That doesn't mean—"

"Tell me who died."

"I can't tell you."

"You can. You won't."

"I—"

"Lies. Just leave. *Leave*, you liar. *Leave*."

I took her face in my hands. She jerked away so that our eyes couldn't meet.

"Look at me," I commanded.

I wanted her eyes—I got them. But they were a fiery combination of anger and hurt. "You're no good for me," she declared with resolution. "Don't you see that? I was fine until you came along. I'm not some—"

I brought her face into mine. I kissed her hard. I kissed her as I'd wanted to when she'd closed her eyes, prepping herself for her first taste of a chili dog, as I'd wanted to when she'd held up the copper necklace at the bazaar and pleaded, "But do you like them on *me*?" I kissed her as I wanted to when she appeared as a hologram at my hotel door, the split second before she forced a smile.

The hell am I doing? Make her think that I love her in order to get her off the boat? Then what? What comical God invented a game we are powerless to resist yet equally powerless to win? Agatha's words from earlier in the day echoed in my head—*rushing wind of emotion.*

I pulled away and leaned into her so that my mouth was at her ear. "Come with me—off the boat." I didn't know how much of that was me acting the part that was necessary to get her off the boat and how much of it was real. There are things we will never know.

She gave a slight shake of her head. "I can't. You'll never love me."

Tell her I love her. Who says I don't? Say it, and get the hell out of no man's land—the hell off the boat.

The truth is revealed by as much as what we don't say as what we do say. For while I held her in the moist tropic air, where our words would fall silent upon the open water, *"remember us"* possessed me, like a chorus riding the waves.

"Thank you," she said with kind resignation, "for not lying." She pulled away so our eyes met. "Why the effort? I'm fine on my own, and I'll be fine without you. Let's stop the charade, shall we? I'm perfectly happy here. Don't bat me around like a cat's toy because you can't make up your mind. I'm—"

"He kills people, Christina. That's what Eddie was talking about. I hired him to blackmail someone, and he did it with murder. Eddie—"

"I don't believe you."

"—showed me the proof. It was a picture and part of the deal." Her hand shot up to her mouth. "I see the picture and then wire the final installment. Eddie must not have liked my calm reaction to a gruesome photograph, although I did my best to turn away."

Guess I decided to tell her. You can file this away: if fake love doesn't work, stick to the facts. Was it the right thing to do? I wasn't sure, but my words were tumbling out faster than my brain was processing the implications: my mouth, again, engaging before my brain. Words without thought— they are the best and worst you will ever hear or say.

"I don't believe you," she repeated with accusing eyes.

"Look around, doll. You think he supports this by selling numbered prints? Think I was the first?"

She backed away from me. "You're lying." Her arms were at her sides as if prepping for a skirmish.

"You block yourself from asking the unpleasant questions," I accused her. "What's Eddie's role in Agatha's life? How about Henny? What do you think—he keeps those street thugs on board for their artistic consideration?"

"You knew this?"

"It's what I hired him for."

"You lying bastard." She stepped back into me. "Tell me the truth, or are you so twisted you haven't a clue what it is?"

"Listen to me. That *is* the truth. He——"

She slapped me hard across the left cheek. "Not about him, about *you*. I don't believe you hired him, knowing he would kill someone. You're not that man."

I resisted the urge to touch my left cheek that tingled with heat. The girl packed some power. "Agatha was recommended to my employer," I said, struggling to keep my voice controlled. "We know what he does. He blackmails people with incriminating pictures, and murder is the most incriminating of all."

"Liar." She gave me a punch-push with her right hand. She turned and took a step away but whirled back around toward me. She flipped up her hand; done with the whole mysterious affair. "Why," she said, her voice calm and flat like a tempest that had run its course, "do you always lie?"

"I didn't mislead you about the chili dogs, did I?"

She shook her head in disbelief. "You're the only joke here."

"You need to trust me. That's all I can say."

She started to talk but clammed up. She eyed me with curiosity, as if seeing me for the first time or, I hoped, seeing me in a new light. "Did you help kill someone?"

"You have to trust——"

"Answer my question. You know I'm suspicious of you. I told you I sided with Eddie, and not to hurt Phillip."

"Trust me."

"This is stupid."

"Have faith in me."

"Why?"

"Remember the chili dogs."

"We're back to that?" she said in an incredulous tone. "That's our rallying cry?"

"It was cheap. Available."

That earned a reflexive smile that quickly dissolved as if she were embarrassed it had snuck out. She held my gaze for a few seconds and then blew her breath out. "I knew there was more money going out than I could imagine coming in. Did I think he was capable of murder? No." She turned back out toward the water and spoke into the night. "I don't know—maybe I purposely kept my eyes tight. He pays me so well. I'm so close to getting my sisters' college funding secured. I want that more than anything. To give them an education and my mother a life where she can stand on the other side of the table. Maybe I just didn't want to know. But you," she said, skewering me with a twin look of bewilderment and pain. "You insult me by trying to have me believe you willingly participate in the murder of innocent people. Tell me the truth, or I'll cast my lot with Phillip and see where the chips fall. Tell him that you're filling my head with wild tales of blackmail and murder."

"No, you won't."

"No," she replied, as if she was disappointed in the sound of her own voice. "I won't."

"You need to—"

"Shhh—" Her fingers were on my lips. "Not again. Not ever. I'm so sorry, but I can't. Don't you see that? Everything he's done for me? And now you tell me he murders people? You can't expect me to read between your lines with enough confidence to believe your tale and toss everything else away.

You need to trust *me*. I can handle whatever you say, but not your lies."

You know the old saying—a good chili dog can only take you so far.

I told her everything.

I had to. I was tired of lying to her. I knew that by divulging my mission to her I was crossing one of those bridges that only goes one way. There was no return trip. Life is full of those bridges. Some are well marked, but most are not. You invariably stumble across the big ones on your own, with no guidance or advice on whether to proceed or not. Such bridges demand purposeful strides.

She took her time digesting the information and lobbed a few questions about Agatha. I softened the blow as much as I could, emphasizing that Agatha himself never harmed a soul. His distance from the crime didn't absolve him of guilt, but I couldn't afford to have her lose her composure in his presence.

"I had no idea," she said. Her hand rested on the rail, her fingers opening and closing. She shifted her weight.

"I know you didn't."

"Do you?" Her eyes implored me. "You don't think I should have seen it? That I—"

"You have no fault here," I assured her. "He's a bright man and works diligently to keep everyone in the dark. There was no way for you to have known."

"Lucille?"

"She'll be returned to her home as soon as possible."

"It's dirty money, isn't it? What he pays me. It's blood money."

"You had no way of—"

"Oh my God, it's blood money. I'm so ashamed."

"Don't be. You—"

"How do I leave?" She abruptly adapted to her new reality.

"When we return to Miami, I'll book you a flight."

"Will he come after me?"

"I don't think so."

I momentarily debated protecting Christina as much as I was giving sanctuary to Riley. Christina would need to view the same pictures that Riley had viewed. She might be able to identify other persons of interest that Agatha had performed jobs for. She would likely be called to testify against Agatha. Best not to tell her that now. It was too great a leap to go from admiring the man to prosecuting him. I emphasized to her the importance of maintaining her relationship with Agatha and giving him no cause for alarm.

"My sisters," she blurted out after my lecture. "And my mother. I'll never find another job that pays me so well."

"I've got good news on that front. As part—"

"Mr. Travis," Agatha rounded the corner. "There you are. And Christina, perhaps you should attend to our guests."

"I was just on my way," Christina replied, properly admonished. She said it quickly, her tone revealing her guilt.

"You may wish to stop by a mirror first, my dear."

Agatha observed Christina as she hastened away. He turned on me, "Tell me what unsettling news you imparted to my beautiful associate that caused her face to contort with such conflict."

"I told her fairy tales weren't real."

He eyed me as if he were truly befuddled, his great mind finally stumped. "Why, man, would you say such a thing?"

38

Garrett, Morgan, and I sat at a bar on Whitehead Street that used to be the Pan Am ticket office. That was back in the day when people were in awe at the glory of flying. They were mesmerized at the dimension of being in two places in one day without using more than a spoonful of that day to span the distance. Now, we routinely split a day with a thousand miles.

When I awoke that morning, the *Gail Force* was docked in Key West. Eddie had informed me the previous night that my funds had cleared, and Agatha had wired $2 million into my account. I'd left instructions to wire the funds to another account, and two more after that. Christina and I chatted privately after breakfast and made plans to meet up later.

I'd just finished telling Morgan and Garrett what I'd divulged to her.

"Beautiful move," Morgan commented.

"You're a sentimental idiot," Garrett opined. "Think that's smart?" It was the type of question that carried its own answer.

"I'll go with Morgan," I responded.

"You didn't see another way?" Garrett kept after me.

"I ran out of options."

"You could leave her on the boat."

"I won't entertain that."

"You know that luck—forget it."

Morgan, who sat on the other side of me, brokered a truce. "It's past. My sister called."

"Franklin's outside business interest?" I perked up, grateful for the subject change. I was having second doubts about my confession to Christina. It's painful defending a questionable decision. Besides, Garrett was right; I'd let my heart compromise my mind. It's oftentimes unsettling that those two warring organs are housed in the same body.

Morgan said, "He hauls in around twenty-five thousand a month from a limited liability corporation that he is the sole owner of. Also, the gag order evidently extends to the former Mrs. Franklin not discussing her husband's finances. Standard stuff, according to my sister. The attorney who fed her this said she doesn't remember a DC divorce that, by the final document, didn't have everyone pledged in blood to never again mention their former spouse."

"Through sickness and health," Garrett cracked.

I asked, "Any business names?"

"Not really," Morgan replied. "Franklin has a limited liability corp called Greenfaire Boulevard. It's public record."

The name sounded familiar. Maybe because of the green carpet in Park Suites.

"When we get back to Miami," I said, getting back to the earlier part of the conversation, "I'm hauling Christina off the boat. We'll show her pictures that you," I nodded toward Morgan, "collected. See if she recognizes anyone else that Agatha did business with. If so, they'll likely be eager to avoid jail time in return for helping the FBI solidify a case against Agatha."

"How stable is Christina?" Garrett probed, still not at peace with my decision.

"She'll be fine," I replied and then padded my comment, for his sake as well as mine. "I spoke with her briefly this morning. She's calm—knows to stay in the role."

"Knowing and doing are two separate acts."

"Where is she?" Morgan cut in, keeping us from getting back into it.

"With Agatha at an art gallery. She's on duty until this evening. We turn the blowers on at midnight—Miami by morning."

We discussed what we would like to see unfold and how we could best influence such an outcome. The FBI would collar Agatha and company, and Christina would either be placed in protective custody or, depending on how the FBI felt about her, be sent back home to Aruba, which might be the safest place for her. With luck, we'd be back on our island by tomorrow evening.

I left the bar five minutes after them. That was just enough time to recall that Garrett was going to say something about luck but decided it was a wasted effort.

39

The Fat Man

"The funds cleared?" Agatha said.

"Yes, sir," Eddie replied. They were in the main stateroom. Agatha had recently completed his necessary stops on the island. He sat behind a desk, his hand resting on a champagne flute.

"Our two-million refund to Mr. Travis?"

"Also transferred, sir."

"And based on our previous conversation, what is it you propose to do?"

"Throw him overboard."

Agatha chortled, his triple chin bouncing like water balloons. "He claims, you know, to be a good swimmer."

"Not that good."

"This may come as a surprise to you, my dear Eddie, but that is precisely what I want you to do."

"I didn't think you were that concerned, sir."

Agatha gave a dismissive flip of his hand. "Oh, not for your reasons. I assure you I navigated my own path. Although, please do not be disheartened, for I take your comments quite seriously. Although in full disclosure I must admit that it was your persistent prodding that led down this particular path. It is best if our Mr. Travis simply fails to exist anymore. Pity we lost that two, but I refuse to renege on my deal with him. Peculiar, isn't it Eddie? One honors the deal, but not the life."

"A real gasser, sir."

"Pardon?"

"A poor expression. Did you contact Mr. Philby?"

"Checking in on me?"

"No, sir. It's just—"

"I'm teasing you. It was his suggestion."

"Sir?"

"Eliminating Mr. Travis."

"Why did he want Travis taken care of?"

"Taken care of?" Agatha mused. "An unusual combination of words, considering their usage. The ultimate diametric phrase." Agatha brought the flute to his lips and held it there, as if savoring the sensation of the tingling champagne. He tipped the flute and placed it back on the table, his hand caressing the stem of the glass. "Mr. Philby believes that our friend Mr. Travis is in bed with the FBI. The most thorough method of eliminating our risk is to make sure that Mr. Travis never files a report—should he be in such a bed."

"My pleasure, sir."

"You may gloat. Your first impression of the man was spot-on."

"Just doing my job, sir."

"It's interesting, Eddie. He, Mr. Philby, is claiming he wants out, doesn't need our money anymore. What do you think of that?"

Eddie shrugged. "It don't—doesn't worry me too much. I was never convinced he was worth the dough."

"Do you believe one's motivation changes materially over one's life?"

"I do not, sir."

"Yes. And for Mr. Philby, it's always been about money. For men like that, there is never enough. But suddenly there is?" Agatha rose, making a great effort to circumvent the desk and plant himself in front of his bantamweight henchman. "Once we take care of Travis, Mr. Philby is next in line. Do you understand?"

"You think he's connected to Travis?"

"Doubtful. But Mr. Philby's disquieting eagerness to disassociate himself from his previous venal behavior has caused me to see the most recent events in an entirely new light. What if his withdrawn interest in our highly profitable business arrangement is related to our most recent job? I shall rest comfortably when he is gone. Do you require further clarification?"

"No, sir."

"You recall our earlier conversation about your childhood neighborhood?"

"I do."

"Recall who you said the winner would be?"

"The first one to see it coming."

"Excellent. And that other matter, Travis?"

"Yes."

"I'm sure I don't need to remind you, but be careful. We do have a boatful of guests. If the opportunity does not arise, do not force it."

"About that," Eddie ventured. "He is fond of Christina. If we should stumble across the two of them together—"

"My dear man, you so much as lay a hand on that child, and I'll have your face sliced open like an onion and twist a prop up your ass. That's your language, is it not?"

Eddie opened his mouth, paused, and said, "Yes, sir."

40

"This is divine," Christina exclaimed. "Isn't dessert for the end? You know, save the best for last?" We were savoring Key Lime pie on a stick with a dark chocolate shell and graham cracker base. And she thought chili dogs were to die for. "I haven't even," she continued between bites, "had dinner."

"The advantage of eating the good stuff first," I observed, "is that it naturally curbs your appetite for healthier foods."

She'd completed her official duties for the day, and we had two hours before the *Gail Force* departed. I was feeling better about my decision to confide in her. At least that's what I told myself. There was no telling how Agatha would react when the hammer came down. I was at peace knowing that when that occurred, she would be safely tucked away from him. We strolled to a converted-house restaurant on Southard Street, licking our sticks clean step by step. At the restaurant, we split—that's two-thirds to me and one-third to her—lobster bisque and hog snapper with roasted red pepper zabaglione. We washed it down with an Australian red.

She chattered excitedly about her day. She closed nearly a million in sales with 40 percent staying in Studio Four-Twenty's coffers. She received no commission as Agatha insisted she be generously compensated regardless of whether or not the merchandise moved. She exhausted shoptalk and then ran the gamut on what schools she thought would best be suited for her younger sisters. I had never asked her their names, and I was afraid to do so now. Afraid that it would draw attention to my original lack of interest, and equally afraid my late-blooming concern would only bring me closer to her and tangle us deeper in the emotional web. Stupid on both ends, but there you have it.

"And you?" I asked as I scribbled on the chit.

"What about me?"

"Savannah? Art?"

"Oh, that. If I wait past next fall, which I think I need to, then I'll need to reapply. I haven't much time to dedicate to my own work, and I worry that I'll need to show them something new. My portfolio's mostly watercolors, some oil. Oil was a tool that intimidated me at first, but I'm getting better at it. Phillip pays for a private teacher, Suzanne, to instruct me. She's encouraged me to be more aggressive. Every picture, she says, is a blank canvas; it's the tools you take to it that make all the difference."

"Any favorite pictures?"

"Of mine?"

"No. Rembrandt."

"Smarty. There is this one that I just finished. It's like that, you know? The last one is the one you love. It's sort of a self-portrait. Rolling hills, the sea...it's nice. It was beyond what I was capable of, but an artist—and this is Suzanne's manifesto—must strive for what is beyond her grasp. She implores me to exceed my expectations."

"I'd like to see your work."

"You would?"

The disbelief and insecurity of her remark shrank me. Here was a woman who wanted to be an artist, who worked hard for her family, yet like us all, desperately wanted someone to care about her. She was forced to place the interests of her siblings ahead of her own. That didn't mean she didn't covet her own dreams and ambitions.

"I'd love to. Is your work back in Miami?"

"Some. But I have a portfolio on the boat. Phillip insists I bring it along." She tilted her head, birdlike. "In the event someone might want to see it."

"And someone does."

"Sure you don't mind?"

"Let's look at it tonight. There's nothing else in the world I'd rather do."

There are times when we make such a statement, and it is spoken as a matter of speech. There are drastically fewer times when the sweeping proclamation is true. This was the latter.

"You really want to?" Her voice was uncertain, causing me to wonder what she thought of me.

I stood up. "You want to get into that school? You want a career in the visual arts?" She stood but remained silent. "Well?" I said.

"I thought you were being rhetorical."

"Answer the questions."

"Yes?" It came out with the timidity normally reserved for an intimidating schoolmaster.

"That won't do."

She puffed out her chest and threw back her shoulders. "Yes."

"Believe in yourself," I said, although I had no authority to speak such a worn decree. Authority, however, is a floating crown, oftentimes available to anyone daring to wear it.

Two steps away from the table, I said, "Your purse."

"What? Oh." She scurried back to her chair and snatched her purse. "I'm always forgetting the simplest things."

"I wouldn't worry about it."

She was, however, afflicted with that particular bug. From forgetting to place the key back above the door of the wine cellar, to doubling back to retrieve her fruit at Freeport, her mind wandered from the detail of the moment. I extended my arm, opening the door for her.

"A novel of manners," she murmured graciously as she slid past me. "I can't wait to tell Mama."

We hiked back toward the boat, ignoring the bustling bar scene. We wove between the swerving stream of inebriated humanity, like seasoned boxers smoothly slipping short jabs, and never granting an inch to anyone who thought they could separate us. She gushed about herself. How many hours a day she reserved for her work. Whom she admired. Suzanne says don't get trapped by what you've done in the past. Suzanne says unless you destroy half of what you do, you're not trying. Suzanne this. Suzanne that. Career goals and detailed steps she'd laid out to meet those goals. It was if by stating that I wanted to see her work, I'd unleashed her to be free and talk about herself. All I needed to do was listen. I suck at that, but that night, I nailed it.

We were passing an alley when she abruptly stopped, and exclaimed, "Pirates tattoo?" She grabbed my arm—having no interest in my reply—and hauled me into the alley. A lady in dreadlocks and a silver headband was just finishing highlighting a colored fake tattoo on a young girl. Behind her, on a wicker bookstand, a speaker crackled out an Ella Fitzgerald song. A yellow squeaky pirate duck perched on top of the speaker.

"You first," I said.

"First, middle, and last, I'm sure." Christina poked her chin in the air. "But I'm in the mood, matey." She pounced on the chair the girl had vacated, and in a singular move, she tied her hair into a rumpled ponytail. "That one," she instructed the lady in dreadlocks as she pointed to a particularly menacing pirate on a board of pirate faces, "will do me just fine."

"No." I intervened as the lady reached for a peel and stick form. "Do something freehand. You can draw, right?"

She leveled her gaze at me. "Yes. I can draw." The simplicity of her reply yearned for a clarifying, perhaps even apologetic remark from me, but instead I went with, "Do an original."

Twenty minutes later, the face of a ravishing female pirate was inked on her left shoulder. It was black, except for her hair, which was wild cotton candy colors that flowed nearly to her elbow, and the eyes, which were small, vibrant blue dots. Christina vowed to keep it for a week. When I refused the lady's offer to me for similar treatment, Christina swatted me and accused me of being a party pooper. She skipped down the sidewalk, urging "party pooper" to keep up with her, swinging her ponytail side to side with a precision a marching band would envy.

"I'm in the right place," I said striding up beside her. "The night smells like party town."

She stopped and faced me. "No," she said with a flirtatious smile. "The night is *redolent* with revelers."

We boarded the *Gail Force*, and Brooklyn flicked me a weak smile as she stumbled toward a rear lounge chair. The rest of the cast assembled, and as his yacht idled out of Key West, Agatha held his glass high and exclaimed, "Let us shake the devil by its tail." An impromptu and roistering bash followed. It endured for close to two hours. Afterward, Christina and I managed to find ourselves alone in the interior stateroom.

"It's late," she said quietly, her voice laced with resignation and disappointment. "I can show you my work in the morning."

"Nonsense. I suffered through Brooklyn gyrating with Vitalis to arrive at this point in the evening. Go get it now. I'm not the least bit tired."

"You sure?"

"Scram, Sam."

She took a few steps and turned back to me. "Let's meet in here. I can control the light. I know you like it outside, but its dark, and the outdoor lamps are too subdued."

"Here's great." *How did she know I always prefer the outdoors?*

She looked as if she were going to say something, but then walked and scuttled away, as if she couldn't settle on a gait. When I'd first met her, Christina was a sultry caricature who strutted like a runway model. She had morphed into a young woman whom I, and perhaps she as well, was just starting to know.

About ten feet out, she halted. She retraced a few steps, and stood as if she hadn't a clue what to do next or what had brought her to that point in her existence—like when Hadley III presented a gecko to Morgan, or when my squirrel friend stopped in front of me on the road outside of Devon Peterson's house. Yet she looked as confident and natural as I'd ever seen her.

"What?" I said, and it sounded foreign coming from me. I'm not one to toss out conversational probes.

"Elizabeth," she stated.

"Excuse me?"

"The girl applying to art school."

"I don't follow."

"My name. My name is Elizabeth."

I gave that a second, although I didn't need to. "After the book, Pride and Prejudice."

"Yes."

"Why didn't you tell me?"

"This counts doesn't it?"

"And Christina?"

"Phillip. He picked it, you know, like a stage name."

"I can't wait to see your work, Elizabeth."

"How'd you know? That first day when you asked me what my real name was?"

"I didn't. I was just messing with you. Last name?"

"Burnham. Elizabeth *Austen* Burnham."

She pirouetted around and pranced away.

I never saw Elizabeth Austen Burnham's work that night. Instead, I leaped over the port side of the *Gail Force,* took a night swim in the Gulf Stream, got bonked in the head by a Cuban with a ukulele, and was reprimanded for trying to pass off Budweiser as an American beer.

41

I wasn't too happy about any of that.

It happened immediately after Christina—I'd decided it best to keep the name Agatha had bestowed upon her until we were off the boat—was out of sight. I was taking a stroll on the deck while waiting for Christina to return. Henny and a beefy stevedore approached me from the bow. I turned, and Eddie was closing in fast from the opposite direction, the moonlight reflecting off his gun. Thinking can be a dangerous and time-consuming option.

I jumped.

Eddie fired off several shots. His shooting justified my decision to jump, which I was second-guessing the moment I was airborne.

Before I hit the water, I realized that Christina would honor our rendezvous and that I'd be a no show. She'd fidget as the minutes dragged on, her impatience and self-doubt swelling within her, and then finally, reluctantly, she'd go searching for me. Agatha would make up some excuse about me being seen last entering Brooklyn's room and, in the morning, say I departed long before sunrise. First off the boat. Maybe he'd usher Brooklyn off as well. Christina would have all the proof she needed that no one gave a damn. Especially me.

When I finally splashed, I was in a terrifically foul mood.

Fortunately, the sea was calm, and my phone had a seasoned waterproof case. Unfortunately, key lime pie on a stick, lobster bisque, hog snapper, roasted red pepper zabaglione, and the Australian red coagulated to create a concrete life jacket. It was a bad time to see the light of Garrett's philosophy of exercising at sporadic times. The heck with it: I'd pretend it was early morning. I wondered if that would work.

I bobbled for a moment to get my bearings and review what I'd just done. I had no doubt my hasty decision was correct. Eddie's shots into the night confirmed his intentions. But why? Now wasn't question time—now was survival time.

No sign of Morgan. No sign of anything, except the snickering lights of the *Gail Force* as it plowed away from me. As my eyes adjusted to the dark, I made out another boat's starboard and anchor light running parallel to land. I got out my phone and punched Morgan's number, but there was no service. At least the flashlight app worked.

Morgan had followed on the port side on the way down. I should have located him after we left Key West. I signaled SOS by using one hand to hold the phone high above my head and my other hand pulsating in front of the phone while my feet vigorously treaded water. Even if the lights running against the shore were Morgan's, he and Garrett wouldn't be searching for me or naturally scanning the water level. My flashlight would be nearly impossible to see even if someone were looking for it. I packed it in.

I didn't have enough resources to tread water for an hour and then decide to swim. A northerly swim of a mile or so should get me to within view of lights on land. I kicked off my shoes and settled into a steady breaststroke. Five minutes later, I stopped.

The sounds of a ukulele softened the night.

While not accustomed to bobbing in the Atlantic at midnight and therefore not intimate with the indigenous sounds of my surroundings, nonetheless, it was odd. It was too early in my ordeal to succumb to delusions. I twisted a finger in my left ear that—courtesy of my plunge, and its preexisting impaired ability—was borderline useless. No, this ukulele was clearly coming from outside my head.

The source revealed itself as a shape darker than night. Refugees in a raft. I stealthily closed in on them, the ukulele beckoning me as if I were a lost soul paddling Dante's purgatory. Ten feet off their aft port, I called out.

"Amigos."

If they were German or French, I could blabber all day. Not so with Spanish. If they were German or French—then I knew I was delusional.

The music stopped. Panicked muffled sounds carried over the choppy surface of the water.

"Take you to America," I offered.

"Who are you?" A man demanded in unexpectedly clipped English.

"Welcome lady."

"Who?"

It was a decrepit flats boat jerry-rigged with a black sail. No more than five inches of freeboard kept them afloat. A dozen or so people huddled on the deck. One good wave and it was Davy Jones's locker instead of Islamorada Key.

I reached out and grabbed the side of the vessel. That lobster bisque was a killer. "I fell off a boat. Perhaps—"

The ukulele bonked me on the head. It was a glancing blow, as if the person on the other end of it knew that a heavy strike would damage the instrument and therefore held back at the last second.

"Ouch." I took my hand off the boat. A skinny old geezer held his instrument at a right degree to his body, like an auction paddle. "You really think that was necessary?" I griped. "Did I make disparaging remarks about the music? You think my evening's going by plan?"

Skinny stared at me, his instrument locked into place as if readying it for another blow.

"What boat?" It was the man who had talked before. He sat in the rear and held a rusted Coca-Cola sign that served as a tiller.

"Does that matter?"

He seemed to consider that. "No. I guess not."

"Don't have room for me, do you?"

"No."

"Mind if I hold on and kick?"

"You kick us to America?"

"He going to whack me with that ukulele?"

He threw out some Spanish toward Skinny, received a reply, and said, "He says if you can kick us to America, he's sorry. If not, he wishes he hit you harder."

"Swell. Listen, there's a boat out here looking for me. If they find me, they'll help you get ashore. Your chances of hearing that ukulele in America increase dramatically if I can get my buddies to locate us."

He exchanged some clipped words in Spanish, and dissension erupted between the ranks.

"You kick," he ordered me. "Nothing else."

My hands grabbed the rear of the boat, and I let myself float for a second to get my wind back. Here's a freebie for you: stay clear of lobster bisque before a night swim.

"I said kick."

Nasty little taskmaster. I kicked.

And kicked.

And kicked.

She's probably sitting there right now. Her portfolio open on the table in front of her. An empty chair next to her. The encouragement and promise of the earlier part of the evening dying with every tick of the second hand. And I told him my name, *she'll think.* I thought he cared. Fool. Fool. Fool. He's a liar, and I'm a fool. A liar, a—

"Kick."

"Yes, suh." I kicked and continued to scan the water. The distant lights of another boat, smaller, like *Fishy Lady,* were slightly behind me, which is where Morgan would be if he was tracking the *Gail Force.*

"Those might be my friends," I said to no one, eager to shake the image of Christina sitting by herself, her posture eroding. I reached into my pocket and fished out my phone. I kept one hand on the boat and rotating my right hand that held the phone, did my best to signal SOS. That ignited another Spanish volcano. The distant lights shifted course.

"We'd like you to leave now," Tiller Man, considering my abrupt imposition on his vessel, said with unnecessary politeness.

If it was Morgan, there was no way he would leave our floating cousins. He harbored a soft spot for smuggling people, having done so on numerous occasions. Much of the merchandise at his thrift shop went to those who arrived in the States with nothing more than the shirt on their back and a relative's address. I kept my signal flashing. The boat was closing fast.

"I can help you," I lobbied my case. "I'll make sure each foot hits soil."

"Help us?" Tiller Man snorted. "You are the one in the water."

"Trust me."

"Why?"

"You want American beer in America, at sunrise."

"Sí."

"I can help you get that Bud."

"They are owned by the Dutch."

"Yes, yes they are." I kept flashing my light. "I see you know your beers. I admire that. Sam Adams, OK?"

He lectured the steerage and then came back with. "You will buy us all Sam Adams in America."

The boat was bearing down at us. It was about the right size for *Fishy Lady*.

"I can do that for you."

Morgan came in slowly. I made introductions while treading water. Morgan spoke the native tongue, and he soon had the whole romper room laughing and pointing at me. Garrett tied their vessel to an aft cleat. We killed the running lights, and transferred the refugees onto *Fishy Lady*. Skinny fired up the ukulele, and Morgan laid down the law. We untied the flats boat, swamped it, and went in dark and silent.

Fishy Lady, stuffed with six children, three women, five men, and a skinny geezer with a ukulele, idled into the mangrove channels of Key Largo a little before sunrise, the eastern sky heralding the arrival of a new life. Morgan never doubted his route. Garrett was quiet, other than he observed the flats boat would have been better off without my extra weight.

The bow crunched onto the sand and I was unprepared for the relief that familiar and reassuring sound cast upon me. Garrett lowered the front ladder catapulting our passengers as they scrambled and fell over one another in a desperate act to get their feet on American soil. Some of them had chosen to jump into the shallow water before we beached. America's "wet-foot, dry-foot" policy allows Cuban refugees who make it to US soil to remain. If caught at sea, however, there are returned to Cuba or another country. The bizarre policy, which applies only to Cuba, is intended to discourage a similar act like the 1980 Mariel boat lift where 125,000 Cubans sailed into Florida.

I rummaged through the red spinnaker bag and handed Tiller Man $500. "Welcome to the States," I said. "Head down that road about two miles—three point two kilometers. You'll find a resort. They might give you a look, but don't worry. You're in America now. Remember, it's a profit scheme. They'll welcome your money. Buy a round."

"Round what?"

"Sam Adams. It's an expression."

"I have much to learn."

"Have a good time."

He addressed his group, and I was the man of the hour. Skinny stepped forward, strummed a chord on his ukulele, and planted a kiss on my chin.

"Roosevelt," he said. "*Gracias*, Roosevelt."

Tiller Man explained, "He was told Roosevelt was the last great American. He insists that is the only English he needs to know."

"We're leaving," Garrett cut in.

Morgan climbed over the bow of *Fishy Lady* while Garrett and I shoved her off the hard sand. Morgan lowered the engines, and as the whining hydraulics delivered their anticipatory sound, I hoisted myself over the port side.

"When'd you see my light?" I asked whoever wanted to field the question.

"Morgan saw it," Garrett replied. "Said it might be raft people. I told him to let it go, to stay on the yacht, but he insisted on swinging by."

"Hope you don't mind," Morgan added. "Beats swimming."

"You jumped overboard?" Garrett said, more as a statement than a question. I had only briefly given him details of my adventure. When Morgan says we go in silent—we go in silent.

"I did. It was either that or wait and see if Eddie had any parting words before he shot me."

"Why does Agatha want you dead?"

"I can only think of the obvious."

"Which is?" Morgan intervened.

"He doesn't want me alive."

42

"That one not good?" New Zealand said to Morgan.

We were at the marina's fish house and had just settled on bar stools as if we'd gotten off a cattle drive. I'd ordered a beer, snapper sandwich, and fries. The brisk Aussie behind the counter had wished me good luck with that and informed me that the kitchen didn't open for thirty minutes. She also said, on my questioning, that she was from New Zealand, not Australia. Morgan had also ordered a beer. He took one sip and tossed the bottle into the trash can on the underside of the bar. That was his morning custom. He claimed a sip in the morning kept him away from the poison until later in the day. Sunday was his exception. The poison had taken his father, and I suspected it was why Morgan had stepped off the boat, leaving life on the water, as well as his charter business. He never confirmed my suspicion. Nor did I probe.

"It was fine," he replied to New Zealand's question. "I just wanted a sip."

She started to say something, but her face flooded with lack of interest, and she moved on.

I wanted to make contact with Christina but needed to approach her off-property. The image of her waiting for me with her portfolio haunted me. She'd told me her name. *Elizabeth*. Laid it all out there. And I never showed. I had to atone. Had to get her off the boat before it went down.

Garrett, picking up the strand of our earlier conversation, said, "Agatha already wired the two million. That alleviates not paying you the money as the motive to kill you."

"That leaves us," I said, "with the conventional 'I knew too much.'"

"But you don't."

"Not that I know of."

"So we go unconventional. You rubbed Eddie the wrong way. When the deal's done, he acts on his own."

I mulled that over. "Maybe. He's a street kid. We can't dismiss that." I took a swallow of cold beer.

Garrett pursued the topic. "Who profits most from your burial at sea?"

I recalled the thoughts that had ambushed my mind before I'd boarded the *Gail Force*. "Daniel Vigh," I addressed Garrett. "A half a billion dollars is the elephant in the room."

"Vigh controlling the play?"

"I can't see that," I admitted. "Yet everything's orchestrated, as if we are someone's dancing marionettes. But Vigh doesn't know I exist—and why would he kill the man who brought him the deal?"

"Your thinking is flawed," Garrett correctly pointed out. "That is exactly why he would want you dead. But maybe we're overthinking. You misjudged the situation and overreacted. They might have been content to rough you up, and you surprised them with your Tarzan dive. Eddie fired off a few rounds for the sport of it."

"I went feet first."

"All we have is assumptions. The strongest of which is that Agatha wants you dead and dispatched Eddie. We can't totally discount that Eddie acted on his own."

Did I misread my predicament? Maybe I'd get a chance to ask Eddie himself—get a few moments alone with him before the feds cuffed him. First, though, I had to appease the worrisome images in my mind of a young lady waiting, her hands on a table, her passion on paper, her dreams laid bare for a man who never came.

"I'm going to find Christina," I announced and left before Garrett had the time to instruct me to keep my head in the game. On the way out, I stopped into the marina's store and bought a new pair of boat shoes, shorts, and a shirt.

"Stuff will dry out, you know." The kid with a lip ring behind the counter noted when I offered him my damp clothes. He appraised my shirt as he held it up to his chest.

"Yours," I told him. "They bring me bad memories."

"You sure?"

I nodded.

"Things not go well with the woman last night?"

"Something like that."

"Tell me about it, brother."

43

I loitered a block away from Studio Four-Twenty, keeping an eye on the front door. I checked my e-mails and sent Kathleen a text.

"Remember me?"

She came back instantly with, "Remember us?"

Christina strolled out the front door of Oceana. I shoved the phone in my pocket. I caught up with her as she entered a deli and got within a few feet of her before she noticed me. She was the quicker draw.

"Leave me alone," she hissed.

"What did he tell you when I didn't show up?"

"I said, leave me alone."

"Not until I explain."

"What tale are you bringing now?"

"I jumped off the boat. It was either that or Eddie was going to shoot me."

"Really?" She squared off and took a step into me. "That is *exactly* what Phillip said you would say if you ever floated into my life again. He said you were seen with that smoking blonde and left early, but if I ever did see you again, you'd invent some tall tale about jumping off the boat."

"Excuse me," a woman with a dog interrupted us. "Are you in line?"

"No," I said.

"Yes," Christina countered.

I grabbed her arm and pulled her over a step. "What did he tell you? I ditched you for the blonde? I passed out? Fell overboard myself? Look at me and tell me you believe any of those."

"You're hurting me."

I lessened my grip but didn't free her. "I don't want you back on that boat."

"You should hear yourself. I don't even know if I still believe what you said about Phillip. Everything was—"

"His days are numbered. Agatha's going down, and everyone around him will be a suspect and questioned."

"You didn't jump. You couldn't have swum that far."

"I got picked up by Cubans in a raft after a skinny geezer whacked me with his ukulele."

"Give it a rest, will you?"

"Remember our dinner in Nassau? The tall, solid black man at the bar you studied? Shining head, no hair? Scruffy thin man with him?"

"I don't—" She gave me an impatient shrug. "What about them?"

"They're my buddies, Garrett and Morgan. They've been shadowing my every move. They plucked me, and the Cuban refugees, out of the water."

She flipped her right hand in the air. "You just keep popping up with bizarre stories. Phillip's a murderer. You're working for the government. Eddie was going to kill you. Ukulele Man and shadow buddies. Do you know what that all sounds like to me? I just want a turkey sandwich. I need to get back to the studio."

"Dude, you in line or not?" A young man with thick eyeglasses shifted on his feet behind us.

I tightened my hand around her arm and repositioned us out of the traffic and against a wall under a faded poster with a ripped corner. It advertised twelve inches of ham, turkey, lettuce, and tomatoes for $3.99.

She winced, and I let go. "Listen to me," I implored her as I invaded her space, aware that I'd worn the tread on those three words. "You'll be in jail within twenty-four hours on a trumped-up accessory to murder charge. That what you want? Think that'll get your sisters through college?" She stared at me with confused eyes, and I was mad at myself for not making her world a better place. "I wanted to see your portfolio. I *want* to see your portfolio." I started to reach for her shoulders but pulled back. "You believe I voluntarily went for a midnight swim? Smoked weed with that blonde? You know better."

"I waited so long," she capitulated. "But you never came. I felt so...so stupid, just sitting there with my portfolio."

I didn't think she ever fell for Agatha's version. The resignation in her voice conveyed how frustrating it had been for her. "That night was no good for either of us," I conceded. "I'm flying you to Tampa today. You're done here."

"I can't just leave. I've got to get my—"

"Forget clothes. I'll buy you new—"

"My portfolio. I left in on the Gail Force. I need to have it."

I punched out my breath. "Can you get it now?"

"Eddie was really going to kill you?"

"I chose not to find out. Your portfolio."

"There's a bash tonight—another work event designed as party. But this time it's Phillip's birthday. The boat's going to sink with the number of people he invited. I'm supposed to work it. I'll get it then. I can tell him I'm not feeling well and leave."

"Can't you get it now?" I marginally modified my previous question.

She shook her head. "I've got three appointments this afternoon in the studio, including two couples from the cruise. I barely have time to sneak out for lunch as it is. There's no reason for me to go there. Won't this evening be fine?"

I didn't think a few hours would mean that much. She would possibly draw greater scrutiny if she broke her routine and dashed off to the boat.

"This evening," I relented. "But I want you on and off. I'll be waiting for you in a car. Call me. I'll pull in and pick you up."

"Are you sure?" Her forehead wrinkled with a brew of concern and eagerness.

"I won't be more than a block away."

"No. About all this? Do I really need to leave?"

I realized I needed to call Binelli and get a timeframe for the feds clamping down on Agatha. I was fine as long as it wasn't before tomorrow, but I needed to be certain that was the case.

"Yes," I reached out and touched her arm—to see if I could do so without her wincing. "Absolutely necessary. Your life's going to change for better or worse. I suggest you choose better."

She curled up the side of her lip. She looked as if she were going to say a lot more than she did. "OK."

I handed her my card so she would have my number. She refused it. "You already gave it to me, remember? First time we met."

"That's right." My mental lapse disturbed me.

"Was this guy really playing a ukulele?" she said in tone intended to lighten the mood.

"A midnight concerto."

"And that's how you found the raft? Through his music?"

"Yes. But I signaled Morgan and Garrett with my phone."

"Dot, dot, dot, dash, dash?"

"You know that?"

"Sailing school."

"That's right. You island people grew up on sailboats."

She gave a tepid smile. "We island people did."

"I like your tattoo," I said in an effort to expand her smile. It worked as she beamed with the pleasant memory of that evening.

"I told you," she said, as if I'd forgotten, "that I planned to keep it for a week."

"What time's party duty?" I said, getting back to business and killing her smile.

"Seven. Party starts at eight. You know the scene—lot of guests don't show until after nine, but Phillip likes me there early."

"Seven it is. Grab your portfolio, and tell Agatha you're sick. If you're not comfortable with that, tell him you forgot something at the studio and need—forget that," I babbled. "He might send someone else. You're sick, got it?"

"Aye, aye, Captain." It reminded me of when Kathleen had given me a mock salute when I'd asked her to keep an eye on Riley. I needed to hear her voice—seemed like it'd been two forevers since that happened. "I need to go," she insisted.

"Get a sandwich first. I'll leave now. I don't want us seen together."

A fly landed on the tomato in the picture. She hesitated, and her posture slackened. "Listen, I feel bad asking, you're doing so much for me, and it's way premature, but I'll need a job. My sisters—"

I slapped the wall, killing the fly and startling Christina. "Your sisters and mother will be fine," I assured her. "We'll talk later." I wanted to wait for a special occasion to give her the good news. Not under a faded and dusty poster of a ham and turkey sandwich with a dead fly on the tomato.

44

"When are you closing the ring on Agatha?" I demanded of Binelli on the phone just as a text came in. I'd ducked into a bar, taken a seat at the counter, and ordered a cheeseburger and a Sam Adams.

"You done?" Binelli asked, not addressing my question.

"Wrapped up my last take."

"Where are you?"

"Miami." I rephrased my question. "When is Franklin raiding Studio Four-Twenty?"

"I don't know. My guess is—"

"I need to know, not to guess."

"Why?"

"Got to get somebody out. Am I safe tonight?"

"Who?"

"An innocent person whom I don't want caught up in the maelstrom."

"Shouldn't be a problem," she assured me. "We're— Franklin's out of town, but he was thinking more like two or three days. It's all paper work now. He wants everything lined up before he brings Agatha in. Agatha will drag in a legion of jacked-up lawyers. We can't afford to have him slip away because of shoddy prep work on our part. Why are you bringing her out?"

"I didn't say it was a her."

"If she were a he, you would have said so. Beside, your heart's your trump card. Remember—first time we met— you saved those two young girls? I can't afford to have you compromising—"

"I can't risk her being thrown into the system. For all I know, Franklin will scream Homeland Security and suspend everyone's rights. This woman will—"

"Take it easy, slim. Just don't clog things up. I won't even remember this call. And it's under RICO."

"Thanks."

"Come again?" She brightened up. "I missed that last comment." She disconnected.

Something she said—*where are you*—no, something else she was about to say. I let it go, for I had another issue. Now that I'd made peace with Christina, it was free to dominate my mind.

Who wanted me dead and why?

I took a long draw of ice-cold beer, and my world got a little better. A bite of the cheeseburger reminded me that somewhere on our circular home, the sun was rising over foreign plains. I brought up the text I'd received while talking with Binelli. It was from Kathleen.

"Hey, floozy. I said remember US?"

I started to reply. Instead, I remembered something that Eddie had said when we'd first met. I shelled out a twenty and started for the door. A giant step back, and I was at the counter again. I grabbed a couple of napkins and took the burger with me.

Garrett and Morgan were on *Fishy Lady*. A pair of nice sheepshead were on ice.

"Couple of things," I announced as I jumped onto the deck. "I think Binelli and Franklin are here in Miami, prepping charges against Agatha. She mentioned Franklin was out of town and caught herself saying 'we' instead of just him."

Garrett said, "Why not just tell you?"

"That tribe's big on need to know. She's likely following orders."

"And has been known to break them at will, which is why we recruited her in the first place."

"But," Morgan observed, "nothing definitive can be drawn by her and Franklin possibly being in town, right? Other than he's moving quickly." He jerked his pole back, but the line went slack. He reeled it in and set the hook on the rod. He placed it under the gunwale and slid it into a rod holder.

"What's number two?" Garrett demanded.

"Eddie didn't act on his own; he was ordered to kill me."

"Why are you now certain of that?"

"At the bar—first night I met him. He told me he lived by a code. About how he never turns on the man who pays the tab. Eddie values loyalty. It's who he is. There's only one reason he came at me with a gun. He followed orders. Agatha instructed him to kill me. It's not in his DNA to act on his own."

"OK," Garrett readily agreed. "We'll lock that in. We assumed it was Agatha in the first place. We're still back to where we were earlier—who and why?"

"Didn't you just say Agatha is the 'who'?" Morgan said.

"Not necessarily." I dropped the lid of the cooler. "Agatha can't be killing his ex-clients. Someone running Agatha wants me dead, and might have given Agatha the order."

"Daniel Vigh?" Garrett eyed me.

"He's my wild theory. He's an uninvolved third party, yet he profits the most. Lot of money."

"Maybe he's your puppeteer."

"Marionettist."

"Who?"

"Puppeteer. Marionettist."

That earned me a deserved blank stare followed by, "It's the same man."

His words flooded back Franklin's comments to me when we met at Tony's and I'd commented on the difference between our business cards. *"It's not the title, it's the man."*

A center console sputtered into the marina. Four men and a dog. The dog was in the bow, its nose pointing toward the dock. It jumped down and disappeared and then popped up on a rear seat. It scampered away a few seconds later. It knew the dock was approaching and couldn't contain its excitement. I'd make a good dog. I didn't know exactly what lay ahead, but I knew my boat was getting ready to dock. I could sense it.

The boat swung to the port and I glanced at the name on the transom.

Anchors Aweigh.

Underneath it was: *USN.*

It's not the title, it's the man.

Had Franklin's title, wardrobe, and blue-blood name clouded my vision of who the man was?

Games are like that sometimes. You can stare at the board all you want. Configure your strategies. Ponder your opponent's position. The board is bland, uncaring. Impassive. Your mind locks up like an engine on an arctic morning. It just doesn't turn over.

And then it does.

I sputtered out words the moment coherent thoughts took form. "Cuff links—Greenfaire—that's who else it could be."

"Greenfaire," Morgan said. "That's Franklin's LLC, isn't it?"

"Pumps him gold every month."

"Cuff links?" Garrett said.

"Navy cuff links. Franklin, a West Point man, sported them both times I saw him, and—"

"Zebra's contract is with the navy."

"Franklin was stationed in Dallas in his early days." I said, recalling what I'd read in Mary Evelyn's report—the day I'd discovered what I like about cats. It had been buried with his other early career stations, Los Angeles and Chicago. They didn't mean anything to me then—just standard big-city stops on his way up the ladder. Mary Evelyn had listed every street address. I started working my phone. "Green-faire rang a bell," I explained. "Franklin lived on a Green-faire something. Here we go. Greenfaire Golf and Country Club. Greenfaire Boulevard circumvents the course..." I waited until my phone confirmed my suspicion. "And Zebra Electronics is located in the Crosswoods Industrial Park. Less than a mile away."

"Think they know each other?" Morgan said.

"It would explain a lot," Garrett said and then solidi-fied his statement. "It would explain everything. Kent Edward Franklin the third—the master marionettist—choreographing your every move."

"I'm willing to bet," I said, disgusted with myself, "that Franklin's been protecting Agatha for years, knowing that

Zebra's contract was set to expire. No way would he trust his fortune to the wind."

"Brilliant, really," Garrett added, with more conviction than was warranted. "Franklin pretends to run an operation against Agatha while all along he's running an operation *with* Agatha. A perfect subterfuge."

I recalled Binelli's comments in Saint Pete. *Everything's a budget decision.* Yet, Franklin showered me with millions. Was it Franklin's own money that I was wiring to Agatha?

"Think he owns private stock in Zebra?" Garrett jolted my thoughts.

"No doubt."

"We need proof. Right now it's just an interesting, albeit compelling, theory."

"I'll call Bin—"

"She's too close. She'll draw attention—"

"She knows that. She—"

"Keep her out." Garrett ordered me.

He was right. I trusted her too much. My theory might be wrong, but if it wasn't, I couldn't place her in an awkward position with Franklin, the man who hired her and mentored her. Conflicted loyalties cloud judgment.

"Keep her in the dark." Garrett kept after me in the event I was wavering. "Let's verify before we chase a false lead."

"We're trying to put Daniel Vigh and Franklin in the same room, right?" Morgan said. "We need a list of Green-faire members. That won't be easy with a private club, but how else can we verify?"

Good question, and one I didn't think on for too long. The longer you think on a problem, the more difficult it becomes. Simplicity and swiftness are your friends. I snatched my phone and brought up Greenfaire's website. I punched the hyperlink to the pro shop. I placed the phone on speaker and situated it on the dash, below the Garmin chart plotter and next to the Icom radio.

"Greenfaire pro shop. Vince speaking." Garrett and Morgan crowded in closer.

"This is Daniel Vigh," I said. "I'd like to schedule a tee time for next Friday."

"Certainly, Mr. Vigh. Usual time."

"You know, I'm not sure. Kent Franklin might join me. Do you know if he's already golfing that week?"

"Lemme see. He's not in town that much...ah, here, well, perhaps you forgot, Mr. Vigh."

"What's that, Vince?"

"You and Mr. Franklin are teeing off at eight-fifteen. This Wednesday. Just the two of you."

"Oh, that's right. Silly of me. Thanks, Vince."

"No problem."

Bam.

Just like that.

45

Quarrelsome gulls screeched at one another, and I wondered what could possibly go wrong in their world.

"Franklin's money," Garrett said as he started pacing the deck, "comes from Zebra. Edward Kent Franklin the third—master marionettist—has been pulling your strings."

"He's been protecting Agatha day and night," I concurred, "while telling others that he's running a sting on him. The real reason for the gag order was to insulate Franklin from Vigh and Zebra; rest of it was smokescreen."

"Pretty slick." Garrett bobbed his head.

"What about the dead agents?" Morgan cut in.

"Not by design," I reasoned. "Franklin lost control, but he's too close to the IPO to pull up now. Zebra goes public, it's payday. When I dropped into his lap? Manna from heaven."

"And now he needs you dead," Garrett added. "Agatha as well. You do the simple math—even years from now—it brings Franklin down."

"Franklin insisted on Peterson completing the play," I said, recalling the feeble argument I'd mounted in Park Suite when Binelli informed me of Franklin's decision. "It was served right to my face—I didn't see it."

"But why," Morgan said returning to Garrett's earlier declaration, "does Franklin need to eliminate Agatha?"

Garrett explained, "He can't afford to have Agatha on the stand. Agatha knows that and will try to eliminate Franklin—"

I completed his sentence. "Before Franklin eliminates Agatha."

"If," Morgan added, "Agatha knows that Franklin is connected to Zebra."

That slammed us into a wall of silence. Garrett ceased his pacing. A sailboat floundered into the harbor, and her crew lowered the main sail. It crumbled like a giant starched bed sheet onto the deck. A thin-legged lady bent over and collected the fabric, bunching it up in her arms with expertise and speed. "Any guesses?" I said.

"If Agatha doesn't know," Garrett ventured, "he may, one day, learn of such a connection. Franklin won't grant him that opportunity. My chip's on the man from DC. He's got a contract out on Agatha as we speak, and he won't use G-men."

"No, he'll knock off Agatha using outside contractors, shut down the sting, and castrate any investigation into his death. Case closed and buried. Zebra goes public and Vigh and Franklin make enough money to buy Miami."

"Franklin," Morgan reminded us, "is not the one who forced you to jump off the boat."

Garrett said, "That might have been Agatha following Franklin's orders."

"There are elements," I admitted, "that we don't know. We can assume that Agatha, at this juncture, is highly suspicious of his relationship with Franklin. Uneasy. Each side doubting their counterparty."

"Erasing you is the first priority of business for Franklin as you lead back to him." Garrett nodded at me. "He let you complete your mission and then likely tipped off Agatha—recruited him for the deed. Exactly what I would have done."

"No need to fawn over it."

"No need to underestimate the enemy."

"The likely scenario?" Morgan interjected before I again defended an indefensible position.

I took his question and went with Garrett's theory. "Franklin instructed Agatha to kill me the moment Franklin got what he wanted, which was Peterson begging his buddy Walderhaden for money. That would have aroused Agatha's instincts. It's just a matter of time before Agatha reaches the intersection that we're at."

The sailboat that had lowered its sail docked two piers over. Its naked mast, like an aluminum pencil, got lost in a sea of other masts, their halyards slapping the poles in a rising wind.

"Christina," Morgan said. "Is she safe?"

"I'm getting her out tonight." I reviewed my conversation with Christina. I was going to tell them that her real name was Elizabeth, but there'd be time for that later. Morgan tossed in a few questions about her future once I got her back to Saint Pete.

"You can't do anything until she's out?" Garrett said after I'd satisfied Morgan's concerns.

I couldn't tell whether his comment was in support or contempt. "That's right," I replied.

"Then let's get her out," he said, and I wondered why I doubted him. "After that, our only choice is to get Agatha. We need him to bring in Franklin."

"Once Agatha is shut down, I'll go to Binelli—"

"Her loyalty to Franklin?" Garrett cut in.

I recalled why Natalie Binelli entered the FBI in the first place; intelligence I'd yet to share with Garrett. "She'll be fine," I assured him with enough confidence to make him stand down. Besides, he'd already won the first round. "We can't bring him in by ourselves." I pocketed my phone and gave our marching orders. "We'll get Christina off, apprehend Agatha, and make contact with Binelli. Agatha will confess to her about Franklin's role in return for avoiding the chair. The FBI will discreetly bury their own bad egg. Agatha will spend his next fifty birthdays in clothing provided by the state."

"Those are loaded bases," Garrett observed. "You got a plan for your grand slam?"

"I do."

I explained everyone's role as we made our way through the docks.

"A cake?" Garrett said when I'd finished.

"A Trojan horse of a birthday cake. Needs to be big enough to slip our hardware on the boat. We all agree?"

They nodded in silent agreement.

Garrett added, "Probability of success?"

"Extremely low."

They nodded in silent agreement.

46

The *Gail Force* towered splendidly above the lesser boats in the marina, her blue lights highlighting the orange sunset, adding an artist's proof to nature's classic and most reproduced work. Behind her, a dozen cranes sprouted between the high-rises in the Miami skyline. They were thin weeds that begat thicker weeds of steel and reflective glass, battling one another for a piece of air.

I sat in the backseat of a car two blocks from the marina. I'd exchanged my marina store outfit for off-the-rack pants, shirt, and a blue blazer. When Christina was safely off the boat and under Morgan's watch, my number was up. I wasn't too worried about gaining admittance. Agatha wouldn't resist the challenge of learning of my survival.

It got a tad murky after that. We planned to neutralize Eddie and Henny and then invite Agatha to depart with us. We were banking on the other hired hands not interfering without Eddie and Henny, although the refrigerators that stood sentry at the base of the gangplank were of concern. One of them was with Henny the night of the ukulele. That indicated that he was likely on Agatha's payroll, and not just a party-boy helper.

Waiting and I don't get along. I told my driver to sit tight and exited the car. I paced the street and dawdled along the edge of the parking lot. She should be aboard by now.

I checked my phone. No messages. No missed calls. I still owed Kathleen a text, but didn't want to get a chain going. *Why, when Christina hits my mind, does it snap to Kathleen? You know why, pal.*

I checked my phone.

7:10.

7:26.

7:34.

7:36.

7:37.

My silent phone sent a loud message.

It got close to eight, and the band hit their opening chord. A steady stream of guests, two by two, approached the ark's gangplank.

A blinking light pulsated from the side of the yacht. It came from a lower stateroom, not far from the room I'd stayed in. A boat idling out of the harbor momentarily blocked my view. It reappeared. It wasn't a sharp light, but rather someone playing with their room lights, the lights staying on for different intervals of time.

Dot. Dot. Dot. Dash. Dash.

Christina had indicated she was familiar with the Morse code signal for distress from her sailing days. Was it her? I breached security and called her. It went to voice mail. I called Garrett, told him the plan didn't go one inning, and to give me thirty minutes before storming the gates.

The one man recognized me as I approached. He whispered into a shoulder mike.

"Your invitation, sir?" the other asked.

My gaze was steady on the man who recognized me. "I believe Mr. Agatha will be intrigued to see me."

He nodded as he listened to his earplugs and then focused on me. "I'll be accompanying you aboard." He smirked at me. "Why'd you jump overboard the other night?"

"Thought we'd all decided to go for a night swim."

He replied by extending his arm up the gangplank. "After you."

I stepped aboard the *Gail Force* for the last time.

Eddie was waiting for me on the deck, a few paces from the gangplank. "Spin around, Beachy," he commanded.

"No," I said flatly.

"Pardon me?"

"I'm here to wish Mr. Agatha a happy birthday and to thank him for the two million dollars. I also wish to let him know that while my employer is immensely happy with the job, I am less than thrilled with my most recent accommodations while aboard this vessel."

Eddie stepped into me. His hands went inside my jacket and felt around my back. I coughed into his face—more like the top of his head. Our eyes locked together, and I said, "I was telling your friend here that I thought the plan the other night was for all of us to take a night swim. What happened, you afraid to jump?"

He stepped back. "Don't know what you're talking about. We heard there were pirates in the water and were patrolling the circumference of the boat. We see you and you hopped the rail." He grinned. "You see? We was baffled when you did your Esther—Esther—what the fuck's her—"

"Williams."

"Yeah, that's right. Gee-zus, I'm gonna miss you." He erupted in a machine gun rift of laughter. He slapped me on the shoulder. "We was stunned. Told Mr. Agatha but he said not to worry on account that you, on that first day, telling him what a good swimmer you was, and boy, you was, weren't you?"

"Where is he?"

Eddie considered my question as a burgeoning throng of people crowded the aft deck. "Make yourself at home. Louis here is gonna keep you company. We'll send for you when we're ready."

Eddie left, and I faced Louis. "Shall we?"

I knifed my way through the crowd and secured a drink. I tossed the cherry. I don't need sugar in my whiskey. What I did need was to lose Louis, find Christina, and get off the boat. I had thirty minutes. Agatha could wait.

I came up behind Brooklyn just as a conversational quartet of two men, another woman, and herself, disintegrated.

"Think they got any weed here?" I said. She shifted her weight to grant me her full attention.

"Hey, there. Where's your dark-haired princess."

"Sadly, she passed on me."

She arched her eyebrows. "Really?" She nudged in closer. "Why are all the good men so totally clueless? At dinner that night, when you ignored her? Ooh…let me tell you, darling, that was killing her. Is it true about the abortion?"

"Come with—"

"She's like a child, under that glitz. She's a homey little thing—takes an effort for her to be a woman. I don't make you two. What's your story?"

"I'll give you an exclusive, but let's get some grapes. Care to join me in the wine room?"

She gave me a furtive smile. "I'll follow."

We traversed our way through the crowd and down to the lower level. Louis kept behind at a constant four paces.

When we entered the kitchen, he closed ranks and inquired where I was going. I told him my friend wanted to see the wine cellar and that Christina had showed it to me the first time I was on the boat. He wasn't concerned when I located the key from the top of the doorframe and unlocked the door.

Brooklyn and I entered the wine cellar. The bottle of Chateau Montelena was waiting for me. It pained me to think of what I was going to do. I turned to her and said, "That nice man who is following us?"

"Who?"

Ditzy blonde.

"There's a man outside the door. He's got the good stuff on him. Tell him I need to see him in here. You stay out." I let my hand grace the nape of her neck. "Our time is coming."

She popped her eyes wide, smiled, and went back out the door. A moment later Louis ambled in and said "What?" as I cracked the left side of his head with a 1973 Chardonnay. It hurt me as much as it hurt him, but fortunately, the bottle was up to the task. It didn't break. He stared at me with a bent quizzical look, winced in pain, fumbled inside his jacket, and crumbled. I confiscated his gun and communication equipment—sticking the earplug in my right ear. "Good girl," I said and kissed the bottle before placing it back in its rack.

I locked the door on the way out. Fifty-four degrees. He'd be fine.

"Hey," Brooklyn complained as I rushed past her.

Christina was behind the first door I knocked on. It was the only door that was locked, but didn't have the "Shhh... we're sleeping" sign. I called her name, my face pressed hard against the door. She answered. Taking a cue from the wine room, I ran my hand along the ledge of the doorframe. Nothing. A couple swept past me, the man groping the woman, the woman telling him to slow down, that her boobs weren't going anyplace.

I again pressed my head against the door. "Is there a hole in the middle of the door knob?"

"A hole?" Christina answered from the other side.

"A small, pin-size—"

"Yes, but it's so small."

"Stick a pin in it and jiggle."

"I don't—"

"Look for one."

I turned my back to the door and smiled as a man with a double-pierced left ear eyed me with curiosity. The door opened, and I backed into the room, closing the door behind me.

Her eyes were a concoction of fear and relief. She hugged me, and I stepped away. She held up an open safety pin. "Here's to Marlo's assistant leaving pins where they don't belong."

"What happened?"

"Henny caught me."

"Doing what? Retrieving your portfolio?"

"I was eavesdropping—standing around a corner listening to Phillip on the phone. It's my fault, please don't be mad," she implored. "I thought maybe I could learn something that would help you. I was there too long, too long to be doing anything other than what I was. You said Phillip was involved in murder, right? I overheard him on the phone saying 'he's taken care of.' I—"

"Who was he talking to?"

"—don't know." Her eyes were anxious as the erasure of doubt left no question as to the direness of her predicament. "He was calm. When he hung up he told Eddie that everything was fine and to take care of Mr. Philby. Do you know that name?"

"Famous double agent. Long dead." While not proof of Franklin's involvement with Agatha, it reinforced my beliefs. "Did he say when?"

"When, what?"

"He was going to take care of Mr. Philby."

"That's when Henny shoved me into the stateroom. I had no idea he was behind me. He told Phillip I'd been listening for a few minutes and overheard the conversation."

"Henny said that?"

"Why?"

"I didn't think he could string words together."

She giggled, and her face relaxed. It didn't last long. "I screwed up, didn't I?"

"Nonsense. What was Agatha's reaction?"

"Said he'd talk with me later, but that I needed to stay in my room tonight. He wasn't particularly mad—I don't honestly think he would ever hurt me—but when Eddie escorted me here, he locked it from the outside. Did you know they could do that, lock from the outside?"

"No. I doubt that's how the yacht was originally designed."

"What are we going to do?"

I extended my arm so that she could hook her arm through mine. "Stroll off the boat, as if we haven't a care in the world."

"Can we do that?"

"We can. Walk steady and with purpose, but not with haste. In less than five minutes, we'll be in the backseat of a car and driving away."

And that's what we did.

And it would have worked beautifully, and everything would have been fine. While that version will always linger, it vanished, and it has no more meaning than the promising smile of woman whom you never see again, yet never forget.

Similar to what she'd done when we'd first had lunch and she'd left her fruit in the container, and later, when I reminded her in Key West that she was about to leave the restaurant without her purse, halfway off the yacht, Christina spun and exclaimed, "My portfolio."

I couldn't be upset with her. After all, I'd forgotten as well.

47

I volunteered to go back to her room with her, but embarrassed by her forgetfulness, and equally aware of my non-invited presence, she urged me to keep my head down for a few minutes.

"It's so packed," she reasoned. "No one will notice me. And you have less chance of being found staying in one place."

Eddie found me. Marched right up to me. No problem at all.

Before we could even exchange opening salvos, I felt the indentation of a gun barrel pressed into my lower back. Henny was behind me. I'd not heard anything on the confiscated communication equipment and wondered how they'd found me so effortlessly. *Louis fumbled inside his jacket. I thought he was reaching for his gun, but it was on the other side.*

Eddie reached up, yanked the earplug out of my ear, and confirmed my blunder. "You *frickin'* idiot. You were broadcasting the whole time. Guess you ain't as smart as you thought. Where'd you put Louis?" Henny frisked me and took Louis's gun.

"He's chilling in the wine room. I'd like a few words with Phillip," I said while I internally berated myself for not taking a nanosecond to make sure the mike wasn't on.

"Follow me. Anything cute, and Henny shoots. It's so crammed, it'll be three in the morning before anybody realizes you're not passed out drunk."

We snaked our way to the pilothouse, where Agatha sat behind the desk I'd noticed the first time I was there. It seemed smaller with Agatha behind it. Eddie planted himself at one end, his gun drawn. He nodded at Henny, who bolted back out the door. Johnnie Darling stood by the instrument panel with a large camera around his neck. He appeared lost. Uninterested. He might be the biggest crack in the pot.

"Mr. Travis." Agatha took a sip from his tumbler and reverently placed it back on the desk. "What brings you back after your swim, and why, for goodness sake, did you jump into the Gulf Stream?"

I wanted to tell Agatha that I knew Franklin used me to secure the Zebra contact, that I knew that Franklin had been protecting Agatha for years, knowing the day would come when he needed his services. The best Agatha could hope for, if he cooperated, was life behind bars. I stood before him holding no cards, which made me dispensable.

"I misjudged the situation," I answered him. "Eddie was patrolling with his gun drawn—evidently hunting pirates—and I panicked."

"Why did you think Eddie wanted to harm you?"

"I reached over him and grabbed a piece of bread."

He belched out a laugh. "So you did. Tell me, did you really swim from that distance?"

"No." I gave him the same line I'd given Christina. "I got picked up by Cubans in a raft, and a skinny geezer whacked me with his ukulele."

"Tsk, tsk. Must you use humor to escape everything?"

The door from the stateroom opened, bringing in the party sound. Henny shoved Christina, hugging her portfolio, through the door and slammed it behind him. The noise vanished like a vacuum, accentuating the difference between our dismal predicament and the frat-house freedom that, despite its proximity, was a world lost to us.

Agatha's cigar rested in the ashtray, his hands unusually idle at his side. He addressed Christina as if she were his only interest. "I believe I asked you to stay in your room," he said quietly.

"I am not to be treated like a rabbit in a cage." Her words, although equally subdued, were crisp and honed.

"Nor was that ever my intention," Agatha replied with kindness. "I understand you are not feeling well."

"No, sir. I'm not."

"Sir? My dear princess. Your formality belies your nervousness and hints at dishonesty."

"I don't feel well, Phillip." She rallied, and I was proud of her. "I just want to get my portfolio and work at home this evening. Why did you lock me in my room?"

"A precaution. You see, my dear one, we are at an unusual crossroads in our business, and your baffling illness—and more to the point, previous eavesdropping—is unsettling."

"Forgive me, for I did not know that being ill or curious were punishable offenses."

"No need for that. Your association with Mr. Travis has gotten quite...intricate. I wonder if that, in some manner, has impeded your dedication to your task?"

She took a step toward him, her portfolio, like a plate of armor, grasped tight in her arms. "You know how thankful I am for what you've done, and I look forward to continuing to work for you. If you find fault in my dedication, say so. I wasn't aware that my private life was your concern."

"My dear, every aspect of your life, since I plucked you off that island, is of concern to me." He spread his hands out. "You are naturally free to do as you wish, and I mean no intrusion into your private affairs. If you so desire, leave."

Christina, taken back by Agatha's gambit, stood motionless, uncertain what to do. Strange that she could not hear me screaming in my head for her to go.

"As I thought," Agatha said. "You cannot leave without him. Either he has laid out other plans, or he has shackled your heart with whispers of love. Therein lies the essence. Mr. Travis presents a problem for us. We have a certain benefactor who keeps a watchful eye on us. We have just come into the knowledge that Mr. Travis has been cooperating with the enemy, so to speak. He is anathema to everything we do. Do you understand that?"

Garrett had been right. Franklin told Agatha that I was a snitch. His ploy was to get Agatha to eliminate me.

Christina stood her ground. "What enemies do you have, Phillip, and why would you have such vindictive people in your life?"

Agatha's face contorted, his soul gnarled by the realization that Christina saw through him and that he was becoming something else, something less, in her eyes. It was a two-person play, and Eddie, Henny, Johnnie, and I were the audience. I would have gladly ended it, but Eddie had never taken his eyes, or his gun, off me. Garrett and the birthday cake were due soon. Now would be a dandy time for a little diversion. I started whistling "Dixie."

"Enough," Agatha spat. He regained his composure and addressed Christina. "Perhaps 'enemies' was not the precise word. Businesses tend to sprout adversarial relationships, and in that regard, we are no different." He reached for his drink, but pulled back, his internal conflict physically manifesting itself. "We cannot have you associating with him."

"I am really not well," Christina pleaded. "Can't we continue this tomorrow?"

"I'm afraid not." Agatha reached for his cigar, inhaled, and rolled his head back, exposing his broad baby-belly neck. He blew smoke into the room. "As much as it pains me, you will be returned to your room where you *will* spend the night. If it's anything a few aspirin won't sufficiently address, I assure you my personal physician will see to you immediately. Say farewell to Mr. Travis."

Christina's eyes narrowed in confusion. "Don't hurt him," she said. She hesitated, as if her mind were computing a thousand equations, and then blurted out, "I love him."

"Ah, my dear." Agatha's breath escaped with his words. "It saddens me to hear that, for he is a cold piece of meat. Why do you think I'd hurt Mr. Travis?"

"Eddie has a gun on him. Is it a water pistol?"

Agatha chuckled. "So he does. A simple observation. Well done, my dear." Agatha redirected his attention to me. "Do you love her?"

"I do." *Where's Garrett?*

"Love," Agatha spun the word out as if he were exhausted with a god who never showed up. "Love is a salvational dream." His eyes latched onto mine. "Do you agree, Jake? That the best we can ever aspire to is the hope we attach to love, and that is what propels us along?"

"If you say so."

"Forgive me; I forgot your heart embarrasses you." He focused his eyes on Christina. "You are young, my angel."

He shifted his eyes to me. They were dull and meaningless. "And you are a pathetic liar." He glanced over toward Eddie. "Proceed."

"No!" Christina cried out as Henny grabbed her shoulder.

The door swung open. A man poked his head in and announced, "Pardon my interruption, sir, but there is a rather large and quite impressive birthday cake awaiting you on the aft deck. The crowd is chanting your name."

"Very well," Agatha said. "Our business here is concluded. Keep him here, Eddie. Henny, see Christina to her room. This time, might I strongly suggest you lock the door. Then return here. Johnnie, you come with—no, better yet, stay here—the usual pictures." Agatha stood and made distinct eye contact with Eddie, who gave a barely discernable nod. As he was about to leave, he said to Johnnie, "Don't rely on the camera."

Christina lipped something to me, but I couldn't make it out.

When the room cleared, Eddie kept a safe distance, his gun leveled at my chest. "Last chance, Beachy. Who you really work for?"

"I'm working with the FBI," I explained nonchalantly. "We know Franklin's been protecting you for years to secure the navy contract for Zebra. He's a major shareholder in the private company. Franklin thinks he's running me, but the jokes on him. It's an elaborate game to close you down and put Franklin behind bars."

"No shit?"

"No shit."

"You shittin' me?"

"Nope."

"Shit."

"You need to move on."

He shook his head. "Know something? I think I believe you. That don't even surprise me. Gee-zus H—even makes sense. And you're tellin' me this, why?"

If I waited till Henny came back, my chances diminished substantially. I could drop, roll, and take Eddie to the floor. I would do it in midsentence, when he would least expect it. I adjusted my weight slightly to my back foot. I decided to go with a rambling statement and hit the deck when Eddie's drooping eyes showed the first signs of boredom. Johnnie wasn't a concern.

I told Eddie, "I'm here to broker a—"

The door flew open silencing my speech and altering my plan. Garrett stumbled in slurring his words, "Where's the men's room?"

"Outta here, blackie," Eddie snapped at him.

"Soooo sorry." He stumbled closer to Eddie. Eddie lowered his gun and put out his free hand to ward off the unruly intruder. "I really need to—"

Garrett let loose with a right uppercut. It requires little windup and is the quickest punch. Eddie staggered but kept control of the gun. It wasn't the first time the Italian wasp from Youngstown had taken a cheap shot.

Garrett followed with a quick left to the stomach, and Eddie doubled in pain, his gun pointing down. I stepped in, confiscated his gun, stuck the barrel in his mouth, and said, "Do you have a hit on Franklin?"

He gargled an unintelligible reply.

"I can't hear you."

Click. Click. Click.

Johnnie was taking pictures like it was senior prom night. Garrett snatched his camera. Johnnie, without protest, sat down like a sullen boy stripped of his favorite toy.

I took the gun out of Eddie's mouth.

"You can eat sh—"

I whipped him on the temple, and he collapsed. I turned to Garrett. "What did you do, talk to every person on the way—"

"Save it. We got major problems. Trouble's—"

"What?"

"—here. Right after I pulled up. Couple of guys in a dark car next lot over. They got flowers out of the backseat and headed in this direction. I lost them after I dropped off the cake."

Hit men with flowers, just like our duo in Washington, DC. What a classic gimmick. I wouldn't be surprised if Marcus Junius Brutus approached Caesar on the senate floor holding a bouquet of Florentine iris and Tuscany poppies, or if Franck Johnson had rapped on Trotsky's door offering him a poinsettia plant. I better instruct Kathleen to never have a man deliver flowers to me; it would be the poor bloke's last stop.

"We were right," I said. "Franklin can't summon his own men without implicating himself. Furthermore, time is paramount; why else such a crowded venue?"

I took two large steps and corralled Johnnie Darling, who had nearly snuck out. I held him by the neck, like a mother cat carrying her young. "Sit." I commanded him. He sulked back down.

"The men you saw are hired hands sent to eliminate Agatha," I summarized to make sure Garrett and I were on the same page. "But they don't know we exist—Agatha likely told Franklin that I'm long gone, although Binelli might have told him otherwise. Either case, we need to get Agatha off the boat."

We concocted a plan, each of us ignoring the fact that if the first dozen plans had worked, we wouldn't be creating another.

Henny never knew what hit him when he came through the door.

Five minutes later, with the wire Garrett had in his pocket, we had Eddie, Henny, and Johnnie tied—the last two with their socks stuffed in their mouths. Eddie, as I'd observed the night I met him, didn't wear socks; therefore, he was the recipient of one of Johnnie's. As Eddie came out of the fog, Johnnie's sock in his mouth seemed to upset him to no end. I took Eddie's gun. Garrett took Henny's and Louis's guns. We had no desire to kill anyone that night, but if we did, it would be convenient to do so with someone else's guns.

Thank goodness, Christina was locked away.

48

There are things in our lives that happen quickly, and we forget them just as fast.

There are other incidents that happen just as suddenly and unexpectedly, yet they linger for a lifetime, for time, which is usually transitory, can also be permanent. It can petrify itself. In the same meaningless seconds that pass when you take a bite from a bagel you could also lose your job, win a game, witness a birth, or experience your first kiss. And until the brain is deprived of its final draw of oxygen, your memory will sear those nervous seconds. Your mind will big bang the experience, splattering it across the galaxies, even though the event itself was nothing but an internal speck of dust.

Death is like that. A wisp of air leaving a body can last a lifetime.

It was early in the morning, and the party was sucking air. The band had already punched out. Phillip Agatha, the maestro—the grand marionettist—was addressing a dwindling yet rabid circle of admirers, their effusive praise a product of their inebriated state.

We had to get to Agatha before Franklin's men did, and despite our efforts, there was no sight of the men Garrett had spotted. Garrett and I had split. At this point in the game, we would rarely be within seven or eight feet of each other.

Not only is it advantageous to keep your adversary unaware of your backup, you never want to give a shooter two easy marks.

I rudely squeezed next to Agatha after his closing comments to his adulating flock. "May I have a moment?"

Agatha glanced at me and for the first time a hint of fear clouded his sparkling eyes. "Certainly." He bowed to his admirers. "If you'll forgive me." He turned back to me. "You are a resourceful man, Mr. Travis. I must now entertain the distinct possibility that I underestimated you. Eddie?"

"He, and the rest of the Wild Bunch, are tied up at the moment. Although technically, Louis is passed out in the wine room but not for reasons one would normally expect."

"Johnnie?"

"Excuse me?"

"Did you hurt him?"

"Your lover is fine," I said. It was a harsh comment without thought, although as the words came out, I realized I'd been suspicious all along.

He gave me a disappointing stare. "No need for that. What precisely is it that you want?"

I took his arm and escorted him over to the port rail. "We're leaving. Now. Franklin has men on board who are here to kill you. You will not survive the night without me."

"I see. This would be a splendid time for you to come clean about you who are."

"Franklin used me to secure the Zebra contract."

Recognition swept over his face. "Yes, we entertained the possibility." His eyes momentarily lost focus and then snapped back. "You see, it is *he* who is desirous of killing *you*. That aroused our suspicions. Eddie was right; sniffed you like a suitcase full of heroin. Tell me, for Mr. Franklin's lack of interest in maintaining our relationship has coincided with your presence; does he have a friend who is in some manner connected to Zebra, or is it he himself?"

"Franklin is part owner of Zebra. He and Daniel Vigh go way back."

"Of course." He nodded his heavy head. "I was just starting to nurture that scenario. So clear now, isn't it? Pride goeth before the fall. All along he's been planning for this moment. The money must be astronomical for him. Brilliant, is it not? And what? Your role was to expose me?"

"Yes."

"You must surely realize that he will rid you as well."

"Occurred to me. You, however, are the first order of business."

He cast his eyes down, rousing unwarranted sympathy from me. This man, who joked and made light as I selected a young girl to die, elicited more pity from me than I mustered for a homeless man in Miami Beach. The sweetness that cloaked the man was the masked genius of his madness.

He gazed back up at me. "Take Christina," he implored me. "She is my Gail. I'm sure you see that. Take her, man. Take care of her. I can make my peace with Franklin. You and I will not speak to each other again."

"You will stand trial for murder. You—"

"Have you forgotten the picture Eddie showed you with Lucille? Remember Lucille, don't you? You can't possibly bring attention to me without incriminating yourself. Now, if all you—"

"She's fine."

"Pardon me?"

"Lucille. She's in a safe house under FBI care."

"I don't know who you're talking about. We have a—"

"A staged picture of a faked death. I assure you, I went to considerable lengths to protect that *profiterole*," I said using the word Agatha had used to describe Lucille in the nightclub.

Agatha brought his right hand up to the side of his head and raked his hair. Clumps of his greased hair were left in grotesque positions, like a still-frame from an accident. "I see." He stared at me, although I don't think he saw me. "Eddie…a wide angle shot…he questioned it."

He turned away and faced the Miami skyline, speaking into the night. "He came to me years ago."

"Who?"

"Franklin. Said the FBI was investigating me, but that for a few dollars, he'd protect me." Agatha pivoted back around. "He said he was going through a divorce. It checked out. I see now that Zebra was on his radar all along. But I don't think you knew that, did you?"

"No. I was brought in as an outsider. He played me as well."

"Yes. I should have realized when he turned an eye to his dead agents that he had more at stake than the monthly stipend I sent him. When did you know?"

"I just made that connection, which is why after I hand you over to the feds, I'm going after him."

His eyes drifted and then came back to me. "And I have nothing to offer, do I? Perhaps we can arrange something. Do not deny your fondness for Christina. Help me, and I will shower her with money. I'm sure she has told you that her efforts go to her family. Think of her, not you."

"You're mad. Her mere association with your sickness has placed her in great harm."

He gave me a vapid smile. "She's had a wonderful life," he said. "You think I would allow harm to befall her, my Gail?

I've gone to considerable effort—lengths, as you prefer—to leave her completely and legally absolved of any knowledge and responsibility. I have documents that attest to her ignorance. Unless you have erred and foolishly spoken to her about my business, she has no concerns."

He paused, as if to give me a moment to publicly incriminate myself, but I wasn't in the mood. Had my desire to help Christina put her in harm's way?

"Take my island princess," he continued. "That is why I have indulged you and given her great leeway with you. I knew I couldn't keep her on indefinitely. Broker a deal with me and—"

Agatha stopped as two men burst through a side door and strode briskly toward us.

"Time's up." I said while keeping my eyes on the men and reaching for my, meaning Eddie's, gun. I felt myself entering an enlightened state as my instincts took command.

"You were a fool to tie up my men."

The man on the rail had his arm down at his side. The glimmer of a knife flashed with his stride. Stupid—who brings a knife to a gunfight?

"Jake?" Christina's voice jolted me from behind me and off to my side.

Marlo's assistant and his damn pins.

The men broke into a run. The inside man reached into his pocket but kept his eyes on me. Were they given orders to kill me as well? Have a picture of me in their wallet in the event that Binelli confirmed that I was alive? That's how I would have run it.

A gunshot cracked the night, and the man who was reaching into his pocket went down with his gun in his hand. Garrett—he was behind me. I hit the deck as another shot, not Garrett, came from my rear. Agatha emitted a guttural humph and launched himself across me and onto Christina.

There were more than two men. They already had one on the yacht. Kept one back, just as I kept Garrett back. Not as stupid as I thought.

I fired twice at the man with the knife as he pulled a gun from his jacket. He hit the rail, but not before he got a shot off. He crumpled onto the deck. I spun to my rear. A man was crouched by the chair Agatha favored at the teak dining table. We simultaneously fired two rounds at each other. I caught Garrett in my peripheral vision as he squeezed off a shot as well. The man fell back, his gun launching a final stray bullet.

Whole thing—three, four seconds. Tops.

I stayed low, gun drawn, and combat alert. I kept my eye on the first man I'd shot. Was he dead? I didn't want him to reach for a gun and make me his last act on earth. I glanced behind me and saw Garrett over the body. He darted past me and toward the other two men. He gave me a glance letting me know that he had them.

Agatha's bullet-ridden body straddled Christina.

"Oooh. I'm cold," Agatha moaned. "Was I too late? Tell me, man."

My instincts vacated my body, and panic took their place. I dragged him off Christina.

She was drenched in blood, her eyes shut. The vibrant blue dot pupils of her pirate tattoo she'd gotten in Key West gazed indifferently over the deck of the *Gail Force*. Her portfolio, spattered with blood, lay at her side. Her outstretched hand touched the thin brown cord that wrapped around two protruding cracked buttons that securely latched the portfolio. I stared at the cord, finding consolation in the meaningless, inanimate object, afraid of the reality that would confront me when its spell was broken. And whether that reality would be the unstoppable force of life or the unconquerable stillness of death.

I ripped open her dress. I leaned over her. I frantically searched for a wound. Nothing. *Agatha's blood?*

She blinked.

"Christina?" Her breath escaped as if she'd been holding it under water. "Look at me. Do you feel any pain?" I searched for any sign of a gunshot wound. They are not always easy to spot.

"I don't think so." Her voice was remarkably calm, and my mind flashed to when I'd first met Riley and shook her hand—how soft and smooth it was compared to her demanding opening lines as she had marched down my dock. "I think...I think I'm just shocked. Is Phillip OK?"

"You fool," Agatha spit out with great effort for his eyes were already gone. He lay on his back, and I wondered if "Splendor in the Grass" would come on at 10:00 a.m. tomorrow and, if so, would anyone hear it? "Your instincts would have left her dead." I had a lifetime to ponder his comment. I came back with, "Remember Riley Anderson?"

"Who?"

"Karl Anderson's wife."

"Little thing." He groaned. "What about her?"

"She sent me for you. That's how this all started."

I raised Eddie's gun, but it wasn't necessary. A sea breeze swirled up and, in the early morning hours after Phillip Agatha's thirty-eighth birthday, swept his life away.

49

Life is a whistle in the night. It pierces the darkness and then is gone, leaving no trace of where it came from, where it went, or what it meant. Agatha had vanished, leaving those behind to form new patterns with their time, and new realities in which to form those patterns.

My reality was this: without Agatha, Christina would have likely died in a hail of bullets, and I alone would have been responsible. For a petrified second, I'd thought she was dead. I couldn't shake it. That second. Knew I never would. The only thing I'd brought her was self-incriminating knowledge of Agatha's business, heartache, and a brush with death.

I had issues with that.

It clipped my gait. Clouded my convictions. The old self-esteem machine took a major hit. *Better be careful what games you play; it's not hard for an egotistical, low-life, jacked-up, throw-down piece of jiminy Christmas shit like you to get out of your league.*

I never found out what a shit bird was, but I made a damn good one. The heck with the cesspool of introspection. I had a message and a gift to deliver.

Although the message and the gift were simple tasks, they needed a nudge from Kathleen's hydrogen and helium angels. I don't believe in angels any more than I believe in epilogues. But after crossing three decades, there are a few things I've learned, including this: you're better off believing that which you know not to be true than believing that which will destroy you.

The epilogue:

We secured the yacht and then made contact with Binelli. A cavalry of FBI agents descended on the *Gail Force*. It was like witnessing a stage being struck after the last performance—the pageantry forever gone. Henny, Eddie, Johnnie, Louis—all escorted off. Even the cooks were held for questioning, Spero giving me Satan's stare as they led him down the gangplank.

Phillip Agatha bled out on the deck of his yacht. Garrett, examining the corpse, mildly observed that Agatha had taken two bullets in the back, likely when he was splayed over Christina. He saved her life, not I. That was a heavy piece for my suitcase, which was already permanently over the weight limit.

Eddie, who knew a thing or two about the system, was the first to roll and cooperate. It *was* Franklin in the picture that Karl and Riley were unfortunate enough to trip on. Eddie said Agatha insisted Franklin be present at a sting, but withheld that he planned to murder the girl. The picture of Franklin standing in the bedroom with a dead girl was insurance for Agatha that Franklin would toe the line, much as Agatha had attempted to do with Lucille and me. We assumed that Franklin, once Agatha was dead, would use his powers to raid Agatha's offices and confiscate the incriminating evidence against him.

Eddie also placed Franklin in Miami the night Riley spotted him in Hollandaise. The fake FBI agent, McKeen, was actually Henny dressing the part. *Big guy with a slug-neck*, Riley had said. I should have seen that. I'd thought of describing Henny to her—the night Morgan came through the door with the Buccaneers cooler of trout and Kathleen insisted I utter "Remember us"—but never did. Nor did I ever show Riley a picture of Henny and Eddie, never got around to even taking one. One never knows what might have altered the course of events, and dwelling on such things is slow poison. The mistakes, like the Black Tears from the USS *Arizona*, would bubble to the surface for years.

According to Eddie, Franklin planned to convince the Andersons to allow Henny to accompany them out of the restaurant. When asked what Franklin instructed him to do with the Andersons, Henny responded, "Take them to the zoo." It wasn't easy for the man from Mahoning Valley to make his statements. His lip was split and several of his teeth were missing. He also suffered numerous broken ribs. He can thank Garrett it wasn't worse.

Franklin didn't speak at all. He put his grandfather's West Point revolver in his mouth. The bullet saved me from ripping out his fingernails.

Johnnie Darling, unbeknownst to Agatha, kept pictures in the cloud. After Eddie did his dog-and-pony show for the feds, Darling gave his version, pinning numerous murders on Eddie, including those of Karl Anderson and Special Agent Lippman.

The death of Special Agent C. J. Leonard was still under investigation. Franklin had told me during our last meeting that Agatha was responsible for the death of both agents. When I reminded Binelli of that, she had no comment. She was caught in the turbulence of the internal investigation. The one who was actually best positioned to broker a deal with the feds? Henny. Turns out he had no blood on his hands. Told you he was as bright as an Amazon box.

Riley volunteered to pay for the $2,139 hotel bill. I told her to skip it.

The monkey ashtray from the *Gail Force* now rests next to the Copacabana ashtray on my dirty glass table.

The navy, shunning negative publicity, renewed their contract with Zebra Electronics. Zebra Electronics filed for an IPO. There was no way the FBI could investigate Vigh without drawing attention to themselves. Daniel Vigh hit pay dirt. Rang the opening bell at the New York Stock Exchange. Even a pile of shit has a top to it.

Two weeks later—I'm not sure of the *precise* time, for time had become suspended and dazed, like a late-fall Sunday afternoon on a sleepy college campus—I hit the hotel.

The hotel was a pink Moorish structure built in the 1920s by an Irishman from Virginia, named after a character in a play from a French dramatist that was turned into an English opera, and is set in a city named for its Russian counterpart.

I'm still clueless on that.

"When do you leave?" Kathleen asked from the stool next to me. My head was down in my drink, my cap low over my eyes. I was doing my best to ignore the Florida flesh parade.

"Eight," I answered her. "Get in around four."

"See her then?"

"Not planning to. The markets close midafternoon. We're meeting at the bank in the morning and plan to see her together. Walk on the beach?"

"Sure."

We slid off our bar stools, and hand in hand, slogged through the cooling sand.

We strolled silently into the listless northern breeze, and she said, "Do you love her?"

And I said, "Which one?"

And she said, "Christina or Elizabeth."

And I said, "No."

And she said, "Are you sure about Elizabeth?"

Her green eyes were steady, unaware that I was afraid of what she might say.

"I am. Believe me?"

"Yes?"

"Why?"

"Beats the alternative," she said matter-of-factly. Like she was picking one loaf of bread over another.

"That's not a good reason," I said.

"You're right. Maybe I should have worried more, but really? As I told you, you're a sucker for me."

"A sucker for you," I said remembering when she first sprung that on me after our lunch downtown. "If there ever was one, that's the goddamned truth."

"Do you think she loved you?"

"Christina or Elizabeth?"

"Loved Christina. Love Elizabeth."

"Don't ask me that."

"Too late."

"No," I said. "Maybe in the middle, but not in the end. Not like that."

We continued in silence, she swinging our hands like we were two kids on a playground.

"When you get back," she said and flicked her green eyes toward me. Her lips formed a corner of a smile. My heart soared like strings jumping an octave. "It will be Saturday night, is that right?"

"I believe so."

"Sunday morning champagne with Morgan?"

"I thought you said no more drinking."

"Prohibition's up," she announced.

"Might be cool Sunday morning. Front's coming."

"I saw that."

"I bought you that outdoor heater."

"You did?"

"I did. Ask you something?"

"No. You can't return it."

"How do you feel when I open a door for you?"

Kathleen skipped a few beats and then said, "Bet I can smoke you to Riptides."

She sprinted down the beach. I had no choice but to run after her.

50

The jet bounced once, as if protesting the loss of its freedom, and then settled in as Aruba—One Happy Island—came up and greeted the wheels of the Boeing. I closed a dull biography of Eisenhower and placed it in the Pan Am bag.

My plan was to verify the good news to Christina's mother and then catch a series of puddle jumpers to Saint Kitts in order to return the Pan Am bag to Angelo. My mind kept skipping to the return trip to Florida, the long flight over the Caribbean, and the empty mind the sea and sky grant you.

By the time I checked into the hotel, it was dark. I'd traveled so far, yet unpacked so little. I'd only brought one extra shirt. I folded it neatly and placed it in a drawer by itself. I stared at the shirt in the drawer. It was on the left side. The right side was bare. After a while, I shut the drawer, recalled Kathleen's and my walk on the beach, and thought: *Did I? Love her?*

Do I?

I headed to a bar.

After a few drinks, I traded the bartender a hundred for a half-full bottle of Jameson. I drove to the windward side of the island. The paved road gave way to dirt and gravel. I left the vehicle and picked my way over the jagged stones and toward the sea. It was the part of the island that never made the hotel brochures. The wind and water whipped delirious waves against the rocks. The rocks stood, like aged and indifferent sentries, knowing the frustrated sea could never shake its liquid shackles.

I settled my back against a stone, and my thoughts went in reverse, making sure I hadn't missed anything that would complicate tomorrow's action. Only Binelli had raised a flag. She'd apologized about sending me into a trap. I'd reinforced that it was my decision.

"One thing did come up," she'd mentioned.

"What?"

"The fifteen million we wired? We were only able to recapture thirteen. Agatha wired out two million, and it got bounced around—we lost it. Know anything about that?"

"Why would I?"

"Just asking," she said. "Lot of money."

"It is. Did it come from the orphans' fund?"

"Naw. We took it from Franklin's estate. It's all going to be partitioned out, anyway, for his sins. That was my idea, by the way. Make you feel better?"

"Don't know what you're talking about."

She hung up.

I wanted to tell her where it was going, so she wouldn't think less of me. Later.

Agatha's dying act, as it had done repeatedly over the past week, flooded over me. The man had saved her life. Without him, I would have brought death to her. Without him, Christina would have become like Morgan's father, and Karl Anderson: both past and present tense. Without him, I would have brought a coffin to One Happy Island.

I took a swig from the bottle, but nothing came out. The bottle was empty, but I wasn't done with it.

Without him, I would have saved Lucille yet let her die. I—who helped a poor merchant, but felt nothing for the homeless, who let Thunder sleep, and who braked for a squirrel—would have seen her take two bullets *while I secured the area.*

You're nothing more than a predatory fish acting on instincts and incapable of reason. Certainly not the hotshot you think you are. Agatha was right; your instincts would have left her dead.

I took a final empty swig of air and tossed the bottle into the sea. I was so far gone that I needed to traverse eternity just to get back to the edge of the universe. The sky was mad with stars—a canopy of witness to the folly below. They were there, Kathleen's and my initials. Was it the whiskey? Who the fuck cares?

I woke up to the incessant pounding of the waves, both in and outside of my head. My head was resting on a grassy patch of sand. My bare feet stuck out toward the sea. I assumed the rest of me was in between. At least I hoped so.

At the hotel, I showered, gathered my papers, grabbed a quick breakfast, and forwent pills that had little chance against a monsoon of a headache. Besides, I deserved the pain.

"Jake?" Christina said as she rose to greet me in the bank lobby. "You look...rubbish." She was perky and bright. She gave me a peck on the cheek. "Although," she added, "you smell like Irish Spring."

Her hair was bundled back, and she wore shorts and a short-sleeved white shirt. She seemed taller, but then again, she'd been doing that to me all along.

"You ready?" I said.

"You don't have to do this."

"We've been over it."

"I know you think we have. But I'm not so sure. You saved me, not Phillip. No way—"

"This decision was made long before that night. We're done talking. Find me a coffee, will you? A pastry would be great as well."

I took a seat on a lime-green couch, decided that only contributed to my aching head, and switched to a leather armchair. I still didn't know her sisters' names. I thought I was being stupid, thinking that if I knew them, it would draw me closer to Christina. Perhaps she had her own reasons for keeping her distance; perhaps those reasons weren't dissimilar from mine. If I got to know them, then what? Stay for lunch, dinner, the night? It had to end.

Christina presented me a coffee and cherry pastry and claimed the couch. She crossed her legs and said, "I don't want to tell Mama that Phillip died."

"I'll let you lead."

"Is that bad? I know he did terrible things, but I just don't know how I feel about him. I haven't had the time yet to sort my feelings." She humped her right shoulder. "I don't know if I'm *old* enough to reason with it, even know enough of life to make sense of it."

"That might be your problem right there."

"Trying to make sense of it?"

I nodded.

"I mean, it's dirty mo—"

"It's an unintended consequence."

"You say that, but I think you planned—"

"We're done talking."

"Mr. Travis?" A young man hovered over us. "We're ready for you now."

I followed Christina into a private office, where I wired $2 million into an account in the name of Elizabeth Austen Burnham.

She wasn't hard to spot. Her daughter looked just like her.

"Mama," Christina said. "This is the man I was telling you about. Mr. Travis."

"Ah, my Elizabeth brings a man back to our island, but not for her, this is right?" she said as she stuck out her hand.

"Mama—" Christina started to protest. I jumped in front of her and, shaking her mother's hand and said, "She will do far better than me, I can assure you of that."

"And what is it you need to tell me, Mr. Travis, other than no man is good enough for my Elizabeth? But that I already know."

"It's a novel of manners," I said, delivering the message that Christina wanted me to.

She took a second and then said, "I don't understand."

"Pride and Prejudice."

She looked at me as if reconsidering my value. "Yes. I've known that. But that is a strange thing to carry down from Florida, and you do not look like a man who travels such a distance to say such a thing."

Christina stepped into her mother. "Let's get some coffee, Mama." She shifted her attention to a woman who was unpacking boxes at the table next to us. "Kensey, will you keep an eye on our things? We'll only be gone a few minutes."

"Certainly, Liz-beth." Kensey eyed me as if uncertain of what I represented.

Christina, her mother, and I took a seat on a shaded patio on the leeward side of the island. As the bars came to life, as people queued up at water sports kiosks, as the flat waters reflected the motionless sky, as I ordered a rum punch and promised to clean up my act starting tomorrow, as the birds—with the unstoppable energy of the living—dived into the water looking for food, Christina calmly explained that I'd bought a great many of her pictures, and the money was sitting in the bank, and "Look, Mama, at these lovely and handsome rolling hills of Virginia," and "What do you think of this school for Alicia and Janie?"

While Elizabeth and her mother shared a teary hug, I slipped out, walked back to the hotel, and caught a cab to the airport.

Be sure to read these previous stand-alone Jake Travis novels:

The Second Letter
Cooler Than Blood
The Cardinal's Sin

Naked We Came, Robert Lane's fifth Jake Travis novel, will be published in 2017.

Visit Robert Lane's author page on Amazon: http://www.amazon.com/Robert-Lane/e/B00HZ2254A/ref=dp_byline_cont_book_1

Follow Robert Lane on Facebook: https://www.facebook.com/RobertLaneBooks

Learn more at http://robertlanebooks.com